YESTL___ N E W S

ADRIAN WILLIAMS

First Published in 2025 by Black & Blue Books. Birmingham

www.blackandbluebooks.com

www.adrian-williams.uk

A catalogue record for this book is available from the British Library.

ISBN: 978-1-0684341-0-5

CONTENTS

PART ONE

NEW HORIZONS

1.

The price of profit

A flitting fly caught Jacob's eye.

He assumed that it must have flown into the lift shaft by mistake, for flies are sun-loving insects and have no desire to sample the stifling atmosphere of an underground dig. When the cage doors opened, depositing a dozen hollow-eyed moles onto Level One of the Kimberley diamond excavations, the tiny creature escaped into surroundings that were as foreign to it as a dung pit would be to us.

Jacob was one of the *Transvaal Mineral Mining Company*'s most inquisitive employees, and the fly's maniacal movements continued to draw his attention in the dry, dusty gloom. Its flirtation with the lamps on the miners' hard hats soon waned; a dance around the overhead spotlights was briefer still. Something else had attracted its curiosity in that oppressive, claustrophobic chamber, and as the observant mole squinted to follow its flight, to his horror, the source finally became apparent. There in the murk, his mesmeric Pied Piper had come to rest upon a human foot protruding from a pile of freshly hewn rubble.

With as much power as his bronchial lungs could muster, Jacob shouted out above the din of drills that relentlessly rat-a-tatted into solid rock all around him.

"Help! Help! Over there, boys! Look!"

His bony index finger pointed into the distance.

Work quickly halted and his colleagues stared towards a scruffy shoe loosely wrapped around a crooked human flagpole atop an irregular jumble of stones. Immediately they moved as one, a mass of straining sinews and perspiration, to dismantle the barricade, and when the mound was no more, to their collective horror and distress, there lay the crushed corpse of their much-respected friend and work mate, Joseph Khumalo.

In a mood of sombre dignity, the men returned his broken body to the world of natural daylight so that a forensic examination could take place at the district coroner's department in town, though they were sure that no meaningful investigation into the circumstances of his death would be undertaken. Their initial feelings of grief for their fallen comrade ran to anger when the coroner's report declared that Joseph had died accidentally, due to an unexpected collapse of rock inside the mine.

Khumalo had been a robust spokesman on safety matters for the Workers Council who vociferously demanded expensive safety improvements from the management, so militant agitators at the site instinctively rejected the official verdict, suggesting the involvement of foul play instead. They ordered the rest of the men to down tools in protest, and an ugly mood developed.

The *TMMC* was overwhelmingly the area's major employer, and its Kimberley Site Manager Marcus Botha demanded that local police mobilise immediately with ruthless force to quell the rebellion. Violent retribution followed, and once the dust had settled, those left standing were left with no choice other than to meekly return to their labours below ground. Within weeks, the disturbance was a distant memory, a futile gesture of defiance against corporate might.

The year was 1958 and South Africa was in the grip of its apartheid governance; a society as culturally and socially divided as any on earth. Human rights were the preserve of the Caucasian lawmakers, while the black majority looked on in envious despair...

Marcus Botha had a formidable history of sweeping troublesome irritants like Joseph Khumalo aside, and the dissident's demise extinguished a potential threat to the smooth running of the *TMMC's* highly lucrative business. Those safety proposals were immediately shelved, and injury (or worse) remained a realistic prospect for the employees he had sought to protect.

This was a time for Botha to make merry - and merry he most heartily, greedily, outrageously, disreputably made. An era of treasure chest accumulation lay before him, and he missed no opportunity to increase his company's profits. He was the King Arthur of his own personal Camelot and revelled in his omnipotence, operating in a world where a subjugated workforce had to yield to his will at the merest snap of his stodgy fingers.

And yet he had begun to grow restless and impatient for greater glory.

2.

Opportunity knocks!

Born in 1927, Marcus Johannes Botha was a tough-as-teak terrier from lower-middle-class stock whose high-end intellect made him stand out from the pack. In the immediate post-war years, he studied at the prestigious University of Cape Town (graduating with a Doctorate in business management) and many of his lecturers considered him to be the outstanding student of his generation. Much of South Africa's economic prosperity is fuelled by the mining and export of its natural resources such as gold, silver, platinum, diamonds, and iron, so it was hardly surprising that precious metal and mineral excavation companies sought to develop the young man's undoubted potential. After sifting through several tempting offers, he duly decided to join the *TMMC*, an organisation whose hard-nosed corporate culture won it few friends and many enemies.

He started his working life as a junior manager, compiling risk assessment reports on the budget requirements and staffing levels required for new digs, quickly drawing the attention of superiors with his ability to make confident and courageous decisions. His reputation grew, and when an opportunity arose to run a problematical site at Kimberley, he grabbed it firmly with both hands. This was a dream come true.

Maintaining control of a rebellious workforce is paramount to the success of such a project and Botha exercised his talents for negotiation, persuasion, and intimidation, significantly increasing productivity and profits along the way. With one breath, he would make empty promises to his employees about improving their working conditions, while in the next he bribed local dignitaries to turn a blind eye over his disregard for safety regulations. On-site accidents were a regular occupational hazard, but any complaints were ignored by the authorities because the disgruntled miners came from black villages and townships. Botha would allocate the most dangerous jobs to troublemakers, who often wound up either killed or crippled in the subterranean madness of the extraction processes, with no questions asked.

His board of directors recognised that they had a winner on their team and in a bold move (driven by avarice rather than sound judgement), they handed him the role of Chief Executive at the remarkably young age of thirty-seven.

He proved more than capable, pushing the company to ever-greater successes, but his achievements were borne out of self-interest rather than loyalty towards his paymasters. Within months, the decision to grant him such power and responsibility proved to be gravely misjudged, for when he saw an ideal opportunity for personal gain, their gamekeeper mounted an audacious assault for possession of the entire estate.

To the business community's astonishment, he called an Extraordinary General Meeting of *TMMC* shareholders and announced his intention to overthrow the chairman and take sole responsibility for the performance of the organisation. Before going public with his scheme, he undertook a cloak and dagger operation behind the backs of his fellow board members to secure support from the major financial institutions, and once that was successfully completed, he put his pitch for victory to a vote.

"Ladies and gentlemen, grant me greater control of the decision-making process here, and we can think about truly dominating this industry! *Billiton*, _RTZ_, etc. - they will all look on enviously while our business grows beyond belief!" His passionate patter had the audience eating out of his hand. "Many leading banks have significant interests in our company, and they have all given me their full support. I implore you to follow suit, and if you've got any sense, you will!"

Here was a man with an almost orgasmic desire to covet and conquer, and the shareholders swooned, won over by his impressive track record and unshakeable faith. Botha duly completed his transformation from boardroom pit bull to King of the Company.

To consolidate his position, he persuaded the remaining board members to award him a series of generous rights issues and share options which increased his wealth far beyond the expectations of other prominent South African executives.

High-flyers in the business community generally rise to dominance by multiplying already impressive family capital, but he had made his mint from scratch through a combination of astute business acumen, dogged determination, and bloody-minded ruthlessness.

Now he had serious money, power and influence, a state of affairs that mere mortals would have been only-too happy to settle for, but satisfying Marcus Botha was another thing entirely. For him, enough would never be entirely enough. With the world of mineral mining conquered, he wanted to parade his power before different courtiers. His gluttonous ego now required a wider selection of fancies from which to feast and plans to kick-start the next phase of building Brand Botha were already in place…

Within five years of his stunning *coup*, the *TMMC* share price had reached an all-time high, then suddenly, without warning, he took the risk of a lifetime and dramatically walked away from the business that had not only made his name, but also given him a free reign to manage as he saw fit. This shock decision to quit at the peak of his powers threw the company into chaos. Inevitably, speculation raged as to what had motivated him to quit.

Was he ill?

No - he had recently taken steps to improve his health by giving up smoking in an attempt to conquer an occasional irritating palpitation of the heart.

Was a revelation in his private life about to be exposed?

Never - his marriage to the aloof and haughty Elizabeth was strong and stable (and will be explored at length later) and anyway, he was always more interested in affairs of the boardroom than those of the bedroom, unless the scandalous behaviour of a rival could be exploited to his advantage.

Did he plan to retire early?

Hardly - he was still only forty-two years old and had barely gotten into his stride.

The board initially demanded that their leader stay on to oversee the transition period needed for a new CEO and chairman to settle in (the roles were split again to prevent a repeat of his outrageous antics) but on reflection, they decided that a clean break was needed to restore public and investor confidence in their business. After an initial wobble, stock in the company stabilised, as scrutiny of the books showed that he had left the balance sheet in the rudest of health. With order restored, threats of legal action against him subsided and both parties went their separate ways without further rancour.

To appease the press, he issued a vague statement revealing that he had quit the *TMMC*, "to pursue other interests," but this wholly inadequate explanation left inquisitors more curious than ever to understand his eccentric behaviour. In fact, he walked away from mining because he felt the industry was too parochial and stifled his potential; an almost rabid megalomania had taken hold of his senses, leaving him desperate to make a bigger mark on the world stage. He was eager to influence the fate of nations, but before he could begin to realise those heady ambitions, there was a major obstacle to overcome. He needed to fully legitimise the Botha Brand.

South African politics routinely suppressed the country's indigenous people, and rumours circulated about Botha's dubious history of exploiting black workers, so for his next commercial venture he made plans to redress his public image.

With his *TMMC* cash and further thanks to the banks, he purchased a dilapidated shipyard on the east coast in Durban, renamed it *MJB Maritime*, and began the task of turning its flagging fortunes around. He recognised that the super-rich would pay super-prices for super-luxury and consequently built the biggest and best ships that money could buy, charging a premium price and profiting gloriously. His recruitment drive sold employees a dream of a better future working under his benevolent stewardship, and to generate further goodwill, he funded building and infrastructure projects in the surrounding villages and towns, thus improving the lives of local people. These activities, which on the surface appeared to be uncharacteristic examples of his (previously unseen) caring, sharing personality, attracted hugely favourable attention.

All was well again, but old habits die hard, and Botha could not resist the temptations of working beyond the boundaries of the law.

Far away from prying eyes, he conducted dubious business deals aboard his very own super-yacht, the *Lady Elizabeth*, developing trade links with many of the tin-pot despots who had established fragile military powerbases across the African continent. In truth, his regeneration schemes were simply devices through which to launder money illegally accrued by these warlords from their nefarious activities. The projects subsequently generated squeaky-clean revenues that went back into the dictators' pockets as entrepreneurial profit and Botha received a fat cut for his part in the proceedings. When striking such deals, he put personal feelings of disgust for his black partners to one side; whenever there was money to grab, pragmatism replaced the inherent racist feelings that lay within his stony heart.

First mining, then shipbuilding, and finally money laundering; he had excelled in different industries by utilising his tried and trusted talents for decision-making and deceit. With profits flowing in at home and a freshly coated veneer of legitimacy surrounding his new business ventures, it was time to move on again.

People with big egos set big goals, and Botha was a standard-bearer for thinking big. His ambition had outgrown the confines of his home country, and he wanted to advance his business and political agendas by becoming a pivotal figure at the heart of one of the world's great democracies. He knew he would find a warm welcome in the United Kingdom (a nation that had chosen to ignore much of the disreputable goings-on in his homeland) and decided to muscle himself into a position of influence through the purchase a national daily newspaper.

By persuading the embattled and disillusioned owners of the fast-fading *Horizon* broadsheet to sell-up cheaply, he supplanted himself in London as its overlord with a determination to become the biggest and most influential publisher in the land.

And so it came to pass that the man whose early career had been spent unearthing nuggets of gold wound up unearthing nuggets of news.

His chosen path to political influence had historically proved popular for entrepreneurs from the UK's imperial dominions. Canadian Max Aitken (later Lord Beaverbrook) was the first colonial cousin to beat Fleet Street's old boys club at their own game when he turned the fortunes of *The Daily Express* around in the early years of the twentieth century. His business successes led him into Parliament as a Conservative MP, then on to a Peerage (during the First World War, he plotted to replace the incumbent Prime Minister Herbert Asquith with

David Lloyd George, and the new man's leadership proved crucial in the Allies' victory). His persuasive powers came to the fore once more during the darkest hours of World War Two when he served in Winston Churchill's war cabinet with distinction. In appreciation of his wise council, Churchill once said, "Some people take drugs; I take Max."

Australian-born Rupert Murdoch mirrored Beaverbrook's publishing achievements by rescuing the ailing *Sun* newspaper in the late 1960's, turning it into the nation's largest selling daily publication. His confrontational approach upset a lot of his staff, but it helped him to sweep away traditional working practices, and when he controversially transferred the paper's production facilities to Wapping in London's East End, he effectively broke two centuries of Fleet Street's influence on the country's print media.

His arrival in London was very much a case of right place, right time. His rebellious, anti-establishment attitude reflected a sea change in a society that was beginning to shake its hierarchical structures apart. Across the land, the working class found its voice through the boundary-breaking achievements of its rock 'n rollers, photographers, actors, and playwrights; even notorious East End mobsters were making regional accents cool. Murdoch marketed his paper towards celebrity-obsessed, gossip-hungry, everyday people, and reaped huge rewards. When he boasted that *The Sun's* influence on public opinion could determine the outcome of general elections, Marcus Botha's eager ears tuned in to the nascent possibilities.

This latest wannabe press baron entered the industry in 1977 and immediately copied Murdoch's winning business model. His re-launch of *The Horizon* in a tabloid format met with great acclaim, and soon, millions of new disciples were dancing to the Botha beat.

The bright, breezy, all-singing, all-dancing paper was as easy to read as *The Sun,* as full of juicy, close-to-the-edge-of-libellous stories about the famous faces of the day, and as neat in size, making it conveniently disposable once done with. The once disenfranchised working class now had a choice of refreshingly irreverent newspapers to reflect their lifestyles and interests.

Botha had hit another winning run. And always, alongside the paper's celebrity news and sports coverage was an editorial page carrying his daily thoughts and opinions, thinly disguised as the rhetoric of his subservient editor. He had advice on who to like or hate, what to think, and how to vote.

Do as I say, my loyal readers, and our shared love for me can only make us stronger.

3.

Broadening the brand

As we sit at our breakfast tables ready to embrace the day ahead, many will habitually catch up on what has been happening around the world overnight, and nowadays there are myriad ways to receive this information; our digital age allows us to stream content via laptops, tablets, or smartphones; we can watch it on our TV; tune in to the radio. Those who are particularly archaic still read it from a good old daily newspaper! Whether we peruse social media or traditional outlets, the fact remains that the morning bulletins often impact on the rest of our day.

Of course, nothing attracts greater interest than the throwaway fluff that neither frightens nor hurts us. Items containing the word, "celebrity," inspire infinitely more interest than civil wars, Wall Street crashes, or Parliamentary resignations could ever do. Like sponges, we gleefully absorb every lurid detail of the mishaps that befall the pompous, the famous, and the foolish. We delight in judging an endless procession of dim-witted, self-centred cretins who seem to find it impossible to keep their willies inside their trousers, or Columbian snow from their noses. The function of the modern media is to make us think that we actually know the people who spend their lives desperately competing for our attention in the scandal sheets, so we can then pour (envious) scorn on their foibles and peccadilloes with a smug sense of superiority.

Those liars.

Those cheats…

We wouldn't behave like them; we'd never be seen dead going down their route.

We're so much better than those bastards!...

Those lucky, lucky bastards!

Our reactions are to be expected, for they are the product of human nature, but they make us vulnerable to the kind of savvy individuals who exploit malleable minds. The mantra of these clever and manipulative operators has remained unchanged and unchallenged since time immemorial.

Give the people what they think *they want!*

Successful newspaper proprietors possess an uncanny knack for understanding our prejudices and pandering to them; they gain trust by playing on our insecurities and moral indignations, until we take the bait by developing an affinity for their publications. Then they enrich themselves by tapping into the loyalty generated.

Marcus Botha was acutely skilled in the art of filling his own coffers with loose change eased from the pockets of the gullible and easily pleased. At the London headquarters of *The Horizon*, from his penthouse office overlooking the city, he quietly reflected on his successes.

I'm one of life's rare wise owls – those keepers of the clues who can plot their route to riches with consummate ease.

I am special indeed!

He kept his thoughts to himself, for there was no audience to hear his self-congratulation; he had no time, or taste, for friends.

Satisfied that he had a salivating capital anxiously waiting to pick over the bones of a new day's diatribe, his brooding, deadly dark eyes stared at the streets below. With an expansive wave of one powerful arm sweeping over the vista, he sagely ruminated.

I don't make the news – I only publish it.

No-one can ever put the blame on me for the stories I tell – I'm merely satisfying the public's desire for sensationalism…

Affectionately examining a mock-up of that morning's front page, he gave an approving grunt.

Blame them…

He was alluding to the movers, shakers, money makers and piss takers whose adventures (and misadventures) provided the stuff of his daily copy.

And thank Christ for the whole fucking lot of 'em!

His short, stocky figure was wedged behind a plush desk of finest inlaid mahogany and as he emitted a rapid-fire gunshot cackle, an ugly, graceless smile broke out across his lips. In earlier years, he would have drawn on one of Havana's finest cigars, but health concerns now guided Botha along a more temperate path. He saw himself as a Messiah of Mass Opinion, and within the confines of his latest Camelot, he insisted that his staff refer to him as the Head Honcho. Under his guidance, *The Horizon*, that tub-thumping canker of incorrigible vulgarity, passed itself off as a campaigning, incorruptible national newspaper, and it had become his very favourite plaything.

As with every other press baron, he was less interested in articulating the stories of the day than in creating a platform from which to direct attention towards his own way of thinking. A large section of the population read his editorials, so he was a considerable media presence, and any politician who was willing to break bread with him could gain access to a multitude of hearts and minds, though this opportunity came at a price. In return for granting them such prime exposure, he demanded an input into shaping the country's future.

Despite enjoying more than a decade of headline-grabbing success, frustration gnawed away at his ego because he had yet to supplant Rupert Murdoch as the chief bully of Westminster. He knew that to become the supreme power broker in the UK, *Marcus Botha Publishing and Communications* must usurp the dominance of Murdoch's *News International Corporation*.

Murdoch struck fear into the soul of every ambitious Parliamentarian. Whenever a political scandal was uncovered, it was safe to say that the paw prints of *News International* were all over the trail. Like voracious prison dogs hunting down escaped convicts through a Louisiana swamp, his press hounds waded deep into the murkiest of waters on the lookout for scoops concerning the private lives of our elected public servants. Information acquired from some of the more pond-life inhabitants of Westminster and Whitehall could make or break carefully cultivated careers, and that knowledge gave Murdoch leverage to shape House of Commons debates on issues close to his heart (and wallet). It was the duty of Botha's own bloodhounds to work the same magic at *The Horizon*, and through a potent cocktail of diligence and skulduggery, exclusives came his way too, yet despite their best efforts (and the impatience of their tetchy taskmaster) his team were still playing second fiddle to Murdoch's marauders.

The two men may have been rivals, but they were strikingly similar in many ways too. By the late 1980's their battles had become a feature of the business community, though not everyone was exactly thrilled about the situation. Their influence on the political map of the country made many red with rage because, as foreign nationals, neither was eligible to cast a vote of their own come election time. Nonchalantly dismissing this inconvenient truth, both men continued to coerce and cajole policy makers into doing their bidding.

While they saw the ritual humiliation of nondescript low-ranking MP's and civil servants as fair game, they were dutifully magnanimous in their praise for the Prime Minister, Margaret Thatcher, whose leadership of the ruling Conservative party ushered in repeals of trade union laws and lowered income tax for high earners, allowing them to flourish. From the moment she came to power in 1979, they recognised her as a kindred spirit and supported her authority without challenge or dissent. The two mighty tycoons used their newspapers to actively support her three election victories, but soon they would expand their influence and power via a different medium…

Throughout the twentieth century, humankind's sense of innocence and wonder had been irrevocably eroded, thanks to the twin inventions of film and radio. The sights and sounds of our darkest atrocities became readily accessible to a mass audience and we could see for ourselves the effects of World Wars, ideological revolutions, political assassinations, and economic depressions.

Since its inception in the 1920's, the mighty *British Broadcasting Corporation* had established a reputation as the voice and vision of truth in the field of news reporting. Initially through radio, then later, television, it responsibly relayed the horrors and outrages of an increasingly wild world directly into the home. Its content and dry delivery established the Corporation as an exemplar of credibility, but from the 1950's onwards, the public wanted more, and became impatient to see and hear the latest game shows and variety spectaculars emerging from the US, many of which were unavailable via the *BBC*. Competition began to emerge from independent commercial radio and TV broadcasters, funded through advertising revenues. These cash rich independent networks were able to outbid the Corporation for the rights to broadcast star-studded entertainment programmes with mass appeal and their news coverage was equally well received. The *BBC*'s monopoly was over. By the late 1980's, another new kid on the block arrived to challenge the Old Guard in the shape of pay-per-view television.

Rupert Murdoch recognised an opportunity when he saw one. He had no interest in bidding for one of the regional television franchises (such as *Granada* in the north or *London Weekend* in the capital), preferring instead to develop an exclusive national service that was only accessible through a subscription charge. No pay - no see. His business plan for the snappily named *Sky TV* included generating income from the installation of the equipment required to obtain the network's transmission signal (an ugly satellite dish and receiver attached to the outside wall or chimney of a customer's home). As per the traditional independent model, *Sky* would also sell advertising time via commercial breaks during shows.

Newspapers slant the presentation of events to suit the whims of their proprietors, and liberal intellectuals raised concerns that a satellite TV network might do likewise. They feared that, unlike the heavily regulated *BBC*, any individual with a self-serving agenda (and deep enough pockets) would have a free pass to broadcast incendiary, provocative opinions, exploiting ignorance and fanning the flames of hatred without a check or balance of any alternative viewpoint.

Examples of the damage done by a partisan media had already littered the century, leading to two global catastrophes and countless other avoidable skirmishes, so the chattering classes pressurised MPs to adopt an aggressive response against what they saw as a genuine threat to democracy. The government had the power to scrutinise Murdoch's plans via a Parliamentary Commission, but where was their will to do such a thing? Tories were always accusing the *BBC*'s hierarchy of 'left leaning,' bias, so they felt that the introduction of competition from a sympathetic friend offered them a chance to redress the balance of political argument. After weighing up the pros and cons, Mrs. Thatcher's subordinates chose to ignore the dissenters and duly rubber-stamped *Sky TV*'s broadcasting licence. A satellite television revolution had begun.

It was a classic win-win situation; Murdoch could expand his media empire and return the favour by providing positive coverage on issues close to the government's heart.

You scratch my back and I'll scratch yours.

Marcus Botha looked on with interest. He saw great appeal in the pay-per-view business, and inevitably wanted a piece of the action. Many months of scheming and negotiation lay ahead to secure sufficient finance for his own television network, but the chance to buy into an emerging niche market with huge potential on every level appealed to his twin motivators of financial gain and ego enhancement. Broadcasting reached every home, and he intended to become the UK's satellite television king. As an added bonus, he considered success in the industry to be the key to reviving ambitions that had lain dormant for far too long, across the Atlantic in the United States.

4.

Star Spangled Botha

At an age when most people are coveting the carriage clock of retirement, Botha wanted to take on his greatest challenge. He craved possession of the most important slice of real estate the planet has to offer, that space on the coffee tables, breakfast bars and television screens of the world's biggest economy. By making his holding company, *Marcus Botha Publishing and Communications,* a big hitter in the United States, he could influence the whole world, not just the UK and its dominions. To him, that was true power: the ultimate achievement.

It would be his second stab at cracking America. Six years earlier, his first attempt had ended ignominiously, thanks to uncharacteristically flawed strategic thinking and a failure to rigorously research the marketplace.

Focussing on the publishing industry, he looked at the business model that had been such a success at *The Horizon* and simply tried to replicate it across the pond. To his cost, he found that the US market had a very different attitude to tabloid news than its UK counterpart.

Starting small, he decided to purchase regional newspapers in fiercely Republican states, reasoning that the locals would think like him and therefore be amenable to his right-wing editorial outpourings. His first acquisition, an underachieving Kansas publication, *The Wichita Chronicle,* provided a gauge from which to test Middle America's taste for more melodramatic news coverage. Would its readers respond favourably to the fire he wanted to start? The answer was not long in coming.

US daily papers tend to be broadsheet in style, while the market for tabloid journalism confines itself to weekly publications such as *The National Enquirer*. To his dismay, *The Chronicle*'s already diminishing readership proved reluctant to embrace radical change and circulation halved inside six months. He hoped this unwelcome outcome was unique to that newspaper and region, but after encountering the same problem from his purchase of two further dailies, Idaho's *Boise Post* and Wyoming's *Campbell County Tribune*, he reluctantly decided to cut his losses and quit the adventure before damaging his reputation further.

Any life long - lived has its share of disappointments, but Botha found it almost impossible to process his first experience of failure and instead convinced himself that this setback was somehow a necessary evil intended to sharpen his focus, should a better opportunity present itself to try again.

He understood the need to move with the times and embrace broadcast news, so it was imperative that he made a success of his television venture on the domestic front in order to attract further finance for his much larger trans-Atlantic expansion plans further down the line.

To win big across the pond he would have to lock horns with two major players: Ted Turner, the genius behind the *Turner Broadcasting System* and *Cable News Network* (who was reputed to be the richest man alive), and his old adversary from the UK battlefield, Rupert Murdoch.

The Australian had turned his attention Stateside some years earlier and desperately wanted to emerge as the cock of the walk. His progress towards achieving that goal was already impressive thanks to some judicious acquisitioning; since 1985, he had effectively owned the *Fox* television network along with several other US newspaper interests. While Murdoch's business partners at *Fox* used their vast experience to advise him how best to develop *Sky TV* in the UK, Botha had to scratch around independently as a novice broadcaster.

It took until October 1989 before the Head Honcho's preparations were completed, and once the finance was in place, he was finally ready to announce his entry into the satellite television business.

At last, I can finally get the gloves on and come out fighting.
And nobody hits harder than me!

5.

The big announcement

Outside Botha's penthouse suite, muttered mumblings heralded the gathering of his senior staff for an editorial conference, scheduled to begin after the presses had rolled for the last time that day. These meetings usually took place every evening between the Head Honcho and his Chief Editor Edmund Cornell, but on this occasion, the paper's sub-editors were included, so they knew that a big announcement was in the offing.

Their leader excitedly ushered them all in, then by way of a prelude to the main event, he began an enquiry concerning the following day's lead story. Looking around the room, he quizzically asked, "Is there nothing big to bite on for tomorrow's front page? I get the feeling that we're going to be chewing on sprats unless you tell me differently, so speak up now if you've got something."

At this, his Showbiz Editor Neill McEvilley stepped up to the plate.

"We've secured an exclusive interview with Gideon Judge." Looking around the room at some of his older colleagues, he detected a vacant disinterest and decided to clarify the importance of his scoop. "I realise that *The Old Testament's* heavy metal music might not be to everyone's taste here, but we all know their lead singer is a big deal to our readers and he's just been discharged again from the Priory. For those of you who aren't up with these things, that's a sanctuary for celebrity lost sheep in Surrey which is proving very popular lately with the rock 'n roll set."

Botha winced at the mention of the clinic, thinking about the wealth of confidential material stored within its walls that was simply crying out for exposure.

"Anyway, he's given us his latest sob story, a tell-all from his time in rehab, so we're good to go for a front-page splash, with the juicy details inside. We can do follow-ups throughout the rest of the week."

This information received a cautious but still congratulatory pat on the back from his boss.

"Good. Good work Neill. They've read it all before in a hundred different ways, but the public never tire of such nonsense, eh? I think this one will have fresh enough legs to run, though perhaps not tomorrow."

McEvilley was aghast.

"Surely we have to go to print as soon as possible, it's a guaranteed winner!"

"It's my call and I say it will keep." No one felt inclined to challenge Botha's authority on the matter. "Anyone else?"

Eve James spoke next (she was the sole female in this forum, for the cut-and-thrust of the newsroom was considered to be a rather macho affair. Her presence was tolerated because she edited the **WOMAN**'s page).

"Do you want a royal story? I've had a tip-off of another bust-up between Charles and Diana - it seems their relationship is at breaking point."

Eyes rolled around the room and Botha snapped, "Anything concrete? Evidence - led?"

"Nothing quotable, but I'm working on it."

"Come back to me with proof and I'm happy - give me guesswork and I'm not. This looks like it will be a big dig to me, and that takes time, so we'll park it for now. Anything from the rest of you?"

"Thatch."

Botha threw a sharp stare at his Political Editor Peter Hawkins for this disrespectful reference to the Prime Minister. For the good of his future career prospects Hawkins quickly corrected himself. "Sorry, Mrs. Thatcher - is meeting a delegation from South Africa to discuss the Nelson Mandela situation."

The change in Mandela's circumstances had been a remarkable feature of global politics. For years he had been left to rot on Robben Island in a maximum-security prison, convicted of terrorist offences, but in the wake of pressure from the international community he eventually found himself re-located to the much more accessible Victor Verster gaol on the mainland, and his release was imminent. His transition from political prisoner to iconic symbol of the African National Congress party's struggle against oppression made Botha feel deeply uncomfortable.

"Yes, yes, that's all well and good," he snapped, without a trace of sincerity, "but we don't want to make too much fuss there; we'll save our political thunder for the PM's next statement on Europe. Too much exposure for one person, even her, can turn people off, and ambivalence is bad for sales."

Hawkins felt that the story merited consideration and courageously dug his heels in.

"Are you quite sure Marcus? I imagine that the competition will carry this as their lead...."

"Our competition will carry gossip, like Eve's royal stuff - though on that, we obviously need to be very careful that we don't get sued." A quick stare in the direction of the token lady was a reminder for her to provide watertight information in future. "Tomorrow will be no different to any other day, and if any of our rivals can run with a bit of gossip, however inconsequential, then they will. A bit of tit-and-bum scandal will sell more papers than any routine political story elsewhere. Do you still need lessons from me on how to suck eggs? Let the broadsheets go with the PM's meeting about Mandela if they wish, but *our* readers, Peter, couldn't give a flying fart! Who really cares out there?" He glanced out of his window, then stared Hawkins down as he continued. "Sure enough, at election time we'll all be in there with our opinions and oratory, and if we can run a Euro-sceptic lead every now and again, all well and good too, but the only time a *Horizon* reader really wants to know about a politician is when they've been caught with their trousers down or their hands in the till."

He scanned the room for any signs of dissent, but his team decided that agreement with the boss was their wisest course of action. "Let's remember what sells our papers. We got the biggest circulation anywhere this year when our very own Daniella Lae walked out on the aforementioned Mr. Judge to drape her knickers around Ben St. Claire's bedpost."

'Easy' Lae (as rival tabloids labelled her) was a minor celebrity due to her regular appearances as a saucy guest on the television game show circuit. She was also the nation's favourite glamour model, whose topless talents regularly brightened the day of *The Horizon*'s predominantly male readership, and she boosted her income with a (ghost written) weekly column on Eve James' page called **JUST FOR THE GIRLS**, providing fashion and lifestyle advice. In an exclusive front-page interview that summer, she had revealed that her tempestuous affair with her ageing rocker boyfriend was over, while in the next breath she declared undying love for St. Claire, a rising star on the professional snooker scene. Her latest squeeze had a precocious talent and wholesome good looks, in contrast to the grizzled Gideon Judge (whose outrageous hell-raising exploits had been making headlines for over two decades). The combination of those three characters in one story meant it was easy to see why that particular edition flew off the nation's newsstands.

McEvilley jumped back into the conversation, looking to stake a claim for favour by reminding everyone in the room that he was responsible for the scoop.

"Remember how we ran that one boss? **PAGE FIVE FILLY SNOOKERS THE SAINT.**"

"Exactly Neill," confirmed Botha, "that headline said it all. Adding Ben St. Claire into the Daniella and Gideon Judge stew gave us sex, sport, and rock 'n roll - that's tabloid gold, with the feel-good factor of a 'boy-next-door-gets-lucky' ending. And with that timely reminder of Judge's newsworthiness, I believe your rehab story will serve us very well."

"Bingo!" cried a jubilant McEvilley.

"But not tomorrow."

The sub-editors threw swift glances at one another, now knowing for certain that the front-page space was being set aside in service of a mysterious grand project that the Head Honcho was about to reveal. "Ok gentlemen, if there is nothing else of world-shattering importance to discuss, we'll move on to the next item on my agenda. For once I'm not unhappy that we've got a quiet day in prospect, because I have an announcement of my own to make which we can use for our headline piece." Without stopping to assess the reaction of his team, he began to elaborate. "As you are well aware, my business acquisition people have been in negotiations with several banks and financial backers recently, and I'm sure you're curious to know what's been going on.

Well, God willing, with the wind in the right direction and so on, it's my hope that this turns out to be one of the most momentous days for broadcasting since the invention of television!" With no trace of discomfort at the pretentiousness of his proclamation, he declared, "I'm going to revolutionise the TV industry; I want to blow away the old guard - finish off the *BBC*, and all the other commercial stations too." The build-up was certainly worthy of the great man's ego and ensured the rapt attention of everyone in the room. With increasing enthusiasm, Botha puffed out his barrel chest and continued to explain his intentions with a rambling prelude.

"Since the *Live Aid* worldwide satellite transmissions of four years ago, it's been possible for broadcasters to reach a global audience of billions - if you've got a message worth tuning in for, you can grab the attention of the whole world in an instant. You can interest, inform, incite and influence people from different cultures, beliefs and backgrounds on every continent, in every country; all at the same moment. That's my idea of real power, and I recognised the possibilities from the outset.

Those rock concerts at Wembley stadium and in the US actually affected a real change - they received worldwide attention, and the *BBC* was flooded with donations from viewers supporting Bob Geldof's mission to feed the people of famine-cursed Ethiopia.

Think of it! At Wembley Stadium, you had millionaires performing in front of a transfixed global audience, telling the rest of us to dig deep to prevent a catastrophe, and between them they raised a fortune for the relief effort. Ironically, of course, as soon as they got off that stage, those very same do-gooders were burying their snouts in troughs of cocaine and indirectly supporting the exploitation of other third-world hellholes like Colombia!" Realising he was drifting, Botha quickly got back on message. "My point is that if satellite broadcasting can help ill-educated hypocrites like that to get their message across so effectively, then what might a smart man achieve with such a tool?

Over the last few years, I've been casting envious eyes at the success of Ted Turner in the USA with *CNN*. There you have a man of great vision. Have you seen his ratings? Staggering within the realms of news broadcasting. Well, I feel the time is now right for me to take advantage of the satellite possibilities that are opening up here in the UK. I'm going to launch my own subscription broadcasting network called *MJB TV*."

Curious glances passed between the assembled gathering. "Before any of you raise the issue, I'm fully aware that it must look as if my rival Mr Murdoch has already stolen a march on me," (*Sky TV* had been up and running for eight months) "but I reiterate what I said at the time of his launch, which is that I fully expect his enterprise to fail. His start-up expenses are truly colossal, and I don't expect him to sign up enough subscribers to turn such an outlay into a profit."

At this, Willie Watson, the Financial Editor asked, "Well if that's the case Marcus, why on earth would you want to follow him down the same ruinous path?"

Botha always grew irritable when anyone questioned his business acumen, so he laid out his grand plan concisely for the gathering to mull over.

"Because, dear Willie, once Mr Murdoch's dreams have collapsed, I'll be able to take advantage of all the costly groundwork he's laid. I'm going to offer him a pittance for his existing pay-per-view customers and advertising contracts. To rub even more salt in his wounds, I'll take every satellite dish that he's already installed too, reducing the costs of my own expansion plans. I suspect that he'll be reluctant to accept my terms, but what other choice will he have? Whatever he gets from me will help to alleviate some of his huge financial losses.

Once the public gets used to the idea of pay-per-view television and becomes dependant on my services, I'm going to expand the operation, reinvesting the profits to take on Mr Turner and co in the US. Are there any questions?"

The phalanx of editors had to admit that their leader's game plan sounded impressive, but none of them had reached their lofty positions without developing an acute sense of self-preservation.

What would all this mean for the newspaper?

When Watson spoke again to voice his concern, it was on behalf of the group as a whole.

"Marcus, does this move into television mean you'll be looking to wind down your publishing output in any way?"

"What you really mean to say is, '*will you be closing down The Horizon?*' and the answer is a very emphatic no. We're making good money here, aren't we? The print media still has a significant value. Even when *Sky* comes a cropper, I can't imagine *News International* winding down any time soon, can you? More's the pity, eh?" Uncomfortable forced smiles greeted his upbeat reply. "I see this new venture as a supplement to the printed word, created to co-exist with the paper. Trust me, your next few - and hopefully most productive - years will be spent right here."

"So you'll not be taking any of us to *MJB TV*?"

"Television is a specialised medium, so I'll be hiring new people who have experience in broadcasting. Take my advice gentlemen and stick to what you're good at. Anything else?" The troops stayed silent. "No? Then on that note, remember this; Ted Turner has a saying: *'Early to bed, early to rise, work like hell and advertise!'* and that's precisely the message I expect you to take on board. Go back to your desks and spread the word! Give me the biggest, boldest headlines you can muster tomorrow morning, and drop some delicious quotes into the mix while you're at it - all attributed to me, of course.

I've got press releases ready for our rivals to chew over first thing too and I'll be doing interviews on the *BBC* and *ITV* breakfast shows. I might be intending to destroy them, but they have a duty to report the news, however unpalatable that may prove to be, so I might as well take advantage of the free advertising! Now be off with you all!"

Botha's editorial team responded to his emphatic dismissal by hurriedly filing from the penthouse suite. Once outside, the International Desk Editor Patrick Faraday turned to Watson and asked, "What do you reckon then Willie? Does Murdoch's business plan stack up or is the boss right to take him on?"

"To tell you the truth, I was surprised that Marcus let Murdoch get out of the starting gate unchallenged in the first place, but he's a shrewdy alright. He's betting that UK viewers will take to pay-per-view eventually, just like the Yanks did - only not quickly enough to cover Murdoch's outlay. He might just have timed his own run to the winning post to perfection - I certainly wouldn't back against the old boy's instincts. Would you?" Watson was an aficionado of the horses, and he regularly punctuated his comments with racing terminology. "That said, who would be stupid enough to take Rupert Murdoch for a fool either? This will be a fascinating battle to watch. I don't think the pay-per-view industry will be big enough for both of them."

"But who do you think will win? Stop sitting on the fence, will you?" Faraday was getting impatient with his friend, who finally drew to his conclusion.

"We all know there's a nasty edge to our glorious leader that gives us the chills, and if he has that effect on his employees, one can only imagine how he comes across to his competitors. You can feel a malice - a killer instinct when you're in his presence - so for that reason above all else, precious Patrick, my money would be placed on Marcus."

6.

The Westminster well-wisher

Marcus Botha should have been basking in the excitement of his big announcement, but something had spoiled his mood. Peter Hawkins' enthusiasm for Mrs. Thatcher's meeting with South African officials was a reminder that great changes lay ahead in the land of his birth. Soon the African National Congress (which at this time was still an outlawed political movement) would be accepted as a legitimate party with Nelson Mandela at its helm, and the black community's long march to freedom was about to become a reality.

This in itself would not have unduly troubled Botha because he had long-since shaken the native soil from his shoes, but among ANC members there was a desire for revenge and reparation. The party's manifesto included a pledge to investigate the illegal activities of white entrepreneurs who had exploited black workers during the apartheid years, and Marcus Botha was among its most prominent targets. It intended to prosecute the miscreants, even seeking the extradition of those who had left the country since committing their crimes. To keep his enemies at arm's length the Head Honcho needed an ally, a Westminster well-wisher who could assist him in navigating those choppy waters, and for some time, one man had been on his personal radar to fulfil that role.

Lewis Neeves was a typical example of a career politician trying to ascend the greasy pole of political power in the late 1980's. Public school educated, a staunch promoter of family values (despite having a cynically compliant mistress tucked away in the Home Counties) and a dedicated courtier to Queen Thatcher, he was obsequious to a fault, and had perfected the art of ducking under the duvet at the merest hint of opposition gunfire, only to emerge offering the Prime Minister his full support when the time came for a counter - attack. Career politicians are a particularly odious breed.

As a boy, he was singularly selfish and rather disliked, though exceptionally bright, and his Berkshire based parents masterminded an exclusive tutorage for their son, first at the independent Heatherdown school and then on to Eton College. They were determined that the apple of their eye should receive the finest education money could buy (while keeping a comfortable distance between him and any local ruffians emerging through the comprehensive education system). Inevitably, Oxford beckoned, and he graduated with a first-class BA (Hons) degree in Philosophy, Economics and Politics from Brasenose College, where an interest in shaping the country's future took root. He became a Young Conservative and enthusiastically undertook research work for the party to get his face seen by those at the core of the organisation.

After deciding that he needed some work experience beyond the Westminster bubble, he spent a decade learning the art of persuasion at the *Saatchi and Saatchi* advertising agency, before finally applying to join the approved list of candidates wishing to stand for election as Conservative Members of Parliament.

Thanks to the contacts he had made during his researcher years, his application was routinely rubber-stamped, and as luck would have it, shortly afterwards a vacancy arose for a safe seat in the shires. After a sudden illness, the sitting MP had passed away, leaving Neeves to contest (and comfortably win) the subsequent by-election. Like everything else in his life, his path to the House of Commons ran a smooth-as-silk course.

The Thatcher Revolution gained someone steeped in the every-man-for-himself philosophy that was so much *en vogue* around the corridors of power. He was a networker *par excellence*, popping up with a ready handshake and a winning smile for every favoured face at Westminster, while carefully avoiding anyone at the dying fag-end of their Parliamentary careers as if they carried some deadly infection. His views on almost every strand of government policy mirrored the thinking at the top of the party and within two years of his by-election victory, he had risen to the post of Parliamentary Under-Secretary at the Foreign Office. With the first rung on the ladder of power now successfully scaled, his emergence as someone with the potential to become a major political player brought him to the attention of Marcus Botha.

The Horizon's editorial column began to mention Neeves' name in favourable terms, and while this in itself was of little consequence (for most of its male, working class target market were more interested in the contours of a Page Five Filly's breasts than the UK's increasing foreign aid bill), he knew that securing Botha's personal patronage would greatly enhance his future prospects.

The possibility of building a synergistic relationship appealed to both parties. They shared the same opinion on the ANC's rise to prominence in South Africa; Neeves was a vocal advocate of white rule there, a stance that the far-right wing of his party warmly embraced. He had become a member of the controversial Monday Club, a collection of old-school Tories (including prominent figures like Mrs. Thatcher's friend and *confident* Norman Tebbit) who wanted to roll back the years to the 'great days' of colonialism and yearned for the restoration of the British Empire. The bantamweight Parliamentarian was now mixing with some seriously heavy hitters and Botha needed no further encouragement to recruit him to *The Horizon*'.

His right-hand man Edmund Cornell received orders to approach the rising star with an offer to write a weekly political piece for the paper. A meeting to discuss the idea further was set up between the honourable member and the Head Honcho himself.

The move had a residual benefit, in that it was made without consulting the paper's Political Editor Peter Hawkins, keeping him on his toes and wary that his position might one day come under threat.

In politics and business, however, offers made to one party usually come with a proviso that benefits the other, and Botha's deal had ulterior motives of particular personal importance.

Before formally asking Neeves to join the team, Botha wanted to secure an understanding that his prospective recruit would strive to keep the ANC at arm's length, should any threat of extradition loom in the future.

"Lewis, let me assure you that any accusations regarding my behaviour back home are utterly baseless. I treated all my employees well. My labour relations record was exemplary."

"Oh, I don't doubt it, Marcus."

"And I have several witnesses who would corroborate what I say - if the need ever arose."

"Of course." Neeves recognised a lie when he saw one, but expediency dictated that he played his part in Botha's game. "Anyway, I shouldn't imagine that anyone would make trouble for you on that score."

"Well even though I have nothing to fear if they did, we're all aware of the perils and pitfalls of regime change - Christ, the Foreign Office has had centuries of coping with the kind of difficulties that can crop up."

"Quite."

"There are countless examples of militant opportunists trying to make scapegoats out of those who prospered under previous administrations..."

"I completely understand your concerns."

Neeves most certainly did, for he was as cunning as they come and knew full well that Botha's protestations of innocence would not be necessary if he really had been a squeaky-clean employer back home. The man from the Foreign Office made a mental note to do a bit of digging back at Whitehall to assure himself that the Head Honcho would not become a source of potential embarrassment in the future.

Deals are often sealed with a nod, a wink, or an ambiguous promise, but knowing the significance of the opportunity before him, Neeves assured Botha of the UK government's full support if the ANC were ever to ask awkward questions about his past.

The tycoon arrogantly assumed that pre-emptive discussions on the issue must have taken place at cabinet level for the ambitious MP to speak with such confidence, but both men were being deceitful in their guarantees.

Discretion is always the watchword of the political animal, so they agreed, if asked, to deny that any mention of the ANC or extradition proceedings had ever taken place between them.

Better to leave those cats in their bags.

Neeves was playing a dangerous game, for if his bogus promise became public knowledge, he risked dropping the government into serious diplomatic hot water. Victory for the ANC at South Africa's next election was a forgone conclusion, so an extradition request for Botha to face criminal charges was entirely possible. Depending on prevailing circumstances, the powers-that-be in Whitehall might see political expedience in playing ball with the new regime, and if they sent the Head Honcho back to his place of birth, that decision would fatally expose the Under-Secretary's grand *faux pas*. Panicking for a split second, he imagined reams of negative press headlines coming his way, along with an inevitable Parliamentary clamour for his resignation. In reality of course, this was a highly unlikely scenario. While most MPs loathed the bullying Botha and would gladly see the back of him, his support for the Prime Minister meant a lot to her, so she was hardly likely to throw him to the ANC's hungry wolves.

That's enough of the negative thoughts, old boy - concentrate on nailing down this newspaper deal!

This is a golden chance to raise my public profile and if I'm selective in what I write, I can impress Tory grandees with my ability to reach out to The Horizon's working-class readership.

His fee would also be a welcome addition to a bank balance that had already swollen considerably since his elevation from the government backbenches. As a representative of the Foreign Office, he was able to accept a number of lucrative consultancies from companies with international interests that recognised the benefit of adding cabinet kudos to their organisations. Financial opportunities motivated Neeves much more than any desire to serve the will of the people and with this in mind, he refocussed his attention when the conversation finally returned to his political column.

"Now to the real business of the day," said Botha (though of course both participants to the parlay knew that the main course was finished and all that remained was the dessert order and a wrangle over the tip). "I understand what makes my readers tick Lewis; I know what they're looking for from my newspaper. Their priorities are:

1) Good quality sports coverage on their back pages.

2) Entertainment gossip and the TV guide.

3) Competitions, crosswords, horoscopes etc. and finally,

4) They want to see a pretty girl with a nice smile and bulbous breasts adorning page five.

That's it. In a nutshell, it's all about no-nonsense amusement for no-nonsense people."

"Oh, I think you're underestimating them Marcus - they take an interest when a big story breaks, surely? For instance, I don't imagine they were entirely ambivalent when the Berlin wall came crashing down."

"They understood what a big deal that was alright, but they weren't interested enough to explore all the ramifications involved. In a case like that they'll want a surface level appraisal of the situation, so they don't look stupid if someone raises the subject in the pub, but that's as far as it goes. Christ, they know all the in-depth stuff is in the broadsheets - if they really gave a rat's ass, they'd read about it there wouldn't they? And that's never going to happen! Football results mean more to my readers than the end of Communist tyranny in Eastern Europe!"

This dismissive appraisal of *The Horizon* readers' tastes painted a depressingly vulgar picture to Neeves, who now began to wonder how he would fit into Botha's plans.

"So where will they find time in their busy days to accommodate a political page?"

"They won't, but that's not what I'm proposing here. Let me clarify my intentions."

"Please do."

And be quick about it because my patience is beginning to strain.

For a second, Neeves wondered whether his much-anticipated dessert was missing from the menu.

"I propose your contribution to be no more than three hundred words in length, rather than a full page. I know that'll be a bit of a squeeze, but in order to remain competitive, I've recently increased the amount of advertising space in the paper and some of my writers have already found their workload trimmed a little. Obviously, I'd be an idiot to reduce our show business, gossip or sports content, so I've shrunk some of our hard news reporting, just enough to free up space for more adverts, and to create a bespoke political column. Many of my readers would still support the lame duck Labour Party if those losers had any credibility, so I think it's important that they get an opportunity to properly assess Tory policies in a way that any layman can understand. The messages need to be broken down into not much more than bullet points that can be digested over a tea break at work."

"Once the sports pages etc. have been taken in, presumably?" retorted the rather disgruntled Parliamentarian. Like all politicians, he liked to hog the stage and Botha's dismissal of his importance pricked his ego.

"Exactly. Your column will be seen as an intellectual treat!"

This respectful change in tone was much more to Neeves' liking.

"An intellectual treat, eh? You could have something there Marcus - I do see that the working class are struggling to grasp what we, as Conservatives, are trying to achieve. This is an opportunity to communicate with people who might normally shy away from political rhetoric, and that challenge excites me."

"I couldn't have put it better myself; your gift for clarity is remarkable. It's obvious I've found the right man, eh? We'll call your column, **LEWIS LETS LOOSE!**"

While musing on this, Neeves suddenly realised that he had agreed to the deal before discussing the terms of his contract. Botha's flattery had infiltrated his defences and the wily old operator quickly rammed home his advantage.

"Now, I don't expect you to undertake such a responsibility on the cheap, but we also have to recognise that this fledgling enterprise won't increase our circulation - not until it gets established at any rate. I'd like to start you off at fifteen thousand per annum - bearing in mind you'll only be asked to submit one column per week (and none at all when you're on your annual holidays)."

Cagey and calculating as ever, Botha did not want to throw too much of the family silver at what was nothing more than a political bribe to an up-and-comer in the government. After all, the fickle Westminster landscape can change as quickly as the London weather, and his man could rapidly go from being the flavour of the month to burnt toast before making good on his earlier guarantee.

Neeves made no reply to this less-than-generous offer and used his silence to exaggerate the measure of his disappointment. Seconds dragged by, but any expectation that the man before him might feel pressured into increasing the pot evaporated in the noiseless penthouse suite. Finally, Botha spoke up.

"I realise that your fee is a pittance compared to what I pay my Chief Sports Correspondent Gordon Rimmer, but I'm afraid we're talking about market forces here and a lot of people buy the paper to read what he has to say."

That comment ended Neeves' hopes of further negotiation, so, through gritted teeth, he decided to seal the deal on a handshake, because when all was said and done, the opportunity to increase his profile would prove beneficial in the long run.

"I fully understand your point of view Marcus and I'm happy to accept your terms," he lied. "When would you like me to start?"

"I'll leave those details with Edmund Cornell - he'll be in touch to thrash out the finer points with you, ok? You're a good man Lewis - a very good man indeed. Welcome aboard."

Both men left the table quietly satisfied at the outcome of their conference; Neeves had put Botha's anxieties over the ANC at ease and secured a weekly political slot in a hugely popular national newspaper as his reward. The arrangement felt like a good day's work all around, though the Westminster well-wisher decided to temper his satisfaction with caution until he knew the extent of Botha's business misdemeanours abroad.

7.

Editorial manoeuvrings

Edmund Cornell was sceptical about the Head Honcho's commitment to the future of *The Horizon*, despite his assurances to the contrary. Half an hour before their evening review, Cornell decided to visit the print rooms in the bowels of the building to judge the feelings of the employees there. He steeled himself for the volley of irreverent sarcasm that usually greeted his rare appearances on the shop floor and sure enough, the mocking arrived right on cue. The first boiler-suited machine operator to catch his eye shouted, "Bloody hell, Jesus is back from on high!"

Others who were close enough to hear above the din of the chugging presses chuckled derisorily (Cornell, in his role as the Editor-in-Chief, was known to the printers as Jesus, while they referred to Marcus Botha as Christ).

"Yes…morning boys." The men delighted in the tetchiness of Cornell's greeting. "Is the FOC about?" Those initials referred to the Father of the Chapel, a quaint old title used in the printing trade to describe the senior trade union representative. (Ironically, the un-Godly language used during the many battles between Christ, Jesus and the FOC would make a vicar blush!)

A passing labourer skirted his broom over the dusty floor and replied, "He's over there loading paper - doing some *real* work." The shop floor had a thinly veiled contempt for all the editorial staff, reporters and sales personnel upstairs.

That crowd have it so easy with their sit- down jobs drinking endless cups of coffee all day.

No deafening noise to deal with.

No arthritic backs for them to suffer in retirement.

Cornell knew that every cog in the wheel of a successful organisation has important tasks to perform, and each one carried its own unique pressures and drawbacks. His role within the hierarchy was to keep those cogs oiled and working to their maximum capacity.

He found the FOC, a hard-bitten but pragmatic man by the name of Michael Brookes, busying himself at his workstation. Trying to grab a discreet word with him was difficult against the surrounding cacophony, so he simply tugged on Brookes' sleeve and mouthed the words, "Office chat?"

The union leader bellowed back, "You'll have to wait 'til I've fed the last of the paper into the presses - I can't just drop everything when you click your fingers!"

This somewhat sharp admonishment reaffirmed the ground rules between them; the management on one side of the divide, the shop floor on the other. Penthouse and Pavement.

Checking his watch, Brookes continued. "Go on in and I'll be with you in five minutes."

Cornell was tempted to scold him there and then for his stroppy attitude, but instead he bit his lip and dutifully retired to the relative quiet of the union office to await the busy bee. On this occasion, it suited his purpose to be magnanimous.

Brookes loved making the management wait on his account, so it was eleven minutes later when the two men sat down to parlay. They were perched either side of a functional heavily chipped MDF desk strewn with scrawled notes about holiday timetables, hospital appointments and various other bits of union paraphernalia. The FOC pushed the plug of an old, cracked plastic kettle into a nearby wall socket, switched it on and finally got down to business.

"What's up then, Edmund?" This first name basis was in accordance with cordial formality rather than friendship.

"I was wondering what you made of Marcus's announcement about the TV network he's starting up?"

"What about it?"

Brookes knew Cornell was trying to draw something out of him, but he mischievously bounced the ball back over the net.

"Well, how do your members feel? Are they frightened for their jobs?"

"No more than usual where that wanker is concerned." Brookes never missed an opportunity to pour scorn on his employer. "Anyway, why would his telly station affect us?"

"I thought I'd see if you were worried that there might be a brain drain upstairs, you know? If our best reporters jump ship to become TV stars, it's possible that sales of the paper might suffer, and I wanted to know if you'd thought about that."

Brookes bristled at the suggestion that reporters were the key to the paper's success rather than his unheralded comrades in the engine room.

"First, I don't see much in the way of brains up there to drain, and second, if any of your lot do bugger off to the telly, Botha will just scrape the bottom of another barrel for their ten-a-penny replacements. New names to churn out the same old crap we're printing now.

People don't buy this rag for the reporting skills of the writers, they buy it for the tits, bits and oops-a-daisy we churn out. That and the sport. Now if some of those sports desk blokes moved on, we might feel a bit queasy, but all - in - all, I wouldn't say we're too fussed. If it wasn't for my men making sure this load of old cobblers gets to the newsstands nice and early every morning, those big-headed bastards you're talking about would be nonentities, not television hopefuls. And don't you ever forget that, right?"

Boisterous rants from the combustible Brookes were water off a duck's back to Cornell, but as he spoke, the FOC's mind turned over the possible implications of Botha's move.

Would it be such a bad thing if the old man spent less time at The Horizon?

During the move from Fleet Street to its new premises on Commercial Road in Limehouse, he had introduced new working practices and machinery, streamlining the operation at a cost of countless jobs.

Perhaps if he took his eye off the ball to concentrate on building his TV network, the union might be able to claw back some of the entitlements that my members enjoyed prior to the East End switch.

Then again, while I'd be delighted by that outcome, Botha's preoccupation with his new venture just might have negative consequences after all.

If he loosened his grip on things too much here, The Horizon could drop market share, triggering further redundancies.

The kettle boiled and he set about pouring tea for himself and his unwelcome guest. This process allowed him a moment to form an opinion on the topic at hand.

"Botha's TV business won't take precedence over this place. Surely not?... Anyway, telly and papers are separate entities. Your hands and feet are both part of the same body, but you don't pick up a knife and fork with your toes to tackle your dinner, do you?" After suffering from his paymaster's progressive thinking in the past, he wanted to convince himself that there would be no threat to his men from this latest scheme. "Besides, how many *Horizon* readers will bother with one of those bloody ugly satellite dishes anyway? All that nonsense is overrated in my book."

Cornell listened intently to the FOC's thoughts, then, for the sake of politeness, took a small sip of tea from the dirty cup in front of him, before rising from his shabby seat.

"Ok, Mick, thanks for that - it was good to get your feelings on the matter. I just thought you should be kept in the loop, especially since the Head Honcho isn't exactly inclined to pop down here for a chat himself."

"If he did, he wouldn't get back up those stairs in one piece - and you can tell him that when you see him."

"Now now...."

There was no parting handshake between the two men, just a knowing nod that their summit had reached its natural end. Departing swiftly from the shop floor (amid more mocking howls), Cornell stepped into the lift and ascended the entire length of the building to the penthouse for his meeting with the boss. The geographical distance between the manual workforce and their proprietor served as a poignant metaphor to describe their diametrically opposed attitudes.

That day's consultation with Botha was Cornell's first opportunity to discuss the TV plans, and after their routine chat on general policy and storyline matters drew towards its close, he decided to seek clarification on his points of concern.

"Right then Edmund, if there's no other business, I'll -"

"Can I stop you there, Marcus?" He interjected somewhat nervously, but with a sense of purpose all the same.

The Head Honcho looked up from an array of notes strewn about his sumptuous desk and rapidly scanned the body language of the man opposite. Sensing a faint air of controlled aggression in his editor's demeanour, he leaned forwards in readiness for any confrontation that may transpire. Cornell paused. He could certainly dig his heels in when he needed to get a point across to his staff, but standing his ground in front of his boss was a different kettle of fish altogether. In his long and noteworthy career, he had never met anyone to match the granite will of Marcus Botha and that fact continually disturbed him. This was the lion's den, and no one was safe when facing the king of the jungle.

"What's on your mind then Edmund? Come on man, spit it out!"

Almost imperceptibly, Cornell withdrew into himself and began what he intended to be a formal address from a position of clear discomfort.

"Mr. Botha -"

"Not Marcus, eh? That's interesting...Can we cut the formalities, *Mr. Cornell*? We're both busy people and time is money. So let's hear it."

"Well, I've had a meeting with the FOC and he's not a happy bunny."

"Is that bitter little arsehole still moaning about our move to Limehouse? Still crying tiny tears into his tea?"

"He's simply concerned that some of his members are becoming nervous for their futures at *The Horizon*." In truth, Cornell wanted to use his earlier conversation with Brookes to obtain a promise of security from the boss for all of the paper's employees. "After all, if your broadcasting venture takes off..." his voice trailed away as Botha's face turned gallows grey.

"I think the word you are looking for, is *when*, isn't it? *When* my broadcasting venture takes off." At this, he stood up and glared menacingly at his poor Chief Editor. "Why should I care about those pricks in the print department? Why worry myself over them and their outmoded attitudes?"

"Well, we wouldn't want another round of industrial trouble here, would we?"

"I'm more than ready for that lot, I can assure you! Remember the last time they started to sabre rattle? From the moment I bought this paper, I wanted to chop at the dead wood down there. Moving to Limehouse was the perfect excuse to get rid of the wastage while retaining those men with essential skills.

And what did the union do about that?"

Cornell plucked up the courage to defend the printers.

"Well, they did work to rule to get their former colleagues reinstated. They took strike action; they picketed."

"*They* picketed? I seem to recall that they dragged in some secondary pickets to help them out - miners, dockworkers - people who had absolutely nothing to do with the dispute! Those interfering swine tried to railroad me into keeping all my dross on the payroll - they thought they'd got me on the ropes with their industrial action and their futile strikes." Botha was one of the biggest scourges of the socialist movement and he now motored into full rant mode.

"Well, I had an ace up my sleeve to thwart those Communist agitators - the trump card in the pack - I had the 'Iron Lady' beside me!" (Commissars at the Kremlin had bestowed this defining soubriquet upon the Prime Minister, born out of a grudging respect for her indomitable spirit, and Botha felt it perfectly summed up her battle-hardened, never-say-die personality.) "Of course, the PM's backing guaranteed me the support of the police - I had that help on hand twenty-four seven to enforce my justifiable right to run *my* business as I saw fit. The outcome was never in doubt from then on - just ask those dockers now! And the fucking miners! While you're at it, the next time you chat to the FOC - that oh-so-effective custodian of the print workers' affairs - you can remind him too!

Who the fuck did they think they were up against? They were just a bunch of angry losers trying to turn back the clock of progress, fighting over a lost cause - the maintenance of dear old Fleet Street's absurd working practices. Yesterday's people preaching yesterday's news - that's all Brookes and those other clowns downstairs have ever been."

"But they have a reasonable concern for their livelihoods here Marcus -"

"Oh, we're back to first names now, are we?"

The interruption broke Cornell's stride a little, but he ploughed on regardless.

"I just think it would make good business sense to give them some reassurance, a scrap of acknowledgement that you understand their anxieties, that's all...."

Botha smirked.

"Are you trying to tell me what makes good business sense now? Are you steering this ship, or am I?"

It had always struck Cornell as curious that Botha paid top dollar to recruit staff, only to then tell them how wrong they were whenever they disagreed with the great man's mental flow. He patronised, demeaned, or humiliated anyone who contradicted his didactic utterances, and issued disapproving lectures on the folly of their mistaken ways as a penance for having the temerity to be so bold.

One of the Head Honcho's infamous silences momentarily darkened the room, before the lights came on again with his next comment, indicating a more positive change of mood. "Look Edmund, you'll be alright you know? Didn't I tell you the paper will continue? Trust me, you'll be enjoying your well-earned retirement before any fundamental changes take place in the media, though between you and me I can't predict that *The Horizon* will be here in the long term. Over the next few decades, it's possible that there won't be any newspapers at all - they're of their time, and it seems to me that their time is drawing to a close. If you doubt what I'm saying, let's recall the history of information distribution shall we?" Another Botha lecture was imminent. "Prior to Guttenberg's fifteenth century printing press, the world relied on word of mouth to pass on information; then books emerged, eventually leading to newspaper production, yes? All this is common knowledge, but time advances. Since the first *Pathé News* presentations shown in cinemas, visual reportage has taken a stronger grip on the public's attention, then once television began broadcasting bulletins into every home, it got tougher still for papers to flourish - yet their special relationship with the people remained intact. But how much longer can we rely on that? Advances in consumerism accelerate the desire for the latest thing - the quickest this and easiest that. People now have an opportunity to get up-to-the-minute rolling news at the push of a button.

For some years, we've been able to catch up with global events through breakfast TV without any need to pick up a morning newspaper. The reality is that people buy *The Horizon* out of habit, or loyalty, or for the non-news items - the gossip and sport. Pretty soon, video screens, like billboards, will be mounted to the walls of buildings, broadcasting headlines to the public for free, and where will the newsstand be then? Or indeed, the newspaper industry itself?"

"So you are intending to dispense with us, eventually?"

"Rest easy. I've already said that you're perched in the tree-top, safe from voracious predators...it's the fodder at the bottom that will get gobbled up. If selling papers comes to an end, I won't need the printing facility, only my editorial staff and journalists - those who can adapt to the requirements of twenty-four hour rolling news, at any rate."

"But didn't you tell our team that TV and the papers were different beasts - separate entities?"

"Our people wanted to be in front of the camera presenting the news, but I'm hiring a more easy-on-the-eye team of broadcasters for that job. Photogenic eye-candy. The quality of the copy that they work with is going to be key to *MJB TV*'s success though, so for the immediate future, if I see *The Horizon*'s bloodhounds doing a better job than any of the television network staff, they'll replace the duffers there. Otherwise, if the newspaper business withers on the vine...." He ran a finger across his throat to make his message clear. With that ominous vision of the future dismissively uttered, Botha sank back into the red leather surroundings of his throne of power.

Cornell had hoped that this was his cue to go, but his boss wanted to see him off with a slice of entrepreneurial philosophy to put in his pocket for later.

"You know your Darwin don't you Edmund? Survival of the fittest and all that? Those who have the will, the fight - the vision to succeed - will always find themselves on top, looking down on the delusional, the misguided and the wrong-headed. Every species, every society, every culture, produces a few strong-minded individuals, an *elite* who wield the power and crush the dissenters. It's nature's way.

Now that the Eastern bloc countries have broken free from their oppressive Communist yoke, let's see whether the lives of the people over there improve all that significantly. I'm ready to wager that any changes will be largely cosmetic. Individuals will emerge, small in number, creating organisations of vast power, with the people below, the *drones*, doing their bidding. Things will remain just as they were under Communism, only these organisations will be professional, and run for profit - which the doers, the decision makers, the strong, will harvest.

And do you think they're going to give a fuck about their drones? Of course not! Why should they? If the drones don't like their jobs, don't like the conditions - fine! Let them do something else for a living. The new elite will give them the

same message that our paper recently issued to the England football manager -
FOR GOD'S SAKE, GO!

The bolshie drones will be sent packing with fleas in their ears and a simple message to take back to their impoverished families: - *'There's always someone else ready to fill your shitty shoes!'* Just you wait and see."

Cornell thought Botha obviously longed to pass the same message on to his own employees. Unsurprisingly, the next words out of his mouth confirmed that view.

"As for my drones down there in the print room - the *little* people - they simply don't *matter*; they don't count for anything in the grand scheme of corporate control."

So there it is, laid bare.

Marcus Botha – the living embodiment of a Nietzschean wet dream.

Somehow, I have to find a way to work with him, for the good of the paper and those poor 'little people' who work here.

"Marcus, I may not agree…..er, *entirely*…with you …but this is your boardroom, your newspaper and I am but a guest player in your play, so with reluctance, I'll stand by whatever decisions you make regarding the future." Cornell knew that this cowardly capitulation was a damning indictment on the decline of his powers of principle. He was well paid, approaching sixty (which meant that he was probably too old to expect another job of this stature in the industry), and the sheer force of Botha's personality had simply ground him down.

Suddenly, a flash of inspiration sprang into the South African's lively mind.

"I tell you what Edmund, I will give you something to take back to your precious printers - oh, and by the way, when did you, of all people, start having sympathy for the forces on the dark side of the street?" He expected no answer, and merely sought to mock his vanquished subordinate. "You want me to reassure them that we're all one big happy family perhaps? Well you can pass this on to the *brothers*. I'll make them an offer of share options in *MJB TV*.

At a reduced rate, significantly below market value, they can invest in my company and help to fund my expansive plans. In return for this fantastic opportunity, they'll get a cut from the significant profits I expect to make. We'll all be in this together - **Solidarnosc!** - eh?" His ironic reference to the Polish trade union that had prompted Eastern Europe's Velvet Revolution was a rare whimsy from the usually humourless tycoon. "Our printers will effectively have to become capitalists to protect their own futures!"

"Just a second Marcus - isn't that the same offer you've made to the reporting staff? Are they drones too in this New World Order?"

The Head Honcho quickly moved to clarify any misunderstanding.

"Remember, the offer to your people upstairs is for *preference* shares, which guarantee a return on your outlay, come what may, whereas the printers will only get the chance to purchase *ordinary* shares, so they'll have to wait until the venture becomes profitable before they get to benefit from the fruits of our labours too. Don't concern yourself though, '*Red Ed*'" (this mocking quip produced a smile displaying the finest dentistry money can buy). "Everyone will do very nicely in the long run, so you never know, we might just get to see those comrades of yours showing up for work in pinstriped suits and braces, like city speculators! They'll have to snap up those shares quickly though, because they'll need something to fall back on when they find themselves surplus to requirements here!"

With that contemptuous comment, the meeting concluded, and Cornell turned to go back to the newsroom. Before he reached the door, Botha left him with one final thought.

"Oh, Edmund, just remember this.... I don't respond well to dissent and I'm good at finding its instigators. When I see a burning building, I can always spot the fellow holding the incriminating matches. Now go about your business."

The Horizon's Chief Editor realised that his boss had rumbled the truth, that his fake concern for the printers disguised his real fears for the future of the paper and himself.

Message received and understood.

Don't ever try to hoodwink your Lord and Master because you'll end up sorry.

Once the penthouse door closed behind him, Edmund Cornell could breathe again. Alone in the stillness of the lift, descending towards his comfort zone where the press pack hunted, he paused to consider just what kind of man his employer was.

Obviously having the mental toughness to make difficult decisions is a necessity in upper management, but he had grave misgivings for the future if it was left in the hands of such short-term, profit driven, narrow-minded individuals as his boss. Throughout an absorbing, exasperating, but ultimately fulfilling career in journalism, he had crossed paths with many dynamic, devious, and despotic chancers, but Botha stood out because of his discernible edge; his character was more akin to that of a military dictator than a celebrated industrialist, and that made him truly formidable.

A generation of city-slicker entrepreneurs looked at his antics with admiration, and *The Horizon*'s Editor-in-Chief increasingly found himself stifling a gag reflex. He could not decide if what troubled him was old-aged sagacity or the unshakeable cockiness of this unsavoury New Breed, whose twisted values celebrated a vulgar, masturbatory worship of all things mammon.

If men like the Head Honcho are having such an influence on the thinking of others, then what are the prospects for society as a whole going into the next century?

Boom and bust had become the order of the day, providing countless opportunities for shrewd speculators to gauge when to enter and exit the money markets. Their reckless profiteering jeopardised the job security of the average person; the average *Horizon* reader; the engine of the corporate machine. In terms he could directly relate to, that meant people like Michael Brookes and the members of his Chapel.

Margaret Thatcher once famously remarked that there was, "No such thing as society," inferring that individuals need only be concerned for themselves and not each other, but surely, Cornell thought, there would soon come a day of reckoning if the "haves" continued to viciously trample on the "have nots"?

Why is this most obvious of observations not ringing alarm bells of concern at Westminster and beyond?

Sometimes his job required him to be a dutiful shit-kicker for the greater good, for the success of the business as a whole. For the Penthouse *and* the Pavement. Yet in Marcus Botha, he saw a man with a singular vision of success, intended for the greater good of himself alone.

During the endless class struggles that bedevilled British industry in the pre-Thatcher days, Cornell had always stood firmly on the side of the management, believing that ever- worsening employer/employee relations were sailing the country towards the rocky shores of anarchy. He felt that trade unions were strangling entrepreneurial spirit, until the Prime Minister introduced legislation intended to clip their wings. Experience mellows a person however, and now, whenever he thought about the managerial governance around him, an indigestive pain tore away at his insides. Though he remained a committed Conservative, the actions of modern entrepreneurs made him wonder whether the balance of power might have tipped too much towards the Penthouse.

Chills enveloped him, as if the shadows of a dozen celestial spirits had suddenly overcrowded the lift, and he wondered how far his boss might be prepared to go to achieve success. A frown burdened his craggy brow, but he cut short his deliberations to avoid slipping into depression, for there was work to be done, plans to be drawn up for the following morning. Returning to the sanctuary of his office, he reached for his ubiquitous dyspepsia tablets and a glass of water. Within minutes, all was well again, his poker face returned, and after shaking out a shrug of resigned compliance, he got back to the task of trying to increase his employer's riches.

8.

Hillsborough and the blame game

As we have seen with Marcus Botha's failure to break into the US publishing market, psychotic levels of self-belief do not make one immune to folly.

He had a habit of reporting events as he preferred to see them, rather than as they actually occurred, and more often than not his skilful use of suggestion and supposition convinced large amounts of people that his version of the facts was indeed the gospel truth. However, there is much to be commended in Abraham Lincoln's oft-repeated remark, *"You can fool all the people some of the time and some of the people all the time, but you can't fool all the people all of the time."* By publishing an incendiary version of events that took place in Sheffield on April 15th, 1989, Botha pushed his luck too far.

That day, an FA Cup semi-final between Liverpool Football Club and Nottingham Forest was held at Hillsborough, the neutral venue of Sheffield Wednesday FC, which resulted in the UK's worst ever sporting tragedy.

To avoid crowd trouble, each team's supporters were segregated at opposite ends of the ground, with Liverpool's fans occupying the Leppings Lane terrace. Disaster struck before kick-off when the police squeezed too many people into one section of the stand, creating a desperate crush. The solution would have been to allow those at the front to clamber onto the pitch so that they could be ushered into another, less congested pen, but some years earlier government legislation had decreed that the field of play at football stadia must be fenced off to prevent spontaneous invasions from marauding hooligans. Vital minutes passed by while the emergency services dithered about unlocking those metal barriers, and more and more supporters lost consciousness, struggling for precious air. By the time the cage doors were finally opened to ease the situation, the damage had already been done. Ultimately, ninety-seven Liverpool fans perished.

Every newspaper raced into print to defend the authorities, vociferously applauding the police for bringing order to the unfolding chaos. At the same time, they took the opportunity to smear Liverpool's followers, suggesting that they were the root cause of the trouble. After all, this was not their first involvement in terrace fatalities...

Violence between football hooligans had blighted the domestic game for twenty years, and improvements in the national transport infrastructure only helped to facilitate bitter tribal rivalries. Gradually, this propensity to create havoc became one of the country's most successful exports too, as many supporters who followed their teams abroad did so with increasing aggression (fuelled by easy access to cheap alcohol).

During the early 1980's, young male *fashionistas* of Milan and Paris strutted their stuff sporting wedge haircuts, polo shirts and cardigans, with branded tracksuit tops and training shoes completing their look, and Liverpool's travelling fans became aware of this exclusive designer clothing from their team's regular appearances in European competitions. Within their number were a gang of young wastrels, intent on initiating pilfering sprees that targeted the continent's chicest boutiques. Their mission was to bring cutting-edge couture back home, and after each international foray, they were the best-dressed chancers in town.

They now had their own unique image: a regional hooligan brand known as the "Casuals," which differentiated Merseyside's young thugs from those in other cities. Of course, most of the club's supporters saw these "Casuals," as an unwelcome minority whose antics did nothing but stain the club's name. This assumption soon proved to be correct in the deadliest of circumstances.

The 1985 European Cup final between Liverpool and Juventus of Italy took place at Belgium's Heysel Stadium, and during a pre-match skirmish, the "Casuals," launched an attack on rival Italian fans. In the ensuing panic, a concrete wall collapsed, killing thirty-nine people. European football's governing body FIFA reacted to the riot by excluding all English teams from its competitions for five years.

With a previous heinous misdemeanour to draw on, the tabloids had a field day, suggesting that Hillsborough's victims met their fate through the reckless irresponsibility of their fellow brethren. Other observers claimed that inadequate policing and the government's policy of caging in supporters may have caused the catastrophe, but the press (particularly *The Horizon* and *The Sun*) ploughed on regardless with wild accusations of unruly behaviour. The following morning, at Botha's insistence, his paper's evocative banner headline read:

HEYSEL KILLERS IN '85.

HILLSBOROUGH KILLERS IN '89.

The rest of its front page contained just one, caustic and unequivocal paragraph:

'Yesterday Liverpool FC's hooligan following heaped further shame on their club during an FA Cup Semi-Final at Sheffield Wednesday's Hillsborough ground. Ticket-less thugs showed a selfish disregard for the safety of others and rampaged onto the terracing, with catastrophic consequences.'

Read all about it!

More red top publications jumped to the same uncorroborated conclusion, colourfully embellishing their stories with lurid tales of drunken supporters shamelessly urinating on corpses. Worse was to come. Some, "witnesses," claimed to see motionless victims robbed on the pitch, while one newspaper reported that a constable was set-upon as he administered the kiss of life to an injured fan.

For a week, hellish headlines and negative news coverage described a scene more reminiscent of a Spanish Pamplona than a football terrace. David Duckenfield, the Chief Superintendent of police in charge of co-ordinating the police operations that day, told Football Association officials that fans had prompted the carnage by forcing a gate open at the Leppings Lane end and pouring into the packed central pens.

The blame game was in full swing, with all eyes turned towards Liverpool Football Club and its travelling fans.

9.

Kick them, then kick them some more

During the post-war years, the reassuringly familiar procession of cargo ships that had once sailed along the River Mersey gradually drained to a trickle, and as a result, Liverpool's docks steadily declined in importance, leading to unprecedented levels of unemployment amongst its population. Increases in the speed and efficiency of transporting goods via road and air had gradually reduced the country's dependency on regional shipping, diminishing the area's geographical advantage. While successive governments spent hundreds of millions of pounds improving London's road and rail infrastructure to compensate for the reduction of the capital's maritime freight (creating new jobs to replace those that had gone in the process), other port cities found themselves starved of investment. They were not in a unique situation by the dawn of the 1980's.

The UK's economy fell into a deep recession and Margaret Thatcher decided to introduce tough fiscal policies in an effort to reduce the tax drain on working families. Inevitably, those measures produced winners and losers, and one of the outcomes of the restructuring process was the emergence of an economy divided by geography. As the southern service sector began to prosper, traditional manufacturing bases in the north received no financial support and slowly began to wither and die in the face of cheap foreign competition. The cancer of mass unemployment spread, devastating areas that relied heavily on endangered industries to provide work for their people, like Clydebank (shipbuilding), Consett (steel) and Stoke (ceramics).

In response to the crisis, the Prime Minister's Employment Secretary

Norman Tebbit advised anyone who found themselves without work to, "Get on their bikes," and chase opportunities wherever they arose. This soundbite was wonderfully received in the Home Counties (where, generally, there were enough jobs to satisfy demand), but across the rest of the UK, the jobless total vastly outweighed the number of vacancies on offer, so his remarks met with hostility and bitter ridicule.

Back in Liverpool, redundancy notices at the docks meant bad news for the entire city. Dole cheques provide less spending power than a weekly wage, so one by one, local shops, pubs, and restaurants inevitably went out of business. Demand for new-build houses declined too; after all, why build what fewer people could afford to buy? At this time, the *BBC* produced an award-winning TV series, "*The Boys from the Blackstuff*," that followed the plight of a team of Merseyside builders whose work had dried up as the city's infrastructure imploded. The show's visceral portrayal of the impact of unemployment led to a nationwide debate on the government's economic strategy, but Parliament refused to buckle under mounting pressure and fought back, accusing the tax-funded national broadcaster of attempting to interfere in matters of policy.

Liverpudlians have a reputation for bloody-minded resistance, and they are more belligerent than stoical when told to just grin and bear hard times. Consequently, it is hardly surprising to note that since the birth of the trade union movement in the UK, Merseyside accents have found a natural home at the top table of most struggles against low pay and poor working conditions.

In stark contrast to London's prosperity, northern cities traditionally struggle to attract inward investment, so for many people outside the capital, the prospect of large scale, long-term unemployment is an unwelcome reality. As a defensive reaction, the residents of these communities have an innate ability to laugh at adversity and their sense of humour is often of a brutal nature. Caricature remains an integral part of a wit's armoury, and jokes abound about skin-flint Scots; unintelligent Irish navvies; in-bred West Country folk etc. For years, variety club comedians referred to Liverpudlians as work-shy *'Scallies'* (short for 'scallywags'; duck-and-divers, always on the lookout to sell contraband goods that have unaccountably, "fallen from the back of a lorry.")

Wherever the scourge of economic deprivation abounds and opportunities to connect endeavour with tangible reward are limited, the more light-fingered members of society will look for alternative ways to prosper, and in this regard, Liverpool is no different from any other city. The devil makes work for idle hands, whether they come from Merseyside, Marseille or Marrakesh, but mud has a nasty habit of sticking and for many people, the comedic perception of Liverpudlians as a feckless underclass has become a ludicrous reality. Once the newspapers were able to link this enduring image with Liverpool FC's hardcore hooligan faction, they had their scapegoats for the Hillsborough nightmare.

This time though, they had fired their shots too soon, and in the wrong direction.

10.

The backlash begins

A heady concoction of pride, passion, good humour and indomitable spirit has carried the people of Liverpool through many tough times, and after the events of Hillsborough, they would need those qualities more than ever. The city's two prestigious football clubs, Liverpool and their near neighbours Everton, came together to grieve, displaying an almost unique solidarity. Parochial rivalries meant nothing, for fans of both sides had lost brothers, sisters, uncles, aunts, cousins, sons and daughters in the crush.

Liverpool FC's directors decided to open their home ground, Anfield, to the public, and soon the playing surface and terraces were awash with floral tributes and scarves from well-wishers across the country and beyond. Everyone needed a moment of reflection to gather their thoughts, console the bereaved families, and bury the dead. Players and staff from the club respectfully attended every funeral.

Closure, however, would be a long time in coming.

In the immediate aftermath of the tragedy, the police had encouraged the notion that Liverpool's fans on the Leppings Lane terrace had been feral, a view that the government and sections of the media gobbled up without question. Newspapers have a duty to investigate the truth, not merely to accept the words of officialdom without scrutiny, and their glaring failure to act responsibly created public unease once contradictory comments from eyewitnesses began to surface. Impassioned local voices asked for hard evidence to back up the tabloid claims and when none emerged, the tide of national opinion began to turn. A belief grew that the casualties were innocent victims of a botched police operation.

Some papers subsequently retreated from their original stance, but Marcus Botha's *Horizon* and Rupert Murdoch's *Sun* stood firm in their support of the emergency services. This was a risky strategy because when pressure mounted on the government to launch an inquiry into the who, when, why, what and where of the incident, they felt compelled to appoint a High Court judge, the Rt. Hon. Lord Justice Taylor, to investigate the facts. He would be thorough in his approach, but in the meantime, the people of Liverpool had already delivered their own verdict on the publications that continued to vilify their kin.

They simply stopped buying them.

11.

Riders on the storm

The Taylor inquiry lasted thirty-one days and published two reports: the first laid out its findings and the second, released six months later in January 1990, made recommendations for the future of organised football matches.

That explosive first report ripped a hole in the press's original version of events. Unannounced road works on the M62 motorway had caused hold ups for supporters travelling to Sheffield over the Pennines, and this contributed to the late surge of people scrambling to get into the ground (a fact that was conveniently absent from the newspaper coverage). According to Lord Justice Taylor, a "failure of police control" was the main cause of the situation getting out of hand and Chief Superintendent David Duckenfield "froze" upon ordering an exit gate to be opened under the Leppings Lane terracing. His decision led to 2,000 extra fans being ferried through a tunnel into already crowded central pens. Crucially, the report concluded that hooliganism had played no part in the events.

With the fans officially exonerated from any blame, the government, along with *The Horizon* and *The Sun*, Botha and Murdoch's flagship tabloids, were now open to criticism and ridicule for their inaccurate statements, and each in turn suffered severe damage to their reputations.

The day after Lord Taylor's findings were published, The Head Honcho and Edmund Cornell were involved in a heated debate about *The Horizon*'s latest regional sales figures which revealed that circulation was drastically down in the North-West area, particularly around Merseyside. Botha reacted furiously.

"Those people are killing my business! They've ruined what was a fantastic story for us with their constant moaning - why are they all so obsessed with bloody football anyway?"

Cornell was used to his heartless rants, but the particularly callous nature of this latest tirade still managed to drop his jaw to the floor.

"Oh, don't give me all that sanctimonious face pulling Edmund, you know as well as I do that whenever we get a major event - particularly a national disaster - it runs and runs, and we get to shift big units. We had our best week of the year following Hillsborough, but this Taylor fella has just given those northern bastards a stick to beat us with. It's not as if the enquiry's handwringing can bring any of the dead back - what's done is done." Anything that threatened to clip the Head Honcho's wings was glaringly wrongheaded to him. "The trouble is that they love to play the victim - they're always at it!" He then mockingly wiped fake tears from his eyes. *"We can't find jobs and it's not our fault* - yes it is! They're lazy, thieving fuckers - everyone knows that! They're looking to shift the blame again here - they just can't handle the truth!

The police and the government agree with me about the degenerate behaviour of those morons at the match. Their track record is public knowledge for Christ's sake! Nobody kicked up a stink when we reported on their rampage at the Heysel Stadium four years back, so I don't see why I'm getting a kicking this time."

During his career in the newspaper business, Botha had slandered huge swathes of the public at some time or other without ever facing a drop in sales before, because he knew that as a rule, people have short memories and very thick skins. With that in mind, this unexpected rebellion left him utterly baffled. "I just can't seem to get through to their thick heads…why are they being so awkward?"

Staring at his Editor-in-Chief, he demanded an answer, but Cornell could scarcely believe what he was hearing. Despite Lord Justice Taylor's in-depth analysis of all the evidence, Botha refused to concede his error.

"It's because the fans who escaped the carnage gave different accounts to the enquiry than the one we printed. That's why our paper is struggling to sell up there, Marcus."

"How can anyone in their right mind doubt that drunken thugs caused that crush?"

"Because they haven't seen any proof! We based our story on statements made by police officers who were at the scene, but there's no evidence to corroborate their accounts. In Belgium in '85 we all saw the rioting for ourselves on TV, but there isn't a single frame of footage from Sheffield that shows any signs of hooligan activity."

Botha still believed in his own version of events, but he had to concede that Cornell had a point about the police being unable to prove their accusations. It was time to deploy damage limitation tactics to make sure that Liverpool's truculence did not evolve into a nationwide epidemic of hatred towards his newspaper.

"Edmund, send for Lewis Neeves, will you? After that enquiry's ridiculous conclusions, I'm going to need a word in the ear of someone close to the business end at Westminster… the cabinet has to understand that we must all hold firm against any further misplaced criticism…."

Within an hour, *The Horizon*'s political columnist strode purposefully into Botha's penthouse suite for their hastily arranged summit, conveying an air of cautious, yet perceptible confidence.

"Good morning, Marcus - I must say I'm not entirely surprised that you've called me in for a chat today."

"Good morning to you too, Lewis. I'm glad you were alert to my summons - as ever, your antenna for detecting trouble is in full working order. It's good that you've prioritised my concerns over spending the day in the House of Commons because I'm rather hoping that you've got some suggestions as to how I - or rather, we - can get ourselves out of the mess that this bloody fool Taylor has left us in."

"To tell you the truth, I'm glad to be out of the kitchen, so to speak, because as you can imagine, for a while at least, it will be getting uncomfortably hot in there. We're going to be under severe pressure from the opposition today - they're chomping at the bit for the chance to do some establishment-bashing at the expense of the government and the police. Even some of our own less-than-loyal back benchers will see the noble Lord Justice's conclusions as an opportunity to ridicule the Prime Minister."

"Treacherous tossers!"

"Quite so Marcus."

"So what will she do now?"

"Well, this is going to take some careful management, but Mrs. T will be as well briefed as ever before she enters the debating Chamber, and I'm sure she'll defend the government admirably. She excels in these pressure situations, and I'm confident that she can ride out the storm of dissent with her usual mixture of charisma and gritty determination, then I dare say we'll be back on track in a week or two. There's insufficient evidence to prosecute any of the policemen involved, so after some huff-and-puff in Parliament we'll be able to let the thing quietly fade away. Of course, the rest of the media will give us a bit of a bashing for criticising Liverpool's supporters so vehemently though."

"Those hypocritical bastards were all singing the same song as us at the start of this - they just didn't have the balls to stick to their guns when public opinion turned!"

"Oh, I wouldn't overreact Marcus, try to put this into perspective. Her Majesty's government expect to get a savaging from the newshounds on this one, and those canine rivals of yours can hardly be blamed for taking the chance to maul you and Mr. Murdoch at the same time, can they? It's just part of the rough-and-tumble that goes with the job, isn't it?"

Botha disliked the schoolmasterly tone of this advice.

"Criticism may be an acceptable peril in politics but it's not something that I care to cultivate. You would do well to remember that."

Neeves gulped uncomfortably.

"Let me reassure you, this whole affair will be so much fish-and-chip paper by the end of the week. We'll all move on, and Hillsborough will soon be forgotten."

"You're sure about that are you, Lewis?"

"Sure enough. Take a leaf from the government's book on how to manage, er, mishaps like this."

"Go on, I'm listening."

"Think about it - since we returned to power in 1979, Mrs. Thatcher has presided over an extended period of mass unemployment, the like of which the country has never experienced before. Then throw in a decade of continual recessions. We've overseen the collapse of the steel industry and spent a year waging war against the miners. We've contended with race riots and risked the lives of our military personnel in the Falklands conflict. On top of all that, we've taken profitable nationalised industries out of public ownership and sold them off to city speculators."

"What's your point man!"

"I'm coming to that. At every turn, we've been pilloried for those actions. Yet we're still here. We are still the ruling party."

"With considerable help from me and my newspaper - don't ever forget that."

"Absolutely Marcus - and you know how deeply we appreciate your valuable support - but do you see where I'm coming from here? Despite all the civil turmoil - the collapse of manufacturing in the industrial north…despite the growing feeling that the rich are getting richer while the poor get poorer, we've still managed to win three consecutive general elections!

We understand our public - they WANT to believe in the authority of government, and Mrs. Thatcher has built such an invincible aura around herself that she can contradict the findings of any judge, lawyer, journalist or politician with absolute conviction, knowing that the people will go along with her. I'd dare to say that if she told them that day was really night, they'd change their sleeping habits!"

"Ok Lewis, you've made an excellent case for the PM's ability to deal with the fallout from all this. So how, in your capacity as an employee of this newspaper, do you suggest that I manage the problem from this end?"

Neeves had no hesitation over his assured reply.

"Just fudge it. You can issue an editorial apology for our original reporting of the incident and throw all the responsibility onto the police for releasing inaccurate information in the first place."

"I'm not happy about that - I rely on those people to back me up when my unions get bolshie!"

"Needs must Marcus. You need someone else to carry the can for this…. unfortunate situation."

"But I still insist they were right all along!"

Neeves became frustrated at Botha's intransigence.

"Oh please! You know as well as I do that the evidence doesn't support that opinion." This comment did nothing to pacify the grizzly bear before him, so he proceeded with enforced empathy. "While personally I wholeheartedly agree with you, it will be necessary for us to eat humble pie if we want to stay onside with our readers." It was important for Botha to understand that he must retract his accusations for the sake of the paper's credibility. "And don't worry about lambasting the police force. Sooner or later a major incident will occur where they'll be called upon to respond in their usual exemplary fashion, and when they do, you can take that opportunity to praise them to the hilt. A few well-chosen words at the right time will put you back in their good books again."

Some of Botha's anxiety began to ease, but there was still *The Horizon*'s poor sales performance in the North-West to deal with.

"All of this nonsense has decimated my circulation figures up there and I need to get those readers back, so how does that happen?"

"I'm sure you'll find that they'll be satisfied with Justice Taylor's verdict and will just want to move on with their lives now. You won't get them all back overnight, but with patience, those sales will return. What's important here is not to let the dissatisfaction of one community spread across the country and I see no evidence of that happening, as long as we draw a line over the thing once the apologies have gone into print. This is a localised issue, trust me."

Neeves was good. Thanks to the calm assurances of his advisor, Botha's dark mood improved, and the wily Parliamentarian was duly dismissed with an (albeit uncomfortable) pat on the back and a word of thanks for the wisdom of his council.

Moving forward, instead of adding salt to an open wound by constantly reminding his readership of that dark day in Sheffield, the Head Honcho vowed to distract them from the issue altogether.

His remedy would be both dramatic and radical.

12.

The new black

Marcus Johannes Botha's barrel-chested stature belied a slight but perceptible weakness of the heart. He had suffered occasional murmurs since childhood, and this evidence of a suppressed vulnerability reminded him that somewhere in the grand scheme of things, a force of nature greater than his own held sway. In a rarely shared moment of humility, he indicated as much to Edmund Cornell during their latest briefing, which began with a liturgy in praise of his celestial benefactor.

"Every day I give thanks to the Big Man in the white suit," he drawled, looking skywards beyond the stars. "I get down on my knees and say, *'Thank you God for giving me the strength to make more money today! Thanks for all of those willing dupes who happily part with their small change every morning to read the rubbish I publish!'* I thank Him for all their outrage and righteous indignation and rejoice that I've gotten away with it again! Ha!" With a thunderous clap of his rugged hands and an arrogant and insincere smile, he turned to his Editor-in-Chief and said, "Right then, to the day ahead. *Wotcha* got for me?" This improper use of English is an easily recognisable tool of the tabloid press; part of the dumbing-down process that makes their one - dimensional news coverage more easily relatable.

Since the summer, at Botha's insistence, *The Horizon* had been sucking every last scrap of life from the collapse of Communism in Eastern Europe and Cornell tamely offered his Lord and Master yet another quirky slant on the same theme. He reminded himself that the Head Honcho had recently berated

Peter Hawkins for wanting to lead with a political story, yet when it suited the boss man to do likewise, it was seen as a legitimate use of the front page.

"Isn't it time to change that particular record now though, boss?" he asked, hopefully. He was concerned that their readers were tiring of the subject, and gently tried to suggest that the paper should tap the veins of other emerging stories instead.

"Christ, no! No! We won't let go of this one 'til every plasterer, car mechanic, dish washer and shop keeper in the country realises the folly of left-wing dogma. I'm not going to rest 'til the entire fucking Soviet rag-tag house of cards is demolished and the lot of 'em have embraced true blue capitalism. This is about FREE markets - FREEDOM! It's about the right of every man - or woman," (he said as an afterthought) "on earth to be able to say what they like, do as they please and keep what they earn..." A familiar Botha punchline inevitably followed his impassioned speech, "...so long as they're saying what I say, doing what I want and spending their money with my businesses! Ha! What say you, Edmund?"

"Absolutely, Marcus!" Cornell smiled nervously, fully aware that one more disagreement with the Head Honcho might see the termination of his contract. His colleagues in the newsroom preserved their perks by sucking up to the boss whenever possible and although he saw their behaviour as toadyism at its most unbearable, he had become equally guilty of late, and died a little every day in quiet recognition of this unhappy truth...

Anyway, what's wrong with a bit of slavish acquiescence here?

After all, Botha's Anti-Communist views echo those of our own readers.

For over a decade, Margaret Thatcher's Tory blues had seen off the Labour red threat at the domestic ballot box, sending socialism scurrying into the shadows of domestic politics. Now, as a 'Velvet Revolution' swept irreversibly through the Eastern bloc countries, bigger, meaner Communist doctrines began to dismantle too.

"Ok then, Eastern Europe is our main focus again today. Get someone from the Chancellor's office to quote a few financial figures regarding increased export opportunities for UK businesses in the region. If you can't get anyone there to talk to you, just make up a plausible number in pounds sterling and attribute it to, *'a source at the Treasury.'* Got it?"

"I'll get someone on it as soon as we wrap this meeting up."

"Good man, I'm happy with that, so now let's address my other business at hand. Did you bring Harry Ellis with you like I asked?"

"Yes, he's waiting outside in Hilary's office."

Botha called through to his Personal Assistant via his intercom.

"Hilary? Send Mr. Ellis in will you please?"

Harry Ellis, *The Horizon*'s Sports Editor, was one of the key cogs in the organisation, because quality sports coverage was the critical factor in keeping its target market happy. When a big sports story broke, sales increased, at which point Botha would joyously exclaim, "Healthy circulation for the paper improves *my* circulation! The old blood pressure always goes down when our sales go up!"

Ellis entered the room not knowing what kind of reception to expect and he immediately caught a withering stare of icy indignation from his boss, followed by a word of warning.

"Before we begin Harry, let me make myself clear - from today I don't want to hear any further mention of fucking Hillsborough." Turning back to Cornell he said, "That's one record we most certainly can change."

How I enjoy making my subordinates feel uncomfortable!

"Now I know what you're thinking - you're wondering how we're going to fill the football pages when there's still only one hot story in town, yes?"

Ellis nodded.

"Well, we'll replace it with...absolutely nothing."

"What do you mean boss?"

"I mean we won't swop it for another football story because I want to see the back of the bloody game altogether! I propose that as of today we'll begin a campaign designed to rid our readers of their insane obsession!"

Ellis and Cornell exchanged quizzical glances.

Has the Head Honcho lost his mind?

Of course, the answer was no; his entrepreneurial instincts were at work and this typically provocative comment was designed to challenge their preconceived ideas about how far public opinion could be manipulated. He had been wrestling with two pressing problems for some time and finally arrived at a strategy to tackle them both. The issues were clear enough: he needed to create a buzz of excitement around his fledgling broadcasting enterprise while defusing the public's interest in the Hillsborough enquiry.

Given that most of his readers headed straight for the back pages of *The Horizon*, he felt that the best way to establish *MJB TV* would be through sport. An obvious route to brand awareness would involve sponsorship of a major football competition, but he had no intention of going down that path with the Sheffield tragedy still raw in everyone's memories, so, thinking outside of the box, he came up with an alternative sports promotion. He had crystal clear ideas for an imaginative marketing campaign, but they needed to be carefully implemented, and Cornell and Ellis were tasked with providing relevant input. To inspire them, first Botha explained the rationale behind his provocative dismissal of, 'the Beautiful Game'.

"Let's look at the facts chaps. Everyone complains about overpaid footballers and their celebrity lifestyles. They're too flash with their cash - they're rubbing our noses in it! There's too great an earnings gap between the fans on the terraces and their heroes on the pitch. We only recently reported that Liverpool are considering upping the wages of John Barnes to ten grand a week - I accept he's their star man, but that's an outrageous obscenity and the public bloody well know it! Crowds at top class football matches have been in decline for the last decade and right here is proof that the game as a major spectator sport is struggling." He consulted a sheet of scribbled numbers lying on his desk. "Ten years ago, the average attendance for First Division matches was, let me see... here we are - 28,692. Last season it was just 19,273, so crowds have gone down by a third in ten years. During the best attended season of 1949-50, about 77 million people watched football, but by last year that had dropped to only 20 million. That's almost a 75% reduction in paying customers - if I lost three-quarters of my circulation, this paper would be history and you two would be looking for new jobs! Based on those facts, it's easy to see that the party's over - the public are pig sick of the threat of violence that surrounds the game. Law-abiding parents can't take their kids to matches for fear of getting caught up in some ruckus or other - women won't go out shopping on a Saturday morning because rampaging gangs of rival supporters are wrecking city centres with their tribal warfare. Police resources are at full stretch on match days to control the mindless morons inside football stadia. Trust me boys, we're moving into a new era - the age of live mass spectator participation in sports is coming to an end, and television-friendly stuff is taking over.

Look at the rise in popularity of snooker for example - twenty years ago the only people interested in that game were old men in smoky working men's clubs, but the 1985 World Championship final attracted a TV audience of 20 million! When did football ever draw those kinds of viewing figures? Snooker has a production line of new, fresh faced, smiling superstars to admire like young Stephen Hendry and Ben St. Claire - role models who can inspire the youth of this nation, instead of those snarling, cheating footballers who deface our screens every Saturday night on "Match of the Day" with their spitting and disrespect for referees. As family- friendly entertainment, snooker ticks every box.

It's my belief that the public prefers to watch its top-class sport from the comfort of their own homes nowadays. They won't have gangs of knife-wielding idiots intent on mayhem chasing them around their sofas, will they? I'm telling you fellas, I've seen the future and professional football over here is dying on its arse. If we can successfully wean the die-hards away from their weekly fix of fear and misery on those wet and windy terraces, the country will be an altogether safer and more manageable place. When was the last time a fight broke out at a snooker tournament? The answer is never."

Harry Ellis was tempted to argue that snooker's renowned hell raiser Alex 'Hurricane' Higgins had been in punch-ups galore with fellow professionals and officials, but he held his tongue. After all, Botha had a point; hooliganism was not a concern in other sports as it was at football grounds across the country.

Cornell remained sceptical.

"So is that the strategy then Marcus? Is snooker, 'the new black,' so to speak for The Horizon?"

"After hearing my argument, is there any good reason why it shouldn't be?"

The tree of inspiration inside Harry Ellis's mind suddenly burst into bloom. Opportunities to grab Botha's attention were rare indeed, so he spoke up with gusto.

"Are we really focussing on the right sport here Marcus? Is snooker an absolutely perfect fit for the demographic of our readership?"

The Head Honcho paused, then drew himself up to his (rather unimpressive) full height and said, "*I* think it is." A familiar menace spread in the atmosphere of the room. "What makes *you* think it isn't?" The delivery was reminiscent of a playground school bully.

What are you gonna do about it?

Ellis gulped. It was too late to back - track now, so he continued with his train of thought.

"Well, I see a couple of issues here regarding snooker and our target market. First - the earnings of its top players are catching up with international footballers, so, if the public thinks that Liverpool pay John Barnes too much, then the same argument applies to Stephen Hendry and the like. And second - didn't the Queen once famously say she likes to settle in front of the telly every April when the World Championship is on? That tells me that snooker's audience demographic is less specifically working class than football's, so a targeted advertising campaign from us won't necessarily reach all of its followers."

Edmund Cornell's eyes raced straight to Botha in anticipation of a typically condescending response, and, true to form, he replied in the manner of an irritable schoolteacher.

"Television coverage of the game has created a boom in participation amongst the working class - our readers. Snooker halls are springing up everywhere at the very time when municipal football pitches are being turned into car parks, and the fact that every strand of society, irrespective of class prejudice, tunes in to watch Hendry, Higgins, St. Claire and co simply proves the *democracy* of the sport."

Democracy was a word often mentioned but rarely practiced at *The Horizon*. Opposition to the boss's opinions tended to result in the naysayer's slow walk to a waiting taxi, never to return.

"Snooker may be *democratic* Marcus, but as I've said, it isn't the absolute perfect fit for our *demographic*. If we want to mount a campaign to promote another sport over football, we need its replacement to be a unique fit for the readership of this newspaper."

"Such as?"

"Well, there's another sport that you seem to have forgotten about - one that's watched and played by millions - participation costs next to nothing and you don't need to join a club to play it. On top of that it's having its own boom time right now, yet the average working man down the pub can still properly relate to the players."

Botha listened attentively.

"And that sport, boss, is.... darts."

"Darts! Replace football with bloody darts! You're off your head man!" Cornell cried. Now was the time to drag this fantastical daydream back to the realms of reality. "Let's be serious gentlemen - football is the world's most popular pastime, after sex."

"Before it in some households - including mine! Have you met my missus?" quipped Ellis, though his attempt to bring some jocularity to the discussion fell flat. The Editor-in Chief continued with his argument.

"Look, there's no point burying our heads in the sand about this - the world will continue following football's fortunes whether this paper chooses to ignore it or not. We're dismissing a global phenomenon here that generates millions of pounds in revenue - one day maybe that figure will be billions - from broadcasting rights, advertising, merchandising and ticket sales. Our punters will demand to read about it on our back pages, so let's not indulge ourselves with mere wishful thinking, please?"

He expected a withering rebuke for speaking his mind, but none came. Something was stirring in Marcus Botha's ever-active mind.

"Harry old man, I think you may have something there..."

Cornell was aghast.

"You can't be serious Marcus! The paper will become a laughing stock!"

Botha turned towards him almost distractedly.

"Relax Edmund, relax. I haven't gone bananas. What Harry says is beginning to make some sense in my head now, but I'm a realist above all else. Of course we're not going to finish football off, I know that's not possible - what do you take me for - a fool? What I'm looking to do is to simply drive it into the corner of the proverbial parking lot. If we can focus the attention of our readers onto another sporting distraction - stretch the popularity of a non-violent, family-friendly game - they can decide for themselves whether their more familiar hate-filled arenas hold the same appeal.

This is about getting the country's menfolk to spend their leisure time thinking and talking about something other than football - an alternative to bloody Hillsborough and all that goes with it. Who knows how my initiative will take off?

The rest of the world can do as it pleases, but this is an independent nation and it's lost faith with familiar things before - the music hall was replaced by television, compact discs replaced vinyl. The same goes for sport - speedway and greyhound racing were once hugely popular here, but not now.

I can't expect the public to change tack if they don't want to, but I can sow a seed, can't I? If our circulation starts to suffer, I'll rethink the strategy, but for the time being, let me have my day. My gut feeling is that the country has had its fill of football and everything that goes with it, and now Mr. Ellis has opened my eyes to a fresh possibility. Expand on what you were saying Harry."

"Ok, think about this. Darts players are just like you and me - they live in the same kind of houses as us and play for prize money that hasn't raced beyond the comprehension of the working man. Like most of us, they don't do any physical training and they're not hidden away from the fans who turn up to watch them perform - more to the point, they'll happily practice in the same bars that you or I would have a pint in. They're approachable, friendly, and don't swan around in the swanky VIP lounges of night clubs looking down their noses at the people who put them where they are today. Darts is a game played by everyday people, watched by everyday people and we, the English - come to think of it, the whole of the UK - are bloody good at it - we've got the best players in the world! It's been decades since you could say the same thing about our footballers."

On hearing that, Edmund Cornell's memory instantly flooded back to the heady days of Sir Alf Ramsay's 1966 World Cup winning side, though the national team had become decidedly average since then and the current crop were struggling to even qualify for the 1990 Finals in Italy. Their manager Bobby Robson had announced his intention to quit after that tournament, a decision that looked like a case of a condemned man cutting his own throat before the Football Association could lower their guillotine.

Botha ended these reflections by taking centre stage again.

"Thanks for that Harry, you've certainly made me think, and what you've said is going to radically alter the composition of my next announcement. We'll lead our front *and* back pages with details of two major events that I'm promoting, both of which I'll broadcast exclusively on *MJB TV*.

I want my network to broaden its scope from merely reporting news to transmitting spectacular events. We need to become a serious rival to the *BBC*, and my plans will grab everyone's attention for three weeks of peak-time summer television next year. I've already booked two exclusive international venues to host the action - The Copa Room at the Sands hotel in Las Vegas, and South Africa's Sun City Superbowl Arena.

Until this morning, I saw the Vegas event as a cabaret extravaganza - you know, singers, comedians, magic acts, dancing girls - the whole nine yards. I was going to call it, *'Viva Variety!'* - but Mr. Ellis's sterling work here has made me think again. Gentlemen, we can forget about this show business nonsense - instead, from Friday 8th - Sunday 17th of June next year, the Sands hotel will now play host to the world's finest darts professionals. We'll call the competition, *'M J Botha's Darts Duals'.*" The speed at which Botha could alter carefully laid out preparations was quite bewildering to the other men, and he revealed the rest of his plans without drawing breath. "My second major event, the one in my homeland, will be the inaugural staging of another new world - class sports tournament, *'The M J Botha Sun City Snooker Showdown'.* This one runs for sixteen days, from June 23rd - July 8th."

Harry Ellis spotted a potential fly in the ointment for the entire scheme and cautiously raised his concern.

"Marcus, I have a question about those dates."

"What about them?"

"It's just that the events coincide with the World Cup finals in Italy."

"Exactly Harry! They will act as perfect distractions to the goings on over there, and with a bit of luck the nation will prefer to watch stuff that it actually excels at rather than continual failures on the football field. Let's remember that Scotland, Wales and Northern Ireland generally fare even worse than England at these tournaments - who in their right mind wants to see a bunch of losers embarrass themselves on a world stage? I'll gradually increase the hype surrounding my events until armchair sports fans across the land are clamouring for *MJB TV* subscriptions. I can hear them all now - *'Never mind the bloody football, get me one of those satellite dishes!'* Imagine that, eh? I know my public. I know my product - now trust me to cash in!"

Ever sceptical, Cornell continued to question Botha's vision.

"Let's not make spur-of-the-moment alterations to your plans just yet Marcus - are you quite sure about the wisdom of taking darts to the entertainment capital of the world? Might it not be wise to think this all through?"

"No, no, no, goddammit! My original idea for the Las Vegas dates was going to be a showcase of the UK's top showbiz talent - Michael Barrymore, Bobby Davro, Paul Daniels, Freddie Starr - all that crowd. I wanted something that would be reminiscent of the glory days at the Sands when stars like Frank Sinatra, Dean Martin, Sammy Davis Jr. etc. used to hold court."

"A *Brit Pack* to replace the *Rat Pack* eh?" offered Ellis (without discernible acknowledgement) as Botha continued to verbalise his thoughts.

"In hindsight, I don't believe the idea would've made much of an impact - I mean, it wouldn't be offering those Yanks anything new, would it? Variety acts have been the staple of the Las Vegas cabaret scene for years - they've seen it all before. Besides, if the acts I've mentioned had real international appeal they'd have already made it over there by themselves, wouldn't they?

The darts thing is different though; the Americans love a novelty, so they'll get a kick out of watching that. It's going to be a one-off competition - ten days and we're gone. Our paper will run competitions for lucky readers to win tickets to the tournament, with flights and accommodation at the Sands hotel thrown in. Their presence will stimulate local interest. It's a guaranteed hit."

Cornell then spotted something.

"Hang on a minute - did you just say, *'ten days and we're gone'*? I thought darts was going to mount a challenge to football Marcus?"

Botha decided to press on rather than rebuke his man.

"To suit our purpose, temporarily it will, but only as a novelty news event. You didn't really believe I thought the sport had long term legs, did you? No, there's no hope of that, though I do remain convinced about snooker having sustained box-office appeal. Darts should offer a lively enough distraction from the World Cup finals to get me up and running, but that's going to be the long and short of it."

Ellis realised that his powers of persuasion were not so special after all, but he was a loyal team member and instead of sulking, offered his boss further helpful assistance over the haste of the big announcement.

"Marcus, do you really want us to run this story before the alteration to your booking has been confirmed?"

"Ah! Very good Harry! I must admit I was putting the cart before the horse somewhat. Yes, keep your powder dry, men - hold back on both announcements until everything's watertight."

Cornell remained uneasy, so Botha asked if there was anything else on his mind, to which he replied, "May I issue a further note of concern with regards to your snooker tournament?"

"I'm listening Edmund."

"Sun City?"

"That's right, Sol Kerzner's leisure resort - the Las Vegas of Africa."

"Would that choice be entirely *wise* Marcus?"

"And what exactly is your problem with me hosting *my* tournament in the country of *my* birth?"

"Well, we all know a wind of change is blowing through the region and that Nelson Mandela's release from prison will probably call time on apartheid."

"Nothing's certain," Botha replied icily.

"No, and that's why I'd advise you to tread carefully. These things haven't happened yet... when they do, I'm sure life in South Africa may very well be rosy, but in the present political climate I don't believe it would be expedient to promote any business venture there."

Ellis chipped in again, this time jumping to the defence of his colleague.

"He's got a point boss - you've only got to look at the flak *Queen* got for performing at Sun City." (The rock band fell foul of anti-apartheid supporters by playing a series of concerts at the resort in 1984.) "Christ, even Cliff bloody Richard took stick when he sang there, and he's got a hotline to God!" Once more, his attempt at humour fell on deaf ears.

Botha had already considered that negative publicity might blight his ambitious scheme, but business is business, and his local connections were laying on the best hotels and facilities, all at favourable rates. Despite the threat of external criticism, he expected a rapturous welcome back home, where a generation had grown up deprived of any meaningful international sporting competition. The prospect of future praise appealed to his ego, but in the present, Cornell continued to rain on his parade.

"Your critics will dismiss this as an attempt to legitimise the current regime and every political commentator and satirist will tear you ..." here, he swiftly corrected himself once again, "Sorry, *try* to tear you apart. How long has South Africa been banned from international sport, Harry?"

"They were formally expelled from the International Olympic Committee in 1970, but their athletes hadn't been allowed to compete at the games for ten years before that."

"There you are Marcus - the South Africans are, not to put too fine a point on it, international pariahs on the sporting scene. You risk damaging the good name of this newspaper....and more importantly, you risk damaging your own too. You deserve a much greater legacy than that."

Botha simmered in his chair, recognising this insincere sentiment as a saccharine afterthought, meant to sweeten the bitterness of Cornell's cautionary pill. Choosing to neither chastise nor reward the flatterer, instead he fired back a broadside of his own.

"It's very good of you to watch out for me Edmund I'm sure, but I'm a big boy and I can guard my own back against stray knives."

Thanks all the same.

He then puffed himself up as if to don protective plating against any further negativity. "You say that my people back home are pariahs of world sport? That South Africans are banned from international competition, yes? Well let me expose the inaccuracy of that statement. There's a certain compatriot of mine by the name of Mr Gary Player who's won nine Major golf championships - including four since your 1970 cut off point. If he's a pariah, would you be so kind as to strike his name from the pantheon of golfing greats? No? I thought not."

It gave Botha immense pleasure to lecture his staff, and another sermon was imminent. "My example proves that nothing in this world is ever black and white, if you'll pardon the pun. Lofty ideals and bans, etc. are SELECTIVE. Let me remind you that no South African has EVER received a ban from a snooker tournament! In fact, our very own 'Perrie' Mans even made it to the final of the World Championships in 1978.

Unfortunately, since Mr Mans retired, we haven't produced another top-quality player, so by staging the event in Sun City, I'm hoping that talented local kids will be inspired to try and mix it with the Stephen Hendry's of this world in the not-too-distant future. And if that's not a good enough reason to take the tournament over there, try this next argument for size…"

Looking on, Harry Ellis could only admire the way his leader hammered sceptics into submission. He imagined the Head Honcho would make a mighty politician and listened with awe at his glorious leader's eloquent reasonings.

"I'm going to stretch the reach of the sport - it's far too insular and needs to expand its global potential. Christ, the World Championship takes place in the same city - Sheffield - of the same country - England - every year! How can that possibly assist the international development of a game? I'll be doing it a huge favour!" Clearly, Botha was not for turning on his choice of venue; in fact, his reasoned arguments went a long way to alleviating Cornell's concerns. "Finally, never forget the old adage, *'There is no such thing as bad publicity,'* - all publicity is good! Let your satirists and the like mock me for what I'm trying to do. Every sound bite and belly laugh those people get will promote my competition, and he who laughs last, laughs loudest.

My readers - my subscribers - they care little or nothing for the goings on in South Africa - they just want to be ENTERTAINED, and I'll do what I always do - I'll give them what they want! Now, is there anything else left to say Edmund? Anything you're still unclear about?"

"No, I think we're done here Marcus." Cornell was tired of this skirmish; he wanted to withdraw from the battlefield and return to his troops in the newsroom, a safe distance away from front line hostilities.

"Harry, how about you?"

"Er, yes - hang on a minute, guys. Now that we're holding back your announcements, we've got no sports headline for tomorrow's morning edition."

"Well done once again Mr. Ellis, you're having a very good day today - very much on the ball! Better get Gordon Rimmer to do a quick follow up on his thing about the activities of agents in big-time sport. Nothing clever - we're only filling space today now after all."

"And what about our front-page Marcus?" asked Cornell. "If we're not going to lead with your plans for snooker and darts, will it be more of the same on Eastern Europe?"

"That depends on whether some other big story emerges overnight, doesn't it? Christ Edmund, anyone would think I was getting obsessed with Communism's collapse."

His editor looked away and wisely bit his lip.

"Ok then, get back to your posts and we'll reconvene once I've confirmed the booking alterations." With that, the aids turned to leave the room, but Botha still insisted on making one more point. "Oh, Harry - make sure that the aforementioned Mr. Rimmer is present in Las Vegas and Sun City. I want daily bulletins from my Chief Sports Correspondent on these tournaments. No ifs, no buts!"

"He's not going to like that Marcus - he'll be desperate to cover the World Cup finals."

"I don't give a shiny shit about what he wants to do, just get him on those planes! Who does that stroppy Scottish fucker think he is anyway?"

The two men had clashed some months earlier over Rimmer's ethical refusal to mine a particularly rich seam of premium gossip for the paper. At the time, he was in a relationship with Professor Susan Somerfield, an eminent psychiatrist working at the Priory clinic in Roehampton, and once Botha discovered that one of his key employees was romantically involved with a senior member of staff at that particular medical facility, he saw an opportunity too good to miss. The Head Honcho tried to pressure his man into leveraging an endless procession of scoops from his lover, exposing the weaknesses, problems, and unconventional habits of the celebrities who checked in for treatment.

Botha's plan failed to take the loyalty of love into account however, and his stubborn minion steadfastly refused to play ball. In truth, the independent, morally upstanding Professor Somerfield would never have yielded to such an outrageous request anyway.

At the time, Edmund Cornell received instructions to dismiss Rimmer, citing reckless insubordination, but the reporter fought back by threatening to expose his boss's unscrupulous methods of gathering information. Cornell feared that the incendiary row would damage *The Horizon*, but as luck would have it, the storm blew itself out at the eleventh hour when the star-crossed lovers at the centre of the quarrel suddenly and inexplicably broke up. This meant that the link to the Priory was lost, negating any justification for a parting of the ways between the truculent journalist and his paymaster.

Nevertheless, the most spiteful and dangerous man in publishing was not about to let sleeping dogs lie, so for him, revenge remained a prescient priority. When an appropriate moment presented itself to strike, he would do so with relish, but until then he insisted that his highest-paid correspondent must dance to whatever tune he saw fit to play, so field trips like the ones to Las Vegas and Sun City were non-negotiable.

Irritatingly, Harry Ellis had reminded him of Rimmer's prickly petulance, but before his anger could spill into a violent outburst, he closed the meeting, hurriedly ushering his editors from the penthouse suite.

Once the door closed behind them, he took a couple of moments for some quiet contemplation and began to brood. The arrogant self-belief of his public and business persona ebbed away, and he sank into the contours of his impressively expensive leather chair, as if to seek shelter from the cruelties of the world outside. Severe indigestion had become his constant companion and a stubby palm spread across his chest, while his other hand tightened its grip on a ballpoint pen, snapping it in two. He forcibly drew in deeper breaths, and in the silence of his office, struggled to regain his composure.

These plans have got to succeed, they must!

Because Christ alone can help me if the whole thing ends in failure!

13.

You win some, but God, you lose some too

The lyrics of *Deacon Blue's* latest single, *"Love and Regret"* rattled around Gordon Rimmer's troubled mind long after he had turned off his car radio and prepared to begin another interminable working week. The music faded mournfully into the distance and his thoughts reconnected with the present as he nimbly dodged a pool of puddles while looking for a parking space outside *The Horizon's* plush headquarters.

It was a typically grey, typically miserable Monday morning; the kind that everyone complains about but still expects from an autumnal London. Rain drizzled irritably over the pavements, soaking a smattering of preoccupied poseurs who were desperately trying to outdo each other with their outlandish City bonus boasting. Overhead, *Horizon Tower* stood majestically resplendent against its murky monochrome backdrop; one of a number of impressive shiny monoliths that had recently emerged across the previously neglected skyline of the capital's East End.

Marcus Botha acquired the building's tenancy and naming rights when he moved his newspaper lock, stock and printing presses from Fleet Street into the modernist, Le Corbusier-inspired premises. Like the man himself, it commanded attention; its drenched entrance hypnotically drew the eyes upwards to a vision of toughened glass that assaulted the senses with its stark reflections of sky, clouds and the surrounding buildings. This was brazen architecture of totemic significance. Very crisp. Very cutting edge.

Somebody somewhere had decided that our new corporate structures should welcome the light of the world onto their shimmering outer walls, before generously passing the glorious gift on for their neighbours to share. That morning however, Mother Nature decided to issue a grim palate of skies to the reflections, from which they could only produce uninspiring canvases of communal melancholy.

Outside the building stood a billboard, which proudly promoted the tabloid troubadour's embarrassingly ironic strapline:

LOOK TO _The Horizon_ - FOR NEWS YOU CAN TRUST!

Rimmer saw it and shook his head, pitying the next unfortunate stooge to pick up their morning paper and find their deepest, darkest secrets laid bare in print. There was always someone ripe for ripping to pieces, someone who would have their life changed forever, whether the damning story at the centre of their personal shit storm was accurate or not. Graphic attention-grabbing headlines were the paper's stock-in-trade, supported by embarrassingly lurid tales, vague enough in content to dodge any retaliatory legal action, should the recipient wish to contest the accusations.

On those rare occasions when the bitter bile of the paper's gossip - mongers did overstep the mark, Botha's lawyers would simply negotiate discreet out of court settlements with the aggrieved parties, who could expect to see a tiny apology tucked away in the recesses of an inside page the following day.

God Bless The Horizon!

Standard-bearer for a nation's moral soul!

A deeply offended (yet always intrigued) readership of millions luxuriated in the knowledge that at all hours of the day and night, diligent _Horizon_ reporters were busily rooting out the misdeeds of our famous faces and lesser lights, exposing their debaucheries and self-destructions for our continued delectation. Oh, how we revelled in every-last word.

"Read all about it!"

The culture at the paper left Rimmer feeling isolated and friendless: an outsider with scant respect for the professional standards of colleagues who routinely trotted out wholly unfounded rumours, cynically massaged to resemble facts. Their irresponsible lack of ethics drained his enthusiasm for the job, and by now, his mood matched the inclement weather.

Will I always be this miserable?

I wasn't like this when I still had Susan by my side.

I don't think I've smiled once since we broke up.

Sullenly he shuffled past the reception desk into a swift lift that swept past floors full of unheralded office staff who busily made magic happen on a daily basis.

Where would any paper be without its editors, sub-editors, salespeople, administrators and accounts clerks?

I find it ironic though, that Marcus Botha allocated more room at Horizon Tower to the team selling advertising space than to the printers and typographers in the basement who actually create our physical product.

The adoption of leaner production systems had inevitably led to widespread redundancies in the beleaguered print room, and the Head Honcho could barely suppress his delight when boasting about the significant cost savings that followed, much to Gordon Rimmer's disgust.

Although he was only in his late thirties, he had already become something of a curmudgeon, and he found *nouveau riche* proprietors such as his boss considerably more distasteful than their "old money" predecessors. This paradox troubled his solidly socialist soul. Of course, he appreciated the need for businesses to remain competitive (after all, enterprises like *The Horizon* are not charitable organisations, they operate in a dog-eat-dog environment) but those printers whose livelihoods had gone were callously tossed aside without so much as a, "thank you," for their years of loyal service. Compassion was in short supply at the new Limehouse HQ.

The whole ethos of the place contrasted starkly with his own experience of job loss six months earlier at *The Daily Focus.*

There, endearingly old school attitudes came to the fore one fateful day when the paper's much-loved Sports Desk Editor Wilfred Moss summoned him for a dose of paternalistic (if most unwelcome) advice. Rimmer had won industry awards for his thought-provoking and insightful contributions on a myriad of sporting topics and life was treating him rather well, so the chat that followed came like a bolt out of the blue.

"Young man, let me start by saying that I hope you feel we've enjoyed some significant successes together, yes? Unfortunately, however, through circumstances beyond our control, there's a need to embrace some significant challenges around here, so I feel it's only right and proper to let my staff know which way the breezes blow."

"What's up then Willie - I'm not getting fired am I? I don't reckon old Weaver," (Lord Neville Weaver, the boss of the *Focus,* who was the longest-established newspaper proprietor in Fleet Street) "has got the cash to pay me off if I have to sue him for wrongful dismissal."

He meant the remark to be light-hearted, but the usually cheerful Moss was in no mood for laughter.

"That's just it my boy," he sighed, "our governor's a busted flush - this place has had it."

An awkward pause passed between the two men, allowing Rimmer to absorb the shock of his friend's statement.

"Christ, the rumour mill was right after all then." His disappointment was palpable. For months, there had been speculation in the business office that the paper was in financial difficulties, though he had chosen to ignore the doom-mongers. "Surely our advertisers can keep us afloat, eh? Blue-chip sponsors will always support an upmarket broadsheet, it's just the sort of association they're after. Surely?"

A resigned shake of his editor's balding head rebuffed Rimmer's hopeful question. The public now preferred sensationalist journalism to the more measured and objective style of *The Focus,* and its circulation had drifted into an irreversible decline.

"It's the law of the jungle I'm afraid - why place your ads with us if no one's reading what we write?" Moss then offered his prize asset some sage advice. "Look Gordon, the old guard like me can pack up altogether and supplement our pensions by writing boring memoirs about the good old days, but a young man like you has to look to the future and that future is with the tabloids. I advise you to strike a deal with one of those at a premium price pretty bloody quick before other less talented writers start joining you in the marketplace. We won't be the last quality paper to go under and your market value will soon drop if you have competition to fight off - that's the forces of supply and demand at work - so cast your line out pronto. There are some big fish out there, but they'll only take the first bait of the day. Once the riverbank gets overcrowded with other anglers, the choicest catches could slip your net."

Rimmer considered the merits of this elaborate analogy and as usual, bowed to the old fellow's considered wisdom.

"So how long have we got?"

"There'll be an announcement at next month's AGM and no doubt we'll linger around for a while afterwards looking for a knight in shining armour to save our skins, but the truth of the matter is that our kind of paper has had its day. It's not about dedicated journalism nowadays, it's *entertainment* that grabs the public's pennies. They don't want newspapers, they want comics. It's all about jokes, puns, titties and bums. Problem pages. Gossip columns. *Celebrity*."

Moss appreciated the importance of seeing a famous face on his front page as much as anyone else, but downmarket red tops had stretched the definition of a celebrity and utter nobodies were now lauded as VIPs, which of course, sowed the seeds for an increase in scoops and scandals thereafter. In a world where pop stars had replaced politicians as relevant headline makers, *The Focus* had lost touch. Its emphasis on publishing real news over showbiz tittle-tattle left it frozen in time; a fossilised relic of a bygone age.

Rather than continue to bemoan the lowering of standards in newspaper journalism, the venerable elder statesman dismissed his soon-to-be-ex employee with a call to action.

"No delays now, my lad - start making some enquiries and move as quick as you can. Don't waste - make haste!"

Within a month, Gordon Rimmer had accepted an extremely lucrative offer to become the new Chief Sports Correspondent at *The Horizon*.

To the outside world, this seemed like an upwardly mobile and perfectly natural move; Marcus Botha secured the talents of a recognised star sports reporter, and in return, the man himself received a considerable increase in salary. Soon enough however, dark clouds gathered over paradise. The ink had barely dried on his contract before the financial woes at *The Focus* emerged and industry insiders began wondering whether Rimmer had been more than a little fortuitous in the timing of his transfer. He got wind of the simmering unrest among his new colleagues one evening, when he inadvertently overheard two disgruntled hacks griping about his good fortune. The first one began with a bilious whinge.

"That lucky bastard Rimmer! Typical galley rat, that one! Jumps off the deck of a sinking ship and winds up here, sitting pretty with a big pay rise - taking up a job that one of us could have had! Can you get your breath at the brass neck of him?"

His equally ill-tempered workmate twisted the knife further.

"I hear the Head Honcho's furious. He reckons he's been had over, knowing he could've got his man for half the price if the troubles at *The Focus* had come to light sooner."

Rimmer realised there and then that it would be wise to watch his back in anticipation of future difficulties.

Things came to a head soon afterwards. He submitted a particularly well - researched piece to Harry Ellis about the parlous finances at many top English football clubs, only to find it staring accusingly back at him on his desk when he returned from lunch. The damning comment - *REJECTED* - was scrawled across the page in red biro. Barely holding his temper, he burst through the Sports Editor's office door to challenge the decision.

"Harry, I need a word with you."

Ellis was deep in concentration, preparing the next morning's back page layout. Distractedly he looked up over his horn-rimmed bifocal spectacles.

"What is it? Be quick Mr. Rimmer - as you can see, I'm busy."

Too busy, perhaps, to explain the rejection of my article?

This was an affront to the new recruit's professional pride, and he tore into Ellis with volcanic intensity.

"Never mind your '*I'm busy*' bullshit, let's sort this out now! Is there some kind of jealousy thing going on here? Am I raising the standards too high for your liking?"

A short silence followed, during which time Ellis composed himself enough to take charge of the moment. His eyes turned chillingly cold (it was clear that some of Marcus Botha's influence had rubbed off on him) and he looked directly at Rimmer, then in measured tones, quietly and precisely began his riposte.

"In the first place, when I say I'm busy, that's exactly what I mean - have you got that, you smarmy fucker? I know you think you're someone special just because you used to work for a toff's broadsheet, but you're here now and you work for Mr Botha. On-a-fucking-tabloid-for-fucking-Marcus Botha, right? Now as it's your lordship and I can see you're upset, just this once I'll make an exception and give you a minute of my time - no more - so say what's on your mind and make it snappier than that piece of crap you've just tried to pass off as usable copy. You reckon you're raising the standards around here? Christ, that's a laugh! You don't know the first fucking thing about writing for a paper like ours!"

Rimmer took a second or two to catch his breath; clearly, the no-nonsense style of writing at *The Horizon* carried over to his editor's critique. For someone who had grown accustomed to praise, it stung like a jab to the face from a heavyweight boxer.

"Exactly what is your problem with what I've written?" he asked, determined to clear the air.

"I just fucking told you, didn't I? There's no snap! NO SNAP! Savvy?" To emphasise his point Ellis provocatively clicked his fingers in the direction of Rimmer's face. "It rambles on and on like two old farts reminiscing over their war stories!

I want facts (this word produced another click of the fingers) - I want opinions - (more finger provocation) and I want as much outrage (one more click) as you can stir into the pot in five hundred fucking words. Do you get that? Facts. Opinion. Outrage. CRASH - BANG - WALLOP! If you can't get me corroborated facts, then use that brain we're paying so much for and serve up your best educated guesses. I need you to rake up plenty of controversy, so our readers will have something to talk about through their dinner breaks at work and in the pub afterwards on their way home.

This is the tabloid world mate and the sooner you get your poncey eloquence off my pages, the sooner you'll start to earn the fucking king's ransom we're paying you. Now go back to work and try to write something I might like!"

With that, Ellis returned his attention to the sheets of paper in front of him, though Rimmer stood his ground, for he was determined to trade punches.

"What if I won't come up with the sort of bog-standard dross you're asking for?"

Ellis looked up once more, irritated by the continued presence of a swatted pest. He had confidence in the authority of his senior role and went for the finishing blow.

"Look pal, you've got to realise where you are and who you work for. Understand who puts the food on your table. Ultimately, you're Marcus-fucking-Botha's man now and that guy has a habit of getting his money's worth out of the people he employs. He knew what he was doing when he signed you up - your reputation gives this rag of ours a degree of kudos. But let me tell you that within these walls that shite means fuck all, so you *will* write what I tell you to write and in the way I tell you to write it, because that's how Mr. Botha wants it, and you really don't want to be locking horns with him. That's the deal you make when you break bread with our boss. Now get back to work and we'll have no more of this Fancy Dan cobblers. Is that understood?"

Rimmer understood perfectly.

The prospect of dumbing down his work pecked away at his vainglorious pride, but as the saying goes, "*he who pays the piper plays the tune,*" and he had no hope of matching his inflated salary elsewhere. Within weeks, his integrity was but a distant memory, bartered in exchange for that fat, but no longer satisfying, pay cheque.

Then the problems with Susan Somerfield started.

They had met two years earlier during the course of his work. At the time, he was at the top of his game working for Wilfred Moss when he received a mysterious 4 a.m. phone call at home that would indirectly change his life...

"Hello, is that Gordon Rimmer? From *The Focus?*"

"Speaking. It's the middle of the bloody night and you just woke me up, so who wants to know? This better be good!" He was in no mood to exchange pleasantries with a stranger after having his slumbers disturbed at such an ungodly hour.

"Er...sorry... I'm sorry, ok? This is Terry Malloy - my agent got me your home number and I promised him I wouldn't call 'til the morning after I'd thought things through properly... but if I don't get this stuff off my chest now, I'll most likely lose my bottle by daybreak and that'll be that."

The distressed caller was the captain of the England football team, so this encounter was clearly going to be significant. Rimmer's journalistic instincts kicked in, snapping his brain cells out of their slumberous state.

"What's up Terry? You're obviously upset - what's on your mind?" Stating the obvious in an empathetic tone was hardly a stretch of his talents, but he knew that when someone wants to talk it is often the best way to get a conversation flowing.

"I've got big problems and I need to spill my guts out to someone … everybody should know about me… I want everything out in the open…"

Over the course of the next hour and a half, the figurehead of the national game proceeded to unburden himself about a collection of personal issues including addictions to drink, drugs, gambling and women.

While all this had the makings of a huge story, it would hardly be the first time that the excesses of a top professional footballer created headline news. The trials and tribulations of George Best (the sport's most glamorous icon of the swinging '60s) were manna from heaven for tabloid newspaper editors; women adored him, men envied him, and his exuberant off the field antics always created a stir. Though his personal issues were similar to Malloy's, it would be fair to say that the two characters were starkly different; Best was a champagne superstar, a mercurial magician, whereas the Tottenham Hotspur and England skipper was a no-nonsense stopper centre-half; a hero for a less flamboyant era. "Good old Terry," was more of a pint of lager guy, a man of the people, not of the gods.

His motivation to become an international footballer came from a deep love of the game rather than any desire for fame, but his talent inevitably turned this private, somewhat shy individual into a public figure. In an attempt to combat the pressures that come with celebrity, he started to pursue the kind of recreational activities that can lead a fragile personality to self - destruct. Soon the thrill/fear of discovery became his biggest addiction of all, until he finally decided to face his demons in that late-night phone call.

Once he had told Rimmer the extent of his problems, the two men agreed to a more formal recorded interview and arranged to meet up the next morning at a greasy spoon cafe ten minutes' drive away from Tottenham's Hertfordshire training ground.

Both parties agreed that secrecy was necessary for a successful rendezvous, but upon his arrival, Rimmer spotted Malloy's irate agent, Maurice Letterman, seated alone at a corner table. This was an unwelcome surprise, because the contrite star had promised to meet without the threat of interference from his professional advisor so that he could talk candidly. Letterman was a leading light in the new cult of player representation that had rapidly taken a testicles-tightening grip on every facet of sporting relationships, and as a trained negotiator, he came ready to broker a sweet fee for the story.

Before the emergence of agents in football, players often found themselves inadequately recompensed when giving interviews to media organisations, but those days were gone for good; exclusive stories increase newspaper revenues, so reps ensure that the headline acts get a share of that bounty.

Letterman understood Malloy's market value all-too-well and had not turned up to sell his asset short. Rimmer addressed him with a politely cautious greeting.

"I didn't expect to see you here Maurice."

"I bet you didn't Sonny Jim - you'd rather have kept me out of this nonsense altogether, but you didn't really think I'd let my boy off the leash that easily did you? I'm not about to let Terry do or say anything he'll regret later - understand? Now, before we go any further, let's talk money. I want to know what sort of joy you're going to spread for us today."

Just as a difficult conversation concerning cash for questions was about to begin, the man of the moment swept into the room. The café's clientele were accustomed to the sight of 'Spurs players dropping in from time to time for a bacon sandwich after training (the dietary discipline of continental players had yet to be embraced domestically) so when Malloy came bounding through the front door, he barely drew a second glance. That suddenly changed when he greeted his agent with a raised voice of agitation.

"What the fuck are you doing here?" His flushed face was a picture of pure bewilderment. "I told you I'm going through with this and there's nothing you can do about it so butt out Mo, for your own sake. We're finished if you get involved."

"Hold your fire Terry my lad. If this madness - this professional suicide - must go ahead, I need to make sure that you get the best possible deal for your story. It's all about making up for the loss of income you'll incur if your sponsors decide to walk away afterwards." He turned to Rimmer by way of explanation. "I tried to talk the boy out of all of this before he contacted you, but he wouldn't listen to reason, so the least I can do is soften the financial blow once the shit hits the fan."

Therein lay another strand of the agent/client conundrum - does the representative truly work in the interests of his charge or is he simply trying to protect his own commission? Some of their ilk have a divisive agenda and cynically pimp their clients' thoughts and talents to the highest bidder for short-term gains, though Rimmer knew that Letterman was more of a strategic planner type who saw the bigger picture. The man from *The Focus* thought he could write a very nice follow up piece arising from that ethical question.

Malloy's frustration with Letterman was obvious and he snapped, "You just don't get it do you? This isn't about money; it's about me; my life and the fuck-up I've become. I've got to turn things around - face the music 'an all that. I ain't lookin' for cash here - I want to get my head sorted out and the sooner I front up to everything, the better things are gonna be. I've got to think about my family now - my wife and kids. Them and the fans - they all look up to me, but I'm a total disgrace. I can't go on like this no longer."

Rimmer was accompanied by staff photographer Eddie Sutton at the meeting, and when tears began to run down the fallen idol's face, the snapper instinctively tried to capture the image for posterity.

"Put your camera down Eddie," Rimmer demanded, "we'll only take pictures on Terry's approval when all of this is done." This kindness brought a relieved smile and a tap on his shoulder from the appreciative footballer.

"See Mo? Gordon's alright - I ain't gonna get shafted here."

Letterman would have preferred to wash his hands of the whole business, but he faced the prospect of breaking up a lucrative partnership, and losing a genuine friend to boot, or reluctantly allowing the interview to proceed uncontrolled and unrewarded. With a sigh, he chose the second option.

"On your own head be it then, Terry. Just be careful."

"Look, if you want to do me a favour," continued Malloy, "then book me into that rehab place you've been going on about - the Priory, yeah? And sort things out with the gaffer at 'Spurs. I'll need some thinking time after all this is done."

Through gritted teeth, Letterman promised to make the necessary arrangements.

Thereafter a formal version of the previous night's conversation took place and lensman Sutton took his snaps at its conclusion. After an exchange of handshakes and assurances of good faith, Rimmer triumphantly returned to *The Focus* with an unsigned blank cheque and exclusive publishing rights. To add more cherries to his cake, he announced a further agreement to write a series of progress reports from the Priory recording Malloy's path to sobriety.

This new deal was subject to a confidentiality agreement, signed by the England footballer and his agent, along with Rimmer and Wilfred Moss on behalf of the newspaper, which was drafted at the insistence of the Priory's legal team to protect the privacy of other patients. It stipulated that any breach of trust would trigger financially ruinous penalties for all concerned. The medical facility's board were obviously anxious about the prospect of inviting a newsman through its doors, but on the flip side, it hoped that a series of features in an esteemed broadsheet would generate positive publicity for the science of psychiatry.

In the end, their fears proved groundless, and Rimmer's dispatches were to be his ailing newspaper's last great coup; Terry Malloy was able to display an openness and candour during the interviews that re-evaluated the stereotypical masculine image of footballers.

Professor Susan Somerfield had responsibility for his treatment, so she came into frequent contact with the cocksure reporter during the course of his follow-up visits. He soon grew to respect her dedicated approach, but something else led him to seek her company after the conclusion of each interview. Quite apart from her professional capabilities, he recognised a looker when he saw one and her combination of intelligence and physical attraction soon had him hooked. He became smitten and found himself showing up more often than was professionally necessary just to have an excuse to be near her. Susan in turn came to realise that there were no hidden agendas lurking beneath the surface of his transparent good intentions, and despite an initial reluctance to drop her guard around him, she grew increasingly comfortable in his company.

Once Malloy felt strong enough to return to the public's buxom bosom Rimmer's contact with the good Professor should have ended, but he was a real charmer and by then they found themselves in the throes of a burgeoning romance. Her colleagues were astonished to find that a journalist (of all people) had broken down her determined defences, but they too were won over by his refusal to divulge sensitive information concerning other patients on the wards.

Everything looked rosy for the happy couple, but within weeks, Rimmer had swapped life at *The Focus* for a new challenge with Marcus Botha and from then on, his world gradually began to unravel.

After joining *The Horizon*, he hastily made an offer on a house in trendy Notting Hill and made plans to set up home there with his ladylove. He could ill afford such an extravagant purchase but a peacock desire to celebrate the increase in his professional standing saw him sign the necessary paperwork for it anyway. He would soon learn the folly of hubris.

Hindsight hurts because it stores our deepest regrets while disregarding our greatest triumphs and on reflection, he not only rued the error of his bricks-and-mortar investment, but also his failure to consider the implications of working for a tyrant like Botha.

As we have seen, the first problems appeared when Harry Ellis demanded that he produce vapid nonsense unworthy of a thoroughbred's skills. The surrender of his professional pride was a bitter enough pill to swallow, but further distress followed when Edward Cornell ushered him into a quiet corner of the building with a request to press Susan into accessing confidential information held at the Priory. There was no doubt that the order came directly from the Head Honcho, and when Rimmer made it crystal-clear that he would not compromise his partner's professional credibility for the sake of a story he was duly 'advised' of the potential damage to his career prospects. From that moment, the drip, drip, drip effect of relentless pressure gradually began to take its toll on the new man's spirit.

Three choices presented themselves: -

a) Walk out on *The Horizon* and kiss goodbye to the best-paid sports reporting job in UK publishing.

b) Pressurise Susan into breaking her Hippocratic Oath.

c) Engineer a separation from the love of his life to keep the prowling menace of Botha at bay.

In consideration of the first option, committing career *hari kiri* would sever his lucrative (and only) revenue stream. He was hopelessly reliant on those mammoth *Horizon* paycheques to service his mortgage repayments, and that left him financially vulnerable to Botha's intimidation. The government's boom and bust fiscal policies had created another sudden downturn in the economy, leading to a spectacular drop in the housing market, and the Notting Hill folly was instantly worth far less than his purchase price, so he faced a very real prospect of bankruptcy if he sold up.

As for option two, he could never ask Susan to rat anyone out, the very idea of such a thing was completely out of the question.

That left one final, fateful choice available. He decided that the only way to guarantee scuppering Botha's plans was to sacrifice his relationship. Susan's career was more important than any selfish thoughts for his own happiness. In a torturous heart-to-heart summit, he summoned up the courage to call time on their union, blaming his decision on, "pressures of work." He knew that his words were ripping two hearts apart.

She was dumfounded.

What he's saying doesn't ring true - surely the rational course of action would be to discuss his problems with me first - after all, I'm a professional listener!

I'm in the right place at the right time to provide the right help, so Gordon's not just leaving me, he's dismissing my abilities too.

A jumble of irrational thoughts ran through her mind.

Why is he really walking away - could he have met someone else?

Are there gambling debts I don't know about, perhaps?

Secret drug use?

No, this is Gordon I'm thinking about, and my man is no Terry Malloy - of that I'm certain.

If he really is suffering from work-related stress, then my gut tells me that Marcus Botha is responsible for it, meaning he's behind the breakup too.

But how can I know for sure when Gordon refuses to open up about the root cause?

Everybody reacts to pressure in different ways, and Rimmer steadfastly refused to go into greater detail regarding his decision, despite her tearful insistence. His major concern was that she might go public with the news if she knew the truth about Botha's intentions, and that would damage the paper's reputation, which would almost certainly affect sales adversely, increasing the possibility of further job losses. Although he badly wanted to get even with the Head Honcho for the destruction of his happiness, he also dreaded the prospect of inflicting collateral damage elsewhere.

His enforced break up with Susan brought the simmering bad blood between himself and Botha to the boil. They were both stubborn, vain men; one, a prodigal employee who had been cruelly forced into a drastic sacrifice, and the other, a bully whose ability to intimidate and exercise absolute control had now been stifled.

Flaming passions, be they of love or hate, spark intense, often regrettable reactions, which is why they produce the most interesting stories. We can readily recognise the intensity of Rimmer and Botha's mutual ill-will.

Clearly, there would be trouble ahead.

14.

Susan's story

O nce the cult of celebrity had become a global obsession, every breath, every move and every step taken by anyone considered to be remotely newsworthy was subject to intense forensic public examination. Perversely, the failures of the famous seem to attract greater attention (and column inches) than their triumphs, and tales of Icarus-like crash and burn behaviour draw delight from a drooling populace. Even the most narcissistic of personalities would be troubled having to deal with that.

Whenever a, "tired and emotional," casualty of the UK tabloid treadmill seeks solace from the madding crowd, they can check themselves into clinics such as those run by the Priory Group to gather their thoughts, recharge their batteries, and rebuild whatever confidence they have lost. After a refreshing re-set, they sweep out of the gates with renewed vigour and a beaming smile for the paparazzi, leaving freshly gleaming trails of stardust in their wake.

Thanks to our intrusive media, a misconception has grown that the clinics cater exclusively for the care of the show business elite, but nothing could be further from the truth; its stock-in-trade is the treatment of ordinary people, with no preferences permissible, irrespective of any perceived fame that Patient X, Y, or Z might enjoy beyond its perimeter walls. To eliminate prejudice from the psychiatric process, the confidentiality of every patient is sacrosanct.

The Priory's most prestigious facility is found just off the Richmond Road, opposite Roehampton golf course on the outskirts of south-west London. Built in the gothic revival style, the clean white structure provides care and comfort for any lost soul in need of succour (although the range of treatments available to the *hoi polloi* depend upon the ability or inclination of the National Health Service to foot the bill). The tranquil chirruping of birds in the surrounding trees subtly supplements the gentle sense of calm, even on rainy autumn mornings such as the one when Professor Susan Somerfield FRCP, FRCPSYCH, MRCGP, MD gazed out distractedly from her second-floor balcony window, in something of a mental fog. Her customary focus was temporarily lost as she searched for clues to unearth the real reason for her break-up with Gordon Rimmer.

Two years earlier, honest, meaningful True Love had entered her heart, and joys that were previously no more than mythical sentiments became happy and cherished companions. She grew accustomed to their company and now deeply regretted their departure.

As a youth, she exhibited a steely determination to follow her dreams, which kept distracting notions of love firmly on the back burner. Good grades were required at medical school to pursue a career in psychiatry, so on the whole, boys were out, and books were in. Of course, pretty teenage girls will always be the subject of interest from sweaty teenage boys, and the attention she received was not rejected wholesale. Her list of suitors was extensive, but while she satisfied her blooming desires to varying degrees over the course of her emergence into womanhood, she steadfastly refused to become embroiled in any serious romantic attachment. That tunnel vision eventually reaped its rewards at the completion of her studies when the medical profession warmly welcomed a single-minded, mature new addition into its ranks.

She began her working life as a general psychiatrist with the aforementioned Priory Hospital Group, treating people for an array of conditions such as depression, eating disorders, neurological illnesses, relationship issues, occupational stress and addictions. Through exemplary dedication, her reputation flourished, and she quickly became a highly valued member of the team at Roehampton.

On a relationship level, men still occasionally entered her life, but none had ever managed to so much as fracture her cool reserve. Acceptance into the Priory fraternity carried infinitely greater relevance to her; at no time did she harbour thoughts of being an independent practitioner, for the Priory facility at

Roehampton was her sole focus and she approached her work with an almost pious zeal.

Until she met her confident, caring Scottish newspaperman, that is.

What made him so special? Although she thought he was, "reasonably pleasant," to look at and kept himself in good condition, those were not particularly important considerations to this thinking woman. What drew her curiosity was that he showed genuine concern for Terry Malloy and his issues whilst conducting his interviews in the Priory's grounds.

Her experience of reporters stretched no further than the baying mob who loitered across the road whenever a celebrity emerged from therapy, and she thought their insensitivities left much to be desired. The second their target came into sight they would pounce, bellowing intrusive questions with an aggressive intent that immediately threatened to dismantle all the staff's hard work. Obviously, her job required an open mind, so she knew better than to tar an entire profession with the same brush, and from a distance, it appeared that Rimmer was cut from an altogether finer cloth than his cohorts. Despite having unprecedented access to the clinic's inner sanctum, he behaved impeccably; he had the keys to the cookie cupboard, yet still refused to gorge on the goods.

Could this Gordon Rimmer actually be a man of honour?

She began critically dissecting his Terry Malloy articles but found nothing to damage the reputations of either the England football captain or the treatment centre that housed him. As she got to know him better, she grew to realise that his integrity was genuine, and this revelation opened up possibilities that had rarely interested her before. Once it became clear that he felt romantically inclined towards her, she accepted his cheeky dinner invitation and thereafter they swiftly became, 'an item'.

The building blocks for a happy future fell seamlessly into place; Rimmer soon won over her friends and colleagues too and everyone agreed that he was a very welcome addition to her life.

What could possibly go wrong?

What indeed.

Reflecting on her current situation, she was conscious that a cavernous hole had opened up in her heart and she needed to arrive at a positive place for the sake of her mental health. If she could achieve some sort of post break-up closure, that might provide an insight into how to help her patients through their own troubles. This notion of turning her bounce-back into a project was a coping mechanism to stimulate the healing process, but in truth, she lacked enthusiasm for the task. She yearned for what had been lost and desperately wanted to turn back the clock.

Come on Susan, snap out of this and get to work!

Concentrate on your responsibilities.

You need to look forward, not back – assess your future options – don't mope around dwelling on the past.

For now, simply stick to doing your job to the best of your abilities and trust that time will heal your wounds when it's good and ready.

Unfortunately, her first consultation of the day was with another damaged soul who she had been treating when she first met Rimmer, and his return to her care only rekindled thoughts of that period of her history.

The exotically named Gideon Judge had been Christened plain old Paul Ramsay and brought up in a back-to-back council house in Erdington, a working-class area of Birmingham. In the late 1960's he formed a hard rock band called *The Old Testament* with three other disaffected local youths who each shared an ambition to escape the drudgery of dead-end manual employment in the UK's industrial heartland. Like Judge, the rest of the band rebelliously adopted stage names from characters in the Good Book (Ezra Scribe, Malachi Prophet and Solomon Wise) and they went on to enrage Bible worshippers, or "the God Squad," as Judge described them, with their outrageous stage antics and amoral behaviour. Earnest religious leaders accused them of being iconoclasts for combining biblical references and rock 'n roll (the devil's music), but that, of course, was entirely the point. They went out of their way to cause ructions in order to attract maximum publicity, and the strategy paid off handsomely as their notoriety drew them legions of fans. Over the course of a twenty-year career, *The Old Testament* had sold more than 100 million records and earned worldwide acclaim, with Gideon Judge centre-stage, ably balancing the roles of vocalist, band leader and angst-riddled lyricist.

This complicated, yet gifted man, lived a roller-coaster life of iridescent highs and pitch-black lows, driven by a constant need for approval and validation. His rise to rock royalty was the stuff of legend, and even in disreputable middle - age he retained the affection of an appreciative public, thanks to his endearingly chaotic lifestyle. He managed to entertain and amuse in equal measure and the term 'National Treasure' described him well. Yet the positive elements in his nature had to co-exist with a much darker side, and his appetite for self-destruction meant that those around him were always on the lookout for signs of the next melt down. His addictions to drink, drugs, friends, lovers, fame and the curses of fame meant that his car crash life regularly required the kind of pit-stop repairs that the Priory Group specialise in. He became such a frequent patron of the Roehampton facility that the staff there could have forgiven themselves for thinking that he had taken up permanent residence.

Upon seeing Susan, he greeted her warmly, like a close friend.

"Hi Prof, as you can see, I'm back again. No surprises there eh? I bet you're sick of seeing my face around this place - it's become my own little 'ome from 'ome."

"Gideon, we're here to help whenever you feel you need it. So how are things at the moment?"

"Well I can't quite understand this, but since I've been back, I'm finding I can relate to the ordinary guys in here so much better. Hanging out with well-known people all the time can really do your head in, y'know? Every time I go out there's a camera shoved in my face, and everyone wants to know what's going on between me and whoever I'm with. I've lost my way a bit and need to find myself again. Maybe I need to lose the hangers-on and get a bit more real, eh?"

Professor Somerfield understood his issues very well. He lived permanently in the moment, at the expense of everything and anyone else, so if he had seen a famous face or two on the wards his conversation would have been full of the rock 'n roll lifestyle, but as it was, his only contact had been with ordinary, everyday people, leading him to believe that their company was what he needed to keep him on an even keel.

It was very difficult to dislike Judge, but his full-on approach to even the most fleeting of relationships meant that he quickly wore people out around him. He had a history littered with relationship failures as a procession of friends, family and lovers all walked away from his stifling personality. Treatment, time, and experience helped him to understand his difficulties in establishing long-term ties and he was now valiantly trying to suppress his natural instincts to overwhelm anyone who became close.

During the course of their consultation, Judge talked about the pain he felt when his recent whirlwind romance with the glamour model Daniella Lae hit the rocks. The unlikely coupling was headline news throughout the spring and early summer; he was twice her age and globally famous, while she was the UK's most popular topless tease, a bright young thing who regularly displayed her ample charms in *The Horizon*. Marcus Botha's publication had a quick-fire turnover of 'Page Five Fillies,' so the girls involved needed to make an instant impact or face a rapid return to obscurity, and Lae (quite literally) stood out from the crowd. Sassy, streetwise and acutely skilled at attracting publicity, she generated interest in her private life by accumulating an extensive list of well-known conquests. Her lurid love life included dalliances with small - time gangsters, soap stars and the occasional First Division footballer, but when she decided to get cosy with a rock 'n roll superstar, the big - time truly beckoned. Suddenly, her face and frame featured in gossip columns and glossy magazines across the planet.

His advisors wisely tried to shoo him away from this dangerous liaison, but true to form, he leapt in feet first, only to end up broken, bloodied and back once more at the Priory's door when the inevitable happened and his sex kitten purred off to pastures new.

Of the many anxieties he carried from his time with Danielle Lae, the greatest was the sudden understanding of his own mortality. She had *joie de vivre* that the ageing rocker initially found hugely attractive, until he realised that for the first time, he had met someone with whom he could not keep up.

Both sexually and as a party animal, Lae was his superior. He was playing second - fiddle to a brazen force of nature who partied harder and wanted to make love longer than him, yet she still looked great the next morning when the cameras rolled. Her appetite for Class A drugs was staggering, though that story remained a well-kept secret amongst her friends, and the hardiness of her constitution left him in the shade. He was no longer the wild one in the room on a night out and his ego struggled to cope with this unwelcome revelation.

Worse was to come when she finally blew him out to take up with Ben St. Claire, the *'Milky-Bar Kid'* of the snooker circuit, whose clean-cut image contrasted starkly with his own. The fact that she now preferred Mr. Bland to the leader of a big - time hard rock band hit him hard.

During his previous stays at the Priory, Judge had always embraced his detoxification programmes with wholehearted enthusiasm (even if he did reacquaint himself with the first chemical stimulant he could get hold of upon his discharge). This time his need was for protection from the ravages of Old Father Time, and no remedy could help on that score. Daniella Lae had held a mirror to his face, and where once stood a proud stallion, all he saw now in its reflection was a wizened and decrepit ass.

Professor Somerfield's first challenge in attempting to restore his confidence was to get him to accept the consequences of the ageing process and embrace rather than repel the inevitable changes ahead. Then she wanted him to understand that his disastrous relationship choices stemmed from an inner self-loathing; that he actively chased unsuitable connections to punish himself later for their eventual failure. Deep down it was his way of paying a forfeit to the Fates that had given him a lifetime of rewards for which he never felt truly worthy.

At the end of the consultation, Susan sat quietly and pondered on the power of love and every other subtlety of attraction.

Are there lessons to learn from Gideon's troubles that I can apply to my own situation?

I'm convinced the answer is no - I didn't fall for Gordon to punish myself in any way.

My prognosis regarding his core character holds firm - he's a good man, a soul mate who's genuinely enriched my life.

He's not emotionally destructive either - of that, I'm sure.

There's more to his walking away than malice...I just need to know what his real reasons were...

She drew comfort from her certainties, her mental strength was such that she could battle with her own demons of mind, heart and soul and remain confident of emerging victorious.

Eventually.

Real closure, though, would only come when she had answers to her questions over the root cause of the break-up.

Oh Gordon, you stupid, stupid man... Open up to me!

God knows, you owe me that much...

PART TWO

EXPOSURE AND CLOSURE

15.

Poor wee Frankie Dodds

During daylight hours, Hampstead Heath exudes an atmosphere of verdant tranquillity, it is a place where several species of birds and assorted woodland creatures share the beauty of their habitat with a contented public. Parents relax watching their children play in peace, and the area serves as a much-loved local idyll, offering salvation from the cigarette smoke, petrol fumes and din of the big city that envelopes it.

When the sun goes down however, the Heath becomes a cruising ground for horny homosexuals to meet, greet and hump, and such nocturnal activities sometimes draw the attention of a different kind of wildlife. Bored straight youths have been known to roam the most secluded spots with violent intent, hoping to administer a severe kicking to any unsuspecting couple they may find enjoying a bunk up in the bushes.

Frankie Dodds found such thugs disturbing, though not out of concern for his own safety (he had long given up on that) but because they were bad for business and might frighten potential clients away. Drug addictions like his are expensive to service and the cash made with his pants down was regular and tax free, with hours to suit. No qualifications are required to fellate middle-aged men looking for illicit sexual relief on a night out in the big city either.

He had been born to well-meaning but financially disadvantaged parents whose years of struggle in a succession of poorly paid jobs did little to shield their boy from the harsh realities of life. A high rise and low expectations existence on Glasgow's Easterhouse estate is inevitably tough.

After a childhood of poorly funded education meted out by last-pick teachers, Dodds found himself spat out of the Comprehensive school system at sixteen without qualifications or prospects. By then he was either stealing from family and friends or picking the pockets of strangers to feed a firmly established heroin habit. When need smothered the last vestiges of his morality he turned to robbing houses, until the long arm of the law inevitably caught up with him and he wound up wasting away what was left of his youth at her Majesty's pleasure in Barlinnie gaol. Surviving the tough regime behind bars without his drug of choice would have been too much to bear, so he resorted to trading the only assets he possessed (to-wit: two serviceable buttocks) in return for regular scores of contraband skag. His usefulness in satisfying the sexual frustrations of some of his fellow inmates kept him free from the razor boys and other assorted bullies for the duration of his sentence.

Upon his release from prison, like many of society's lost souls, he left Glasgow life behind and hitchhiked to the bright lights of London, and whilst the ripest fruit from the tree of prosperity remained far beyond his modest reach, there were still plenty of less tasty pickings for a streetwise vagabond to pluck.

He moved into a dilapidated squat in Kentish Town because of its reasonable proximity to Hampstead, an area that was altogether too grand for his tastes, but whose Heath gave him ample opportunities to ply his trade. Once his pockets were sufficiently filled, he would scurry back to the security of his modest bolthole and shoot up in peace.

When it was too cold or miserable to work outdoors, he left his home number on a calling card inside all the local public phone boxes, together with a vaguely cryptic message: - **PROFESSIONAL HELP FOR PERSONAL PROBLEMS**. The same scrawled invitation adorned the walls of gent's toilets in local pubs and supermarkets too. Of course, he was not alone in offering intimate services to whoever might be interested, and scribbled contact numbers catering for anything from standard sex to acts of extreme fetish festooned the washroom cubicles of many establishments in the vicinity. Competition was fierce and some of the more aggressive streetwalkers tried getting tough with Dodds to frighten him away, but the dishevelled little man had nothing to lose, so he simply shrugged off their threats.

One black and bitter night during the autumn of 1985, he answered a call in the hall of his bed-sit from a prospective client. After discussing terms, he made the necessary arrangements for a rendezvous and promptly showed up on the corner of nearby Islip Street thirty minutes later. It was past midnight, the local public houses had long since bade farewell to their sparse sprinkling of Tuesday night customers, and inadequate street lighting encouraged those of a sly or subversive disposition to make their mischief.

From an adjoining side road, the driver of a shiny new BMW family saloon flashed its lights towards him as a sign of recognition. The two men engaged in a brief exchange of words, then Dodds furtively checked the street for prying eyes before slumping into the passenger seat. His client examined the pale, skinny specimen sitting next to him with disappointment, for he was the epitome of a modern-day Dickensian street-urchin.

The shambling phantom was twenty-five years old, yet he looked closer to forty. Sporting a straggly mullet of black hair tinted with blonde highlights, his *Lonsdale of London* sweatshirt threatened to overwhelm his emaciated chest. Turned-up baggy jeans exposed sockless ankles, and scuffed Nike trainers completed the sartorial ensemble.

"Where to then?" asked the deep, broad Cockney voice behind the wheel.

"Gaisford Street, two corners down - drive past the shops and it's the second house on the left." Dodds delivered the reply in a hoarse brogue, and a strong waft of nicotine accompanied his stale body odour to fill the gleaming vehicle with a deeply unpleasant stench.

The car stopped outside a near-derelict squat where he passed his days in a heroin-hazed slumber with a bunch of like-minded companions. Sometimes Dodds would escort his needy men to seedy alleys, but if a client preferred a little privacy, he would take them back to the comforts of home, so long as they ignored the general mess and used needles. This guest was particularly concerned about having gay sex in public, hence the invitation to chateau shithole…

Dodds had a sharp eye for detecting danger and had worked out that his client would be neither troublesome nor violent. He was also confident that the man had nothing to do with law enforcement (which was a matter of equal importance), so after ticking those boxes in his head, he ushered his latest very dear friend through the front door.

The Cockney voice introduced himself as, "Graham," which was obviously a false name, though this detail fell on deaf ears, for anonymity is the watchword in the prostitution game. Aged about fifty, approximately five feet eight inches tall, he carried a comfortable (but not considerable) potbelly. An unremarkable character, he was 'typical of the trade.' With his jet-black hair slicked into a slightly-too-long side parting, he reminded Dodds of the comic actor Reg Varney, who had been one of British televisions' most recognisable faces in the 1970's when starring in the hugely successful situation comedy, 'On the Buses'. That show used to reduce his family to all-too-rare fits of laughter back then, and he welcomed the remembrance with a small smile.

Upon entering the building, no one else was awake, but traces of that evening's communal activities accosted their senses. Smoke from a dozen spliffs lingered in the air of the Bohemian living room, where used roaches overflowed from a chipped glass ashtray onto a heavily scratched and burned coffee table. In the kitchen, two Bells whisky bottles stood empty on the sink and the sound of drunken snoring emanated from the other rooms upstairs as Dodds led the way to his fusty bedroom.

Turning to face the older man, he asked, "What's it to be?"

With a look of wary mistrust and anxious anticipation, his guest replied, "Prices as agreed?"

"Yeah, it's £5 for a blowie or £10 for full sex."

Graham had risked a great deal to put himself in this situation, so he was determined to satisfy his lustful urges completely.

"A tenner it is then."

Pausing to consider the BMW parked outside, the streetwise junkie before him then reconsidered their deal and decided to try maximising his earnings potential.

"You can do it without a condom if you like...for twenty-five?"

This temptation proved too much for Graham to resist.

"OK, that would be good," he said, before adding a rather pathetic, "thanks."

Sweat started to drip from his forehead and with a trembling hand, he reached out to touch the young stranger, who recoiled slightly by way of a reflex motion. This was a business transaction to him, not genuine intimacy.

"Once you're done, you're out of here, right?"

"Yeah, yeah,... Don't worry about me on that score. Here's your money. Now take your clothes off, get into bed and lie still...."

16.

Secrets and lies

"Graham", or Barry Shackleton to use his real name, headed back to his home in Maidstone, sated yet also ashamed in equal measure. No longer able to suppress his homosexual urges, in recent years he had been paying men for sex while keeping the secret of his guilty pleasure hidden from all who knew and loved him. His friends readily described him as an honest, hard-working and dependable fellow, with an open heart (and open wallet), ever ready with an offer of help whenever family members or pals ran into difficulties. Inherently modest, he would never make a big deal of the special something that made him stand out from the crowd, yet this generous, genial man was indeed different.

For Shackleton was a professional darts player with a host of tournament victories and television appearances to his name.

His successes on the circuit provided him with a very comfortable living and allowed him to give up the carpentry trade that had sustained his wife and kids in the days before the limelight came his way. Aficionados of the sport rated him dangerous enough to upset any of the big boys at the top of the tree on his day and his new BMW saloon, supplied by a local car dealer in a sponsorship arrangement, stood as a testimony to his everyman appeal. On the surface, Barry Shackleton was a positive role model.

He had married for love, yet Ruth, his best friend and *confident* for a quarter of a century, knew nothing of his true sexual preferences, and as he turned off the M20 motorway, he thought deeply about his despicable acts of betrayal. Before leaving the house to aggressively ramrod a down-at-heel young heroin addict in a shitty north London squat, he had kissed his wife goodbye, lying that he was heading, "up north," to play an exhibition match for a handsome fee.

"Good luck, love," she said as she waved him off.

He was using this untruth with increasing frequency to explain his late-night absences from the homestead, letting her believe that, although the travel was a nuisance, such bookings provided, "a nice little earner," and he intended to ride the good times while he could. All lies, damned lies, for in reality, he had a different kind of ride on his mind that night.

When his darts career took off, Shackleton moved his family away from the urban stresses of Dagenham to start a new life down by the river Medway in Kent, from where they could support his wife's widowed mother, who had become infirm and lonely after the death of her husband. Without hesitation, he dutifully welcomed her into his home, and she saw out the rest of her days in comfortable repose surrounded by precious loved ones. One mid-May morning 'Nana' passed away, content in the knowledge that her daughter had done very well for herself the day she pledged her future to such a stalwart. For the most part, this was true, but skulking in the shadows, deep within that worthy soul, unspoken urges lurked.

Shackleton had left school at fifteen and spent a couple of years labouring on building sites before being called up by her Majesty's armed forces to complete two years of compulsory National Service. He undertook basic training at the Ministry of Defence's cold, grey and gritty army barracks in the North Yorkshire town of Catterick, and quickly learned that the parochial locals there treated Cockney voices with wary suspicion (and more than a little contempt).

When his posting orders finally arrived, the army decided to send him overseas to the Southeast Asian dominion of Malaya. Catterick had been the furthest distance he had ever travelled from London, so the news thrilled him, and he looked forward to embracing a different culture a world away from the concrete conurbations of home. History recalls however that his time abroad would be far from the paradise of his expectations. As a political greenhorn, young Private Shackleton knew nothing of his country's desperate attempts to preserve its global importance through military means and he was hopelessly ill - prepared for the horrors that lay ahead.

The raw recruit and his wet-behind-the-ears band of brothers found themselves dropped into the middle of a war zone as Communist insurgents fought to free themselves from the yoke of the British Empire. Fortunately, the survival skills that ratty sergeant majors had drilled into those impressionable innocents on the windswept Yorkshire moors came to their rescue on several occasions over the next few months.

Friendships forged in the heat of battle run deep and during this time Shackleton struck up a particular attachment with a somewhat sensitive middle-class boy from the West Country called Malcolm Meekins, who the rest of the unit regarded as a bit of a loner. Glances exchanged between them while on sentry duty suggested the possibility for more of an alliance than was strictly permissible within the remit of Queen's regulations, and Malcolm soon became rather more than just a close comrade.

Discretion was very much the order of the day, and any soldiers caught indulging in acts of a homosexual nature faced the indignity of a dishonourable discharge via a court martial. To make matters worse, their stories would emerge in the newspapers back home, spawning local gossip and finger pointing that could prove devastating for family members to bear. More enlightened times eventually challenged such intolerance, but in the immediate post-war years, homosexuality was still an illegal act, carrying with it a prison sentence, and young men in combat situations were expected to uphold the dignity of their regiment, regardless of whatever personal yearnings they may harbour.

Under those circumstances, the two frightened adolescents had to conduct their illicit affair without any hint of suspicion from their comrades, and the tenderness they shared proved invaluable in the lonely and often-deadly chaos of their surroundings. This was Shackleton's first real expression of affection beyond the boundaries of his immediate family, and like many first loves, it was intense, but also brief, and had run its course long before his National Service ended.

Upon his return to civvie-street, he turned his attention towards learning a trade and put the experience to the back of his mind, thinking it was just something borne out of the stresses arising from such a torrid tour of duty. His native East End of London seemed a lifetime away from the horrors of

Malaya, and Dagenham's occasional pockets of villainy and street violence paled by comparison. With his evenings taken up at Walthamstow dog track or down the local with the lads, all-in-all, these were happy times. At weekends he would race home after watching West Ham and spruce up before heading off to the Alexandra Palace or some other dance hall in the hope of catching the eye of a nice, uncomplicated girl with a sense of fun and a cheeky smile.

He met Ruth at the aforementioned 'Ally Pally' and when love blossomed, he thought his homosexual desires would dissipate forever, but over time the stirrings that had remained latent for so long began to resurface, until he could contain himself no longer.

Many men and women experience feelings of restlessness during middle-age; their children grow up and leave home; mortgages get paid off; the chains of responsibility begin to loosen, and relinquished freedoms of youth re-establish themselves. Some calm these ripples on the pond of life by indulging in a simple guilty pleasure; perhaps the purchase of a hot-rod sports car, or a holiday to an exotic location. Others take lovers to quicken pulses. A few go so far in placating their restlessness that they risk destroying the happy families they spent decades carefully nurturing.

Shackleton's mid-life crisis revolved around his need to have sex with men. Lacking the courage to look for one long-term male partner (for he knew that would destroy his family, whom he truly loved) he sought sex for sale instead; casual bunk-ups with strangers for a cash consideration. Job done, satisfaction achieved, then back home to the wife and kids. Nobody need be any the wiser.

With his latest rent-boy rendezvous successfully completed, he headed for home deep in thought, saturated in the stale sweat of his guilty deceit. Little did he know that his evening's rigours would, in the space of a few short years, scatter the shreds of his tattered reputation to all four points of the compass.

By then, Gordon Rimmer, Marcus Botha and three million readers of *The Horizon* would know every intimate detail of his secret life.

17.

The first fly falls

An impatient knock on the door of Frankie Dodds' room received no answer. Its ashen faced instigator had moved into the Gaisford Street squat a couple of months earlier and immediately made himself at home, commandeering a bedroom opposite the elfin Glaswegian's. He coughed several times before gagging on some phlegm that he spat out onto the frayed carpet at his feet. Increasingly angry, he knocked several more times without any response before calling out, "Frankie! Frankie, you little shithouse! Answer the fucking door, will you? I want my money! I need that fiver you borrowed on Tuesday night - I've run out of fags and I'm skint, so hand it over! Come on you tight cunt - open this fucking door!" The strain of raising his voice brought on a further coughing fit. "Doddsie, if you don't bring out my money right now, I'm gonna come in there and get it, and you ain't gonna like that!" The only response was an icy silence. "Right, you little twat, I'm coming in."

The coughing man was drunk, and he leaned aggressively against the door with all the weight he could muster, snapping a tiny rusting chain on the other side that stood as an ineffectual barrier against unwelcome intruders. As he burst into the drab, damp, dreary room, a fetid stench of neglect and decay made him recoil, filling his lungs and making him gag once more.

The source of the foul odour became glaringly obvious when he saw Frankie Dodds lying completely rigid on his dirty mattress. Barely weighing five stone, the tiny, fully clothed shell of a man was open-mouthed, colourless and quite, quite dead.

Once the intruder had satisfied himself that the body was indeed cold and lifeless, he promptly relieved the room of its cash, cigarettes and any trinkets that could be comfortably pawned for profit, before quietly slipping away. Those who traverse the cesspits of life are rarely inclined to mourn the passing of a fellow traveller.

The drunken wretch confided his deadly news to two of the building's other resident squatters (leaving out any mention of his ill-gotten gains, thus avoiding the need to share out the spoils). Between them, they decided against notifying the police about the deceased, for fear of attracting unwelcome attention to their own illegal activities. Instead, they made plans to remove his corpse from the premises under cover of darkness.

That night, the three men unceremoniously leaned an unloved, unmissed bundle of bones against the small wall of a side street leading to Wolsey Mews; far enough away from their squat for him not to be recognised as a fellow housemate. Lying there, the skeletal frame looked like a sleeping vagrant in the shadows: out of sight, out of mind.

Out of luck. Out of life.

When the body was discovered, it was duly removed by the authorities for forensic tests to take place, and a local coroner declared that the heroin-addicted rent-boy's cause of death was unsurprisingly AIDS related. Frankie Dodds, of no fixed abode, no discernible past, present, and certainly no future, was buried in a pauper's grave; just another fatality chalked up to the latest scourge of society's underclass.

London's magnetic pull attracts aspirants, dissidents, dilettantes and the careworn, all hoping that its alchemic properties will turn their dreams, hopes, or mundane practicalities into gold, yet only a fortunate few emerge victorious in the lottery of life. The rest soon discover that there is much more mud and misery on those lonely streets than ever was the stuff of glister.

18.

Viva Las Vegas!

Fast forward four years to the summer of 1990, where we find Gordon Rimmer in the departure lounge of Heathrow's Terminal 4 waiting to board a British Airways plane bound for Las Vegas. He is there to cover the '*M J Botha's Darts Duals*' tournament alongside a motley bunch of second-rate tabloid sports hacks and a sprinkling of elder statesman from the broadsheets.

This unwanted commission left him bristling with anger, much to the merriment of his hale and hearty rivals, who, over a few pre-flight drinks, burst forth with ever more colourful taunts mocking his displeasure (none of which were suitable for publication should they have wished to commit them to print).

The Horizon's marketing team had gone into overdrive to hype the Head Honcho's televised darts and snooker events, describing them as, "monumental," additions to the sporting calendar. Their efforts left Rimmer wary of a fateful tap on his shoulder demanding his attendance, when he desperately wanted the plum job of reporting on the football World Cup finals in Italy instead. Throughout spring, he would check the sports team's duty roster, hoping that another, lesser light might be saddled with the dubious honour of supporting Botha's vanity projects, but Harry Ellis kept the paper's plans close to his chest. Finally, after weeks of anxious limbo, Rimmer confronted his editor directly to get some answers.

"Yes, your Lordship? What can I do for you today?"

"I need to know my itinerary for *Italia 90* Harry - you haven't told me where I'll be staying or which other matches you want me to cover besides England's.

Time's ticking on, you know."

This suggestion of tardiness was just one of the many things that got under Ellis's skin about his biggest irritant, so he carefully chose the wording of his reply to cause maximum displeasure in return.

"Well, I can't argue with you there - time does indeed have that annoying habit of tick-tick-ticking away, but I wouldn't let it get to you too much, because you won't be going to Italy anyway." He saw Rimmer as a pompous, self-important egotist, with an over-inflated opinion of his abilities, and took great delight in bursting the upstart's bubble.

"What do you mean I'm not going? I have to go! You've got to send your Chief Sports Correspondent to the World Cup finals! It's the biggest event of the year for Christ's sake!"

Ellis stared disdainfully over his spectacles and cleared his throat before revving into another acidic riposte.

"I didn't know you were hard of hearing - would you like to have your ears checked out? You can book a test through your expenses account if you're concerned. Perhaps I'll get a great big sign made up to stick on your desk, so you get the message loud and clear because YOU'RE NOT GOING TO THE BLOODY WORLD CUP! Have I made myself understood now?" It felt good to trample over the precious ego of a disliked colleague, and to humiliate him in front of the rest of the team (who were nosily ear - wigging the conversation through the sports editor's open office door) was better still. "You're off to Las Vegas to cover the boss's darts thing, then you'll be going to South Africa for the *Sun City Snooker Showdown*. Have you got that, or would you like me to say it again?"

The two men glared defiantly at one another.

"What's this really all about Harry? If you've got a personal issue with me, let's take it upstairs to the Head Honcho right now!"

A sadistic smile crossed Ellis's lips.

"We can if you like old son, because I'd love to see the look on your face when Mr. Botha spins you around and kicks your arse straight back out the door for daring to bother him. See, packing you off to Las Vegas and Sun City is his idea - he says he wants our best man covering his tournaments to give them the biggest profile possible, though Christ knows why he thinks that's you. I'd have sent Sammy Biddle - he's never let me down when I've given him darts or snooker gigs in the past. I don't see what you can contribute that he can't."

Rimmer tried to turn this antagonism to his own advantage.

"Exactly Harry! You've hit the nail right on the head! Sammy's your man - so can you let Botha know the way you're thinking and swing it for me to go to Italy instead?"

"No."

"What! Why the hell not?"

"Because he expects people to do what they're fucking well told around here, so that's exactly what I'm doing. I've said that to you before - are you a bit stupid or something?"

"But this could damage our circulation during the World Cup weeks."

Rimmer's arrogance astonished Ellis.

"Listen here, you! I could dig up a slug out of my garden to write a piece about the World Cup and our punters would still read it. What you do is easy enough to replicate - we're talking about a sports column in *The Horizon*, not one of Shakespeare's fucking sonnets! Now follow your orders - your itineraries will follow in due course!" With the dispute apparently done and dusted, the disconsolate Rimmer turned to leave, but to his surprise, Ellis called him back. "I haven't finished yet. Close the door, will you? I don't want the others outside hearing what I've got to say."

Despite all his bluff and bluster, he knew that the omission of *The Horizon's* Chief Sport's Correspondent from the world's premier football tournament would reflect badly on the paper, so some weeks earlier he had asked the Head Honcho to rethink Rimmer's attendance at the *Sun City Showdown* (hence the roster delay). That very morning, Botha finally agreed, but with significant caveats.

"Look, I've had to be the bringer of bad news because that's my job," (Ellis declined to mention the pleasure that the task brought him) "but there's still a chance that you can change your fate. When the Vegas job is over, the boss expects you to fly straight to South Africa, but I've spoken to him on your behalf, and he's prepared to cut you a deal - only if your copy from the darts malarkey comes up to scratch, mind. *Italia 90* won't have gotten into its stride until the *'Darts Duels'* thing is over, so play the game and you might - just might - get to the World Cup after all."

"What are the terms of his deal then?"

"The boss says you can only follow the football if England reach the knockout stages of the competition. If that task proves to be beyond them, the agreement is off - his reasoning is that domestic interest in the World Cup would wane without any home nation involvement. So come up with a clever approach to your coverage of the darts - that's what we pay you for anyway - and it might get you on that plane to Italy."

Rimmer's destiny now lay at the feet of England's finest footballers: a prospect guaranteed to stick in the craw of every true-born son of Scotland! This deeply unsatisfactory bargain left him frustrated, fed-up, and bound for Las Vegas in the company of a gaggle of alcohol-fuelled adversaries, most of whom he barely knew, because nearly all of the big guns were heading in the opposite direction to Italy. Eleven hours later, dog-tired and still childishly sulking, he dragged his weary bones out of McCarran airport into the Nevada sunshine, where a waiting taxi whisked him to the Sands hotel, his home for the thick end of the following fortnight.

As he checked in and scanned the reception area, he began to question Botha's choice of venue for the tournament. The hotel had long since lost the lustre of its golden years, when the *Rat Pack* performed to rapturous audiences in its Copa Room. Frank Sinatra, Dean Martin, Sammy Davis Jr., Joey Bishop and Peter Lawford were the kings of casual cool and their much vaunted, *'Summit at the Sands,'* show was considered to be the high-water mark of the cabaret scene, the very zenith of glamour. Thirty years on, the place had gone to seed somewhat; with its peeling paintwork and faded carpets, it felt entirely unsuitable to host a televised tournament. Once it was a stop-off point for Presidents and Hollywood royalty, but soon it would be answering the call of a wrecking ball as part of this progressive city's constant regeneration.

Of course, Rimmer knew nothing of Botha's original plan to re-invent the *Rat Pack* magic with a Union Jack twist. In that context, with a clever use of lighting and imaginative camera angles, the place might just have managed to restore a bit of its old lounge lizard slickness, but soft-focus lenses cannot work miracles, and slick tricks were never going to glamorise grey and grizzled professional darts players like Jocky Wilson or Eric Bristow!

After settling into his room on the seventh floor, Rimmer went downstairs to the tournament's practice facilities to acquaint himself with the players, who were busily acclimatising to their new surroundings. Much of their talk concerned Barry Shackleton's drastic diet, which had left him looking shockingly emaciated. His radically altered frame was playing havoc with his game too, because he had recently slipped out of the top ten in the world rankings. One of his fellow competitors was overheard saying, "It's not natural for a darts player to be so thin - look what it's done to his sharpness! When he lost his weight, his form went too - it's pitiful to see how he's playing now. On top of that, he never socialises with the lads anymore either - he'll be up in his room now tackling a sprig of lettuce while the rest of us get stuck into all this free grub downstairs!"

That evening, Shackleton was not alone in playing the anti-social card, for Rimmer chose to shut himself away in his hotel room too, resisting the temptations of the celebrated Las Vegas Strip to do some further background research on the stars that he must pass comment on the next morning. While his colleagues in the press corps were hitting the bars below, he kept his foul mood to himself and concentrated on finding imaginative angles to enliven his column. The pressure was on to impress Marcus Botha back home if he wanted to secure his trip to the World Cup finals once all of this nonsense was over.

Eventually, sleep called, replete with welcome dreams of Susan Somerfield. As he slept on, he was completely oblivious to the sufferings elsewhere of pale, frail Barry Shackleton, but very soon, that sickly man's sorry story would provide reams of inspirational copy for every scribe in town.

With this in mind, for now, our attention turns to his room: his troubles....

19.

Another one bites the dust

You sleep badly, intermittently, with a head full of anxieties and dark dreams. In the morning Ray Evans, one of your closest friends and fellow competitors on the circuit, knocks on your door to ask if you want to join him downstairs for some breakfast, but you answer back saying that you don't fancy anything; you're not hungry. You're never very hungry anymore. He asks the same question again because he couldn't hear what you said, and you realise that your ever-weakening voice has not carried far enough to be heard outside. It's an effort to extricate yourself from the sweat-stained sheets on your bed, but you get up to open the door so that you can speak to him directly.

"Morning, Ray. Listen mate, I don't fancy any grub this morning. I'm not feeling too clever, see…"

"Jesus, Barry! You look fucking terrible!" The face that greets you is a picture of concern. "Do you want me to fetch a doctor?"

"No, no, I'll be alright", you reply, before thinking better of the offer. "Well, I suppose it wouldn't hurt to get a couple of pills down me, so ok, will you do that? Cheers Ray, you're a pal - if you can get 'em to just send someone up here that'll be good. I'll be resting up all day 'til show time tonight."

"When are you due on?"

"I'm the third match up. Playing Colin Brandon. What about you?"

"I'm on first - I've pulled the big one - bloody Bristow. Looks like my stay in town's gonna be short and sweet then, eh?"

You console him over his unfortunate luck in the draw and hope that he does himself justice.

"If you can take Bristow out, we'll all have a better chance at the title."

"Yeah, and pigs might fly! Just take care of yourself Bazza." He turns away but looks back and speaks again before you can close the door. "I know I've said it before, but this crash diet is doing you no good at all. You need to get some decent scoff down you!" He pauses in the hope that you will change your mind and join him downstairs, but a shake of your head makes it clear that you're not up to it. "Fair enough, well at least I've had my say. I'll make sure that reception sends a quack up to your room. All the best for tonight, ok?"

Sometime later - you don't know when - a doctor arrives to perform a routine check-up and he states the obvious by confirming that you're running a temperature. He prescribes some pills, gives you a shot of something or other to cool you down and advises you to go to the local hospital immediately to undergo some more extensive tests. You promise him you'll go once your participation in the tournament is over and despite his grumbles, he knows that he can't change your mind. After seeing him off you spend the rest of the day quietly contemplating the job at hand.

At six thirty, you are showered, changed, and ready for the call to take your place in the backstage area and practice facility downstairs. You are only-too aware of the way the other competitors look at you, observing your discomfort and ill health. Some, like Ray, ask if you are ok, while others are secretly pleased that you are clearly in no shape to play top class darts. That sums up the dog-eat-dog world of professional sport.

Then there's the seemingly endless wait to go on. Everyone else is practicing hard, propelling dart after dart into the practice boards with metronomic efficiency, but you decide to sit quietly and compose yourself before your turn comes to perform. You read a good luck telegram from your agent, the venerable Mo Letterman, who says he's going to follow the action on TV back in Essex via his new satellite dish, and that he'll be there on stage with you in spirit.

You're furnace hot, then iceberg cold, and both sensations are distracting and uncomfortable.

Steady Barry, steady.

Just think about what you've got to do to win this match tonight.

Some people have come a long way to see you play, so put up a good show for them.

For the wife and kids back at home too.

No!

Don't clutter your head with all that extra burden, old son.

Do this for yourself - for your own pride.

Think like a professional.

Act like one.

Steady yourself so that you can give of your best, for you, and you alone.

Concentrate on that and the rest will take care of itself.

Somewhere in the dimly lit auditorium, a tannoy plays your theme song, "*I'm Forever Blowing Bubbles.*" It's the football hymn beloved of West Ham fans the world over and from the other side of the stage curtain you hear some muted, drunken (or at the very least merry) Cockney voices in the crowd joining in, which lifts you from your lethargy. But the sound seems distant; almost artificial; it doesn't feel like the usual live experience of a big-time darts audience.

The curtains open and a Master of Ceremonies bellows out your name by way of introduction. Lights suddenly glare into your face, and you struggle to see the people beyond the stage. Cheers break out and applause distracts you, yet the crowd seem to be so far away; it's as if they are hardly there at all. You can't make out whether there are a hundred, a thousand, or ten thousand people here. You hear their individual shouts of encouragement though.

"Come on Barry!"

"Show 'em who's boss!"

"You can do it!"

You stop shuffling and try to stride purposefully across the stage, taking your place next to the ebullient MC. An enormous ice bucket overloaded with bottles of Budweiser beer sits on a shiny glass table embossed with an obligatory *MJB TV* logo. The alcohol is for the benefit of the players, most of whom will happily imbibe throughout their matches without suffering the slightest detriment to their skills. You, of course, will abstain to try to keep your focus.

You see a towel draped over a chair next to the table. It's got your name stitched across it and you grab it to dab the sweat from your head and neck. You're going to need that towel tonight. The lights are giving off so much heat, and your brow immediately runs another river of salt water.

Noise levels rise once more as your opponent, the very tricky Colin Brandon, enters the arena. You look around at him, nodding a friendly acknowledgement. The MC describes him as hailing from, "England's Charrrming Coastal County of Corrrnwall!" and you smile at the extent to which hype infects even the inanest of introductions in this city.

You both have a couple of three-dart practice throws into the matchboard and then it's showtime; the moment to switch on. Distractingly though, you're bitterly cold again, as if you've gone out for a walk in a blizzard without a coat. So why are you sweating? You think you know the answer but, as ever, you don't want to submit to your deepest fears.

Sharpen up!

It's time to play - time to go to war!

I can do this - I know I can.

If only I can stop these bloody shivers from making my hands shake so much.

The MC settles the crowd down so that battle can commence, and for the benefit of the uninitiated amongst the audience, he explains the tournament rules. You were told in advance that this is necessary before each match to encourage curious locals to follow the proceedings, but for the pros, the real darts fans here, and the TV audience at home, it's such a fucking nuisance. You're desperate to just get on with the job. While he prattles on, Brandon meets your eye and mouths, "Blah, blah, blah!" bringing a rare smile to your face, before the business end of his interminable spiel is finally reached.

"To the triumphant victor go the spoils of war; a place in the next round awaits… while for the unfortunate loser, it's a case of…..c'mon everybody, repeat after me….ON YOUR BIKE, TAKE A HIKE!" This little catchphrase seems to go down well in the already convivial atmosphere. "Are we ready?….Then LET'S PLAY DARRRRRTSSSSSS!!!"

The match referee, who up until this moment had cut such a peripheral figure that you failed to notice him, tosses a silver dollar coin into the air, intercepts its descent with a shovel-like grab and asks you to nominate whether heads or tails will lie face up when he unpeels his palm. You correctly call, "Heads" and get the opportunity to throw first.

You press your right foot against the 'oche' (the line measuring the mandatory seven feet nine and a quarter inches distance from the thrower to the board) and raise your first dart to eye level, drawing a bead on the target.

The crowd hushes to an expectant and reverential silence, though you are no longer remotely aware of their presence. Your first dart hits its intended mark in the treble twenty scoring area with laser like accuracy. Shots of twenty and another sixty follow.

The scorer roars, "One Hunnndrrred and Forrrty!" with an overblown gusto, and an appreciative roar greets the call. It's a great start, and after Brandon has taken his three throws there's another cry, this time of, "One Hunnndrrred!" You've taken the lead. The game continues until you're eventually left with a potential three-dart finish of one hundred and nine. Your first dart scores eighteen, followed by treble seventeen, leaving you requiring forty more to win. If your last dart finds that tiny red baize bed at the apex of the board, you'll score double twenty ('double top' as it's known in the trade) and take a one-nil lead. With a mastery that recalls your glory days, the arrow flies true, hitting the target with a reassuring thud and the crowd collectively scream, "YES!" The first game is yours.

Eventually, you take the first set, and the match then begins to settle into the natural way of things, nip and tuck, back and forth, but overall, you still have control. Everything is as it should be.

Then, from nowhere, your sweats start to kick in again.

Perspiration drips from your fingers and you are unable to grip the darts with your usual finesse. Your vision switches from sharp focus to blur and back again. Your powers of concentration start to wane, and your mind wanders off into spells of vague nothingness. Your precious tungsten tools slip from your grasp once, twice, and then for a third time. Palpitations paradiddle on your heart. The room spins, slowly at first, then ever more quickly, and you suddenly find yourself wanting to vomit. Despite your best efforts, dizziness takes hold of your senses, and you lose balance. Such is your recent weight loss that there is no discernible thud; you barely graze the polished wooden floor, but teams of security and medical people immediately burst into the lights, rushing the stage to administer assistance to your stricken frame.

"Keep back!" someone cries from the middle of the mêlée. "He needs air!"

For your part, you know nothing of this because you have succumbed to a state of unconsciousness. Your concerned opponent and the referee keep clear as paramedics check your vital signs to see if your airways, breathing and circulation are still functioning, then you are placed onto a stretcher and whisked away.

Amid the confusion in the arena, the MC uses all his professional showmanship to re-establish control over proceedings.

"Let me assure you ladies and gentlemen, there's nothing to worry about here - it seems that Barry has unfortunately fallen victim to the heat from our television and stage lighting rigs, so as a precaution he's going off to hospital and will be monitored overnight. He's in the best hands possible - the medical facilities here in Las Vegas have the unnn-disss-puuu-teddd reputation of being the finest in the whooole wiiide worrrlllddd! So, right now, let's all send our verrry best wishes to a true gladiator for a speedy recovery. From everybody here at The Sands Hotel and Casino - altogether now! - GET WELL SOOON BARRRY!!!"

He allows the crowd's applause to die down before putting an arm around the shoulder of your bewildered adversary. "Now let's raise the roof for our winner - by virtue of the retirement of his opponent, I give you...Colllin Brrrannndon!"

In and out of consciousness you drift, occasionally catching muffled shouts of, "Emergency - coming through!" and, "Please, clear the way ahead!"

Within minutes, you are taken into a waiting ambulance. A siren wails, but you know little and care less, unable, as you are, to resist the peaceful lure of yet more sleep...

Flickering eyelids signal your return from slumber and an uncomfortable oxygen mask engulfs your face, while an intravenous drip feed keeps your left arm occupied.

Busy paramedics fuss and flap over you in that claustrophobic space, inducing a nausea that results in an expulsion of vomit. If your collapse wasn't embarrassing enough, now you're throwing up over your helpers. One of the ambulance crew replaces the mask, wiping your face and mouth while uttering words of comfort in response to your unease.

"Just try and relax sir, we'll be there soon."

Dizziness then renews its acquaintance with the insides of your skull and soon everything is vague once more…

The next time you open your eyes, all is white. Your vision gradually sharpens into focus, and you see before you a hospital room. Looking beyond your bed with its stiff, starched sheets and rigid mattress, you follow a plastic tube's journey from a saline bag perched above your head into a barely perceptible vein in your arm. Your mouth is dry; your lips are dry. You ache all over and feel so weak. Each laboured blink is an effort, and you wonder how on earth this natural reflex became such a chore. You want to speak but struggle to make yourself heard.

"Nurse....Nurse..."

A sharp intake of breath follows each puny utterance, but eventually you gather enough strength to push your vocal cords into effective action and summon some assistance. A tall, very burly black man with a reassuringly friendly face responds to your call, and his toothy smile radiates warmth as he speaks.

"Hi sir, how are you today? My name is Darryl, how can I help you?"

"Please... where am I? How long have I been here? Can you tell me what's going to happen to me? When can I get out of here?"

"Woah there my man, steady on now! Let's take those questions one at a time, shall we? Well, this facility is the Santa Maria Hospital and Medical Centre, and you arrived here last night. All I know is that you got wheeled onto this ward from ER a couple of hours ago after one of our doctors there ran some initial tests on you." He sees the distress in your look and tries to keep you calm. "I'm sure there's nothin' to worry yoursel' about - you know, it's jus' routine kinda stuff - that'd be my guess." In an effort to deflect your concerns, he tries to change the subject. "Say, you've created quite a stir aroun' here, man! We've had British reporters hangin' aroun' the hospital all day 'cos of you! To tell you the truth, they' bin a damn nuisance, but I kinda like the buzz of it all!"

This one doesn't take himself too seriously. but you know that his cheerfulness is a show of kindness towards you. With a baritone chuckle, he goes on. "I hear you're one of those guys playin' in that darts show over at the Sands - well you wuz, anyways! I don't see how you gonna be able to land none of them pointy lil' cocktail sticks into no target way over there from way over here!" The nurse's grin illuminates the room once again. "As for how long you'll be residing at our plush li'l establishment Mr. Shackleton, well I really ain't the man to ask."

"It's Barry....call me Barry will you, Darryl?"

"Ok sir - Barry - but that's jus' got to be our li'l thing, ok? The folks round here don' like too much familiarity 'tween the patients and the staff. I gotta call you Mr. Shackleton in front of the other staff members."

Nurse Darryl places your weak free hand in his and a formal, if feeble greeting takes place.

"Anyways, like I say, I ain't heard nothin' 'bout when you'll be well enough to be discharged, but I can tell you that this room is private, peaceful and quiet - you' gonna get plenty of rest in here." He means well, but this news only adds to your stress, and you try to raise yourself from the bed.

"Oh God no, I'm having none of that! I know how much it costs to stay in these bloody places - there's no National Health Service over here to cover all this - not like back home. I've got to get out."

It's obvious to the nurse that despite your apparent notoriety, you would find an extended stay in a hospital like this beyond your budget, so he tries to address your concerns.

"Relax sir - sorry, er, Barry - relax. Take my word for it, all that's gonna be taken care of without you havin' to part with a single dime. Jesus, those news guys outside would happily pay for everything just to get a single word with you."

"You think so?"

"Sure thing, man. You jus' leave all that to Darryl. Now jus' lie back an' be cool, ok?"

You are too weak and too tired to argue, so you smile feebly at your new friend and trust to his judgement. Within minutes, you're out for the count again and the mysteries of the here and now are left for others to solve.

20.

Sin city epiphany

Once the evening's drama drew to a close, the (disappointingly small) crowd drifted from the arena into the hotel casino's seductively open arms, where its slot machines, roulette wheels and card tables lay in readiness to welcome their thrill-seeking prey. Casinos act as bastions of hope for every optimistic fantasist who dreams of beating the house and breaking the bank, though in reality, the odds of that happening are ridiculously long indeed. Hotels like the Sands spend a great deal of time and money designing their mesmeric lures and those efforts are not undertaken to give a sucker an even break; their sole purpose is to drain every spare dollar and dime from the pockets of any poor deluded fool who wants to take on the challenges within.

'*Welcome to the Jungle,*' my pretties!

After the press corps had 'phoned in their reports, they dutifully observed the time-honoured traditions of their trade by repairing to the bar to debate the key incidents of the evening. Naturally, the major talking point on everyone's lips was the collapse of Barry Shackleton.

"It's no surprise those stage lights got to him, the old boy's lost so much weight and that's bound to take its toll. He just looked lost and bewildered out there." This was the considered opinion of *The Daily Mirror*'s Stanley Potts, and the rest of the sporting sages concurred with his assessment. They were collectively wise after the event, yet all of them had blithely ignored the signals of Shackleton's fragility throughout the flight from London and none thought it significant that he had stayed cooped up in his room from the moment he arrived at the hotel.

"I tell you what", murmured Geoff Betts from *The Daily Star,* "his game's been going to pieces for months now and I wouldn't be surprised if he's close to packing it all in. His glory days are long gone and at his age it's hard to turn back the clock."

Just then, a familiar metallic chink of gold medallions and sovereign-covered fingers announced the arrival at the bar of one of the darts scene's leading characters.

"Blimey Geoff, what are you talkin' about, *his* age? He's five years younger than I am, you fucker!" Thus spoke Ted 'Sunny' Day, a genial former World Darts Champion from the 1970's who now made a lucrative living as a TV pundit.

"Pull up a pew, Ted."

The reporters gathered around the darting grandee for an insider's update on Shackleton's condition.

"How is Barry then? Any news?"

"No, I ain't heard a thing - I've only just finished doing my summary on tonight's matches for the telly people. I reckon the medics will keep him in hospital overnight and see how he feels tomorrow. If you ask me, the heat's got to his noggin 'cos of that bloody silly diet."

"That's what we were saying."

"I mean, who ever heard of a darts player going on a *diet* for fuck's sake! We're *meant* to be fat bastards!" His audience laughed raucously; all stags together; each one wondering just how *'TV's Mr. Darts'* managed to keep his potty mouth in check during broadcasts when he struggled to construct a single sentence without profanity once he ventured beyond the camera's gaze. "If I get a whisper, you lads will be the first to know, ok? Now who's gonna fill my fucking glass with a whisky, you tight tossers!"

The conversation and drink flowed merrily on, while beyond this masculine enclave, Gordon Rimmer kept himself to himself, choosing to take in the sights and sounds of the Strip instead in the hope that Las Vegas's unique atmosphere might help him unwind. He thought that the real sports stories were happening at the World Cup finals in Italy, yet here he was, thousands of miles away from the action, covering a tournament with no discernible global appeal.

This whole thing is just ridiculous.

At least he could do his sulking in a place he loved, for America's most brash, flash adult pleasure palace always bought a smile to his face, even when his thoughts were at their most sour. He had an enduring fondness for the city's rough edges, but just like the Forth Bridge back in Scotland, it seemed to be in a perpetual state of renovation, and he wondered whether he would recognise the place in ten years' time.

Major reconstruction plans were afoot, and he hoped that some traces of its naughty, tacky character would remain after the changes took place. By ripping everything up and starting all over again (the Sands was already earmarked for such a fate) the city risked killing rather than curing the patient's ills, though he readily accepted that an appropriate upgrade here and there might not go amiss.

Nevada's curious desert jewel goes by the favoured nickname of 'Sin City,' and for good reason too, because when daylight turns to dusk it transforms into a magnificent neon orgy of spectacle, unrivalled in its exuberance. As Rimmer walked along Las Vegas Boulevard, car horns tooted, whistles blew, and lights dazzled in a contagion of visual excess, while dime-a-dozen street hustlers, loan sharks, pimps, and decorous showgirls all made their gloriously individual contributions to the ludicrous extravaganza. The *Sturm und Drang* delighted him, adding further colour to his treasured collection of Vegas memories (which ranged from being a privileged observer of epic world championship prize-fights to acting as his pal Eddie's best man when the idiot married a one-night stand hippy chick at a *'Drive—Thru Chapel of Love'*).

From a personal perspective, he thought that the union of Las Vegas and the sweet science of boxing made for an infinitely more compatible partnership than most of those, 'Love Me Tender,' marriage pacts ever would. Fighters bravely put their lives on the line in pursuit of glory, and once that first bell goes, there is no going back until the referee declares a winner, whereas spur-of-the-moment matrimonial gambles like Eddie's can be painlessly annulled in the time it takes for a next-day hangover to wear off. No harm done.

Maybe I'm unhappy about this darts nonsense because there's no real jeopardy element in the sport?

After all, Eric-bloody-Bristow is hardly risking mortal danger if he loses here, is he?...

If Rimmer only knew that somewhere downtown there lay a broken man in a hospital bed who, like the boxers he so admired, had pushed himself to the very limits of human endurance. The full extent of Barry Shackleton's troubles were yet to emerge though, and the newsman remained completely unaware that one of the biggest sporting stories in years was about to land on his lap…

For now, the charms of Las Vegas continued to permeate his musings.

Despite its failings (and many a ruined gambling casualty will bear witness to those), he saw a city of celebration rather than one of despair; a bastion of hope where lives can change on the spin of a wheel or the turn of a card, and he felt very comfortable with that. Wherever he looked, he saw people on a spree. Everywhere, everything and everyone was primed to hoover up cash from the wave upon wave of sensation-chasers drawn into Sin City, all of whom were determined to indulge their hearts' desires.

Blue collar Latinos and blue-rinse Bible belt ladies of leisure poured into the hotel casinos, intent on mercilessly plundering small change from an endless array of slot machines. Ring-a-ding buzzers and bells sporadically signalled the sweet sound of silver coin success, reminding everyone that pay-outs were tantalisingly possible (though in the end, most of those who came in hope were destined to return home lighter in their pockets).

While the majority of amateur speculators put their faith in Lady Luck to give them a generous smile, others believed in a more cerebral route to riches. Over on the roulette tables, frustrated students of calculus consulted notebooks full of complex hieroglyphic formulas, each one trying to predict the final resting place of a single, fidgeting ball at the conclusion of its frenetic travails around a shining, spinning wheel. Happily, for the ever-polite croupiers and their eagle-eyed floor managers, none of the weekend Einsteins on view appeared to be proficient enough at unravelling the mysteries of mathematics to emerge victorious.

Passing the entrance to the recently opened Mirage casino, Rimmer spotted some bellhops and waiters from his hotel. They were still eagerly anticipating the chance to gamble away their hard-earned dollars, despite bearing daily witness to the folly of taking on a house that always wins. Nothing else that he observed on his wanderings captured the irrational mania inherent in Las Vegas more vividly.

"Place your bets, ladies and gentleman, please!"

Of course, gambling is not the only vice synonymous with Sin City, for temptations of every kind are close at hand and sex is pursued with the same vigour as a winning bet. During his stroll, he saw Texas high rollers chasing good-time girls, drunken hen parties flirting with hopeful high-school jocks, and chubby bald 'executives' spinning dubious tales of boardroom dynamism to lonely divorcees. Every night the Strip is crowded with chancers, dancers and romancers, and they all want to return to the reality of their workaday lives with a winning tale to tell from the gaming tables or the boudoir.

Whenever he became reflective, his thoughts turned to Susan.

What would she make of all this madness?

Would she denounce or pity the imbecilic fools who continue to bet, bet, bet, while they lose, lose, lose?

Would she chastise or advise the sex pests?

I know my girl well enough – she's endlessly fascinated by the complex workings of the mind, so she'd judge each case on an individual basis, then help those who have difficulty separating the fun from their addictions.

Whilst surveying the all-go, Day-Glo street scene before him, he suddenly wished that he could ask her what she thought of Vegas's infamous kitsch, though he felt confident enough to assume she would embrace it all with the same enthusiasm that he did.

Christ, I miss her so much!

Just then, he arrived at a decision that was going to alter his future. This was a moment of epiphany.

The second his contractual obligation to Botha's vanity projects was over, he would quit *The Horizon* and stake his future happiness on trying to win his woman back. He knew that this would inevitably cause ructions up in the Penthouse, but what was the worst the Head Honcho could do? Life was already miserable working under his tyrannical pressure and all Rimmer could see from now on was the shining light of freedom.

If his career was finished then so be it; despite loving his profession dearly, he needed Susan more. The house would have to go of course; he would just have to take the financial hit and move on. Somehow or other he would work off the debt. What mattered above all else was having her by his side, come what may.

It's only taken one evening here to make me understand the gambles I need to take to be a winner for the rest of my life!

21

Rimmer nets a catch

After spending a couple of hours soaking up the local atmosphere, Rimmer returned to the Sands' lounge bar for a nightcap. By now, most of his fellow scribes had drunk their fill of liquor and made for the welcoming repose of their beds. Only Alan Hawkins of *The Daily Express* and *The Daily Mail's* Ray Chatham were still drinking, slouched on a sofa near the door. Rimmer found both men objectionable, so to keep his distance, he took occupancy of a stool up at the bar. When they saw him however, Hawkins mischievously shouted over.

"So, how's Botha's boy tonight then? Been sending him a 'Wish you were here' postcard, have we?"

Chatham dutifully backed up his friend.

"No Al, I reckon he's been on the prowl for some female company. I thought bookworms were his thing though - I didn't reckon he'd be eyeing up the showgirls, eh?"

The industry grapevine had heard about Rimmer's break-up with his fancy lady professor, and this was an opportunity for some prime ribbing. As their bearbaiting was just a continuation of the abuse that flew around on the plane from London it was easy to shrug off, so, much to the frustration of his tormentors, he smiled serenely back and made a mental note to get the first punch in himself next time.

"You've read me wrong boys, I'm just here to work, same as you."

"Ok pal, we don't want to touch on a sore point," replied Chatham, insincerely. "Fancy joining us for a drink?"

By drawing him into their company, they hoped he might let slip something about his troubled romantic or professional relationships, which they could then turn against him when the right moment arose.

"Thanks for the offer, but I'd just like a bit of 'me' time tonight."

With that unequivocal snub, the two slightly inebriated hacks recognised the futility of further button pushing, so they downed the dregs from their gin and tonics and left him to his thoughts.

A smattering of the room's occupants were shell-shocked losers seeking salvation from the temptations of the gaming tables; all alone with their frets and regrets, they quietly reflected on their, "might-have-been's," and, "if only's," in peace. At the opposite end of the bar, a very large, heavily set man seemed keener on drinking than thinking and he appeared to be paying particular interest to the new arrival. Rimmer's radar was picking up distress signals.

"Hey you there! You boy!"

The voice was curiously familiar, causing him to shoot a swift glance in the direction from whence it came. The man was indeed addressing him, but he was in no mood to attract trouble, so rather than offer a response, he chose to scrutinise the label on his half-drunk bottle of Budweiser instead.

"Hey, you - you on the stool! Did I hear right - did those guys just say you work for Marcus Botha?"

Rimmer quickly realised that the familiarity in the voice came from its South African origin, like that of his paymaster. It sounded slurred from too many drinks, but on closer inspection, its owner appeared to be ruggedly friendly rather than angrily hostile. Recklessness comes easily in Las Vegas, so after deciding that the man was not some bar room drunk picking a fight, he replied, "Yeah, I work on his British newspaper, *The Horizon*". His anxiety increased however when the stranger stumbled towards him, with an expression which could be read as either a glazed-eyed smile or a malevolent sneer.

"Seeing as you're on his payroll then, tell me, what do you think of good old Marvellous Marcus?"

The question presented Rimmer with a moral dilemma. If the brute closing down his personal space was a fan of Botha's (or God forbid, even a relative!) then wisdom dictated that he should lie and praise his boss to appease a potential aggressor. On the other hand, if the beefy Boer felt the same way as he did about the Head Honcho, then he could reply honestly, and with impunity.

To lie or tell the truth?

Think quickly now!

A spiteful decision by Botha had taken him halfway across the world to cover an event that was nothing more than a promotional gimmick for *MJB TV*, so he chose to speak his mind and to hell with the consequences.

"I think the man is an absolute bastard!"

"No, no, no...that's wrong - so very wrong...the word you're looking for is *cunt*! He's an absolute *cunt*! Ha!" With that, the kindred spirit chinked his glass against the bottle of his new drinking buddy and said, "Pieter Hertzog is the name, what's yours boy?"

The condescending use of the word, "boy," seemed calculated to place the South African in a position of superiority, but Rimmer chose to ignore this presumption and introduced himself nonetheless. The conversation continued in a typically macho vein.

"So what's with the sissy drink you've got there? That sort of piss-water is never going down *my* gills, for sure! I'm a scotch type of guy - that's a man's drink. Not for the faint hearted - well, not when drinking it to excess is concerned at any rate! Ha! What say you, are you up for it? Will you take a real man's drink with me?"

Hertzog was clearly used to getting his own way and Rimmer felt disinclined to provoke an argument, so he accepted the offer.

"Barman, when you're ready, two more of these, please."

"That's the spirit!"

Sports journalists are notorious for their relationships with alcohol, so he was comfortable in the company of hard drinking men and could usually keep his own end up in the boozing stakes. As the contest grew tougher however, he resorted to a spot of unsportsmanlike cheating to preserve his dignity; whenever his new acquaintance took a bathroom break, Rimmer maintained an illusion of authenticity by getting the barman to substitute the odd shot for iced tea. Quite why he felt compelled to undertake a late-night whisky-downing session with a total stranger was difficult to fathom, but something told him to stick around, as things might get interesting. Soon enough his instincts bore fruit.

"So, Pieter, somehow old Botha must have really gotten under your skin - why do you feel so bitter towards him? There's got to be a tale to tell there?.." A journalist's curiosity is habitual, and questions asked by the good ones will irrigate the stoniest soil during the most casual of conversations.

"All you need to know, my friend, is that once upon a time I used to draw my water from the same stagnant swamp that you do now and I'm a happy man indeed to be free from his clutches - I'm free as a bird. Free to drink myself to a stupor and loosen my tongue a little without having to look over my shoulder all the time like I did back in the bad old days..."

Rimmer sensed embryonic possibilities from this reply. Allowing Hertzog a little brooding time, he lay in wait for a follow up, but instead the South African turned the question around. "So what about you then boy, what's your story?"

Not wishing to give the game away that he was a reporter, he thought on his feet, saying, "I'm a photographer on the paper and Botha has had me working on glamour model portraits for a couple of years, but now I want to get away from him too."

"What, you're one of those guys that takes the topless shots of pretty girls eh? They're the best bloody things in your British newspapers - there's no other good reason to buy those rags!" Hertzog's frame shook with another self-satisfied guffaw, but his initial respect for Rimmer's fictitious occupation suddenly ground to a halt as a thought came to mind. "Wait a minute - did you say you want to move on? Why? You've got the plum job on the paper! Hang on - you're not a bloody *poofter* are you? Seems to me your country is getting overrun with fairy boys!"

Rimmer issued an assurance that his sexual inclinations were strictly straight and his motivation to quit *The Horizon* was purely professional.

"For a long while I'd been pestering my editor to help me move into action photography - sports stuff, you know, but each time it was suggested, the boss man insisted that I stayed put. I was being stifled."

"You mean you wanted to be developed! Ha ha! That's a good one, eh! Be developed!" Hertzog gloried in his pun for some minutes while this fabricated back-story unfolded.

"In the end, under an assumed name, I submitted a portfolio of sporting photographs that I'd shot independently, and the paper became interested. When I revealed myself as the guy who'd taken them, I'd proved my point and got my transfer. Naturally, once Botha heard about this - he pokes his nose into everybody's business at the paper - he wasn't happy about an upstart like me getting one over on him. To get his own back he made sure that I was sent here to take pictures of this daft bloody darts thing while all the top snappers are at the World Cup in Italy. I've had enough of being messed about by him, so now I'm looking to move on."

"That's a bummer, boy. Bummer boy - we're back to the poofters! Ha!" Once more, the drunken oaf laughed uproariously at his own comments, completely oblivious to the embarrassed looks he drew in the room. Everyone within earshot chose to abandon the bar area to avoid his bigotry. "And as for holding your own - I bet those girls used to help you out a bit there didn't they? After a hard day behind the lens staring at naked dollies, I'm sure you must have been tempted into paradise once or twice, eh?"

Rimmer satisfied his companion with a couple of lurid tales of imaginary dalliances with well-known 'Page Five Fillies', then when he felt that the conversation had become relaxed enough, he probed once more for an answer to the Botha question.

"Oh I don't know that I want to go there...I don't think so..." A shadow fell over Hertzog's face and a frown set deep across his rugged features. For what seemed like a few minutes, but was really only several seconds, he hunched over his drink in quiet contemplation, tuning out from the noise of the bar and the activity in the casino beyond, before resurfacing with a renewed purpose. "Ah, fuck it. I don't suppose it'll hurt. Not here. Not anymore. The whole thing is yesterday's news - it was a long time ago and a long way away."

"What hold did Botha have over you Pieter?"

Hertzog fixed him with a world-weary stare and Rimmer understood the depth of experience that those eyes had soaked up.

"Be very careful of that man... He doesn't take kindly to being crossed and when things don't go his way, he has a habit of taking matters into his own hands..."

"What exactly do you mean?" From the fly-fishing days of his youth, Rimmer knew when his bait was about to be taken, and now the conversation was entering similar territory.

"As things stand, I don't reckon you've got anything to worry about. After all, you might have outsmarted the bastard - as you like to call him - but the bottom line is that he's got a top sports photographer on his books now instead of a mere tittie-snapper, so he's better off despite himself, isn't he? But if you take your talents elsewhere, well… I'd advise you to keep your head down and choose a new employer as far away as possible, because he's a *very* vengeful fellow."

This prophetic warning gave Rimmer chills after his decision earlier that night to quit *The Horizon* for real, but his immediate urge was to get Hertzog's secret out into the light and not allow negative thoughts to cloud his concentration.

"What happened to you Pieter? You've come this far, you might as well tell me the rest."

The South African knocked back the remains of his drink and ordered another, then when the barman moved away to serve somebody else, he quietly replied.

"October 27th, 1956. June 18th, 1958. The 7th and 12th of February 1961. Those dates - and more - are indelibly etched in my brain, boy."

"But why?"

COME ON, you fucker!

Just get your story out!

The big man gave a resigned sigh, then finally stirred himself to speak again.

"Because those are dates when I killed people on the orders of Marcus-bloody-Botha."

BINGO!

The hours spent drifting towards drunken oblivion with a total stranger were worth it after all. Rimmer had been hoping to hear a bit of salacious gossip about his despised boss, something relating to dirty tricks or corrupt business behaviour if he was lucky, but instead, the mother of all scoops had landed in his lap!

Glory, glory, glory!

A late evening spent with a kindred spirit, twisting an imaginary knife into Botha's back, had just turned into a twenty-four-carat gold discovery to trump anything else he was ever likely to uncover for the rest of his career.

Think, Gordon, think.

Stay calm.

They say the devil is in the detail and thus far, he had nothing more to work with than a wild uncorroborated statement from a random lush. He needed to reel his catch in; gently, oh so gently.

"Ah come on, I thought you were going to tell me what really went on between you and Marcus - I'm tired and it's too late in the evening to listen to this game-playing bullshit."

Hertzog's voice became steadier than it had been for the last hour as his eyes focussed on a fixed point somewhere on a distant horizon.

"Bullshit you say? No, no, no…What I'm saying is not bullshit, boy - it's the truth, the whole truth and nothing but the truth etc, etc…"

He went silent again, so Rimmer gently tugged on the hook.

"You can't seriously expect me to believe that a man like you - a thoroughly decent fella by my reckoning," (he lied) "could actually take someone's life -"

"Keep it down boy! I'm not sharing this with the world!"

"Sorry!" Obviously, such a conversation needed the sensitivity of hushed tones. "It's just that I can't imagine you doing such a thing on Botha's say-so. No, I'm not buying that one!"

Still staring straight ahead, Hertzog replied, "You can believe what you like boy, but I'm telling you I know what it's like to snuff someone's lights out, just like that!" He slammed his powerful right palm onto the bar, drawing anxious looks from other drinkers a safe distance away, and Rimmer imagined what it must be like to get on the wrong side of this bear of a man. He thought about treading cautiously, but by now the catch was inexorably moving towards his net.

"Alright Pieter, steady on mate, I get it! If you say it happened, then I suppose I've got to take your word for it, but you can't just make a statement like that and leave it hanging there - let's have some meat on those bones! Marcus-bloody-Botha didn't just decide one day to have someone killed, then click his fat fucking fingers and send you off to do the deed, now did he? There's got to be more to it than that, so what were his reasons?" He was taking a chance by being so bold, but it was time to bring his fish to the surface.

"I worked for him at the *TMMC* - have you heard of them?"

"Of course, the South African mineral miners."

"The very same. I had a position of trust in the organisation in the days when Botha ran a diamond dig in Kimberley - I was his, 'go-to,' man whenever there was a problem with some *kaffir* that needed sorting out."

"Such as?"

"They'd either want more money or an improvement in the safety equipment, some shit like that - those black bastards are always moaning - and I was given the job of, 'negotiating,' with them directly. Sometimes that meant making sure they were kept quiet permanently."

"How did you do that then?"

"How do you think boy? Jesus! It's a good job they only get you to take the bloody pictures at your paper - you're not bright enough for anything else!... I'd take them for a little drive to discuss their grievances - somewhere nice and quiet - then introduce them to my revolver. BANG! The rest of the *kaffir's* friends would soon get the picture and there'd be no more trouble from then on."

Rimmer continued to reel him in.

"So how did you explain everything to the authorities? I mean, even in South Africa I strongly doubt whether they'd look the other way when there's a dead body to dispose of."

"You obviously don't know my country very well! You have to remember who my boss was - MJB was a very powerful WHITE man who didn't want any mess affecting his business and the mining of minerals is very big business. The country's economy relies on the industry being run efficiently and economically, so it's in nobody's interests to stop production just to investigate the death of some darkie. Once the deed was done, I'd simply chuck the body down a mine shaft and issue an official statement saying that an underground accident had killed one of our workers. A friend of mine in the police force would give the, 'accident,' scene a quick once-over, then write up a favourable official version of events in his report and life moved on."

Rimmer's thoughts went to the families of the alleged victims, and he wondered at the callous brutality of such a corrupt regime that could dismiss their concerns as insignificant when placed against the needs of a major industry to turn a corporate profit.

"How did you feel about the job you were asked to do Pieter?"

"How do you think I felt? I don't care whether I was asked to kill a *kaffir* or a white man - murder is still murder however you cut the cake! I've come a long way since those days - I'm the corporation's Operations Manager now - but I can never forgive MJB for what he got me to do."

This display of humanity failed to convince Rimmer of Hertzog's remorse in any way, though the big man became significantly withdrawn after revealing his shocking news. The confession sounded genuine enough and there was obviously much more to explore in the story, but the atmosphere had (understandably) taken a turn for the worse and the big man suddenly decided that his evening's drinking and chatting were done.

Satisfied that he had picked a difficult lock, Rimmer decided to wait until the morning before assessing the true value of his plunder, and if the glints of gold that he could see now were still visible in the cold light of day, he would quiz Hertzog further, with the clarity of a sober mind.

22.

Death or glory?

Pieter Hertzog half-crushed Rimmer in an embrace and congratulated him on his drinking prowess, while still finding it necessary to remind him that, "Real men hit the bar at a reasonable hour, not when the fucking night is drawing to a close!"

It was three in the morning and for his part, the man from *The Horizon* was relieved that his companion had finally called a halt to the destruction of their livers before the entire evening descended into one big boozy blur.

They shared a hotel lift; the South African's room was on the ninth floor. Rimmer got out at seven, but before he could stagger into the cavernous corridor, they arranged a second summit at the same bar at noon. It was key for him to keep close to the big fellow, because he had to go over some details of their earlier conversation again with a clearer head, though for now, he resisted any further mention of Marcus Botha and murder for fear of spooking his stool pigeon into silence. With this in mind, he suggested that their next meeting should involve nothing more demanding than idle bar-room chit-chat, at least until he could find an appropriate moment to return to that all-important confession. It was going to take subtlety and guile to cajole Hertzog into corroborating his sensational story.

Once ensconced in room 742, the over-excited Rimmer looked for some medicinal assistance to becalm his hiccupping heart. Adrenaline, when mixed with copious amounts of alcohol, rarely make for the best of buddies. An ever-ready box of Paracetamol (that staple requirement of the long-distance traveller) stood next to the sink in his spacious bathroom, and he hastily released two tablets from their silver foil, gulping them down with tap water. Leaving the cold tap running, he sluiced its reviving liquid over the back of his neck and face to regain some semblance of mental sharpness. Caffeine was another essential weapon in his battle against the forces of drowsiness, so he boiled a kettle before consuming the first of several nocturnal coffees. With dogged perseverance, he painstakingly recorded every word of the conversation that had taken place in the bar, then took stock of his situation.

What should I do?

How do I play my hand?

His first instinct, as ever, was to be professional; he must tell the London desk about his scoop. Then he pressed the pause button in his head and considered his options.

Do I really want to let The Horizon know what I've got?

Why pass my (albeit sketchy) information on to Harry-bloody-Ellis?

What has that son-of-a-bitch ever done for me?

All he'll do is immediately alert the Foreign Desk, and in no time, one of the paper's investigative reporters will be on the next Vegas-bound plane to personally grill Hertzog over every tiny detail of his revelation.

Before anyone can say, "Thanks for the tip-off," my story – along with all the ensuing career enhancements, garlands, and glory – will be in the new guy's grasp.

My pivotal role in breaking the news will be reduced to a marginal footnote.

Not bloody likely!

No fly-by-night is going to steal away my exclusive book/TV/film deals – no thank you!

I'm an experienced newspaperman, not some wet-behind-the-ears cub who can be shoulder-charged out of the picture.

Within any hierarchical organisation, there is a pecking order of importance, from the omnipotent boss at the top of the ladder down to the lowliest underling, and innate, odious, unfettered snobbery festers between every rung. This divisive trait is particularly prevalent in competitive occupations like journalism. Investigative reporters are the trade's superheroes, they are the heavyweights who will happily risk mortal danger on the front lines of war zones or scrape life's underbelly to gather their harvests from the murky cesspools of the criminal underworld, while at the bottom of the printed word's credibility ladder reside the gossip columnists and sports reporters, whose work seems shallow and distinctly paperweight by comparison. So much of a paperweight's output relies on speculation without corroboration - '*which celebrity has been cheating on who?*' or, '*which star player is looking for a new team?*' On slow news days, they can fill their copy with educated guesswork and pass it off as genuinely researched reportage, without damaging their paper's reputation or sales. They rarely interview the deep thinkers of the day, and instead often have to generate interest from the ill-considered thoughts of egocentric ignoramuses who have little to offer outside of their arbitrary talent.

This slur is clearly an outrageous generalisation, but perception is reality where pressroom jealousy and prejudice are concerned, and paperweights luxuriate in the vacuous unreality of the entertainment industry, rubbing shoulders with the rich and famous, so in the eyes of the front-page sages, they are fair game for mockery and disdain.

Of course, this kind of petty one-upmanship means nothing to a newspaper proprietor, particularly any owner of a tabloid, where frivolity sells, and the core readership prefers light relief from the world's problems. Investigative reporters might receive the backslapping respect of their peers during the award-giving season, but these are pyrrhic victories, for in an increasingly competitive world, the last laugh always goes to the sports desk and gossip columnists, because it is their headlines that will empty a newsagent's shelves every morning, while the efforts of the heavy artillery routinely go unnoticed.

Despite all this, an excited Rimmer wanted the chance to take 'serious' journalism on and bring his story to life in his own inimitable style. With the decision to go it alone now made, he reflected on what Hertzog had said and suddenly a glaringly obvious point struck home.

Jesus Christ! How stupid could I be?

While daydreams of glory were filling his head, he had blithely ignored the piss-drenched puddle he was about to step into. If his scoop proved to be correct, it would destroy the man who pays his wages: the man who controlled his immediate future. Suddenly things became very clear, and his focus returned.

I could never have contacted Harry Ellis, because that sycophantic toady's first call would have been straight to the Head Honcho and there was not a hope in hell of the story ever seeing the light of day then!

Another, more sinister thought now crossed Rimmer's increasingly agitated mind.

If Botha really is the type of man who can ruthlessly order the killing of discontented African mine workers, then surely, he'd have no qualms over bidding a swift adieu to an impertinent, overpaid sports reporter in the same manner?

This consideration was a game changer; his story might lead him into very treacherous waters indeed. That pounding heart of his missed a beat and a bowling ball weight of anxiety hit the pit of his stomach with a heavy thud.

Shit!

Should I let the biggest scoop I'm ever likely to stumble on slip through my perspiring palms, or do I stretch out my stride like an Olympic runner heading into the home straight and break the tape in defiance of the consequences?

Decisions, decisions, decisions…

How can I even think of suppressing something as big as this?

I'm a fully paid-up member of the, 'Publish and be Damned!' brigade, and after all, isn't there a moral obligation to think of too?

This is the kind of opportunity that fed my dreams back in the provinces, so surely I've got to plough on?

And yet…

Oh, who the bloody hell am I trying to kid?

I'm out of my depth, just like when I was a seven-year-old boy and that bullying bastard of a schoolteacher, Mr. Pearson, threw me into the deep end of the pool at the local swimming baths just because I was making my classmates laugh.

Back then, I couldn't really swim, and he knew it, but somehow I managed to scramble back up to the surface, grabbing the side rail in a flailing frenzy of panic and terror…

Hang on a minute though - I survived that and everything turned out well in the end, didn't it?

The other kids complained to their parents about that arrogant arsehole and he was suspended - he even came within a whisker of getting the sack before I asked the headmaster to take pity on him.

He came back to school as a whimpering poodle, not the rampaging pit bull he was before.

I won that war.

Aye, Gordon Rimmer knows what to do when bullies behave badly!

Hmmmm....like I said before, who am I trying to kid?

Pearson probably had some good in him all along that would have surfaced in the end, with or without my intervention.

Anyway, putting him in his place is hardly on the same scale as taking on Marcus Botha - that guy is one of the world's most powerful businessmen, an international tycoon, not some ten-a-penny little Hitler lording it over a few knock-kneed kids at a rural Scottish primary school.

If I find any truth in Hertzog's confession, I'll be inviting some serious shit through my door...he'll be looking to KILL ME!

By the time Rimmer finally swapped his anxieties for the comforts of slumber, the first rays of sunlight had already begun to penetrate the dusk. When he awoke, the Strip was buzzing with business and the heat coming in from the Nevada desert could fry eggs on the pavement outside.

His sleep had been deep, but altogether too brief. He dreamed vividly of his parents and their strong Presbyterian sense of right and wrong. He heard his mother's voice convincing him that, "criminals always get caught in the end." (Clearly, the stark realities of the UK's rising crime statistics and its ever-increasing percentage of unsolved cases had failed to permeate his soporific thought processes!) He saw a tearful child somewhere in South Africa receiving news that their father would not be coming home from work because of, "an accident at the mine."

He had slept in his clothes and when he awoke, he rose from his bed and disrobed, then automatically stumbled into an icy shower to reassemble his thoughts. Staring back at his reflection in the truth-telling bathroom mirror he was troubled no more. Unless he was forcibly stopped from doing so, he intended to root out the truth about Marcus Botha's past, wherever those investigations took him; whatever the risk to his professional future and personal safety.

Death or glory indeed.

23.

A spanner in the works

Rimmer still had a job to do reporting on the darts event before his investigation into Botha's criminal behaviour could begin in earnest. His first task of the day was to check on the health of Barry Shackleton after the poor man had (literally) fallen victim to the expectations of that sparse but passionate crowd the previous evening. Despite being unfit to perform, *'The Dagenham Dynamo'* (a professional nickname conjured up by the agile mind of Maurice Letterman) had drained every last drop from his rapidly evaporating canteen of talent and in the process pushed himself beyond the limits of physical endurance.

During the unseemly scramble to remove his prone body from the stage, Rimmer spotted some of Botha's marketing team engaged in animated conversations with tournament officials, making sure that the timetable for the rest of the evening stayed on schedule.

What price compassion when there are ratings to chase, eh?

Curiously, this lack of sympathy for the player's plight extended to all areas of the arena, for as one, the audience and assembled press felt that Shackleton was right to play on, despite his considerable distress. The *Dynamo's* spirited determination to ride the *Darts Duals* gravy train may have satisfied their expectations, but his gamble backfired so spectacularly that now this pitiful disciple of the great god Mammon lay suffering in a downtown Las Vegas hospital bed. Rimmer thought to question the wisdom of his unholy worship.

What a joke!

Lead them to the altar where the dollar sign shines and they all cry, "Praise be!"

Then again, who am I to talk?

A stale stench of hypocrisy wafted over his pious condemnation of greed, and he reluctantly reminded himself not to judge the morality of others.

Didn't I trade away my relationship with Susan to stay on Marcus Botha's payroll?

People in glass houses shouldn't throw stones – isn't that how it goes?

Thinking about his lost lover reminded him that at some godforsaken hour during the night, he felt a misguided, delusional desire to call her and clumsily fumbled for the phone before reason spoke to his senses and sleep became a better option. Now that he was more *compass mentis*, he noticed the receiver lying on the bedside table and returned the errant device to its stand. Immediately it rang with a series of recorded messages from reception instructing him to contact his London office. He ignored the requests and instead made his way out of the door into a descending lift, deciding that his early morning fragility made it wise to avoid any dealings with Harry Ellis.

The lobby area buzzed with animated reporters shouting instructions to their colleagues back home via the hotel's excellent telecoms facilities. Rimmer's newshound nose smelt traces of a sensation surfacing and he immediately regretted his decision to stay so long in Pieter Hertzog's company the previous night, scoop or no scoop. That drinking binge might now impair his ability to respond to unfolding events.

Recognising Bob Lawrence from *The Independent* (a man whose professional coverage of sporting events was much admired) he decided to say hello.

"What's up, Bob? Why are all the press boys going nuts?"

Both men understood the importance of concealing a story from a rival to preserve exclusivity, but whatever was causing the commotion appeared to be common knowledge among the assembled hacks, so Lawrence had nothing to gain by being evasive.

"Haven't you heard? Christ alive! Where the bloody hell have you been?"

Rimmer's thoughts immediately turned to Shackleton, and he feared the worst.

"Is it poor old Barry? He's not dead is he?"

"No Gordon, no - he's still receiving treatment after his little, er, 'turn'."

"Well, what's going on then? Has something happened out in the *real* world away from all of this crap?"

This casual remark infuriated Lawrence because, although he was predominantly a boxing man, his fascination for all sports gave him a genuine enthusiasm for the darts commission and Rimmer had shown it a complete lack of respect.

"Look here pal, this event might not be the be all and end all of the sporting calendar, but it's keeping a bunch of travelling fans and media boys cosily occupied for the next week, all *apropos* of your gaffer. I'd expect you to show a little bit more gratitude, particularly as you're actually representing his poxy paper."

"Ok, ok, point taken. Sorry."

Satisfied that he had sufficiently admonished a surly upstart, Lawrence then opened up about the big news that the rest of the press pack were already addressing.

"You won't need to go scrambling around in the *real* world for your headlines tomorrow because in a matter of hours, the *real* world will be turning up here. We've got a major story on our hands." He could see the almost painful look of enquiry on Rimmer's face and played him a little more. "You were right that the story concerns poor Barry Shackleton, but it's not about how he is…apparently he's as well as can be expected at the moment - under the circumstances…"

"Jesus, this isn't 'Twenty Questions' is it? Can't you just give me the goods? Please? What the bloody hell has happened?"

"The story isn't about *how* Barry is - it's *where* he is that's got everyone in a tizzy."

"What do you mean? You're not going to tell me he's been abducted by aliens, are you? I know this is Roswell country, but do try and behave!"

Lawrence failed to appreciate this mocking levity.

"Look, I'm only going to say this once, so either listen up or you can bugger off and bother somebody else, ok?"

Rimmer held his hands up by way of another apology and nodded; he knew the wisdom of playing ball when somebody had information that he needed.

"Barry isn't being treated in a general ward…he's in the hospital's AIDS unit!"

The news sounded too ridiculous to contemplate.

"What? WHAT DID YOU SAY?"

"Oh I'm pretty sure you heard me alright."

This positively surreal turn of events threw a spanner in the works of Rimmer's Botha investigation, but the incredible new development simply had to take precedence.

No wonder the sports desk was trying to get in touch with me!

They must have gotten wind that a big story was breaking and were only trying to kick their man into action.

"How have the other boys reacted to this?... I'm absolutely stunned Bob ... aren't you?"

This not-so-secret secret news is SO bizarre - SO unexpected - I need to know that my reaction is understandable.

"Who wouldn't be stunned?" replied Lawrence, "I doubt that anyone in their right mind would ever expect to see a headline like **DARTS STAR IN AIDS SHOCK!** We're all in bloody disbelief! Now run along will you, 'cos I'm going to be busy with this for the rest of the day. Every other laggard hound is descending on the hospital as we speak, so I suggest you get your skates on too if you want to get the full low-down on what's what."

Before racing off, Rimmer remembered his manners and thanked his fellow hack.

"I owe you one."

"I'll make sure I collect it too," came Lawrence's perfectly justified reply; after all, in the information gathering industry, back scratching goes both ways.

Quid pro quo.

Of course, he could afford to be helpful because his own report had already reached London, but at least he had given a rival a sporting chance to play catch up, for which the man from *The Horizon* was genuinely grateful.

Before departing for the hospital, Rimmer paused for breath to (finally) contact HQ and let them know he was (belatedly) on top of the situation. The call went directly to Harry Ellis and drew a predictably angry response, so in trying to take the wind from the bellows on the other end of the line, he quickly blurted, "Never mind all that Harry -," but was cut off without ceremony before finishing his sentence.

"Fuck you and your 'never mind' bollocks - I don't want to hear any excuses, you smug prick! What have you been playing at?"

"You already know then?"

"What do you think I am, fucking stupid or something? Did you honestly imagine I would be stuck in the dark over this? It's the biggest bloody sports story of the year, for Christ's sake! This is a dream come true and you've fucking missed it!" The editor's callous attitude to Shackleton's plight was hardly surprising; after all, news is news; bad things happen to people all the time, and most of what we see in the media relates to those bad things. "So what have you got for me? Mr. Botha called me up to the penthouse for a progress report and I had fuck all to give him 'cos you couldn't be reached, so I had to blag my way through a very awkward conversation. Do you have any copy at all or are you over there scratching your arse, getting pissed, chasing skirt and playing the tables?"

Rimmer was at a loss over what to say in reply; after all, he had indeed been drinking until the early hours and sleeping it off as the dam burst. He attempted to stall.

"I'm onto it right now Harry... information is sketchy at this point."

"It's so fucking sketchy that the whole wide world and his dog now knows Barry-bloody-Shackleton is a bum-bandit! Meanwhile, *The Horizon* pays for the competition which exposes his disgrace, yet we're pissing into the wind without any clue as to why we're getting wet!"

His inflammatory words were a blatant attempt to get under the skin of a more enlightened enemy, who immediately hit back with some fire of his own. Rimmer could accept that the criticism coming his way was entirely justifiable, but he felt duty-bound to defend Shackleton and challenge his governor's lack of empathy.

"You seem a little sensitive about the gay thing Harry - is there something you're not owning up to?..."

Ellis was in no mood to play games though.

"Don't get smart with me you lazy bastard! Just get us exclusive rights to an interview with the invalid - can you at least manage to do that properly? Throw some money at it - whatever's necessary. Grease the palms of anyone at the hospital who can get us his unfettered attention. Back home, our *proper* journalists will cover the family angle by speaking to his wife and kids." This intended slight found its target with precision, and he followed it up with a damning verdict on his wayward Chief Sports Correspondent's performance thus far. "I want you to know I think you're a fucking disgrace."

The line went dead, leaving Rimmer to reflect that he had given Ellis (a man who openly despised and distrusted him) the perfect opportunity to deride his professionalism. He bore his verbal crucifixion resolutely, knowing that if he managed to expose Marcus Botha's misdeeds successfully, a spectacular resurrection was within reach. For now though, that opportunity must remain under wraps while the sensational situation before him unfolded.

Time was of the essence, and the "laggard hound," had to get a move on. A press release the previous evening revealed that Shackleton was undergoing supervision at the Santa Maria Hospital and Medical Centre, so Rimmer knew where he needed to be. After hastily flagging down a taxi, he took stock of events.

Who in their right mind would have seen this one coming?

Darts and AIDS?

Those words are incompatible, surely?

Very few things can reduce an experienced reporter to incredulity, but here was just such an occasion.

To most people, darts is the sport of the jolly beer belly; a pub pastime, enjoyed over a pint with friends. It symbolises a cherished image of working folk at leisure. By contrast, the very mention of AIDS conjures up images of leather-clad, moustachioed men cavorting with vest-wearing young Adonis's in cavernous nightclubs, or needle sharing low-lifes quietly pursuing a miserable oblivion. Rimmer began to look beyond stereotypes, realising that the deadly virus is obviously no respecter of social demographics. Newspaper editors, however, prefer to paint simpler pictures than that for their readers, devoid of monochromatic subtleties. Shackleton might well have been the unfortunate recipient of an injection from a contaminated needle (a possibility which, in itself, opened up a myriad of tangential speculations), but if gay sex turned out to be the root cause of his condition, he was in big trouble. The national dailies understood the moral majority's discomfort with non-conformist expressions of love and sexuality, and if it emerged that he was a closet homosexual, they would rip him to shreds.

With foreboding, Rimmer wondered how far Edmund Cornell (under the supervision of Marcus Botha) would go to coerce *The Horizon*'s readers into demonising the poor beleaguered wretch. For years, the paper had spouted barely disguised gay hate via a plethora of bigoted jokes and innuendos, arguing that its rhetoric reflected the tastes of, 'normal, *right-thinking* people.' Society in general had become more open-minded, but the Head Honcho was a shrewd judge of his target market and knew how to stir their ire.

Then Rimmer's thoughts turned to Shackleton's unfortunate wife and kids. A torrent of terrible publicity and immense pressure was heading their way, whether they knew it or not.

They were public property now; fragile innocents caught up in a savage circulation war, and Botha's mighty spin machine was ready to gazump any rival bids for their reactions.

They had his sincerest sympathy.

24.

Nurse Johnson negotiates

Darryl Johnson wondered just how much Shackleton knew about the seriousness of his predicament; whether he was aware that the deadly HIV virus was responsible for his collapse, or that it had inexorably led him to this treatment ward for AIDS sufferers.

Does he understand the impact that the news'll have in his home country, or realise how it's gonna affect his friends and family?

The busy nurse saw a chance to do a bit of good all-around and began addressing his other duties with half a mind on how to make that happen. He set himself three objectives: -

1. To help Shackleton get all the expensive medical support he needed without crippling his family's finances.
2. To chaperone some lucky newspaper reporter towards a career-boosting scoop.
3. Most importantly of all, to fill his own pockets with extra funds with which to play the card tables in this casino-obsessed city.

Gambling was the motivation for his pilgrimage from Louisville to Las Vegas six years earlier and if his plans bore fruit, a welcome windfall of extra stake money would soon be coming his way.

From a window on his second-floor ward, he shot a glance at the plethora of pressmen loitering expectantly outside. They had found themselves banished from the premises by security staff, but the concourse was a safe haven beyond the hospital's jurisdiction where they could gather without causing a nuisance. For the right price, he intended to offer one of them an exclusive interview with his *cause celebre*, but he knew he must tread carefully. He needed to make his pitch without drawing the attention of his fellow workers, because brokering such a deal would breach hospital policy and result in instant dismissal, which he could ill afford. He wanted his plan to result in a sublime high, but it was a one off, bereft of residual aftershocks, and an addiction like his relied upon a steady income stream to guarantee regular fixes. Clearly, his anonymity had to be a prerequisite of any agreement struck and although he wanted to confront the reporters *en masse* in the hope of starting a bidding war, those left disappointed might expose his scheme.

Tricky, tricky.

My best option is gonna be to target one candidate.

But how?

He wanted to find someone inquisitive (or desperate) enough to ask him questions relating to the English patient, so like a hooker on the Strip he decided to stroll past them in his working clothes to draw their interest. Just as he nervously reached the foot of the staircase leading outside, he heard a Scottish accent at the reception desk breathlessly introducing himself and enquiring as to the whereabouts of Barry Shackleton.

Why is this guy so late on the trail?

He immediately assumed that, rather than being *behind* the other reporters, (who he knew were just sports journalists already *in situ* covering the darts tournament) this one must be *ahead* of an expected avalanche of big shots from the national broadsheets.

The voice belonged to Gordon Rimmer and Johnson reacted swiftly. Sensing an opportunity, he swooped, instantly wrapping his long strong arms around the bamboozled newsman's wiry frame and bundling him towards the exit.

"I'm sorry Sir", he said, "but Mr. Shackleton can't be contacted at this time – he needs to rest. If that situation should alter however, I'm sure the hospital will notify all you gen'men of the press in due course." With this, he gave Agnes behind the reception desk a cheeky wink, which she duly reciprocated.

On the surface, all was well; Nurse Johnson had dutifully represented the interests of both the patient and the hospital to the best of his ability. However, instead of ushering Rimmer out of the building, he neatly sidestepped the interested party into an adjoining corridor and, in hushed tones, quickly set about presenting his enticing proposition.

"Man, I don't know who you are or who you represent, but if you wanna conversation with that guy upstairs, you gotta go through me to make it happen."

His opening hand left no room for ambiguity. If he failed to strike a deal with this complete stranger, his job was in jeopardy, but as any true gambler will testify, *"fortune favours the brave"*.

"Are you saying that you can definitely get me in to see Barry - Mr. Shackleton? You're promising me direct access?"

"That's right - no questions asked - for a price."

Dodging the financial barrier, Rimmer wanted to know more.

"Is he well enough to conduct an interview right now?"

"No way - not yet, the guy's been real sick so you'll have to wait a while. All I can say's when he's good an' ready, you'll be the first to know - if you got the dough."

The canny Scot was determined to get the biggest bang that his bucks could buy, so he squeezed some conditions into the arrangement.

"When you say I'll be the first reporter to know, I want to be the ONLY one to get that message. Is that clear?…er, I didn't get your name?" He failed to notice the prominent nametag displayed on Johnson's uniform, but in the excitement and adrenaline rush of the moment, neither man saw this lack of observation as a giveaway sign that he was not the heavyweight journalist of the nurse's imagination.

"Call me Darryl - listen man, you don't get shit 'til I see the colour of yo' money."

"We'll talk about payments when I know I'm dealing with the right person - for all I know, you might be trying to fleece me and my paper." Rimmer needed proof of Johnson's credibility in order to pacify Harry Ellis and *The Horizon*'s finance department.

"Ok, ok, I guess that's cool. So what d'ya need to know, brother."

"Can you tell me if our man contracted the virus from a penetrative homosexual act?"

"Say what? Well he sure as hell didn't get it playin' darts!"

This crass response did nothing to suggest that there was any real rapport between the patient and his nurse.

"Come on, you must know as well as I do that he might have picked it up through an injection from an infected needle."

"Hey, I know what's what round here when it comes to the causes of infection, but all's I'm sayin' is what's it to you anyways? Either way it came from a prick!"

Johnson broke into a toothy chuckle and Rimmer's patience began to stretch.

I need to establish a relationship of trust with this man, but Christ Almighty, he's really hard work!

To show good will, he declared the reason for his interest in the specific details of Shackleton's condition.

"The readers of my newspaper would be more sympathetic to Barry's plight if they could blame a contaminated needle for his troubles rather than a gay liaison."

"Why? Are you sayin' the folks back home in England gonna like him better if he's a junkie than a fag?"

"Who said anything about drugs? Maybe he's had a blood transfusion somewhere that's gone wrong, eh? This is just the sort of speculation that I want to clear up. Look, if I send back an accurate report, they can make up their own minds, can't they? I'd prefer the story to be based on truth rather than gossip, pure and simple. I'm only interested in Barry's newsworthiness, I'm not out to assassinate his character." This reply was true from his own perspective, but he could not speak on behalf of his paper, for he knew that *The Horizon* would print sensationalist headlines and sell masses of extra copies in the process if it could, "out" Barry as a closet homosexual.

"Listen man, that guy up there is screwed whichever way it turns out - y'see, a sport like his, well, that's a man's world, and now all those guys are gonna turn their backs on him - though not literally I guess!" Another broad grin swamped Johnson's face as he enthusiastically chewed on gum. Nurses grow hardened to the unpleasant nature of illness and death, but time was short, and the exasperated reporter was not prepared to pussyfoot around any longer.

"Can we concentrate on the business at hand? I have to find out exactly how Barry contracted this virus - do you know or not?"

The reply only increased Rimmer's frustration.

"Look, I'll be honest wit' you, I don't know for sure - but I can find out. He talks to me - I can get the whole thing down straight..." Johnson's voice trailed off a little by way of apology and he sought to distract his man by turning the focus onto Shackleton's predicament. "He's a nice guy, y'know? A nice guy who's gonna get thrown to the wolves if he don' have somebody to watch his back. I get it that you need to know what's goin' on, sure 'nuff... all's I'm sayin' is with you guys guessin' over what he might or might not have done to get this thing... well, it jus' means the poor fella's life - what's left of it anyways - is gonna turn out pretty shitty from here on in, no doubt 'bout that. I know those are the breaks, but I feel for him, man."

Rimmer would have been more convinced of the hustler's sympathy if he had not insisted on payment for his part in presenting Shackleton's story to the world. That lure of lucre now came to the fore in the conversation.

"I share your sentiments, but it's important for me to know what's really happening here, either from the man himself or his medical notes, so let's cut to the chase - how much is it going to cost me to get the goods? What if I give you, say, a thousand dollars?..."

"A thousand? I thought I was talkin' to a serious player here - a man's gotta eat ya know! In this town, I could blow that with the turn of one card." Johnson began to fear that he had picked the wrong person with whom to chance his arm.

"So how much are you looking for then? And be reasonable if you want to do a deal."

There was a brief pause for arithmetical calculations, followed by a confident reply.

"Make it ten grand."

Although the precise details of Shackleton's illness would soon be common knowledge, it was vital for *The Horizon* to get this kind of information first. There was only one choice.

"Done. Now when will I know?"

"I ain't doing no scratchin' around 'til I see you foldin' that money into the palm of my hand."

This was a challenge to Rimmer's authority as the paymaster of the deal, but he refused to buckle under pressure and wrestled back control of the negotiations.

"You'll get five hundred only for now." At this, the nurse's grin disappeared. "The rest will follow if I get my answers by this afternoon at three o'clock. Here's the number of my hotel - leave a message at reception for me, ok?"

Johnson reluctantly decided that the stipulation was reasonable enough and nodded his compliance. "

Oh, and one more thing Darryl…"

"Shoot."

"If you can get me a face-to-face interview when we speak next, there'll be another ten thousand in your pot - now how's that for a winning hand?"

Johnson's grin returned, and his pearly-white teeth shone like the Nevada sun.

"Sure thing man - you can bet on it!"

At three o'clock precisely, an anxious Rimmer picked up a small bundle of notes that were waiting for him at the Sand's hotel reception desk. The first one was from Pieter Hertzog, and it stopped him dead in his tracks:

Sorry boy, but something has come up and I've had to check out earlier than expected. If you're ever in Jo'burg and find yourself short of a drinking buddy look me up - Piet.

He had been hoping that the big Boer was still sleeping off the effects of his excesses from the night before, but instead he had flown the nest without confirming his nocturnal drunken boasts. The note was accompanied by a contact number, and this left Rimmer with a dilemma; if he wanted that face-to-face, on the record meeting, he would have to follow his man to South Africa by covering the *Sun City Showdown* and give up his World Cup Finals ambitions.

Fuck!

Come on Gordon - now's not the time for bitterness - without Hertzog's help, the trail linking Botha to murder is colder than Christmas in Lapland.

His story had better stack up now!

There was no time to dwell on his disappointment because the Shackleton scoop had to come first. While the invalid remained out-of-bounds to visitors, there was a chance to steal a march on the rest of the assembled press and secure the big interview they all craved.

After sifting through some aggressive reminders from Harry Ellis to stay diligent, Rimmer read one more scrawled scrap of paper signed *DJ*, containing another phone number and the words: *Give me a call.*

He got through to a tiny office tucked inside the Santa Maria Hospital and Medical Centre's AIDS ward. When he asked for Nurse Johnson in his lilting Scottish brogue, an unfamiliar female voice frostily replied, "I'm sorry sir, but private calls are forbidden during work time."

The management at the hospital had issued a directive to staff members warning them to be suspicious of anyone contacting the ward with a British accent in case it belonged to an inquisitive journalist trying to disturb their celebrity patient's rest. Before she could cut the call, Darryl Johnson swept into the tiny office and gently eased the telephone from her hand. He had been hovering around in readiness to pounce and the second he realised that Rimmer was at the other end of the line he sprang into action.

"Is that for me, Rita? I've been waitin' on my bookmaker all day - let's hope it's good news, eh hun?"

The amiable nurse was a notorious flirt and none of the female staff members at the facility could resist his cheeky charm, so he flashed a reassuringly toothy smile in her direction, and she immediately responded in kind.

"Now Darryl, what have I told you about this nonsense? No more calls at work, understand?" She wanted to sound firm with her friend but simply came across like a supply teacher struggling in vain to discipline a loveable naughty schoolboy.

"Ah, you won't tell on me will you? Looks like I finally got a winner, so maybe I'll treat ya to a burger when we get off, ok? Now can I have a li'l privacy hear for a minute, jus' 'til I know how much I've won?"

With a cute pout, Nurse Rita replied, "Well ok…but be quick, yes? Just make sure no one in authority sees you?"

"Don't you worry none, hot stuff!"

Once he was alone in the office, he returned to the phone to hear Rimmer's voice.

"Darryl, is that you - are you free to talk?"

"Yeah, it's cool - we're busy though - mainly jus' keepin' your pals away from Mr. Shackleton. Listen, I get off in an hour, can you get here?"

"Absolutely - where will you be?"

"Meet me outside the laundry room - ask someone when you arrive and they'll show you the way - but remember to use your head in how you talk - you Brits ain't too welcome round here jus' now."

"Can I expect good news?"

"The best baby - the best!"

At the stipulated time, Rimmer was already in place to greet his inside man.

"So, what have you got to tell me then?"

"You got the bread?"

"Don't worry about that, if you've done your stuff I'll look after you ok."

Johnson was cautious to reveal anything without some more tangible proof of the reporter's honesty.

"What you asked from me was tough man, it's real hard for anyone to get near Mr. Shackleton - the doctors want him to be left in peace to get over his sweats. Maybe ten G's ain't enough…"

This was too much; no matter how desperate Rimmer was for answers, he refused to let the cocky nurse fleece him.

"Look pal, have you got something for me or not? Don't fuck me about or I'll walk away right now."

Fearful of his bird fleeing the nest, Johnson decided to stick with the original deal.

"Hey, wait, wait a minute man. You gotta expect a guy to try for a bigger pot don't you?" An impatient silence answered the remark, broken only when he finally imparted the information that his patron needed to know. "On the question of how Mr. Shackleton got stuck with his AIDS thing - he mumbled somethin' to me this morning about how he's bin payin' guys for sex an' how dumb he's been. He reckons he's been HIV positive for some time."

At last, there was real news to report, though it would need verification from the invalid himself during the course of a formal interview.

"And when can I see him?"

"Well the thing is…I told him that you were gonna set his family straight with dough, ok? I know that was a bit sassy of me, but I don't want the guy bein' exploited jus' on account of his getting' this dumbass virus. You cool with that?"

Rimmer was tempted to say that if there was any exploitation going on, then Nurse Johnson was the culprit, but he held his tongue to push for that all-important interview.

"I promised you before that I've got Barry's best interests at heart so of course my paper will cover his costs, that's guaranteed. We're sponsoring the darts event, so we've got insurance cover for any player who's been taken ill."

"What, your boss is already payin' Mr. Shackleton's hospital tab? I knew I'd picked the right guy to deal with when I first spoke wit' you!"

"Also, as proof of my integrity Darryl, tomorrow I'm going to make out a personal cheque for £50,000 to Barry for exclusive rights to his story."

"You've got that sort of cash? Man, I'm in the wrong business!"

"It won't be my own money - I'll get my editor to transfer it from *The Horizon*'s coffers into my account. If it comes from me, that should cover the paper's tracks, and when anyone asks how I got past you to talk to Barry - as I'm sure they will - just say you thought I was a concerned family member who's worth a few quid and wanted to help out, rather than a cash rich hack hustling for an exclusive, ok? By my reckoning, the worst you'll get from your bosses is a slap on the wrist for being naïve, especially if Barry speaks up for you, and he ought to be up for doing that with fifty thousand big ones in his back pocket, thanks to your smart bit of negotiating. Happy with all that?"

"Damn straight! Well ok then, thanks to *your* cool dealings Mr. Newsman, I can confirm that our guy will see you tomorrow. He's been feeling better today so he should be up to talkin' now he knows he'll be taken care of. We gonna play this jus' like you said - describe you as a close family friend who's flown out here to see that he's bein' looked after properly. Y'all be a legit visitor - the first one he's been allowed to have. So far, so cool, but don't forget me here - none of this li'l play of ours is gonna happen if I don't see my slice of the pie. Right here. Right now." With a defiant look in his eye, Johnson held out his hand. "Jus' to keep this whole thing on track." Rimmer gratefully handed over the first instalment of the agent's fee for his under-the-counter service to journalism and they arranged a visiting time. "I'll make sure I'm aroun' to supervise your interview - so I know for certain that Mr Shackleton can stand up to the ordeal."

It had been a highly productive meeting, and *The Horizon*'s man-on-the-spot delightedly relayed its outcome back to his London office from a side street payphone, out of sight of the hospital and beyond the radar of the huddled press pack.

Harry Ellis had gone home, and an office intern took the call. She was more than a little reluctant to take responsibility for the message and asked him to ring Ellis directly at home.

"No, whenever possible, I try to avoid speaking to him - I can't stand the fucking prick!" He heard the girl gasp on the other end of the line and immediately knew that there would be no long-term future in the newspaper trade for such a fragile flower. "Don't worry, he feels the same about me so I'm not picking on him - and if you're going to work at *The Horizon* you'll hear quite a bit of that kind of industrial language, so you'd better develop a thicker skin pretty sharp-ish, ok? Now, have you got a pen handy?"

"Er, hold on - yes."

"Right, jot this down, kiddo. Just let Mr. Ellis know I've got a source at the hospital who can confirm that Barry Shackleton contracted the HIV virus from another man - that's a world exclusive for our paper and it's cost us ten thousand dollars in cash. Better than that, I've secured us the exclusive rights to his story - we'll be having a formal interview tomorrow. Access to the patient is costing us another ten grand, which also goes to my contact here, and we're paying Barry fifty grand in pounds sterling to spill his guts. For now, to keep the paper's fingerprints off the fine details of the deal I'll sign this cheque myself, so the money needs to be transferred into my bank account pronto."

"Can I stop you there?"

"What's up?"

"Are you talking about two different currencies? Is that twenty thousand dollars in total and fifty thousand pounds?"

"Aye love, and I'm glad you noticed the difference. With the exchange rates, the U.S. end of things won't run out as expensive as it looks. Well done for picking that up." The girl blushed and allowed herself a little self-satisfied smile. "Now, I understand that any medical fees incurred during the tournament are covered by the terms of our sponsorship, but I've also promised that we'll foot the bill for his continued treatment when he returns to the UK." Rimmer had added this last detail to the negotiated deal because he felt Shackleton's story was such a blockbuster that the paper should be duty bound to provide him with comprehensive care. "Oh, and one more thing - this is VERY important.... Tell him that I'm prepared to forgo my next assignment at the World Cup finals. I'll cover the poxy *Sun City Snooker Showdown* instead - but only if he agrees to give me *carte blanche* to write the Shackleton story as I see fit. No interference. No re-writes."

"Er, what's *carte* thingy again?"

"Uh - you'll go far at this place!" The intern's new-found confidence instantly disappeared.

"Just pass the message on as I said it and if Ellis gives me the ok, I'll confirm the terms of the deal with my go-between. Now have you got all that?"

"Confirm...the...terms...of...the...deal...with...my...go-between. Ok, got it."

"Good girl. If Ellis gets that message precisely, word for word, I promise to bring you something nice back from my travels, ok? Now what's your name, my lovely?"

"Stacey - I'm Stacey Brown."

"And what's your favourite perfume, Stacey?"

"Well I buy 'White Musk' when I'm in the Body Shop."

"Consider it done, missy - you'll be turning all the boys' heads in the office!" Rimmer knew that flattery and bribery were still effective tools to use when dealing with impressionable young hopefuls in the support team, and his gesture restored Ms. Brown's self-belief while giving her an incentive to follow the instructions diligently.

Passing up on his football adventure was a major frustration, especially as securing exclusive access to Barry Shackleton's tale of woe would have guaranteed him the switch from South Africa to Italy, but he was now able to pursue two major scoops unfettered by obstructions.

If Ellis accepts my terms, I'll have leverage to tell Barry's story without any editorial interference, then Botha's snooker competition puts me in the right place at the right time to ruin the old bastard!

So long as I can locate Hertzog, that is...

When morning broke, Harry Ellis called Rimmer to rubber-stamp his deal, though the editor avoided congratulating him on getting the interview that the rest of the industry craved. Ellis knew that Botha wanted his man to be on Sun City duty rather than at *Italia 90*, and the Head Honcho received the news of the changed plans with considerable interest. He even asked for precise details of Rimmer's new timetable, including flights, car hire and accommodation information.

This request baffled Ellis

Why on earth is the boss involving himself in the booking process here?

Does he expect our Chief Sports Correspondent to fiddle his expenses account?

If Marcus is looking for a pain-free way to get rid of him, then a dismissal for financial misconduct would do the trick – and wreck his reputation at the same time...

Here's hoping – that would suit me very nicely!

25.

The interview with the invalid

Gordon Rimmer entered the Santa Maria Hospital and Medical Centre via a side door, and immediately found himself challenged by two burly members of its security staff. For obvious reasons, they were keen to know the nature of his business.

"I've come to visit a patient - a Mr. Shackleton. I'm a close relative and when I found out he was here, I got the first plane over from the UK to give him my support. Apparently, I'll be his first non-medical visitor."

"By who's authority are you on the premises, sir?"

Like a thoroughbred investigative reporter, he remained calm under the pressure of his interrogation.

"I called ahead and arranged my visit through a nurse on his ward - Nurse Darryl Johnson."

The men muttered something under their breath and Rimmer heard one whisper, "Darryl's cool so we should let this guy go on through." Like a biblical Red Sea, they parted, allowing him to pass.

"Ok sir - do you know where you need to go?"

"Uh, aye it's the...er... the signposting is easy to follow, thank you." He decided against broadcasting his direction of travel, though he assumed that the men knew he was heading for the AIDS unit anyway. Upon his arrival, he nodded to the omnipresent Johnson (who was patrolling the ward with watchful zeal) and cautiously entered Shackleton's private room.

The two men had never met before and their early moments together were uncomfortable, though this was hardly surprising given the situation. Speaking weakly, the patient enquired about the reaction back home to his collapse, and was gratified to hear that for now, at least, everyone had shown great concern for him.

"I'll be honest Barry, everybody I've talked to is utterly stunned."

"They know what caused it then I suppose… why I keeled over? They know about my… pneumonia?"

"Well there are plenty of newsmen out here and it's our job to get to the bottom of these things, so aye, we know your collapse was brought on by pneumonia. We've all seen the diagnosis." Rimmer paused before revealing what else everyone knew, preferring to dance around the subject rather than wade in with a bombardment of heavy artillery. "I'm afraid it didn't take long for us to get to the root cause of your, er, condition…"

Shackleton appeared edgy and he wilted under the reporter's watchful gaze, but the battling instincts that had helped him fight back from many a losing position on stage kicked in as he desperately tried to avoid any mention of his deadly virus.

"Yeah…I've not been well for some time…the weight loss, you know?…I haven't been looking after myself properly…"

Rimmer realised now that pussy - footing around the truth would be dishonest and unprofessional.

"Barry, don't. We know."

The invalid still stalled, though an expression of panic betrayed him.

"Know what? What are you talking about?"

He was praying for a miracle, hoping against hope that the press were following a bogus trail to a mistaken conclusion, but no; God had decided against benevolence and it was time for him to confront some cold, harsh home truths.

"I'm sorry, but we know that you are HIV positive and have now contracted the full-blown AIDS virus … and it's obviously front-page news."

Shackleton's heart stopped beating temporarily and he closed his eyes as tears began to run freely down his emaciated cheeks.

"Jesus, no. No! Oh, no, no, no…"looking skywards he whispered, "Take me now!"

It was an awkward moment, a terrible moment for a man who suddenly realised that the secret he had harboured for over a year was finally, yet inevitably, public knowledge.

Rimmer hasn't turned up here to talk about my on-stage collapse – he's bagging an exclusive interview with the first professional sportsman in the world to fall victim to AIDS!

I didn't grasp the significance of the fifty grand fee for my version of the story 'cos I've been doped up all the time.

How could I be so stupid?

No paper would pay serious money to a darts professional who just fell over!

A waterfall of tears rolled down his face.

I can see it all clearly now – the UK press are gonna line up pictures of me, Rock Hudson and Liberace.

We'll be in a 'Gay Plague' rogues' gallery…

"My wife. My kids…" his lower lip trembled terribly. "Do they know yet?"

"Everyone knows. We were hardly likely to miss the fact that you're in the hospital's AIDS unit, were we?"

"Am I? I suppose I must be. When you're in a private room you don't think about stuff like that. The state I've been in, I couldn't have told you day from night, never mind what bloody ward they put me in."

"As far as your family are concerned, I've alerted London to say that your condition is stable and you can have visitors now, so they're on a flight over here as we speak. My boss Marcus Botha has taken personal responsibility for their protection, and he promises to keep them well away from the rest of the press pack."

"Oh yeah, of course Botha's gonna be all over this - I'm only here in the first place to play for his fucking trophy! That's just great…I'll be fried alive…" Shackleton fully understood the bind he was now in; he was at the mercy of a mercurial showman who would delight in making an exhibit of him. Like an evil Victorian ringmaster parading some poor, mutated creature before a gawping public at a fairground freak-show, the Head Honcho was going to subject him to mass mockery and ridicule.

Rimmer grew concerned that he might lose his interview.

"Trust me Barry, I can assure you that your side of the story will be dealt with sensitively. I've got no interest in causing undue distress to you or your family."

The browbeaten patient lifted his heavy eyelids.

"Who are you trying to kid, pal? Yours is the bloody paper that pushed Ollie Collins into an early grave when they found him with that teenage boy, so do me a favour and tell it like it is. This is gonna be bad….it'll be so bloody bad for me."

Ollie Collins was a successful comic actor with a three-decade-long body of work spanning theatre, television, and the silver screen. He was also a closet homosexual with a *penchant* for adolescent boys. When *The Horizon* discovered that he had struck up a sexual relationship with a fifteen-year-old, its editorial demanded his arrest. Public outrage followed, effectively destroying his career. Two days before the start of his trial for underage sex offences, a neighbor found him dead in his Waterloo flat beside an empty bottle of pills.

Rimmer recalled *The Horizon*'s front page headline the next day - '**FROM QUEER TO ETERNITY**' - with embarrassment and not a little shame. Though he considered the predatory behavior of Collins to be odious and contemptible, what stung him was the way that the headline suggested homosexuality itself was the menace, not one dirty old man's misguided corruption of a minor.

Of course, Shackleton's prediction of being, "fried alive," was all too accurate.

Before the origin of his virus was established, skilled wordsmiths back in Limehouse developed contingency plans to cover every possible scenario. If a blood transfusion had sealed his fate in some way, the paper intended to lobby Parliament to implement a ban on the import of unscreened blood supplies. However, should the truth emerge that he became HIV positive from either drug abuse or a homosexual act, then a *blitzkrieg* of mocking puns and word plays were locked and loaded, ready to fire at their hapless victim. When *The Horizon*'s world exclusive finally ended all the speculation by, "outing," him across its front page, homophobes everywhere felt obliged to bury their sharpened knives into his side.

Marcus Botha's purchase of the broken and beaten invalid's story allowed him the dubious honour of serialising one man's miserable demise in minute detail. To mitigate some of his own responsibility for what was to come, Rimmer felt obliged to try to limit the damage.

"Look, I can't speak for the way things will be handled in London, all that's out of my hands, but what I can do is offer you a non-judgmental hearing from our interview. Check out my track record - you'll see that I don't go in for finger-pointing witch hunts. I just want to know what's happened - you have my guarantee that there'll be no fabrication of the facts." His words went unnoticed, for Shackleton cut a distracted figure, consumed with a million thoughts and terrors. "Barry, did you hear me?"

"What? Oh, oh yeah. I get you. If you stick to your word, then that's all I can ask for I suppose, but I'll make a promise to you too - if you let me down, I'm gonna make sure that my missus goes after you and your paper in the courts. Just remember, I won't care how nasty it gets for me in there 'cos I'll already be '*brown bread*' by then…" His fatalistic use of Cockney rhyming slang showed that he fully understood the terminal implications of his diagnosis.

Rimmer reassured him on this issue by saying, "I've got a cast-iron promise from my editor that my copy won't be interfered with, so you can rest easy that there'll be no grounds for litigation."

This assurance pacified Shackleton enough for the interview to commence, though in truth he was in no position to refuse *The Horizon*'s generous terms and conditions anyway. The situation had already escalated beyond his control, so now he had to make sure that the paper got its money's worth from his tale of woe.

Painfully recalling sketchy details of his double life, he occasionally broke down, shedding more tears of guilt while begging for the forgiveness of his cherished family.

"My Ruth has always been such a rock for me, but I just couldn't bring myself to tell her the real cause of my problems. I dunno for certain, but I think I was hoping to die without her ever having to know the truth."

Rimmer decided that this was a good moment to wrap proceedings up for the day so his man could rest after what had clearly been a particularly stressful experience.

"Thank you for your time and more importantly, your candour. Now as an additional support to your family, I'm going to push for some tests to be completed on your wife at *The Horizon*'s expense, just to make sure she's not in the same …difficulties as yourself."

"What for? We stopped having sex the moment I realised the seriousness of my situation. She's safe mate, don't you worry about my girl - leave her be."

Seeing an opportunity for one further revelation, Rimmer trod gently to keep his star player on the pitch for just a little while longer.

"But what about the period when you must have been HIV positive before you'd had the news confirmed? Barry, didn't it occur to you that your wife was at risk throughout your...confused years?"

Shackleton suddenly looked like he had taken a bullet.

"Jesus Christ...I never thought about that!" He turned even more ashen. "I've been in a bubble of my own making for so long, I didn't think about the consequences of what I was doing at all... Please, for fuck's sake, save my Ruth!" The potential consequences of his behaviour had finally struck home. "God forgive me, I can honestly say that I must've been in denial the whole time. This kind of thing doesn't happen to people like me...I just saw myself as a family man with a problem. Are you telling me that you've never had problems in your life that you couldn't get to grips with?"

The question took Rimmer back to his split with Susan Somerfield, but this was not the time or the place to open up that particular sore. He was astonished at Shackleton's ignorance of the harm that could have come to his life partner.

"This isn't about me Barry, it's about you. So you didn't even *think* you might infect her?"

"Fuck you, sunshine! Who do you think you are - my judge and jury? Nothing like that ever crossed my mind - if I thought she was in any danger, I'd have got her to a doctor straight away, wouldn't I? Well? Wouldn't I? What makes you think I'm any bloody different to you?" In his consternation, the sweats returned. "Look, I've had enough of this - that's all I'm gonna say today, so leave me alone, you self-righteous bastard! I've done enough damage to the people I love, and I won't say anymore 'til I've spoken to my wife. Now just fuck off! Nurse!" He pressed a bedside buzzer and his faithful guardian immediately rushed into the room.

"What is it Mr. Shackleton - what's the trouble sir?"

"I'm done in Darryl.... I need to rest. Get rid of him for me, will you?"

Johnson immediately feared that his golden goose might have laid its last egg.

"That's a wrap for today then sir - let's go, ok?" Without any outward show of fuss, he ushered Rimmer from the room. The two men walked to the nearest elevator and he asked, "Did you get what you needed?"

"Yes thanks. I'll have to come back tomorrow though."

"That's supposin' I can get him to see you again, you mean!" Johnson wanted his benefactor to understand how hard he had pushed his patient, and that the chance of any further interviews may be in jeopardy.

"Er, of course, you're right Darryl. Look, I really do have Barry's best interests at heart you know…will you be sure to tell him that?"

"I will, but he's gonna need some persuading to let you back into his confidence…" This was clearly a hint for further funding.

"When I need your help again, there'll be some more money coming your way, ok?" Rimmer knew the importance of keeping Johnson sweet; he had to maintain exclusive access to Shackleton and the lure of extra cash was sure to do the trick. With this new offer, the familiar beaming smile returned to the nurse's face.

"Sure thing man, but just remember to be good to the guy, yeah? He's gonna need some friends now."

On the family front, when the time came to face the music, Barry Shackleton inevitably hated the tune. His children felt utterly humiliated and refused to see him, sinking his leaden heart further still.

To his amazement and eternal gratitude, Ruth stayed loyal during those darkest hours. She had undergone the necessary tests (HIV specialists would subsequently declare her free of any infection) but at that moment her future lay in limbo and the shock of recent events still left her in a dazed state. Acting on autopilot, she instinctively clung to certainties for succor, cocooning herself in the love of Barry and their girls. Despite what he had done; despite his deceit; the actions that threatened her very life; she simply found it too hard to abandon him to the prowling ravenous wolfpack outside. The whole thing seemed like some sort of horrible dream, and she desperately wanted to wake up and find the man she loved still by her side, ready to play happy families again.

The Horizon had put the family up in a private residence well away from prying eyes, and a well-drilled security team were on hand to shield them from unwelcome attention. From there it was a fifteen-minute cab ride to the hospital over on Paradise Road where she could check on her husband's condition.

Oh, the irony of that road name!

Paradise couldn't be further away.

Sometimes truth is too terrible to contemplate, and it was going to take time for Ruth to grasp the entire ghastliness of her situation. Barry's estrangement from their kids meant that she would have to divide her energies between keeping a bedside vigil for him and matriarchal duties back at the hideout; there was simply no thinking time left with which to take everything in.

I used to worry about you losing so much weight - remember me saying you should get yourself checked out for cancer?

You said you were ok and you'd stop your, 'diet', soon - that you were only on it to live longer for the kids' sake.

You told me those blotches on your skin were a rash from a tournament in the Far East that had turned nasty, and I believed you.

I believed you!

What would I know about bloody AIDS?

Watching him rest, she caught herself staring at his skeletal frame. She hardly recognised him; it seemed like someone else was lying there; a stranger she had never seen before. A shiver ran down her spine at the thought that for some time, whenever they were intimate, she unwittingly faced a death sentence from his loaded gun. She had only ever known the Dr. Jekyll side of his character and this Mr. Hyde before her now was more like an alien being than the love of her life.

My decent, caring Barry - my good Dr. Jekyll - is dying.

How am I going to cope without the man who has made me so blissfully happy?

This stranger - this Mr. Hyde - who's cruelly destroyed my family and robbed me of everything I hold dear - he's a man of mystery to me.

How long has he been around, whispering into dear old Dr. Jekyll's ear, putting me in danger?

Oh, how did things come to this?

And why, why, why?...

26.

Farewell, my lovely

Two days had passed since Shackleton spoke to Rimmer and the patient was in a low mood. Not even the arrival of his ever-loyal wife Ruth the previous evening had been enough to lighten the spirits of this disillusioned, downcast man. Outside a chorus of bird song reminded the good people of Las Vegas that a new day was dawning and the ward beyond his private room slowly coughed and spluttered into some small semblance of life. First to greet him was Nurse Darryl Johnson.

"Hey, what's up fella? How you doin' today?"

"…Oh, I'm as well as can be expected I suppose…"

While this response was vaguely up-beat, the tone of his voice gave the game away.

"Hey come on man, things are lookin' up! You got your family here now and -"

"I've got my wife here Darryl, but no, I haven't got my kids. They're stuck in a private apartment and won't see me…they don't want to know their own dad."

"Now see here, that ain't the way brother," said Johnson, encouragingly, "they'll come round - jus' you wait and see. You jus' got to give 'em some time, that's all."

Shackleton muttered something to himself.

"What was that, Barry?" the nurse asked.

"I said time is something I don't have."

"Oh come on, that's no way to be goin' about your business. You gotta be strong - be positive. Whatcha need to do is show your kids that you're gonna take good care of them."

Shackleton was less than receptive to his amiable friend's good vibes.

"And how do I go about that exactly? My life is fucked, my career's finished - just how do you think I'm gonna make things good? Those kids are my whole life and they fuckin' hate me for what I've done."

"Well now, think on - that's easy fixed! Jus' keep talkin' to the newspaper guy - every time you rap wit' him it's gonna be - *kerching!* Cash in the bank! Once the family sees they're gonna be ok, things'll be sweeter than the maple syrup on your breakfast pancakes baby, jus' you wait an' see."

Nurse Johnson was genuinely concerned for Shackleton's well-being, but he also had some *kerching* of his own to think about and that became a key driver in trying to motivate his grumpy patient, who sat up in bed mulling things over before replying.

"You don't understand mate - that bloke made me finally take stock of all the bad stuff I've done. He brought it all home - I never really thought enough about it before - how much I've hurt the people I care most about…"

"Listen, I'm tellin' you man, if you bite the bullet hard and talk to that dude again, his paper will pay you enough money to set your folks up for good. Surely that's worth the trouble, 'specially if you want to make it up with your kids. Am I right?" Nobody could accuse Johnson of a lack of effort, but other patients needed his attention too, so reluctantly he had to leave his meal ticket to stew in peace. His efforts were not entirely in vain though, because as he walked off, Shackleton called him back.

"Darryl, can you do me a favour? Can you get me an English paper from somewhere? I feel a bit more up to reading something today."

"You sure that's really a good idea Barry? Wouldn't it be better if I got you a book or somethin' instead? Maybe a sports magazine?"

The invalid was undeterred.

"Please, if you could, I'd really like a copy of *The Horizon*. I want to see what Rimmer has actually written about me."

Johnson was extremely reluctant to comply with the request in case the published article turned out to be a hatchet-job piece, so he decided to be diplomatic and just say, "I'll see what I can do."

Las Vegas is a city that wants its visitors to forget the stresses and strains of the world beyond and there is little interest in clogging up its newsstands with foreign titles. It was going to be difficult to comply with Shackleton's request, but the intrepid nurse needed his trust, and he had friends in the hotels who could always be relied on to rustle up anything for their guests. He called a favour in from a long-standing gambling pal at the Golden Nugget on Freemont Street and by mid-morning he was sifting through a day-old edition of Marcus Botha's flagship tabloid, surveying the reams of copy that had been devoted to its lead story.

Jesus, either Barry is a really big deal in the UK or none of those guys have ever been to 'Frisco!

While most of the articles were vitriolic (indeed, some were positively actionable), Gordon Rimmer's interview and personal column reflected his promise to be honest, yet non-judgemental, leaving Shackleton a degree of dignity.

Barry says he's only interested in our man's stuff, so I guess it'll be cool to give him what he wants.

On his next tour of the beds, while dispensing lunch to his patients, he duly handed the paper over.

"Now don't you start gettin' all over - excited by that girl with the big titties on page five", he said with a toothy grin, before immediately regretting the comment in view of the circumstances of his patient's condition.

"No need to be embarrassed mate," was the reassuring reply, "now let's see what's what, eh?" The front-page headline - **SHACK BACK ON THE RACK – FAMILY ROW LEAVES HIM DAYS FROM DEATH** - drew a despairing grimace of horror from the man at the centre of the story and he visibly shrank at the extent of the coverage that had been devoted to his tale of woe.

"Fuckin' hell - 'aven't they got anything better to do than to dwell on me and my problems?"

It was always going to be a risk letting him see the reactions of the press back home, but Johnson quickly pointed out Gordon Rimmer's contributions, accentuating the positives contained therein.

"Read the stuff that our guy wrote man, never mind the rest of that shit!"

Shackleton had to agree with his nurse that the journalist had been true to his word.

"Yeah, Rimmer has done right by me, I can't grumble about his article. But as for the rest of those…bastards!…

"Don't you worry none 'bout them sir, you ain't talkin' to any of those crazy dudes anyways - it's our guy who'll see you alright."

"Mmmm…."

"Come on Barry! Maybe I should get him to pay you another visit tomorrow, yeah? Wouldn't that do you some good?"

Shackleton brooded for a while, then disconsolately looked up and said, "Let me think about it. I'll tell you what I've decided to do in the morning." There was finality about his words, so Johnson thought it best to let him rest, hoping that his mood would lighten by the break of the next day.

Once the door closed, silence enveloped the room; it had a presence; a menace. It controlled the thoughts of the miserable depressive lying cocooned in its grip. Dark thoughts cluttered his head, multiplying like the viral infection that ran riot through his blood cells.

He stared at a plastic knife resting next to his plate of untouched food and paid particular attention to its serrated edge, calculating the odds of being able to slice his wrists successfully. If he failed, the press would be more intrusive than ever, heaping further misery on his wife and children. The application of any great pressure in the cutting motion might snap the flimsy utensil in two, but he possessed great skill and dexterity in his fingertips and had confidence in their abilities; after all, those nimble digits were responsible for providing him with a comfortable living over these last few years.

Should I take my chances with the knife?

From underneath his pillow he produced a suicide note, written during the night in between bouts of broken sleep. Re-reading the words, he carefully reviewed his options. Then inspiration struck. There would be no need to risk the plastic blade.

He picked up a pen lying by the newspaper at the side of his bed and compared it to one of his beloved tungsten darts. Feeling its weight in the fingers of his right hand, he caressed its barrel as if he was preparing to sink it into the bullseye of a championship board. His left hand then went to work, tracing the outline of his jugular vein. Bringing the pen's nib towards his neck, he lined them both up. Before proceeding, he offered up one final prayer to the vengeful God who had seen fit to punish him so cruelly, and begged that he would be able to stay quiet during the completion of his final act…

The next few seconds were too terrifying to contemplate, but with as much power as his weakened body could muster, he jabbed the pen inwards, penetrating his skin and piercing the vein in the process. Blood erupted from his body like an Icelandic geyser. With every ounce of effort left in his perspiring, expiring body, he fought to supress the screams that would alert the ward to his distress. The previously intimidating silence now became his friend, his ally, his co-conspirator.

As the bedsheets stained to a deep crimson, there was no noise of any kind; only stony silence; until a passing orderly routinely looked in on the room and saw the body, the bed, and the mess, before hurriedly shouting out for assistance.

All too late.

When support staff arrived to assess the scene and remove tragic Shackleton's bloody corpse, they discovered his suicide note tucked inside a pillow and immediately alerted the hospital's management to its poignant contents -

Please Darryl, if you get this message first, for God's sake hide it somewhere safe and only show it to my missus. Tell the authorities I've had an accident or something or my family won't get any insurance money.

Ruth, my darling, the last few days have been a living hell from which I know I can never escape. I had hoped that my little time left on earth would be spent with my loving family by my side, but sadly that is not meant to be now. I got Darryl to fetch me an English paper and seeing what it said about me was bad enough, but when I saw the look of anger on our kids faces in the picture on page 2 I knew that this was the right time to go.

I am truly sorry for what I have done to you all but I cannot expect forgiveness, so the sooner I am out of it, the better. You have made me much happier than I ever deserved to be and I would have lived in misery and confusion for the rest of my days if you had not come into my life. You made sense of everything.

Love, I don't want you to see me fade away, or have to empty my waste and feed me through a straw. That would be our future and you deserve better. I can't stand the idea of our kids thinking you are mad to still be with me either.

To tell you the truth, I am frightened of going home as well, what with the name calling and stuff I would have to deal with. I am not strong enough to put up with all that so I'm better off just ending it here.

You and the kids will be closer again when I'm gone.

I want you to know I did my best for you all and I know I was crazy to risk hurting you, but I can't explain my feelings well enough to make you understand what it has been like to live a lie.

Love you always

Bazza. X

Within hours, an internal review of staff procedures took place and Nurse Johnson had to explain the exact nature of his relationship with the deceased. Sensibly, he had already rehearsed his responses.

"I was Mr. Shackleton's go-to guy - I ran errands for him, jus' like I do for anyone else on the ward. As for lettin' him speak to that press fella, well, I got suckered into believin' there was some sort of family connection between them. Guess I was guilty of bein' a li'l naïve there. Anyways, later on, when he told me he'd given Mr. Rimmer an interview, it looked like the experience had brought him some comfort - though in view of his actions afterwards, I suppose that might not have been the case."

He admitted to giving the pen to Shackleton, but this act received no reprimand because psychologists see the writing of letters or attempts at crosswords etc. as positive stimulants for a patient, and nobody could have anticipated that he would use the implement to end his desperate life. The tribunal duly exonerated Johnson from any blame for the regrettable incident and he quietly returned to his life as a hard-working nurse and after-hours small-time gambler.

The Santa Maria Hospital and Medical Centre was perfectly accustomed to dealing with all kinds of commotions, but the manic British press pursuit of an unknown sportsman from an unknown sport kept the wards chattering for a while. Life goes on though, and the daily dramas of the present are more than enough to concentrate busy minds, so all that media madness quickly drifted into the dim and distant past…

Back in London, for a week *The Horizon* indulged in an orgy of scaremongering and speculation about the growing threat of the *'Gay Plague,'* but knee - jerk reactions from self-proclaimed 'right-thinking' observers conflicted starkly with the more balanced observations of its Chief Sports Correspondent. **The Rimmer Review** added much needed insight to the debate and drew considerable admiration from envious editors elsewhere in the newspaper industry. His stock had risen and the serious broadsheets were circling, so the prospect of doing more worthy work away from Botha's grasp (at a competitive salary that might even match his current King's ransom) became a tantalising possibility.

Barry Shackleton's family received the grim news of his demise with a mixture of resignation, devastation, and despair, but before they could fully digest its impact, a second wave of media hysteria surrounded them. On their return home, news emerged that the official verdict of suicide invalidated the terms of his life insurance policy. This was a further cruel blow which left them not only bereaved, but penniless too (save for *The Horizon's* blood money). A nation's sympathy focussed on Ruth and the children, and Botha took further advantage of the situation by organising a campaign entitled **SUPPORT THE SHACKLETONS – LET'S CONSIDER THE *REAL* VICTIMS OF AIDS** through his paper. Cash donations began to pour in from across the UK. He publicly took care of the funeral arrangements too, flying the deceased's skeletal body home for a service and burial in Kent.

Once those formalities were completed (attracting more front-page headlines), the crazed circus that had painstakingly captured every facet of this tragic tale dusted itself down and rolled out of town; on to the next story; the next scandal…

27.

Challenges and disagreements

In the end, '*M J Botha's Darts Duals*' turned out to be a tremendous exhibition of precision and skill, including several epic encounters. To nobody's great surprise however, its impact on the Las Vegas tourists and gamblers was negligible. Attendances were embarrassingly poor, and only avid devotees from the British Isles cared enough to view the spectacle. While their vociferous support from the front of the auditorium did raise the roof on occasions, they could not mask the fact that behind them, row upon row of empty seats told a sorry tale for the cameras. Back in the UK, the tournament had barely raised a mention beyond the rather biased confines of *The Horizon*'s sports pages.

Despite the unprecedented national media coverage of Barry Shackleton's extraordinary revelation and subsequent demise, very few people linked those events to Botha's televised flop, leaving him frustrated and furious in equal measure. Consequently, his much-anticipated increases in satellite dish sales and subscription sign-ups to *MJB TV* failed to materialise, signalling a need for some creative (and illegal) accounting to disguise huge quarterly losses.

Financial advisors informed the Head Honcho that his private investors and the banks had enough faith in Brand Botha to continue their backing in the short term, but patience (a commodity more precious in business than any Transvaal gem) was rapidly wearing thin. With *Sky TV* landing all the early punches in the pay-per-view broadcasting war, Botha appeared to be trapped on the ropes, helpless to repel Rupert Murdoch's blows. *MJB TV* was already just weeks away from going into administration, so its future hinged on the success of his, '*Sun City Snooker Showdown*'.

Meanwhile, week one of the month-long *Italia 90* World Cup had passed and the England football team were struggling to reach the knockout stage of the competition. Progression depended on the players achieving favourable results from a group stage pitting them against the Republic of Ireland, Holland and Egypt. After uninspiring draws against the Irish and the Dutch, they faced the ignominy of elimination at the first hurdle should they lose to the Egyptians, and thus far, their performances had drawn widespread ridicule from a frustrated nation. Marcus Botha offered up his own thoughts on Bobby Robson's boys during a meeting with Edmund Cornell.

"The national team is a disgrace - their manager is clueless, and our post bag is bulging with letters from critics grumbling that enough is enough. Surely this is a reminder to everyone that football is on the ropes? A successful snooker show on *MJB TV* is just what the doctor ordered to cheer those people up. The Sun City tournament will tip the balance my way, for sure."

Edmund Cornell countered Botha's braggadocio with a cautious reply.

"I hope you've read the signs correctly Marcus, but there's still the Paul Gascoigne factor to contend with. That lad has magic in his feet and if he sparks the team into life, public opinion will change completely."

'*Gazza*' was an unpredictable maverick and his performances thus far had been the only bright spot in England's World Cup campaign. Pundits were unanimous in suggesting that without his world - class skills the side would already be booked on the first flight home, but while he was pulling the strings, faint hopes for success remained. An exhausting weight of expectation lay on the young man's shoulders, for the entire future of English football as a national obsession was coming under scrutiny.

Botha did not take kindly to his Chief Editor's caution.

"Don't doubt me, Edmund. We've got star names of our own performing in Sun City - bigger and better ones. If Alex Higgins, Jimmy White and Ben St. Claire do their stuff over there, we'll be home and hosed. Our darts coverage may not have had the desired impact, but snooker is a much more suitable sport for television and we're targeting those armchair punters who are angry about the football team's ineptitude. We just have to sell our product better, that's all."

"How are you planning to do that then?"

"How are *we* planning to do that...we're in this together, you and I." The Head Honcho's dead eyes stared directly at Cornell, sending him a chilling warning not to distance himself from the task-at-hand. "*We*'ll do it by spending more bloody money on advertising - shouting from the highest rooftops, extolling the virtues of our wonderful network as loudly as possible! It's the only way. There'll be more billboard posters, more slots on free-to-air television, and all my publications - *The Horizon,* its sister papers in the regions and my magazines - will splash full page ads across their centre pages. If it means cutting our content to the bone to find the space, then so be it - we'll do whatever's necessary to make sure that *MJB TV* takes off."

For the first time, Cornell detected desperation in his master's voice. If that was indeed the case, then the implications were dire for everyone currently sheltering from the heavy weather of recession underneath his financial umbrella. In an unusually bold move, he risked incurring Botha's wrath by questioning the plan.

"Are you quite sure that sacrificing more news content is the best policy to pursue at this time? Our most recent figures show that before Gordon Rimmer brought in the Shackleton interview, we'd been suffering from a perceptible decline in our circulation."

"And don't I know it! I'll tell you now Edmund, as you're supposed to be captaining this ship, I hold you entirely responsible for that underwhelming performance."

"Yes, well I suppose that's your prerogative, but we've commissioned some market research to analyse our sales dip and it suggests that the reductions in content that we've already made to increase advertising space, together with our recent price rise, were the factors driving away our missing readers."

"Don't give me that old rubbish! The price increase was in line with similar action taken by our competitors. We all acted as one in a proportionate response to increasing production costs."

"I agree with you that the price hike was unavoidable, but with the greatest respect, the squeezing of column inches undermines the talents of my staff and endangers the future of the paper."

The Head Honcho stiffened in his seat and clenched his fighting fists.

"You've got a fucking nerve - you must think I was born yesterday! If our readers are being driven away, it's because you can't do your bloody job properly! I'm having to increase our advertising revenue as a consequence of the shoddy job you're doing editing my paper. You've lost the plot when deciding on the running order of our news items and you're overpaying our writers!"

This attack stung the vastly experienced and capable editor because he had taken *The Horizon*'s daily sales to an all-time peak of three million before the recent dip (though Botha quickly forgot those successes as his temper raged). The doors and windows of the penthouse started to rattle from his roars, but still Cornell stood his ground.

"On the subject of our writers, may I remind you that I warned you against hiring Lewis Neeves?"

On hearing this, Botha leapt to the defence of his political poodle.

"That man's column adds credibility to this newspaper. It gives us a unique advantage over our rivals in the way it challenges our readers."

"It doesn't challenge them Marcus, it *bores* them to tears. Our market research tells us -"

"Bugger the market research!"

Undeterred, Cornell continued to make his point.

"Look, we've paid for this analysis so we might as well reference it, and it tells us that our readers skip the political page entirely. The truth is that they're simply not interested in anything Lewis has to say."

Botha wanted to take advantage of Neeves' position of influence in Parliament, so to butter him up, **LEWIS LETS LOOSE!** now took up an entire page of the paper each week. Rather than accept criticism for this decision, the vexed proprietor continued with his passionate rant.

"You question my decision to bring Lewis Neeves here, but whose idea was it for us to shell out a king's ransom to get that big-headed fucker Rimmer?"

Cornell took the retort on the chin.

"Well, er, that was me, absolutely. And what a wise move it's proven to be!" He defended his star signing despite the fact that the Chief Sports Correspondent's extraordinary contract had created friction amongst the paper's lesser lights. "Gordon's coverage of your dart's tournament was exemplary, and he got us the scoop of the year with his exclusive access to Barry Shackleton."

"I should bloody well hope he did - if my own man couldn't manage that when the story broke right under his nose at *my* tournament, he'd want shooting, not praising! Besides, he wasn't all that hot in Las Vegas because he didn't steer anyone towards my fucking network!"

"Oh that's grossly unfair! My journalists are here to write bulletins that are interesting, inventive and attention-grabbing - it's not in their remit to sell satellite dishes or subscriptions for *MJB TV*."

This unwelcome and unwise response stretched Botha's patience to breaking point.

"Edmund, during the course of this conversation I've reached a conclusion which I don't think you're going to like. Every branch of my communications empire needs to pull together to achieve the synergistic benefits I require and with that aim in mind, I expect *The Horizon* to help my pay-per-view business to bud. If it can't do that with you at the helm, I'll make the necessary changes to make sure that it does. Do I make myself clear?"

"Look, I can only be held responsible for what goes on here - it's completely unreasonable of you to expect me to sell your other wares as well."

Botha replied with typical pomposity.

"To paraphrase your naval hero, Admiral Nelson, at the battle of Trafalgar - *I expect every employee to do their duty*. No ifs, no buts. As for the performance of our paper, it's my opinion - and that's the one that counts - that your decisions have cost me money and reduced our circulation, so I am serving you notice that unless there's a significant improvement in our sales figures over the next quarter, I'll be honour bound to take corrective action to arrest the malaise. Sort it out or else - that's what I pay you for."

"How? By reporting less news and printing a page every week that nobody wants to read?"

The boss had heard enough dissent for one day.

"Just do your fucking job or expect the consequences - now get out before I sack you on the spot, you cheeky bastard!"

Cornell understood the futility of further debate, and so, somewhat relieved to escape with his physical well-being intact, he withdrew from the (utterly one-sided) meeting to review his future. With a final flounce of frustrated fury, he slammed the penthouse door on his way out and for a couple of seconds the noise reverberated around the otherwise silent and vaguely eerie room.

Botha glared at the door and his eyes narrowed.

How dare a nobody like Cornell question my business acumen!

He better watch his step if he wants to stay healthy…even at my age, I'm not about to go soft on my subordinates…

I need the money this paper brings in – more than ever right now – and if he fails me in this regard, he'll pay a heavy price!

28.

Edmund gets to work

For several weeks, Lewis Neeves had been vigorously defending the government's hugely unpopular overhaul of the rates system via *The Horizon's* political page. Margaret Thatcher's radical Community Charge (or "Poll Tax" as it became known) related to the contributions charged by local councils to cover the costs of services such as policing, refuse collection etc. It decreed that the haves and have-nots must pay the same flat rate, regardless of their financial circumstances; in essence, increasing the tax burden *pro-rata* on the cash-strapped poor. Public anger towards the scheme manifested itself in acts of civil disorder, and in central London, a two hundred thousand strong anti-Poll Tax rally descended into a full-scale riot with pitched battles breaking out between the police and protesters.

The government response was to stay firm and implement the legislation, regardless of the flack it received. During the months that followed, thousands of ratepayers faced prosecution for refusing to pay their new bills and Magistrates courts across the country struggled to cope with the huge backlog of cases.

Conservative MPs began to fear for their re-election prospects and to add to their anxieties, economic pressures saw interest rates rise alarmingly, further squeezing the finances of beleaguered homeowners. The Labour party now had a significant lead in the opinion polls and debate raged over Mrs. Thatcher's position as Prime Minister.

A year earlier, Sir Anthony Meyer, an inconspicuous Tory backbencher, had taken her on via a '*stalking horse*' leadership challenge, in the hope of stirring one of the party's bigger names into aggressive action. At that time, none of them had any real stomach for the fight, even though to everyone's surprise, he received thirty-three votes from supportive colleagues in the seemingly futile ballot. From that moment on, dull but incessant murmurs of rebellion grew louder.

The Right Honourable Lewis Neeves was ambivalent to all this unrest. He represented one of the country's safest seats in the south-east of England and it had a reliable record of returning right-wing Conservatives to the Commons, regardless of external pressures, so his Parliamentary future was secure. He believed that the Prime Minister's fighting qualities were more than a match for any malicious troublemakers too.

His support for the Poll Tax conflicted with the opinions expressed by *The Horizon*'s readers, but their concerns disinterested him. Although they represented the working-class demographic that the legislation detrimentally affected, they could not directly influence his career; that power was in the hands of the Prime Minister, and to a lesser extent, Marcus Botha, both of whom were obdurate advocates of the controversial tax.

To remind those key allies of his usefulness, he dedicated his latest column to another of their favourite topics, the government's fractious relationship with its partners in Europe. Mrs. Thatcher vehemently opposed the increasing influence of the European Court of Human Rights on matters of UK law, so he wrote a toadying article in support of her views. Before he could submit his copy, Edmund Cornell called. *The Horizon*'s Editor-in-Chief had just reached his office after his intimidating morning meeting with Botha.

"Ah, good morning, Edmund, what can I do to delight you today? Let me guess…Has one of my naughty Commons colleagues been behaving badly again? Have you caught a big fish from the cabinet, perhaps? Might I hazard a guess that you really have nothing concrete to go on - just salacious gossip that makes for an eye-catching headline? Oh, if only a government insider could supply you with an appropriate quote to flesh out your tale, eh! Is that what this call is about? If so, then of course I'm only too happy to help."

Neeves harboured a simmering resentment of Cornell, and these playful musings were a charade designed to irritate him. "How's this? *I have no knowledge of any alleged wrongdoing concerning my dear friend and I am confident that these (as yet) unsubstantiated accusations will do nothing to damage his/her reputation in the eyes of the Great British public, etc., etc.'*

All rather bland stuff, I admit, but the words, '*as yet*' will sow seeds of suspicion in the minds of our dreary unwashed, suggesting that your allegations may have some credibility. If the mud you sling has any substance, we can expect my unfortunate ally to resign in two shakes of a lamb's tail. You'll get a week's worth of headlines from the whole episode, while I shall - very reluctantly, of course - look to fill the vacancy by trotting off to join the other runners and riders in the promotion sweepstakes. Have I read the scenario correctly dear boy?"

I can sense this vulgar little man's distaste for Westminster merry-go-round power plays.

He's as much of an oik as his readers and as such, has always had difficulty empathising with the subtle machinations of state affairs.

What fun it is to yank his chain!

Neeves' smugness raised the hairs on the back of Cornell's neck, but wisdom dictated that he should refrain from reacting to the MP's gentle provocation.

"Look Lewis, my call concerns your column, not Westminster tittle-tattle. I want to ask if you could try to make it a bit more… *populist* in the future, ok?"

"Populist? Would you care to elaborate on that description?"

"I mean that with our circulation down just now, everybody has to do their bit to help increase sales, so could you…I don't know…maybe lighten your pieces up a bit?"

"Lighten them up? Come-come, Edmund - the business of government isn't some sort of situation comedy, you know."

Cornell stopped short of reminding him that one of the *BBC*'s most successful programmes of the time was, "*Yes Prime Minister,*" a satire that mischievously poked fun at the absurdities of political decision making, because a dry fish like Neeves would fail to see the irony in his last grandiose statement.

"All I'm suggesting is that you try to connect with our readers a little more, because our research suggests that they're skipping past your page rather than digesting what you have to say."

Ego is an integral part of every MP's makeup, causing them to take umbrage at the merest hint of criticism, and any inference that their words of wisdom are being ignored leaves them feeling particularly piqued.

"Now look here, I was hired with a specific remit - to provide the paper with an insider's guide to life in government. The format allows me the freedom to have my say on whatever I think are the important issues of the day. If you want a clown for a columnist, you can pick one up from the nearest circus and send me back to the Commons!"

This vainglorious posturing was too much for Cornell to stomach, so he decided to remind the diva on the other end of the line of a pertinent fact concerning their professional relationship.

"Well I'm not looking for a clown Lewis, but if I'd had my way I wouldn't have hired you either - the political slot was the boss's idea, not mine."

"And you'd do well to remember that my friend!" interrupted Neeves. "When it comes to your - our - newspaper, I answer to the proprietor only, and he says he's very pleased with my contributions, so I'll thank you to mind your own bloody business!"

At least now the kid gloves were off; their guards were down, and a proper row could commence.

"That's as may be, but I've just come from a very heated meeting with Mr. Botha where he let me know in no uncertain terms that every contributor to this newspaper needs to up their game. If you don't feel the need to change your approach, how about writing something to promote *MJB TV*? You could say that subscription television offers freedom of choice for viewers when set against the *BBC*'s compulsory licence fee. Would that kind of subliminal support suit you better?"

"What on earth are you talking about Edmund? Do you expect me to help him sell his satellite dishes too? Am I a market trader now?"

"Marcus wants everybody to pull together to fire up his broadcasting revolution. Our TV guide is under orders to feature exclusive articles relating to programmes on his network. The sports desk has to marvel at his televised darts and snooker tournaments. He's got our gossip columnists raving about any stars who'll agree to appear on his flagship Saturday night chat show, *'In Town Tonight!'* And now I expect you to demonise that bloody license fee! Have I made myself clear?" There was little doubt that he had. "Or if that's too much of an ask, the next time you share a cup of Earl Grey with our boss, you can tell him why your head is stuck so far up your own smug, self-satisfied and sanctimonious arsehole that you refuse to help him out of his present difficulties. Shall we hazard a guess at how that particular conversation will go down?"

Neeves quickly processed the points raised and two trains of thought emerged. On the one hand, he needed to address Cornell's caustic attack without losing face, and on the other, he was curious to know more about Marcus Botha's troubles. He would deal with the former issue now and the latter later.

With studied gravitas he replied, "On reflection, I agree that we should all do our best to assist our employer in any appropriate way possible, so in my very next *Horizon* column I shall vigorously defend our put-upon taxpayers by drawing swords with the *BBC* over its outrageous subsidy." Typically for an experienced politician, this compliance came with a proviso. "However, although I will gladly support Marcus on this particular topic, I need hardly remind you that it is my privilege - and the privilege of any contributor to a free press - to speak my mind on any subject against anyone - friend or foe alike should the need arise - unfettered by the diktats of others. Now have *I* made myself clear Edmund?"

"Perfectly, thank you Lewis. I'm happy we've arrived at a working arrangement."

Conciliation had been undertaken, and an understanding reached.

Cornell allowed himself a little chuckle at his obstinate sparring partner's pomposity. The *"freedom of the press,"* angle is routinely used and abused by journalists to service their own agendas, but he knew that if Neeves should ever utilise that freedom to criticise his own paymaster, he would swiftly find his avenue of expression road blocked with a decree that he must never, ever, push his luck again.

29.

Botha brazens it out

The Head Honcho felt entirely comfortable when it came to ruffling the feathers of his employees, so upsetting Edmund Cornell that morning left him utterly unmoved; a shouting match was indeed a trivial matter when taken in context, after all, he had been equally indifferent when sanctioning the murders of his militant mineral miners two decades earlier. Scientific studies on leadership suggest that there are more psychopaths running large corporations than are to be found residing in the darkest recesses of the prison system; their lack of empathy makes them perfectly suited to the world of big business, where the ability to make ruthless decisions without the hindrance of remorse is of enormous advantage.

While his ease in the area of confrontation was obvious, the row had dredged up issues that were beginning to spin out of control. He had built his kingdom on a bedrock of extraordinary self-belief, but some truths are irrefutable: the slightest hint of failure can expose previously solid foundations to signs of subsidence.

Despite his bluff and bluster, his judgement calls of late had been uncharacteristically poor and the alarming losses at *MJB TV* suggested that his entry into the satellite broadcasting business was a huge mistake. He had deliberately come into the industry late, anticipating that *Sky's* enormous start-up costs would destroy its first-mover advantage, but his strategy proved inaccurate. The early adopters (those people who absolutely <u>must</u> have the new this; the latest that) chose subscriptions with Rupert Murdoch's network rather than Botha's and his business model was not diverse enough to attract great interest.

To compound his problems, many *MJB TV* customers experienced transmitter difficulties from its inferior equipment. Murdoch and his backers had indeed spent a phenomenal amount of money on infrastructure, but the technical know-how of his engineering team was robust. He had stayed strong; stayed in the game, and slowly but surely saw a tiny trickle of return on his investment, while his rival's pockets haemorrhaged cash in a frantic attempt to compete.

Botha had temporarily dodged a bullet by publishing less-than-honest financial results, but discovery of his deceit would see him face a barrage of litigation that no mere mortal could repel. Astonishingly, he now decided to push his luck still further.

Desperate times call for desperate measures, so in an act combining gross arrogance, outrageous greed, and a complete disregard for the laws of the land, he propped up his ailing business by misappropriating four hundred million pounds from the *Marcus Botha Publishing and Communications* employee pension scheme, putting the futures of thousands of ordinary men and women at risk. We have seen that he felt no guilt at the prospect of ruining other people to achieve his aims, but the need to keep his astonishing crime under wraps was of critical importance.

A thousand thoughts ran around his head.

Business is business and my financial needs are far greater than those of my employees.

I pay their wages, don't I?

I put food on their tables and rooves over their heads.

Without me, they're nothing, so it's only reasonable that they make an investment in their long-term futures by supporting their boss in his hour of need - whether they know they're doing it or not!

Sometimes you have to think outside the box if you want to win, and I NEED TO WIN!

When my tournament proves to be a major success, subscriptions and sales of my satellite dishes will quadruple month on month, of that I'm certain.

My network will prosper, then the pension money will be paid back and everything else will fall into place.

As if to contradict this optimistic appraisal of his prospects, his chest began to tighten. He closed his eyes and concentrated hard on staying calm until the crushing pain eased.

Gordon Rimmer had better come good for me in Sun City – he doesn't know it yet, but he's not going to get another chance!

PART THREE

UNDER AFRICAN SKIES

30.

The Taker

On the outskirts of Johannesburg, an African National Congress cheerleader addressed a ragged assembly of locals, bursting forth with impressively impassioned rhetoric.

"Soweto will be the symbol of the new South Africa! Get ready, for our time is here! Our time is now! Cry freedom!"

The crowd listened intently, but their feelings were many and varied, for while the majority fervently hoped that their man spoke the truth, not everyone was so enthusiastic. Soweto's problems had cast a shadow upon the world's conscience for decades and many of those who gathered for the speech were battle scarred from their continual struggles; they had seen their hopes scattered like dust to the four winds so often that there was a reluctance to get too excited by (as yet) undelivered promises.

Lenka Molome was one of those who looked on guardedly, never daring to dream the same dreams as some of his friends and neighbours. He was eighteen years old and a study of pouting suspicion and mistrust.

What does all this talk of freedom mean for me?

I've only ever seen poverty, hardship, trouble, violence - it's tough enough just surviving in this shitty shanty town.

How free can I ever really be round here?

So now I'm supposed to believe that good times are on their way?

Fuck yeah!

He spat on the dusty ground between his feet.

When things get better for my family and me, then I'll believe all this talk, and not before!

In Europe one year earlier, a Velvet Revolution had emancipated Eastern Bloc states from Communist oppression, and now that same momentous wind of change blew through the crisp, late afternoon air of Gauteng Province, South Africa. Significant steps towards an unconditional dismantling of the apartheid political system were underway. The ruling National Party had lifted its ban on the ANC, and its leader Nelson Mandela was now a free man. Upon his release from prison, he took the opportunity to tour the globe, discussing his plans for the country's new dawn with prominent world leaders, while his foot soldiers maintained the momentum back home through speeches, marches and other non-conformist activism in defiance of their white supremacist rulers.

That day's Soweto rally was taking place outside the Regina Mundi Church, to the north of the Moroka district (named after former ANC president James Moroka). This was the very heartland of the black resistance, and its church galvanised support, helping the congregation to picture a Utopian fantasy of heaven on earth through political change and personal empowerment. As Fields of Dreams go, the place was hardly the stuff of Hollywood, but it had a relevance to the townsfolk, adding resonance to the rhetoric. Eventually the mass chanting of ANC propaganda songs began to wane and the crowd slowly dispersed, leaving their dreamlike euphoria behind to return to the here and now.

Lenka Molome walked back down Old Potchefstroom Road towards home on the edge of Maetla with a sulky expression and his shoulders slumped. His attendance at the gathering had nothing to do with spiritual or political enrichment; he was there for financial gain. His stealthy, skilful fingers were well versed in the dark arts of the pickpocket, and he was looking to reap a healthy harvest. Never mind that those he sought to steal from were, in the main, as poor as him.

If you don't get given, you learn to take.

He felt legitimised in his intentions. Legitimised, but still broke. Every time he, 'accidentally,' bumped into someone in the crowd, he was rumbled and told to, "Fuck off," in no uncertain terms, so after a few such spats he wisely decided to keep his busy hands to himself. In Soweto, 1990 style, the name of the game was simply to get through another day unscathed, and the young man was street-smart enough to know when to quit his little caper for the sake of his future well-being. He could not hide his disappointment, but on those mean streets you find ways to get by.

I'll get more chances to duck and dive tomorrow.

Though life was tough, he supposed it could be worse, and decided to count his blessings by thinking about the people who meant the most to him. The first of those, his mother. Bettina Molome, was the glue that kept his family together after their rotten father had walked out one drunken night, never to return. Nobody missed the contemptable swine's brutal nature, but he had been the principal breadwinner, so his departure created a significant cavity for her to try to fill. Ever the multi-tasker, she worked tirelessly to make their basic dwelling habitable while scraping a meagre living as a sewing machinist in a downtown Johannesburg sweatshop, and when she got home, she utilised her considerable cooking skills to turn plain but affordable food into hearty nourishment.

There were two Molome children, Lenka and his elder sister, the beautiful but fragile Dikeledi. Her sufferings weighed on his mind every waking hour, for she was terminally ill, having fallen victim to the wretched curse of AIDS that cast its shadow over the entire continent, and her end was in sight. His desire to see her well again bordered on the obsessional, though he had no clue how to make that happen.

His only other close connection was to an aggressive little street gang, a unit strong enough *'to take arms against a sea of troubles'* if ever the need arose (not that he would relate to any of that Shakespearian tomfoolery; the realities of Soweto street life were more dramatic than anything dreamed up by the bard of Stratford). He felt a sense of brotherhood and belonging in their rag-tag company.

The young punk's controlling desire was to be a bigger man than his father ever was. That drunkard's dead-end dogsbody job had failed to drag the family out of poverty, so he intended to hustle, thieve, and fight his way to a better life because they needed him to start pulling his weight. Now that he was all grown up, it was time to get mean.

Don't mess with me – I'm a bad boy player!

He refused to clutter his mind with the implausible pie-in-the-sky bright new dawns of the ANC's activists; his future would be fashioned through his own words and deeds. This wannabe gangster yearned for recognition and respect; he craved the admiration (and more than anything, the fear) of the townsfolk. He wanted them to depend upon his patronage and be forever grateful; to look at him in awe. His long-suffering mother would surely then see beyond his criminal activities and take pride in his achievements.

I'm ready to change my own future – I don't need brother Mandela's help!

Soon he was home, pushing the flimsy and wholly inadequate wooden gate aside to get to the front door. Through the kitchen window, Bettina anxiously watched him approach and with a triumphal roar, shouted, "The boy is back!"

Dikeledi lay uncomfortably on the moth-eaten sofa in their tiny living room and recognised increasing relief in her mother's voice each time, "the boy," returned safely. He was too old to control now, so every moment that he was out of the house brought a dread of the trouble he might bring back. As he swept indoors to greet his skinny sister, they embraced in a loving hug.

"How's your day been?" she asked, hoping that some joy might have found a home in his rebel soul.

"Up to no good is my guess!" bellowed a world-weary cry from the kitchen.

"If you want to know mom, I went to the ANC rally up the road." With a wink aimed at Dikeledi he shouted, "Our great days will soon be here!"

His mother smiled to herself, hoping that her wayward son had finally absorbed the message, though her wisdom and maturity suggested that he was merely spinning her around for his own amusement.

"You listen good to those words, young man," she advised. "Brother Mandela is going to open up doors of opportunity for everyone in this town soon enough, you'll see. You are lucky – you'll live the best years of your life free to go wherever you want – to do whatever you want – to *be* whoever you want to be. That is if you don't squander them behind the bars of a prison cell."

Her problem child bristled at this barbed reference to his petty criminal activities (she was well aware of the delinquency inherent in his day-to-day existence), though he understood the sincere and absolute love at the source of her words of warning.

If only I could make mamma understand what it's like to be a teenager in the township. Maybe then she'd cut me a bit of slack.

Yeah, keep dreaming boy!

With her admonishments ringing in his ears, he visibly withdrew into himself, and the brooding returned, drawing Dikeledi's concern.

"What is it Lenka? What's wrong?"

"Nothing sis, nothing's wrong." His reassurance was just so much worthless effort, for both siblings knew that a cloud of old had returned to rain on the troubled youth.

He was dwelling on his mother's optimism for the post-apartheid world. Opportunity might, just might, come knocking for him, but when he looked at his pale, frail sister curled up in the foetal position, nursing a severe stomach-ache behind her fixed smile, he thought only of *her* opportunities, of *her* future. Or lack of one. And it made him want to cry. His poor Dikeledi would not see the arrival of this much-vaunted Utopia, for her time on earth, a time that had been plagued with little, save misery and hardship, was rapidly running out.

For over a decade, the HIV/AIDS virus had sown its insidious seeds of death across the globe, but its impact did not strike everywhere with equal ferocity; whereas Europe, the Americas, India and Australasia saw sporadic evidence of its dreaded blooms, on the African continent it was already delivering a bountiful harvest of carcasses. There were differences in the nature of its pollination too. The developed world still saw the scourge as a '*Gay Plague*', predominantly affecting homosexual men, but in Africa, both sexes felt the Reaper's scythe in equal numbers. There, the indigenous population felt the worst effects of its deadly spread, and because of a scarcity of finance, education, and treatment (in some regions these resources were not available at all) they could not rise to the challenge of combating it. As a result, while life expectancy of the continent's white population was comparable with the rest of the planet, blacks died much younger and at a far greater rate.

In South Africa, the Caucasian élite saw shantytowns as blots on the landscape; places where pestilence could find a safe haven; yet the country's finest medical minds began beating a path to these areas in their desire to understand more about the virus. The fear was that it might start to spread to the white world (which would not do at all!) so the government needed accurate data on the specific demographics most at risk and the number of carriers.

Statistical research showed that the black community had a liberal attitude to anal sex and was more sexually active than their white counterparts. These cultural differences were enough to suggest the possibility of an HIV/AIDS epidemic breaking out in the villages and shanties, but there was also an altogether more sinister contributor to the alarming number of carriers.

At the beginning of the 1990's, estimates suggested that almost a quarter of black males there would admit to committing the heinous crime of rape. Rape of women; of children too (South Africa had some of the highest incidences of child and baby rape in the world). A separate and hopelessly inadequate schools syllabus for black children (known as the Bantu Education) was set up to provide only basic skills for a labourer class, so it was tragically no surprise that, in some areas, girls were more likely to be raped than to read. The youths even had their own slang term for gang rape: *jackrolling*.

Lenka Molome and his feral friends had twice participated in brutal sex attacks on girls, showing a complete disregard for the physical or emotional damage suffered by their vulnerable victims. Sexual responsibility was low on their list of priorities, but he was soon to understand the dangers surrounding unprotected intercourse when disaster befell his sister in miserably vivid fashion.

Mercifully, Dikeledi did not succumb to HIV (and later, its deadly sleeping partner) through some random savage act; her troubles began after having consensual sex with an infected local boy. They were unaware of the dangers involved, such was the chronically poor state of sex education in Soweto at the time. Soon her young lover was dead and now her own funeral would not be far away. The fateful deterioration phase had begun, and her brother knew that unless divine miracles suddenly came into season, their time together was short.

"Get to the table you two, dinner is ready," their mother yelled.

That evening, there were three plates filled with enough chicken and potatoes to leave them all satisfied, though in truth, Dikeledi had no need for more than a morsel of the fayre on offer.

"Poor baby, does it hurt to eat?"

"A little mamma, but I'm alright, really I am."

A knowing glance from the matriarch said it all. She was prone to melancholy in her daily ways, and when her beautiful daughter entered the world, she assumed the responsibility for naming her. Dikeledi means, 'Tears' and this clairvoyant act reflected the harshness of the challenges that her child would eventually endure. By the time a baby boy joined the cast, Mr Molome had taken centre stage, determined to represent the masculine lineage appropriately. The boy's name, Lenka, means, 'Taker', and he was raised to grab every chance that came his way in life; legal or otherwise. In this respect, and only this, the son learned well from the father.

To lighten the mood, the ever-optimistic Dikeledi spoke up.

"What's tomorrow gonna bring, little brother? What are your plans?"

"Me and the boys are off to the city…" Bettina swiftly shot a glance towards her wayward son, eager to know more, "…to look for work." He stared hard at his mother's accusing look. "What? Why do look at me like that mamma? You're always telling me to get a job and now you give me the dead eyes when I say I'm gonna do just that!"

She steadied her heart rate for a second, then said, "Just make sure that is all you do up there tomorrow my boy. I don't like that crowd you hang out with - they are no good, the lot of them!"

"Be still mamma, they're my friends - they'll look for work too." To temper his mother's wariness, he brightened with false reassurance. "You should relax - your baby boy will make you a proud woman. You'll see. Our great days will soon be here! - remember? I took it all in today, see?"

31.

Chaos in the CBD

The next morning at ten o'clock, the youngest resident of the Molome household stirred from his deepest slumbers in response to a vigorous assault on his obstinate front door.

"Hey Lenka!"

"Come out, man!"

"It's time to get your arse out of bed!"

Around the back of the tiny home, a further cry of, "Wake up you lazy *kaffir!*" seeped through his bedroom window.

Mother Molome had packed herself off to work some hours earlier, so Dikeledi opened the door, intent on shooing the unwelcome invaders from the premises. Wrapped in a shawl and shivering from fever, she looked considerably distressed.

"Go away! He's not at home - you've missed him. He's trying his luck in the city, so you'll have to fend for yourselves today."

For a second the motley crew fell silent, though they were all of one mind; they could see the ravages of the AIDS virus upon her, but her pretty features were still discernible, stoking a burgeoning furnace of teenage lust amongst the assembly. One or two thought of what they would like to do to her if she really was on her own in the house.

Just then, her brother appeared, breaking the awkwardness of the moment.

"Don't listen to my sister, yeah? I'm here - I'll be out in a minute." Wearing just a pair of scruffy shorts, he rubbed his eyes and returned to his room to get ready for the day's action as Dikeledi brusquely shut the door on his expectant friends.

When he emerged, their unit was complete. They were eight in number and Molome made nine; all kitted out in their obligatory cheap replica football shirts, crappy denim jeans, and fake Adidas or Nike trainers. One of the gang, a swarthy, arrogant wannabee who carried a permanent king-sized chip on his shoulder, issued a challenge to the latecomer.

"Do ya want to play with the big boys today Lenka? Are you up for some *real* fun?"

His street name was, 'Hitman,' because of his propensity to cause violent confrontation, and he had his sights set on making mischief. Their eyes met and Molome rose to the bait.

"Sure thing! You know me - I'm always ready to play! So what's cookin' in your kitchen today?"

The Hitman smiled, then replied, "Put this on your plate, man."

He slowly produced a .25 calibre Browning automatic pistol from the back of his jeans. The weapon was small and light, so it was easy to conceal underneath his overhanging football shirt, and he began waving it like a trophy over his head in front of his impressed audience.

They surveyed Molome's face for a reaction, but he remained calm, while realising that things were going to get serious. He knew he must not show any outward signs of weakness, or his tawdry gang of desperados would smell blood and duly install his rival as their new Alpha male. Expressionless, he asked, "Where did you get that from?"

Evasively, the Hitman answered, "I know people," implying that he had the more impressive gangster credentials because of his access to weaponry.

"Big fucking deal, brother! Anyone can pick up a gun round here, we all know that! Waving a wand is one thing, but using it is something else, big boy!" Molome thought he had reasserted his authority by defiantly ridiculing his rival's power play, but there was more to the Hitman than mere peacock preening; he had a strategy designed to win control of the gang.

"If you're such a fucking tough guy Lenka, you can have this thing to play with today. Show me you know what it's for, yeah? Let's see if you can put it to good use and get us some money." With this, he handed the pistol over. The cold steel of the firearm made Molome's body stiffen, despite the brilliance of the July sunshine.

He always knew that he was going to have to prove himself one day, and now the time had come to step things up a gear. Obviously, it was not going to be a simple task for his motley crew to slip into town, steal some cash and hastily scuttle back to the sanctuary of the township, but if he completed his mission successfully, he would cement his standing as the leader of the gang.

I need to show them all why I'm the Taker!

Scowling defiantly, he stuck out his chin and rallied his troops.

"Let's go then - who's with me?" The sheep dutifully gathered around their shepherd, and with the gun as his staff, he marched them to the bus station, bound for the Central Business District (known locally as the CBD).

Four years earlier, as part of the gradual dismantling process of the apartheid system, the government had repealed regulations which prohibited black people from leaving designated ghettos and entering 'white' neighbourhoods without an identification book (known as a *dompas*, a word that in Afrikaans means, "stupid pass"). With the Pass Laws gone, Molome's disaffected youths were free to wander around central Johannesburg unchallenged, but despite the relaxation of the legislation, wherever they went, suspicious Caucasian faces trailed them.

Under such claustrophobic conditions, Molome realised that the gun was more of a poisoned chalice than a trophy worth idolatry. Tucked into the back of his waistband, he had its shaft wedged between his buttocks, which made walking uncomfortable, and he could not pretend to be cool like his big screen heroes. Clearly, movies really were different to reality. His shirt flowed loosely over his trousers to conceal the metallic meal ticket from view. Crucially he could still get to it quickly if needs be.

The gang were growing impatient and their eagerness for some sport was apparent.

"So what are we waiting for?" asked one.

"Yeah, when are we gonna see some action?" complained another.

"Is that weapon in your trousers as useless as the one in your shorts?" joked a third.

At this challenge to his manhood, Molome snapped.

"Just shut the fuck up will you? Are you all fucking stupid or what? Do you really think I'm gonna wave this thing around in broad daylight, you dumb asses?"

The Hitman reacted to his agitated rant and decided to apply a bit of pressure.

"Well what are you gonna do with it then? We want some money and you've got the right tool to get it. So get busy, yeah?..."

Like two rutting stags, they stared confrontationally into each other's eyes in a spaghetti western style stand-off. The general hustle and bustle of shoppers shuffling through those busy streets faded into the background as an uneasy stillness filled the space between them, and the other gang members became acutely aware of the importance of the moment.

Suddenly the focus of Molome's gaze diverted when he caught sight of an overweight middle-aged white man approaching a First National Bank ATM machine directly behind his adversary. The familiar lunchtime cashpoint queues were conspicuous by their absence, and he recognised that this was the right time, the right place to make his move. In the blink of an eye, he pushed the Hitman out of his way and produced his pistol, pressing it to the small of the man's back. His cohorts were quick to respond, forming a circle around their target, crowding his space and disorienting him.

"Right, you fat bastard - get as much money out of that cash machine as you can, then give me your card and pin number, or I'll blow you away to your white fucking heaven - have you got that?" The man began to breathe heavily, breaking into a profuse sweat (a condition mirrored by his assailant). Two thousand rand passed between them.

"So what's the pin number, fatty! Come on - I want it NOW!"

Gasping for air, the confused victim whispered, "Six… one…seven…" Despite the fact that he had just tapped his four-digit code into the machine only a few seconds earlier, his stressed mind went blank and he struggled to remember the last number.

"Hurry up!"

"He's playing for time!" warned the Hitman.

Molome jammed the gun harder into the man's back to sharpen his thoughts, but due to the pressure of the situation, he started to sway, then lose control of his balance, and within a further second or two, he had collapsed to the floor. People passing by suddenly became aware of the scene playing out in front of them and a woman screamed in panic.

"Jesus, you've shot him!" shouted one gang member and their cordon fragmented to reveal the prostrate victim gasping for air on the pavement.

"Let's get out of here!" bellowed another, racing away in no particular direction.

The undisciplined rat-like rabble then splintered off to every point of the compass with as much haste as they could muster, leaving their weapon-wielding leader rooted to the spot. Shaking uncontrollably, he stood over the fallen man and felt a dozen pairs of eyes boring into the back of his head. Just then, someone called out for police assistance and in an adrenaline-fuelled torrent of emotion, he pointed his pistol at the gathering crowd to keep them at bay, while taking a dozen purposeful strides towards the clear white light of escape. An imaginary neon sign flickered into life before him, emblazoned with a simple message: "RUN!" and he bolted as the sound of sirens cut through the chaos.

The chase was on.

In central Johannesburg, taking flight was not the easy matter that it would have been in the township; here the police force cared about crime; here perpetrators of criminal acts were much more likely to face the full retribution of the law. Especially if they had black faces and committed their offences against white folk.

Soweto's streets were familiar to the hunted punk, but he found boltholes of refuge harder to find in the CBD. After the briefest of pursuits, he found himself trapped in a dead end behind the Glen Shopping Centre, off Harrison Street, only two blocks from the crime scene, with the police bearing down. He skulked behind two refuse bins in an alleyway and aimed his pistol directly at a young patrolman who was bravely racing towards him.

"Stay back or I'll shoot!" he roared.

The fresh-faced officer was barely out of cadet school, yet he had the confidence to take control of the situation.

"Put the gun down on the floor, sir. It'll be better for you in the long run if you do as I say."

No one had ever called Molome, "sir," and the word temporarily threw him, before his aggression returned.

"You've got to be joking me, man! Just how the fuck is that going to be better for me? You dumb white piggy!"

The reply was no more than a defence mechanism, for he knew the hopelessness of his predicament. Less than ten minutes earlier he had been staring down the Hitman, and here he was, involved in another life-changing situation. The officer replied, "Look sir, you haven't killed anyone, and you haven't tried to hurt me. Right now, you're only looking at assault with a deadly weapon - nothing more than that. Try to think clearly and don't do anything to make things worse."

"What do you mean? What about the fat guy?"

"No shots have been fired - yet."

In the confusion of his escape, there was no time to assess what had actually taken place and now it dawned on Molome that the man at the bank had dropped to the floor without the help of a bullet. As his heartbeat began to slow, a patrol car arrived on the scene, and he knew that the game was up. His thoughts turned to his mother; to Dikeledi too. He imagined their faces contorted in grief once they knew of his disgrace. The prospect crushed him. By the time the rookie constable approached his makeshift barricade and gently removed the gun from his nervously shaking hand, he was sobbing uncontrollably.

Once the other two officers from the patrol car took over, he quickly regretted the wisdom of his meek surrender. Without ceremony, they bundled him into the back of their vehicle and reined a series of hefty blows on his face and body, to the unrestrained anger of their youthful colleague.

"Hey, leave the guy alone! He gave himself up! Get your hands off him!"

Further police support reached the alley to find all three arresting officers trading punches. Raised voices and bruised egos combined to create an unedifying mêlée, but when the dust eventually settled, the young patrolman found himself pinned against a wall in receipt of a severe reprimand from several of his disgruntled peers. Meanwhile, a single siren heralded the patrol car's departure, with a handcuffed Lenka Molome in tow, and order returned to the CBD's streets once again.

32.

The Carter clan

The Houghton suburb of northern Johannesburg embodied the white South African dream; it was affluent, middle-class and a world away from the mean streets of Soweto. And that was exactly how its residents intended it to stay. For all the talk about the eventual handover of power to the black majority, Houghton and similarly leafy enclaves around the country were determined to pull up their drawbridges and keep themselves to themselves.

Professional people abounded; doctors, lawyers, teachers, and police officers enjoyed everything that South Africa had to offer there in terms of quality of life. The community was close-knit and weekend garden barbeques were commonplace.

On the Saturday after Lenka Molome's arrest, charcoal crackled below sizzling skillets of chicken and prime beef at the Carter family home on the corner of Sixth Street and Fourteenth Avenue. The furore at the CBD during the week inevitably provoked much discussion amongst the invited guests, because the youngest Carter boy, Dominic, was the rookie police officer who had faced the gunman down before entering into a scuffle with his own roughhouse colleagues.

His parents, Julius and June, were United Kingdom nationals who had immigrated to South Africa in the late 1950's. Solidly middle-class and conservative in their ways, they found the post-war shift towards socialism at home rather distasteful, initiating a desire to pursue a better existence in a more convivial atmosphere abroad. At the time of their departure, June felt a pang or two of disloyalty for abandoning Harold Macmillan's Tory government to their fate at the hands of the progressive proletariat, but she accepted that there was little they could do by themselves to resist the disruptive power of militant trade unionism. And they were much too polite to try anyway.

Back in London, Julius had worked in the forensics department of New Scotland Yard, and he met June when she took a job as a laboratory assistant at the same facility. It was a case of love at first sight and their colleagues instantly recognised the comfort they derived in each other's company; they were two peas from the same pod, so it came as no surprise to anyone when their short courtship turned into a, "til death do us part," marriage. With enthusiastic ardour, the intrepid adventurers immediately began making plans for a new life overseas.

Any UK national blessed with a good education, bright prospects and money in the bank could expect a hearty welcome in the thriving Southern hemisphere, and after discussing every option thoroughly, they chose to make South Africa their home. Once the necessary paperwork was completed, they said tearful farewells to friends and families and set off to plant roots in one of Johannesburg's picture postcard suburbs. Houghton society was quick to embrace their new neighbours, and their switch from New Scotland Yard to the South African Police Service proved equally seamless.

As is reasonable to expect, not every new experience was a welcome one, and Julius and June found their adopted country's apartheid laws morally reprehensible. Their hostility to Fascism during World War Two meant they were uncomfortable about living under rules based on racial lines, but they were pragmatic traditionalists at heart with a deeply ingrained respect for the law and kept their dissent to themselves. Despite their misgivings, they thought that their adopted country offered an idyllic lifestyle in which to start a family and in the fullness of time, they established a modest dynasty with the birth of their sons, Cornelius and Dominic.

The ever-so-slightly-out-of-touch parents had burdened their children with Christian names more commonplace at an English public school than the stockbroker belt of Johannesburg, but still the boys thrived. South Africa's climate, food and environment are particularly conducive to the production of healthy specimens, and a schooling in the rules of rugby and cricket taught them to play hard, but also to play fair. They harboured a collective sense of right and wrong, and upon the completion of his studies, the eldest, Cornelius announced his intention to join his father in the police force.

He possessed a high degree of intelligence and rapidly developed the necessary skills to forge a career as a detective inspector. While the job often taxed him, he found it stimulating too, and putting bad guys away gave him a sense of elation that could never be replicated in a conventional nine-to-five occupation. He rapidly matured, both inside and outside work, and before his twenty-second birthday he had met Kim, the woman who was to become his life partner. Like his parents, they wasted no time in exchanging vows, and before long, the Carter lineage expanded once more.

As we have seen, when Dominic was old enough, he joined, 'the family business,' too, and together this second generation of public servants worked at the CBD station house on the corner of Delvers Street and Market Street. Their colleagues quickly noticed the differences in their temperaments as the younger sibling struggled to find his feet in a rigidly autocratic organisation. He lacked his brother's effortless charm, and the gentle pragmatism of their parents also failed to filter through to the passionate youngster.

Dominic was something of an idealist; politically savvy and impatient to see his country shift towards racial equality. He wanted to be part of the process of integration and warmly embraced all the challenges to come, though his enthusiasm for a level playing field in South African society perturbed many senior figures and fellow students at the police training college. One trait that he did inherit from his parents was an innate self-confidence, and this gave him a thick enough skin to ride the comments of, "*kaffir* lover," and, "black boy's bitch," that had dogged him ever since.

Julius and June applauded their youngest son's disdain of the apartheid system and were proud that he chose to challenge the *status quo* as part of the law enforcement community, rather than from the safe distance of a journalistic or broadcasting career. Their boy was made of tough stuff, though it concerned them that his principles left him at loggerheads with others in the service.

Trying to shield Lenka Molome from a vicious assault had not endeared him to his fellow officers, so the weekend barbeque was an opportunity for the Carter clan to discuss the issue privately in familiar, familial surroundings.

Cornelius, Kim and their children arrived early, laden with gifts of beer and cuts of beef for grilling. The older sibling already knew that his brother's brawl had led to much heated debate at the station house, so as soon as the provisions were refrigerated, he got down to filtering the facts from the fiction. Taking Dominic to one side in the spacious garden at the back of the house, he commenced his interrogation.

"I hear you had a bit of fun on Thursday - want to tell me about it?" His attitude was both protective and authoritative. The response was predictably defensive.

"If you're asking about my dust-up with those two goons who were beating up my suspect, what's there to tell?"

"Well, for a start you can explain to me how you think that kind of behaviour looks to the public? How do you expect civilians to have faith in the police department when they see its officers fighting amongst themselves?"

Dominic's youthful passion expressed itself more vociferously now.

"So what do you want me to do then, Corny? Am I supposed to look the other way while two of our guys knock the living daylights out of a defenceless black teenager? Is that the kind of thing you think civilians should see instead?"

"Of course not…but they'd rather see a suspect being restrained than officers whacking the crap out of one another - surely you can see that?"

"You're defending them then, aren't you? Admit it!"

As a progressive member of the department himself, Cornelius bristled with indignation.

"Don't throw that racism garbage at me - save your lectures for the boys on the beat."

"Well that's the problem! The behaviour of some of those bastards is every bit as bad as anything I've seen from the criminals we're supposed to put away."

"Dom, you know the procedure if you've got an issue with a fellow officer, so why didn't you report the incident to the desk sergeant at the station?"

"Oh come on! You know old Hendricks plays deaf when it comes to criticism of his patrolmen. Anyway, he was horsing around with Inspector Daalmans when I got back and they both promised to rip me a new arsehole if I hit one of our own again."

"What - 'Chrome-Dome' Daalmans was there?"

Douglas Daalmans suffered from galloping alopecia and was particularly sensitive to any mention of his balding pate, so his colleagues at the stationhouse wisely reserved their mocking comments regarding his affliction until he was out of earshot. He was also notoriously old-school with regard to the treatment of black suspects in custody, and Cornelius knew all about his reputation for brutality.

"Too right he was. He frogmarched me into one of the interview rooms and said I'd better watch my back out on patrol in future. He was threatening me, saying that if I wind up getting hurt, well that's just too bad. Something tells me *he* won't give a shit about what civilians will think if one of his pals catches me off guard and lets loose with their baton."

"Well take his advice then, dummy! Can't you keep your crusading instincts in check for now? That crazy bastard was bound to get worked up when he heard about an officer protecting a black suspect - you know what he's like. Look, these apartheid days are all but done and dusted, so just try to keep your head down until the new regime is up and running. That's when you'll be able to make your mark."

"So until then I'm supposed to ignore what I see and let those racist assholes get away with common assault?"

"I'm just telling you to use your head a bit more, ok? That's if you want to keep it on top of your shoulders at any rate."

Dominic huffed, puffed, and fumed, but he recognised the wisdom in his older brother's advice. Care must be his watchword from now on if he wanted a productive career in law enforcement. To lighten the lecture, Cornelius returned to the topic of Daalmans and his shiny skull.

"Did his Gorbachev mark start throbbing when he tore into you?"

"I swear it changed colour! It went from deep purple to bright red!" (The mark in question was the result of a baseball bat whack that Daalmans received from a black activist during the 1976 Sharpeville riots, and when Mikhail Gorbachev became General Secretary of the Soviet Union, the officers of the CBD immediately likened his famous birthmark to their aggressive colleague's battle scar.)

"Boy oh boy! I would have loved to have seen that crazy head of his throbbing in the sunlight!" They giggled heartily as they had always done, before Cornelius closed their conversation in a more sombre tone. "Seriously though Dom - promise me you'll be careful from now on, eh? You're the smart one here - we can't afford to lose good guys like you!"

With that, they touched hands and rejoined the gathering.

Their mother guessed the nature of their chat and decided to put a positive spin on the week's events.

"What do you think of your brave younger brother then Corny? He confronted that armed robber in broad daylight. A lot of civilians could have been hurt - killed even - but Dominic brought him in without a single shot being fired."

"Oh, he did well this week mom - really great - but he got lucky too, and I was just out there telling him to be careful in future. He needs to learn how to draw on the experience of his fellow officers - the good ones anyway - 'cos they've got a lot to offer an enthusiastic pupil in difficult situations. If he's open-minded enough to accept their differences - how they approach the job, all of that - then one day, their knowledge and skills just might save his life."

Cornelius then exchanged a knowing glance with his father. The old fellow also understood that maverick behaviour was an unwelcome hindrance in the police force. Julius appreciated his eldest son's ability to get into Dominic's head and felt grateful for his influence. He knew that the boy had to find a way to add maturity to his fiery nature or that hot head of his would end up bringing sadness to their happy home.

33.

Feeding fears and pointing fingers

The exhausting journey from Las Vegas to Johannesburg had taken its toll on Gordon Rimmer. Thus far, he had endured twenty-one hours of travel time (including a lengthy stop at Hartsfield-Jackson airport in Atlanta, Georgia) without rest, and as his plane finally touched down on African soil, his spirits were flagging.

Long haul flights made him stressful at the best of times, but events back in Vegas only exacerbated his discomfort. While watching TV in the departure lounge at Hartsfield-Jackson, he caught a *CNN* bulletin that revealed the news of Barry Shackleton's suicide, and his thoughts immediately went out to the deceased's family; particularly the children who had turned their backs on their father in his final days.

How will the UK's press react to this?

For a week, his bone-shaking AIDS story had left residual aftershocks back home. The tabloids in particular fed on the public's fear of this incurable, mysterious virus, asking questions such as: -

IS SAME - SEX INFIDELITY ON THE INCREASE? (*Daily Express*)

THE GAY PLAGUE - HOW FEARFUL SHOULD WE BE? (*The Horizon*)

HOMOS IN HIDING – DOES YOUR HUBBY THINK IN PINK? (*The Sun*).

On another day, Rimmer would have had an opinion on all the issues raised (particularly how they veered from reasoned debate to rabid hysteria, depending on their target audience) but at that moment, all he could think about was reaching Sun City in one piece and crashing out on a comfortable hotel bed. He picked up a Volkswagen hire car at Jan Smuts International and began the final leg of his journey in a fog of fatigue. The airport, situated to the north-west of Johannesburg, is a two-hour drive from his destination, but it seemed like ten.

Gambling was banned in South Africa, but when the government declared the land of Bophuthatswana to be an independent state, and therefore not liable to the same restrictions, shrewd businessman Sol Kerzner took advantage of the opportunity to create an adult playground there. Consequently, Sun City officially opened its doors for business on the 7th of December 1979.

Rimmer found his way to the Entertainment Centre (the venue for the *Snooker Showdown*) via one of two busy Skytrains that convey guests from the remote parking lot, and by the time he finally reached the main hotel, he needed to pinch himself to know that he had left Las Vegas at all, for the same kinds of distracting ostentation screamed their demands for his attention. Such was his state of exhaustion however, that slumber proved more attractive than the neon nonsense of his surroundings, so he found his room and closed the world away until the break of the following day.

In the morning, though his head still kept fuzzy company with the last remnants of jet lag, he found a newsstand selling UK newspapers and surveyed the headlines. *The Guardian*'s left him feeling particularly uncomfortable: -

DID PRESS INTRUSION INDUCE SHACKLETON SUICIDE?

He paused to reflect on his role in the tragedy.

Should I shoulder some responsibility for what happened?

No – I'm not having that – I was only doing my job!

Barry would have killed himself whether he gave me that interview or not – the man was in a terrible state of fear and confusion.

If the story had gone to some other hack, they would probably have gone on to savage him – then I might agree that the press had pushed him to his fate.

At least I was sympathetic to the poor man's plight…

Despite his protestations of innocence, he was fearful that he may indeed have played a part in the suicide of poor, desperate Barry Shackleton. Whatever the rights and wrongs of his role in the proceedings, he was powerless to affect the views of others on the subject and as a professional journalist, he needed to recalibrate his brain and concentrate on today's stories, today's news. Distressing as Shackleton's death was, he had a new job to focus on and must immerse himself in the here and now.

Rest In Peace, Barry, I did my best for you…

I truly did…

34.

A disappointing arrangement

Gordon Rimmer exhaled deeply for a second and took stock of his manic week. Within seven crazy days, he had: -

a) bagged the biggest sporting scoop of the year.

b) passed up on his dream assignment at the World Cup Finals.

c) flown to Africa to cover Marcus Botha's meaningless snooker tournament.

d) begun an unsolicited investigation into the same man's nefarious past.

The logistical difficulties arising from that final task would require some serious thought, because Botha's accomplice/ accuser Pieter Hertzog was a resident of Johannesburg, and as we know, Rimmer was stuck in Sun City.

For now, while the world's finest snooker stars prepared for the *Showdown* in the practice area, he decided to familiarise himself with the spectacular complex that played host to the event. Besides the ubiquitous slot machines, shopping malls, nightclubs, bars and restaurants, there were two world class golf courses on the site. Adventurous nature lovers could even book a safari to the Pilanesberg National Park.

Let's see Vegas try to match that!

A magnificent addition to the resort, *The Palace of the Lost City,* was due to open in 1992 replete with sculptures, artworks and magnificent fountains, and Rimmer recognised a country waking up from its repressive recent history and looking towards the future with confidence. Listening to local voices around the restaurants and gaming tables, he felt a perceptible buzz of anticipation about the upcoming tournament. South Africa's lengthy expulsion from most international sports had denied its homegrown cricket, rugby, and athletics superstars the opportunity to display their talents on a global stage, so its government saw this chance to host a potentially significant snooker competition as a stepping stone towards global acceptance once more.

To show their commitment, they offered generous financial support to Sun City's administrators, ensuring that all sixteen gladiators of the green baize received £20,000 worth of bets in the casino and an unlimited bar tab. Predictably, snooker's self-styled, 'People's Champion,' Alex '*Hurricane*' Higgins took full advantage of the facilities before and after his exuberant appearances on the practice tables, creating considerable anxiety for Botha's ever-present public relations team. It was important for them to surround the event in positivity, so they attributed his excessive behaviour to natural high-spirits and a relish for the challenge ahead.

The proceedings gained extra sparkle when Ben St. Claire and his glamour model girlfriend Daniella Lae breezed into town. South African television schedules always made space for snooker's annual World Championship, so St. Claire was a familiar face to the locals, and Lae's appearances in celebrity magazines during her fling with Gideon Judge had made her hot property too. The paparazzi were persuaded to expect a charismatic couple in the Bruce Willis and Demi Moore mould, so an explosion of flash bulbs greeted their arrival. Hopes were high for a procession of push-and-shove melees between security men and celebrity snappers during the following fortnight, but once the dust had settled on that choreographed pantomime, photo opportunities of the pair at play were rarer than hen's teeth. To the frustration of an expectant press, they proved to be inexplicably camera shy, preferring to spend their time holed up in their hotel room, leading local hacks to rip up the Willis/Moore analogy and mock their behaviour as, "Garbo-esque."

While the hotel staff were jumpy around Higgins and distracted by the attention drawn to the St. Claire/Lae romance, they had no such anxieties regarding snooker's two greatest players. For a decade, Steve Davis had been the undisputed king of the sport; his mastery only matched by an obsessional dedication to his craft. Ever the consummate professional, he would spend hour after hour at the practice facility, honing his skills on one table while keeping a close eye on twenty-one-year-old Stephen Hendry, snooker's New Kid on the Block, who meticulously matched his endeavours on another. Hendry had shaken the snooker establishment that April by sensationally claiming the world crown (becoming the youngest player ever to do so) and his sights were set on eclipsing all of Davis's heady achievements over the coming years.

All the elements were in place for magic to emerge over the following few days: Higgins, an incendiary force of nature, was primed to explode at any moment; St. Claire lay poised to unleash his pulse-quickening potential; Davis and Hendry, two polished diamonds of precision and artistry, were ready to astonish all comers with their unparalleled brilliance.

Yet still Gordon Rimmer had the feeling that there was something missing; a can't-quite-put-your-finger-on-it *something*. Then it finally dawned on him.

I'm the only UK sports reporter here – nobody else gives a toss for this nonsense!

I expected to see one or two of the Las Vegas crowd, or some new faces flown in directly from London perhaps, but the specialist darts correspondents must have gone straight back to the UK while everyone else has trotted off to Italia 90.

Their editors all know that Rome, the venue for the World Cup Final, is the place to be – not sodding Sun City!

Away from the practice tables, football-frenzy had grabbed many of the snooker stars too. Pockets of players relaxed by drawing on their betting allowance to predict the outcome of World Cup group matches shown on the local TV networks.

Football is a universal religion now – Botha will never alter that!

What a mug!

Crowds are only down in the UK because of hooliganism and mass unemployment – social and economic problems – not from a lack of interest.

There's no hope of snooker or darts ever seriously matching football's popularity.

Naturally, Rimmer felt envious of his peers, but he becalmed his green-eyed monster somewhat by acknowledging that this isolated and ignored corner of the world might provide him with a bigger story than anyone could possibly imagine.

There was one more day of acclimatisation and practice ahead for the tournament competitors, and he spent his downtime profitably by following up his one and only lead on the Botha investigation. Back in Las Vegas, all hope of maintaining a dialogue with Pieter Hertzog got lost in the media scramble for the Barry Shackleton scoop, but the trail had not gone completely cold because the big Boer left his home number at the Sands hotel reception with his farewell note.

Rimmer made the call, which went straight to a recorded answer phone greeting.

"Hi Pieter, it's your new pal from Vegas! Gordon - the tabloid tittie snapper! Remember I told you I'd dropped the glamour model stuff and moved into full-time sports photography? Well you'll never believe where your best mate Marcus-bloody-Botha has sent me now? I'm in Sun City to capture the action from his new snooker tournament! You must have heard about that? I'll be busy for the first week 'cos the early stages are day/night affairs, but once rounds one and two are completed it'll be an evening-only event, so I'll have plenty of time to kill during the afternoons - easy money, eh! I can be in Johannesburg in a couple of hours, so let's meet up if you're free, ok?"

He left his contact details and an anxious couple of hours later, Hertzog got in touch to say that they could meet at his office in the *Transvaal Mineral Mining Corporation* building (one of the Central Business District's most impressive structures). He would need to know the time and day well in advance in order to rearrange his own busy schedule of meetings.

"If you'll do that for me boy, then I'm happy to oblige," he said.

Rimmer needed quantifiable information concerning the Head Honcho's complicity in multiple acts of murder and thus far, all he had to go on was Hertzog's drunken boast made in a faraway bar of a faraway land. Getting his man to confirm the slaying of *TMMC* employees would be another thing entirely in the morning light of a domestic dawn, and such a conversation was hardly likely to occur inside the very nerve centre of the company in question; nobody drops bazookas into their own back yard.

With only a small window of opportunity at his disposal he had no choice but to accept the terms on offer, though the best outcome he could now expect from the encounter was a strengthening of their relationship. If things went well, he intended to press for a further (hopefully more enlightening) meeting free from the interested glances of suspicious colleagues.

Disappointments notwithstanding, the rendezvous was duly set up for seven days hence, time enough for him to prepare a series of open-ended, informal questions that he could casually drop into their conversation without arousing suspicion. This was critical because Hertzog's testimony would clearly have serious implications for his own future.

The challenge was frightening and exciting in equal measure, but all that lay a week away and there was more mundane (but necessary) work to be done beforehand in Sun City...

35.

Here comes the Judge!

To the *Snooker Showdown* then. The early rounds ground on towards the inevitability of a final between Steve Davis and Stephen Hendry, while Gordon Rimmer struggled to create extra interest for his readers back home. Then, on day four, an unexpected stroke of luck came his way when Gideon Judge blew into town, with the stated intention of consoling his good friend Alex Higgins after the enigmatic maverick's early exit from the tournament.

Higgins had long-since faded as a major force in the sport, and his fondness for the gaming tables and bars around the complex hardly helped his match-play preparations. Now that his part in the proceedings was over, he decided to have some fun, and Judge's timely arrival increased the prospects for mayhem. To add further spice to this volatile cocktail, there was the possibility of a confrontation between the rocker and his old flame Daniella Lae, so Rimmer puckered up to steal more kisses from Dame Fortune's inviting lips.

First, the Barry Shackleton scoop - now if I'm lucky, there's another big story brewing here!

And that'd be on top of the chance to expose Botha to murder charges …

If this hot streak runs on, I'll soon be able to quit The Horizon for a better job - and with more money!

But surely I can't get lucky again?

Well, why not?

I've been a good boy, haven't I?

Didn't I protect Susan from my boss's predatory snooping?

Dammit, yes!

This really could be my year after all!

He spotted, '*The Wild Man of Rock*,' with, '*The Hurricane*,' propping up one of the hotel's bars and audaciously introduced himself.

"Hello boys - bad luck Alex. I didn't think you got the run of the table yesterday. With a bit of luck you'd have won that match," he lied, receiving an irritable grunt for his troubles. Turning his attention to Judge, he said, "Remember me Gideon? I'm Gordon Rimmer from *The Horizon* - we met at the Priory when I was covering Terry Malloy's rehab story."

"Jesus, not another fuckin' newshound! What have I gotta do to escape you lot!" The reply was just playful exasperation at the kind of press intrusion that everyone knew he really craved. "Blimey mate, this is some small world - I've just been back there for another week of treatment from your missus! You've got a good 'un there my friend." Clearly, Judge knew nothing about Rimmer's split with his partner, but then, there was no reason why he should; he only became aware of the tenacious Scot after noticing him around the Roehampton clinic during Malloy's recuperation. "I couldn't figure out at first why they let you through the door there 'til I heard you were seein' Professor Somerfield."

"Well that isn't exactly true - we didn't get together until after those interviews with Terry began."

"Is that right? Christ, what an operator you are then! Not only do you manage to get past the security and bag yourself a big exclusive story, but you end up banging one of the staff as well! How did you do that, man? Hey, Alex - this guy is one sharp fucker!"

An embarrassed Rimmer replied, "Well perhaps it's because I stuck to my word when I said I wouldn't expose anyone else who was there while the Terry Malloy series ran. Cast your mind back - did I ever mention seeing you at that time?"

"My memory ain't exactly trustworthy, but I don't remember seeing any tall tales coming out of that place, no. Fair play to you, man - I feel a bit more comfortable now, so do you wanna join us?"

Higgins, however, was less enamoured of spending time in the presence of the press, so he took himself off to one of the card tables while Rimmer broached a sore subject.

"Do you know that Daniella Lae is here with Ben St. Claire?"

Judge's face turned a little pale at the mention of her name, but he refused to duck the issue.

"Yeah, and while I'm here I want to have a private word with her if I get the chance - get stuff off my chest. I want to help her - just like your missus has helped me. The prof has put me on the right road again - in fact, thanks to her, I'm actually off the booze! I know that's hard to believe, but I'm trying. Obviously, given my chequered past, I can't say how long I'll stick to it...after all, a promise of sobriety from me ain't really worth much, is it?" Rimmer threw a quick glance at the singer's drink. "It's pure orange juice - check it out, go on, taste it. That's why *The Hurricane*'s so quick to scarper - he's told me I'm no fuckin' good to him if I'm not up for a party!"

With the purity of the refreshment quickly confirmed, Rimmer's next question concerned the details of Judge's intended advice to Lae.

"You don't strike me as the secretive type Gideon, so what is it that you want to say to Danielle exactly?"

"Oh no, no way man, you don't get me like that! I'm not goin' into specifics with you. I just want her to be honest with herself about some things, you know?"

"Well, I can't honestly say that I do know, unless you give me some details, but it sounds like there might be a scoop hidden in there..."

"If there is, it's gotta come from her, not me. Professor Somerfield got me to realise that it's truth that counts, nothing else. All the rest is just so much bullshit and while I'm here, I want to share that with Dani."

"Well, if the pair of you do meet up, I hope your little chat goes well - though, to be perfectly frank, I doubt that she'll be too pleased that you're here. Neither will Ben. Anyway, you know where to come afterwards if you want to shed some light on the things you're hinting at, ok?"

"Sure enough, Mr. Newspaperman. But hey, wish me luck, yeah? For your old lady's sake?"

Rimmer thought it unwise to complicate their developing relationship by correcting Judge's assumption that Susan was still his partner, so he made his exit with a hearty, "Good luck," and returned to the action at the tournament.

Alex Higgins had quickly grown tired of this sober version of his friend, so

Judge decided to quit the bar and enquire at the reception desk for St. Claire and Lae's room number. A star-struck female receptionist happily passed on this private information.

"That would be Room 212 sir - and can I just say that I'm a huge fan of yours!"

The rocker did not hear her compliment, for without pausing to consider the consequences of his next move, he rushed up to the second floor unannounced.

Knocking on the door with a bellicose cry of, "Room service!" the incorrigible rogue burst in on the couple; newly regained self-confidence bursting from every pore of his impetuous, but well-meaning frame. He was on a mission of Salvation, hoping to encourage his former lover to confront her alcohol and drug addictions.

In typically chaotic fashion, during his dramatic entrance, he managed to stumble into a bedside table, sending a fog-like white mist of high-grade cocaine into the air. While snooker's hottest property frantically snorted up the residue from several broken lines of Class A illegality, a startled Lae screamed in panic.

"Gideon! What do you think you're doing, you idiot? Get the fuck out of our room!"

The mayhem left Judge even more bemused than usual and he stared at her boyfriend's wired expression in disbelief.

"Bloody hell - she hasn't got you into it now, has she? You're supposed to be the fuckin' *'Milky-Bar Kid'*!"

By now, Lae was hysterical.

"Ben, kick this old bastard out right now!"

Slavishly following his girlfriend's order, St. Claire swung a frenzied fist into the face of the intruder, bloodying his nose. The blow lit the touch paper for a serious ruckus to begin, and Judge dragged the younger man to the ground, laying into him with a barrage of knuckle bruising punches and vicious kicks. The commotion was audible to terrified guests in the neighbouring suite, and they immediately contacted the hotel reception desk and the police, raising concerns of a danger to life and limb.

Hotel security staff raced to the room and quickly separated the two men, but despite their best attempts to keep the incident under wraps, luck was not on their side. Before they could clear up the mess, four police officers arrived at the scene to conduct interviews with the individuals involved.

When the (cocaine) dust finally settled on the unruly fiasco, Gideon Judge, Ben St. Claire, and Daniella Lae were all taken down to the nearest station house for further questioning.

Police officials charged the glamour couple with possession of Class A drugs, while crisis managers from the hotel saw to it that Judge went on his merry way with nothing more than a caution for damaging a chair during the scuffle.

Once again, Gordon Rimmer found himself in the right place at the right time when a big story broke. With customary aplomb, he informed the London office about the alternative Sun City Showdown that had just erupted, and his paper reaped another rich harvest of sensational headlines.

The repercussions were catastrophic for both Ben St. Claire and Daniella Lae, as their carefully crafted images were now in ruins. Lae had built her career on being a bright, breezy buxom girl with an ever-ready sunny smile for the boys, but now the public saw a darker side to her character. As for her boyfriend, since bursting onto the snooker circuit he had been cashing in on his wholesome image, and this tawdry episode effectively destroyed his marketing value.

Using all his experience, Rimmer followed the scoop up by offering Judge a chance to explain his side of the story to *The Horizon*'s readers back home, and he grabbed it with both remorseful hands. Fights and drug-fuelled escapades in hotel rooms are a staple storyline of the rock fraternity, so if anything, the chaos caused by his dysfunctional meddling saw his popularity increase.

36.

The dirty work recruitment commission

"Lenka Molome. Lenka Molome! Get off your arse you *kaffir* cunt! You've got a visitor."

The surly youth's battered body lay like a crumpled sack of rags against the far wall of a holding cell underneath the CBD station house while a broadbeamed police officer barked impatiently at him to stand up.

He had been taken into custody the day before and was paying a high price for his fighting spirit as he gingerly nursed the catalogue of fresh bruises bestowed upon him as a welcoming gift by his gaolers. He was a slippery eel, difficult to bring under control, but a generous helping of kicks, punches and baton blows had finally brought him to submission.

He hoped that the visitor would be his mother, come to rescue him in an echo of the aid she provided during childhood whenever overambitious playground confrontations with older boys proved unwise. Though he had silently prayed for her maternal protection through the night, a small part of him also dreaded the prospect of facing her disappointment and wrath. He was always fretting that she might unearth evidence of his many misdemeanours and the prospect of seeing a familiar disapproving look on her weary, worried face now haunted him.

During the long dark night, his fear-driven desire for escape threatened to bring on a river of tears, but now a pretence of defiance returned, and the unbowed youth asked, "Who is it? Who's come to see me?"

"No one you'd know, but this guy might just turn out to be your best friend."

He painfully raised himself from the cold stone floor and prepared to face his fate. Like many a poor wretch before him, he was escorted to an interview room and told to sit quietly on a battered wooden chair.

If this busted thing I'm sitting on could talk, I bet it would have some stories to tell! How many of my people have been smacked about on it, I wonder?

He faced a plain desk on which an arrest sheet lay, logging details of the charges brought against him and the time of his incarceration. Behind the desk was another simple functional chair, though that one did not exhibit the ravages of its twin.

After being left alone to stew in his own juice for a minute or two, the door opened again, and two thick-set white men entered the room. They were strangers to him, and the former displayed a curious scar across his hairless skull. His demeanour suggested an air of menace and he took up residence on the vacant seat behind the desk, while the other man stood by his side. Though Molome was exhausted and sore in equal measure, he looked at both of them with the alert wariness of a cornered animal.

After a moment or two of silence in which the protagonists weighed each other up, the scarred man began to speak.

"I'm Detective Inspector Daalmans. What is your name young man?"

Disdainfully, the prisoner replied, "You've got it there in front of you, why are you asking me?" He could not read too well, but he knew that his particulars would already be on the sheet staring up at the inspector.

"Don't get smart with me my lad, or you won't be able to answer back like that again 'cos you'll be nursing a broken jaw! Now I'll ask you one more time - what's your fucking name?"

The silence reappeared, before a response eventually came.

"Lenka - I'm Lenka Molome."

"That's better," returned the inspector, "just so I know which black bastard I'm talking to today. You all look the fucking same to me when my men drag you from our shitty little cells. Wouldn't do to pick the wrong one out, would it?"

Either out of bravery or gross stupidity, Molome replied, "Depends what you're getting picked for."

Daalmans ground down on his teeth and his scar changed colour from purple to red; he was itching to add to the cocky young buck's punishment, but he was aware of the task at hand, so contented himself with seeing that through.

"You've got some guts young man, I'll grant you that, but I'll let the gentleman here judge whether that makes you an asset or a liability."

He searched for any change in Molome's expression. Interest? Curiosity, perhaps? There was fear and bloody-minded defiance, but no deference; no understanding of the superiority of the white-skinned authoritarian figures in the room. Pointing a thumb in the direction of the man to his left, he said, "This is Mr. Pienaar and he has something he'd like to discuss with you, so I'll leave him to tell you what's on his mind while I go outside for a coffee, ok?" Glancing sideways, he spoke again. "Any trouble sir, and you know what to do?"

"Yes, thank you Inspector. If this one starts to get a little frisky, I'll just call for your men and they'll quickly show him the error of his ways." This was a clear warning that it would be unwise for Molome to try to take advantage of the removal of supervision from the room.

"Be sure to shout good and loud and don't hesitate sir - these township blackies move quickly."

"I'm sure everything will be just fine. That's right, isn't it boy?"

There was no answer.

Daalmans was reluctant to walk away without satisfying himself of the other man's safety, even though Pienaar was a large, strongly built man who would have been more than a match for any show of aggression from the youngster.

"Just be watchful sir - he's a bad sort, this one, I think."

"Thank you again, Inspector. I'll holler if I need you." With that, Daalmans left the two of them to their discussion. Pienaar maintained a penetrative gaze on the youngster. "Do you smoke? Can I offer you a cigarette?"

The street-smart youth had learned long ago never to look a gift horse in the mouth, so he replied, "Can I have the packet?"

"Ha!" Pienaar burst forth with a short laugh that would convince nobody of its sincerity. He passed over the cigarettes and said, "If you do what I ask, there'll be plenty more where they came from and a lot more besides."

Molome stiffened in his chair. At eighteen years old, he had been sexually active for some time and was wary of older men and their advances.

If this Pienaar character is coming on to me, he's gonna need all those cops outside to keep me from kicking his teeth in.

"I have a little proposition for you."

"What do you mean?" Two black fists clenched underneath the desk.

"I mean, if you can do a big favour for a friend of mine, I can do the same for you."

At this, Molome bolted from his chair and assumed a battle position.

"Fuck off man - leave me be I tell you! Come near me and I'll smack your head up good!"

Pienaar raised his outstretched palms towards the excitable youth.

"Calm down boy, calm down! It's nothing like that. I'm not one of those fairy fellas - God no! Now sit back down and relax." The aggressor stood his ground. "Sit down, or I'll call in the inspector and his friends. I don't think you'd like that."

Molome nervously returned to his seat and Pienaar began to explain his proposition.

"Now you've already shown me that you're a fearless kind of guy who can take on a challenge, so I'm here to offer you a once-in-a-lifetime chance of a leg-up in life. You interested?"

"I already told you - it depends." There was less conviction in the young man's abrasive attitude now and his attention became more focussed on what Pienaar had to say.

"I had a tip off about you from my friend Inspector Daalmans, and I've asked him to do a bit of digging on my behalf. He spoke to the investigating officers on your case, and they've been to your house…it seems you've got a sister who's…not very well. Am I right?"

Molome's stomach knotted. With a wobble of consternation in his voice, he replied, "What's that got to do with you? You leave my sister alone! It's me who held up the fat guy in the CBD, me that you've got to worry about - not her." The frightened child inside him was evident in his response.

"All I'm saying is that with some money in your pocket, you might be able to make her better, that's all…"

Suddenly the atmosphere changed, and a light switched on in Molome's head.

What was it that the officer in the cells said about this man?

'He could just be your best friend' - Yeah - that's it!

Maybe this is the moment I've been waiting for - the chance to be the king of my castle!

But hold on - stop and think for a minute.

Why would this man want to help my sister and me?

It was time to ask some important questions.

"How much money are you talking about and what am I gonna have to do to get it?"

"I'm offering you the sum of one hundred thousand rand, which is enough money to get Dikeledi - isn't that her name? - the very best treatment available."

The young man's heart began to beat to a rhythm of tribal drums.

If I can save my little sister's life, I'll be a big boy player after all… and mamma's gonna admire me too - then she'll soon forget about this scrape I'm in.

"Could this treatment…could it make her well again?" He was not only showing his ignorance and innocence, but he had also dropped his guard enough to trust in Pienaar's words.

"Absolutely. For that money, it can be done."

Pienaar obviously knew that there was no cure for the boy's sister, and that the ill-educated Molome would be blissfully unaware of this unpalatable fact.

It was time for further questions.

"So why are you gonna make all of this possible? Why say these things to me? I mean, I've been stuck on the wrong side of a police cell all night, haven't I? There must be other people on the right side of the law who can do this favour for you?"

"Before I tell you how you can help me - and as a consequence, how you can help your sister - let me tell you something about myself. I work for the secret police. That's why I have this access to people such as you."

"What - you mean prisoners?"

"Suspects, Lenka! Don't give the justice system a helping hand, boy! The law states that you are innocent until proven guilty, so until a court of law says that you have committed the crimes for which you've been accused, you're an innocent citizen. Remember that, because as such, you'll be free to roam the streets again until your trial begins… so long as somebody raises the required bail money to assure against your non-attendance in court, that is."

It took time for the raw teenager with no understanding of the intricate workings of the legal system to break down this information. None of his delinquent peers had ever returned to the streets between the time of their apprehension and the beginning of an inevitable prison sentence, so if he got out now, he would be unique within his community. This generous benefactor was not only promising to get him released on bail but also guaranteeing him a small fortune that would make his sick sister well again.

Maybe this stranger really IS my best friend!

But why?

"To get to the point Lenka, a very dangerous individual has entered our country, and this person can cause everyone a great deal of ...inconvenience. He is an enemy of the people - your people especially - and his presence could negatively affect the chances for a peaceful transfer of power to the black majority. We need to stop him from doing that. Do you get my drift?" Molome said nothing, but undeterred, Pienaar continued his pitch. "Now, neither the police or the secret service can be seen to have anything whatsoever to do with this man's....removal, because the repercussions would be disastrous for the image of our New South Africa. We want to show the world that we can achieve radical change peacefully and responsibly here - we must be able to prove that this country can once again be a great place in which to do business. Are you following this?"

The boy understood him perfectly, and the sooner both parties knew where they stood, the sooner he would be free to tell his sister and mother about his unexpected windfall.

"You want me to knock this guy off for a hundred thousand rand? I'll do it. Where will I have to go and when do I get the money?"

Pienaar's face broke into a genuine smile.

"Good boy! When I saw you, I knew you were tough enough to help me out. You're clearly a leader because your little gang of *bandidos* gave you the gun and the responsibility for that shake-down outside the bank."

Molome's chest swelled with an ignorant and misguided sense of pride.

"Now you've got a chance to do something positive with those qualities you've shown. Think of this as a service to your country."

I'll be doing a service to a country that's done absolutely nothing for my people other than keep us down for generations.

Ah, what do I care?

I want that cash!

"Your application for bail will be posted as soon as we leave this room and upon your release, we'll work out the details of what we'd like you to do. Just sit tight, tend to your injuries and lie low until we contact you again, ok? But hey - no silly business - you understand, boy? No petty crime, no fights - just lie low and if everything goes to plan, there should be a happy conclusion for you, your family and your country."

With that, Pienaar adjourned the meeting by calling for Daalmans to return and the detective inspector ordered his gaoler to lead a slightly bewildered Lenka Molome back to the holding cells.

Within twenty-four hours, a local court judge had reluctantly accepted a bail bond posted on his behalf, and the Soweto punk was back on the streets. The bruises adorning his body were battle scars that he could now show off to his friends and he looked forward to the prospect of making some serious money. He was important to someone at last.

The murder errand was a means to an end; little more than a side issue. He gave no consideration towards his intended victim; instead, all he thought about was how the killing would turn him into a *somebody*. He could scarcely wait for the call to get to work.

First though, there was the wrath of mamma Molome to face.

He returned home before she got back from work and occupied himself with trying to sell a tall story to his fretful sister that his arrest was part of a scheme that would eventually make her well again. When Bettina wearily walked through the door, she saw him, and an icy silence gripped the air. Tears filled her eyes.

"Get out."

"Mamma -"

"Get out!"

Dikeledi hastily intervened.

"Mother, let him be - can't you see he's been hurt?"

"Hurt! A man suffered a heart attack because of the actions of my son! And you think I care that he has been hurt by the police? He deserved everything he got - they should have hit him harder! Might have knocked some sense into his stupid head!"

"At least let him speak up for himself, please mamma? Hear what he has to say before you throw him out into the street."

"What is there to hear? You want me to listen to more lies from his lips? He shames me!" With that, she wiped her eyes, looked directly at her boy and repeated, "Lenka, I am ashamed of you."

After these damning words, both of her children began to cry too, before her son stood up to defend himself.

"I did what I did for you and Dikeledi, mamma. I did it for the family."

This justification enraged Bettina and she flew at him, raining ineffective feminine slaps at his already battered body as she roared, "You did NOT do these things in my name! You have NOT been brought up to be a thug - don't think you can get away with saying that rubbish under this roof!"

Her attack was easy to fend off and the boy shouted back, "You've got it all wrong! Look at me - I'm free, aren't I? Why would I be free if I had really done anything wrong?"

This stopped his mother in her tracks.

He's right - why is he free to come back to me if he had really committed this crime?

"But the police - asking me a whole lot of questions about you - bothering Dikeledi, when she was having such a bad day of it too! Explain yourself boy."

"I've been given a special job to do - by the government!" he replied, with his usual immature mixture of defiance and delusion.

"Job? What job? What about the police? See how they've hit you! How do you explain your bruises?"

"The whole thing was a set up - it's all been done to give me a story so I can cover my tracks."

"What are you talking about?"

"The arrest, the working over, it's all been done to make me look like a bad boy, so no one suspects me of working for the government. They're gonna make me rich!"

His mother's disbelief turned to fury.

"Liar! Tell me why the government would go to such trouble to get a wrong-headed eighteen-year-old boy from a shanty town to work for them - do you think your mother is stupid?"

"It's true, it really is - I'm gonna get enough money to make Dikeledi well again. I was telling her all about it just now before you got home."

Bettina's scepticism remained.

"If this nonsense is as you say it is, answer me one thing - why you? Of all the people in South Africa that they could get to play James Bond, why would they go and pick up a teenager from Soweto? Eh?"

"They needed someone who couldn't be traced back to them and I got lucky, I guess. Look, it's something to celebrate - good fortune has finally come to this house!"

Dikeledi spoke up in defence of her brother once more.

"It must be true mamma, or he'd still be rotting in a police cell waiting for his trial. How else can you explain them letting him come home? He MUST be telling the truth!"

There was a lot of information for the head of the household to process and she took some thinking time before speaking again.

"Then what is it that the government want you to do for them?"

"I can't say."

"You cannot even tell your own mother?"

"No - in case you have to answer questions in the future, it's best if you don't know anything."

"Then it is dangerous - I knew it! Do they want you to spy against the ANC?"

"No, no, it's nothing like that. And I'll be fine - don't worry. I was told I'll be helping the freedom movement so you should be proud of me. I'll be ok and Dikeledi will get the drugs she needs to make her well again. It's all gonna be good from now on - I promise."

"None of this is making any sense - why would the government want to help the freedom movement? They are the very people who are keeping us down! I want to know the truth boy!"

"It's complicated - too complicated to explain."

"What, now you are so smart, you can play government games that are over my head? Since when did you become Professor Molome!"

"I'm telling you to trust me and all of this will turn out well, ok? There are secret things I can't talk to you about because I don't fully understand them myself, but I'm not locked up am I, and you can't explain that away, can you? For once in your life, you're just gonna have to put some faith in me."

Confusion and anxiety began to overheat poor Bettina's brain. She wanted her son to have nothing to do with this bizarre nonsense, despite the fact that he must indeed have made some kind of pact with the authorities.

"I don't like it Lenka - go back and tell these government people that you do not want to get involved in their schemes."

"I can't do that now or I'll be put away for the hold-up of the man in the CBD. They know how to get their own way."

His mother sat down, grudgingly giving in to the fact that she could do nothing to alter his immediate fate. If, somehow, he really did manage to get money for the family and provide Dikeledi with a second chance at life, then maybe one day they might all look back on this crazy moment with a sense of pride rather than shame. It all sounded insane, but with cautious reluctance, she sighed and resigned herself to letting him stay in the house.

"Ok, young man, I don't understand what's going on here, but you do not have to walk the streets tonight. I still don't like any of this though."

The war of words was over, and an uneasy ceasefire broke out between the combatants. Bettina trudged into the kitchen and began to prepare dinner, then she set three places at the table. Dikeledi wrapped her skinny arms around her brother, smiled sweetly and whispered, "James Bond!…Mamma is so funny."

While washing vegetables in the sink, their mother saw the flashing headlights of a car passing by her window. There were two white occupants in the vehicle, and it parked up in a shaded area fifty yards from the house. Her boy had seen it too because he bolted outside through the back door to speak to the man in the passenger seat. It was dark by now and she struggled to see what was going on very clearly, but an exchange of some sort took place before the car pulled away. As he stealthily crept back into the house, trying to avoid suspicion, she immediately challenged him.

"Who were those men?"

"What men?"

"Don't give me your smart lip, Lenka! I watched you sneak out to talk with them - were they government men?"

He knew better than to try to pull the wool over her eyes again, particularly as she had allowed him to remain in the family home.

"Yes mamma."

"I don't think you should be talking to white men around here, especially like that, skulking around in the shadows. What if you were seen?"

"I won't have to do it again and besides, the man in the passenger seat is going to speak up for me to get my charges dropped, so I've got to keep in his good books." Bettina had concern written all over her creased features. "Look, I promise I'll be careful - I've got to be. I've got you and Dikeledi to think about." With that, he produced an envelope bursting with notes. This was his advance payment for the "special job". "There's sixty thousand rand in here mamma - that's more money than we've ever seen in our lives! You can book Dikeledi in to see one of those fancy doctors in Johannesburg now…that's if you can get one to take a black girl on as a patient."

The ever-sceptical Bettina winced uneasily.

"It looks like blood money to me."

"If it saves Dikeledi's life, it's just good money. Now take it." The cash passed to his mother and they spoke no more.

After dinner, he went to his tiny room to focus his mind on the job he would have to do. That wad of notes was not the only item passed to him by Pienaar (the car's passenger). He also received another .25 caliber automatic Browning pistol with which to commit the hit, and he promptly stashed this away from the prying eyes of his mother underneath the floorboards upon which his tattered mattress lay. Ever since his petty criminal activities became a lifestyle choice, that secret space had proven useful to hide any money or trinkets gleaned from a day's pilfering.

This gun looks just like the one I got caught with the other day - Pienaar and

Daalmans must think that I fool around with these things all the time!

His instructions were to return to the CBD the next morning and head for the *Transvaal Mineral Mining Corporation* building on Market Street for 8.30 a.m. The target had an appointment there thirty minutes later and would be driving into the visitor's car park (Molome knew the make, model, colour and registration number of the vehicle so there could be no mistakes). The hit had to look like a carjacking and required speed of thought and deed to avoid giving his victim any idea of impending danger.

Pienaar had plotted an escape route for his stooge to follow and given him an assurance that the local police would not give serious chase. At a designated post box on the corner of Fox Street and Sauer Street, a secret service man was to meet him and exchange the murder weapon for a bag containing the rest of his cash. Crucially, he would also receive a signed guarantee from his benefactor granting him immunity from prosecution. The document would verify that his actions during the original hold-up case and this subsequent shooting were in defence of his country, bound by South Africa's Official Secrets Act.

The only remaining issue would be to get home in one piece with his bag of swag. Once there, he could plan the next phase of his life as a wealthy young man (by Soweto's standards at any rate). A small part of his brain even thought that he might earn a medal rather than a prison term for his murderous act!

Before turning in for the night, Molome reminded himself of the description that Pienaar had given him of the intended target.

"He is a white man, he has sandy brown hair, and if you hear him speak, he does so with a Scottish accent. His name is Gordon Rimmer."

37.

The price of pressure

London, July 4th, 1990.

To everyone's great surprise, the England football team managed to defy expectations by progressing to the semi-finals of *Italia 90* and across the country, lapsed fans, disillusioned by years of failure, began to rediscover their affection for, 'the Beautiful Game'.

When we last came across Bobby Robson's boys, they faced an embarrassing elimination at the group stage of the competition, but a nervy 1-0 victory over Egypt saw them progress to the knockout rounds. Further hard-fought wins at the expense of Belgium and the Cameroon took them into the semi-finals and suddenly, the country dared to dream.

This was very bad news indeed for Marcus Botha. The Head Honcho saw the *Sun City Snooker Challenge* as his last chance to resurrect *MJB TV*'s fortunes, but the tournament was completely ignored as terrestrial television schedulers held the viewing public hostage in a football frenzy.

Once again, Gordon Rimmer had bagged a sensational scoop for *Horizon* readers, this time about the hotel ruckus involving Gideon Judge, Daniella Lae and Ben St. Claire, but just like his best efforts in Las Vegas with Barry Shackleton, the story had failed to attract public attention to another of Botha's lavish productions. His boss was enraged.

The sports fans of this country should be gripped by the sensational snooker I've put on in South Africa, but instead, they're all going nuts over the bloody World Cup!

The whole thing is a disaster - my ratings are through the floor!

True to form, the exasperated tycoon refused to blame himself for his plight.

Rimmer hasn't done the job I told him to do - I didn't need another splash about that crazed lunatic Judge, and I certainly didn't need him to ruin the reputation of my top Page Five Filly either!

I ordered him to plug my network and its sports output, but instead, the stupid bastard has got one of my star players banned from my own bloody tournament!

Well at least I can do something about punishing him for his ineptitude.

Today is the day that he finds out what it's like to let me down!

His heart started to palpitate. He found himself continually clenching and relaxing his left hand to relieve a tingling sensation that pestered his arm. His brain throbbed and he sweated profusely now; he was physically overheating.

Pull yourself together man, this won't do!

He loosened his tie, but his breathing became ever more erratic. Desperately sucking in air, he reached for a crystal decanter at the side of his desk to pour himself a drink of iced water, but suddenly his powerful frame tensed up and the glass crashed to the floor, soaking an impressively expensive rug. Drawing on all his reserves of willpower, he managed to buzz his intercom and raise the alarm to his personal assistant.

"Hilary! Hilary! It's my heart!…Hilary! Come quickly …Help me!"

His able aide burst into the penthouse suite to find her employer face down on top of his desk in a state of semi-consciousness. She reacted with haste and professionalism, first by alerting the building's Occupational Health department to the drama and then ringing 999 to summon an ambulance. Moments ticked agonizingly by before on-site medical staff reached the room and set to work on keeping the prone body alive. The chaotic scene mirrored poor Barry Shackleton's collapse at the Las Vegas darts fiasco just a fortnight earlier.

Paramedics from the nearby London Bridge hospital raced to the scene and immediately took charge of the proceedings, applying ECG pads to Botha's constricted chest. He was breathing, though weakly, and with great haste they whisked their Very Important Patient away to undergo emergency surgery.

He would need all of his renowned strength, resolve, and pig-headedness to avoid the Grim Reaper's summons, but he was up for the fight. There was so much left to achieve on earth; so many scores to settle; deceits to conceal. Battered and bruised he may have been, but the old bulldog was not ready to relinquish his stage just yet.

38.

Actions and reactions

Once the initial shock of Botha's collapse subsided, Hilary called Edmund Cornell to tell him that the Head Honcho had suffered a serious coronary seizure, and their boss was now undergoing an emergency operation at London Bridge hospital; his wife Elizabeth would be by his side presently. When it was prudent to do so, Cornell contacted Mrs. Botha and she informed him that her husband's chances of recovery were good, but he would obviously be out of commission for some considerable time, leaving *The Horizon*'s Editor-in-Chief with sole responsibility for the paper's performance. This was the opportunity to shine that he had been waiting for, and he promptly set about informing the rest of the staff of his temporary upgrade in status.

At last, I've got a chance to trust my own judgement - thank you God!

I'm not proud of myself for thinking this way, but as far as I'm concerned, the broadcasting arm of Botha's business can go to hell - I'm only going to concentrate on improving The Horizon's fortunes.

I want to run this paper more successfully than ever, and if I can do that, I'll keep my job.

By my reckoning, one guarantees the other.

Later that morning, during a particularly dull Parliamentary debate, Lewis Neeves received a note requesting his presence in the Commons' lobby, so with much relief he excused himself from the proceedings post haste. A researcher who shared his office in the bowels of the building was on hand to pass him an important fax that requested an immediate response. When he discovered that the message was from Cornell, his enthusiasm turned to irritation until he read its contents.

For the attention of the Right Honourable Lewis Neeves MP.

Marcus Botha taken to London Bridge hospital following a massive heart attack.

Surgery in progress. Please contact me at your earliest convenience.

Regards

Edmund Cornell

Neeves' mind kicked into overdrive, and he followed the young man back to their tiny office to make that call.

"Is there anything I can do, Edmund? Do you think I should contact his wife - offer her my support, perhaps? I mean, I don't actually know her - we've never met, but…"

"I think everyone at the hospital is doing their best to help Marcus and I've already passed on the good wishes of all *The Horizon's* staff to Mrs. Botha. I just wanted to keep you in the loop before your colleagues there got wind of the story and started gossiping. If rival papers want you to respond to the news, just dead bat them, ok? The paper's business will carry on as usual, with me at the helm for the foreseeable future."

"Oh… oh, ok. Got it. You can rely on me."

Like Cornell, he secretly rejoiced at the stricken man's misfortune.

This could be a real stroke of luck!

If Marcus ends up dying on the operating table, I won't have to worry about defending him, should his dubious past ever becomes public knowledge!

Such are the worth of friendships and alliances in politics.

39.

Three scenes

Johannesburg, July 4th, 1990.

By daybreak, Lenka Molome was already up and out of the house. He needed some thinking time before the madness of the day ahead unfolded. The moment had arrived to fulfil his tough guy dreams, yet now that fantasy was about to become a raw reality, and he found the brutal truth of the situation unnerving. He was going to take somebody's life and had barely slept as the enormity of his task struck home. When Pienaar made his enticing proposal, Molome thought only of the bounty money and the power it would bring, but now he understood why the callous act of snuffing out another human being carried such a premium price.

He was frightened. Scared stiff. He wanted to run away; to hide from his obligation and forget the whole thing.

Why did I ever pull a gun on that fat man in the CBD in the first place?

I should have known I was never going to get away with that!

I was even dumber agreeing to do what Mr. Pienaar said…

Why won't my heart stop pounding?

These hands of mine are shaking so much – how am I gonna shoot straight?

I'm sweating buckets already!…

I'm not cut out for this sort of life – I should have waited for Mandela to come to power, then everything would be alright – that's what everybody says anyway.

If only I'd listened to them…

Ah, fuck it – that chance has gone!

It's too late to change the past, and now I'm gonna be responsible for the death of a complete stranger.

He found it impossible to keep his doubts at bay.

But what if I change my mind?

What's gonna happen if I don't shoot this Gordon Rimmer?

I suppose the law will come down hard on me for the ATM hold up, and Pienaar will be mad that I failed the task – failed in the service of this rotten, stinking, unfair, unjust country…

If I do take a coward's way out, how can I look my sister in the eyes, knowing that I've thrown away this chance to make her strong again?

I can't do that, no way…my mind's made up – I'll see the plan through…

Ahhh, but Jesus – so much can go wrong!

What if some stupid cop interferes with my getaway?

What am I gonna do if the secret service man doesn't take the gun off my hands?

What if he doesn't have my bag of money?

Shit – this is all driving me crazy!

His befuddled mind struggled to dismiss these negative thoughts, but he knew that no amount of dwelling on ifs, buts or maybes would alter the situation.

Snap out of this Lenka!

If everything goes like Mr. Pienaar says it will, I'll be rich and Dikeledi will get healthy.

Then everyone will look up to me round here.

Yeah, I like the sound of that – I'm gonna be a hero!

As if on autopilot, he boarded a bus heading for the Central Business District and swiftly made his way to the *TMMC* building. Taking up his position at the appointed time, he nervously waited until the target vehicle (a 1988 red VW City Golf; 1.8 engine; registration number JJM868 GP; just as Pienaar had described) came into view. Everything was as it should be. The VW manoeuvred into a vacant parking space reserved for visitors and the engine stopped. Behind the steering wheel was a white man with light brown hair who he knew to be Gordon Rimmer. Under his breath, he psyched himself into a frenzy that matched his rapidly racing heartbeat.

That's him - now do the job!

He quickly closed in on his target, pushing past a couple of passers-by in the process. Withdrawing the pistol, he straightened his shooting arm (just like he had seen people do in the movies) and cocked the firing mechanism. As he squeezed the trigger, he instinctively closed his eyes, and his sensory perception went into overload. The noise of the weapon and the flash escaping from the barrel was more intense than he had expected.

Jesus, was that loud or are my ears playing tricks on me?

I bet everyone in the whole street will have heard it!

Shattered glass. Blood. Screams. Silence…It was done.

Here we go again!

He started to run, racing as fast as his bruised and painful legs could take him; out of the car park and down the street towards the bus station in Selby several blocks away; following the route that Pienaar said would carry the least threat of resistance. He travelled a hundred yards before suddenly realising that he had made a critical error. His orders were clear - he must hang on to the weapon and swap it for the cash in the secret service man's bag at their rendezvous point, but in his haste to quit the crime scene, he had dropped the gun in the car park.

Shit - you've left the bloody thing behind - you fucking idiot!

It was too late to stop and turn back; too late to worry about the repercussions.

Molome ran like the wind, heading for the post box on the corner where Fox Street meets Sauer Street.

Pienaar's man will be wearing sunglasses and a pale blue business suit, carrying my money in a canvas satchel.

That money holds the key to my future.

I must GRAB THAT BAG!

He was almost there now. He stopped, panting, breathless and highly agitated.

There's the phone box, but something's wrong…

Where is the man in the pale blue suit?

WHERE IS THE MAN WITH MY MONEY?

He looked up and down the street; across the road; everywhere. There was no man carrying a canvas satchel. No man. No bag. No money.

Fuck – Pienaar has set me up!

The hopelessness of his situation suddenly struck home.

There would be no cure for Dikeledi now, and his mother was certainly going to disown him for what he had just done; his dreams of earning respect from the township's hard men lay in tatters too. Suddenly, behind him came a roared order that interrupted his thought processes.

"Stop! Police! Drop your weapon and hit the ground!"

He turned around to see two armed police officers training their rifles on him.

Why are these lawmen chasing me?

In his confused state, he was still struggling to make sense of the dramatically unfolding events.

Of course!

There were no orders issued for them to back off and let me escape.

But how can I drop a weapon that I no longer have?

As they gave chase, his pursuers had obviously failed to notice the pistol lying on the ground by Rimmer's hire car. Molome thought his only hope of escape was to convince them that he could still create carnage, so in desperation he shouted, "Let me get away or I'm gonna shoot this thing!" He clamped his hands together, raised his arms, and pointed his trigger finger.

The sound of rifle fire reverberated in the air, much louder than the pistol crack heard during the attack moments earlier. This shot came from a police bullet, and it struck straight through Lenka Molome's chest, sending him crashing to the floor.

A searing, burning pain fried his insides and a stream of crimson splattered across the pavement, running on into the road. His head span and a cacophony of different noises all melted into one around him. His eyes blurred; shadows were all he could see against the angry skies of an overcast Johannesburg morning. With the final seconds of his wasted, unfulfilled life ticking away, mumbled words escaped from his red-choked mouth.

"Pienaar and Daalmans - bastards!… Didn't mean to hurt you, mamma… God, I'm so scared…Dikeledi - wanted money - to make - you - well…" His eyes closed on the world for the final time. "I love you both… so, so much…"

....

Detective Inspectors Sneddon and van Hoosen took the following statement from a hospital bed in the Brenthurst Clinic on Park Lane, Johannesburg: -

My name is Gordon Alexander Rimmer and I am the Chief Sports Correspondent for The Horizon newspaper in the United Kingdom. I came to South Africa to report on an international snooker tournament called the "Sun City Snooker Showdown" that is being sponsored by my employer Marcus Johannes Botha.

After checking the itinerary, I found that I had time to travel to Johannesburg to catch up with an acquaintance whom I had met recently in the United States by the name of Pieter Hertzog.

We arranged to meet at the Transvaal Mineral Mining Corporation building on Market Street, where he works. He had advised me that there were designated parking spaces available where visitors could leave their vehicles. My car was a hired Volkswagen Golf. I do not remember its registration number.

Our rendezvous was set for 9 a.m. so I reached the car park with ten minutes to spare. I found one of the designated spaces and parked up, but before I could open the driver's side door, a young black man came out of nowhere pointing a gun straight at me. I watched him squeeze the trigger and my heart stopped for a split second. I remember leaning back into my seat in an attempt to dodge the bullet. I heard the shot and the side window shattered. Then I recall moments of severe pain.

People crowded around me and I began to panic when I saw blood start to soak my shirt. Soon afterwards, paramedics arrived and bundled me into an ambulance. I believe I fainted then, By the time I regained consciousness, I had been operated on to remove the bullet in my side.

I have no idea who the gunman was. The only person I know at all in this city is Mr. Hertzog. I do not know where he lives, but as I mentioned earlier, he works at the TMMC building. If you want to speak to him, you can reach him there, but I cannot see how he can help you with your enquiries, except to confirm that he knows me and to verify my story.

I have already been told by everyone here that I was the victim of a, 'carjacking,' and that this is quite a common offence in these parts. One of your colleagues shot and killed my assailant as he tried to make his escape, so I doubt that I will ever know why he tried to do such a thing.

The medical staff at the hospital say that I have to rest but if you need to check on my background, I have given them the phone number of my former boss, Wilfred Moss, who can help you. Also, my parents and Professor Somerfield from the Priory Hospital in Roehampton, England are flying here to be with me and I am sure they will be able to assist you with your enquiries wherever possible.

Gordon Rimmer

....

At a crowded bar in the well-to-do Sandton area of the city, a world away from the frenzy of the Central Business District, off-duty Detective Inspector Douglas Daalmans is sharing a beer with an old friend.

"What's new, Douggie?"

"That dopey young bastard didn't do his job properly - he didn't finish your guy off. I told you not to leave it to one of those fucking *kaffirs*! They're all too bloody flaky - they can't be trusted with any responsibility."

"Keep your voice down man! We need to stay calm, there's no need to panic. Understood?" Reluctantly, Daalmans nodded. "Ok, let's look at the facts as they stand. Are you sure Rimmer is going to pull through?"

"It looks like it. My sources say he's fit and healthy, so he should be strong enough to come out of the other side. MJB won't be happy, you can bet on that."

The detective inspector's friend shuffled uncomfortably in his seat and shot quick glances from side to side to make sure that no one else was eavesdropping on their conversation.

"Don't you worry about him - there'll be no heat to speak of over this. We're old-time sparring partners, so he's sure to cut me some slack after all the jobs I've done for him in the past. I'll probably just get a severe bollocking over the phone and that'll be that. Besides, there was no real necessity for the... favour that he wanted me to undertake anyway - our friend in the hospital was just a nuisance to the old dog, nothing more. MJB has more pressing business interests to worry about right now, and anyway, I'll bet Mr. Rimmer will be a much more pliable commodity in future after his nasty little...experience. Now, let's review the one positive outcome to take away from this mess."

"And that is?"

"That the king-sized moron who was tasked to do the deed is no more, so there won't be any repercussions to concern ourselves with. Let's drink to that, eh?" Mischievously, he then decided to tease Daalmans a little. "Of course, even if young Molome had still been around to tell tall tales, I'd have been alright - the mysterious Mr. Pienaar left no tracks to trace. Things might have gotten difficult for you though…"

Daalmans fidgeted awkwardly in his seat at the thought.

"That's as may be, but there's no way I'd have taken the rap on my own - just remember that." His warning to the man sitting opposite him was clear.

"Douglas, I'm only pulling your leg just a little bit, that's all - don't start getting all melodramatic on me here. Anyway, it's immaterial now as the dead can't speak, so just relax, ok?"

Daalmans wanted the stray strands of the puzzle tied up as quickly as possible to put some distance between the two of them and the dead youth.

"What happens when Rimmer gets out of hospital? What if he wants to carry on snooping?"

"Gordon Rimmer is a sports reporter - if he was an investigative journalist, he might have been keen on poking around for a bit longer, but those guys are a different breed. It's simply not in this one's blood - he'll want to get away from here double quick, I guarantee it. And if he does decide to get nosey, he'll just have to meet with another little accident, won't he? Only next time it'll be better thought through." Daalmans remained wary, so his friend continued to reassure him. "Look, if not for the snooker thing, Rimmer would never have been over here in the first place, so he wouldn't have had the chance to ask questions about MJB's affairs. Trust me, once he's fit enough to go home, he won't give this place a second glance. Chilly English winters spent covering domestic football matches will seem like paradise!

Just to make sure though, find out who's investigating the shooting and see what they know about his intentions, then we can act accordingly. If I'm right, we'll be able to put the whole thing behind us and never have to dirty our hands with this kind of business again. We're too old for these games now, and the young bucks clearly can't be trusted to follow orders properly. Now speaking of orders, it's my round - same again, is it?"

40.

Unanswered questions for curious minds

Half a world apart, Susan Somerfield and Elizabeth Botha stared at the helpless invalids resting peacefully before them on crisply starched white linen sheets and silently prayed for divine assistance. Both women were completely unaware of each other's hopes, concerns, anxieties, and fears, but they were prepared to set aside their rational misgivings and plead with any deity, real or imagined, for the strength to cope with the days ahead.

Sitting beside a screened-off hospital bed in Johannesburg's Brenthurst Clinic, Susan gazed intently at Gordon Rimmer for the first time since their break-up. She had shared his spotlight for two years and the nectar from love's bloom still tasted frustratingly sweet, but she was a spurned woman, and that fact hurt her deeply. Her desire to hear his breathless pleas for a reconciliation had received no reward, and to compound matters, she now sported a physical reminder of his rejection in the form of a subtle frown on her otherwise flawless face.

Gordon, for Christ's sake, get out of my head – you do me no good!...

She immediately regretted her petulance and blamed it on the exhausting journey from London.

This is a time for rational thinking, not childish tantrums – you're sulking like a pre-pubescent whose favourite pop star won't reply to her love letter!

Earlier that week, Wilfred Moss had contacted her in a state of some distress with news of the shooting, and the information struck home like a Great White's bite.

"And there's more, Sue," he said. "Gordon asked me to get you over there… can I tell him you'll go?"

His words shook her into a cocktail of confusion.

"What's this all about Willie?"

"I'm afraid I don't know for sure. He spoke to me shortly after his operation - they've taken the bullet from his side. He sounded so groggy that I didn't want to push him on details, but it was obvious he needs to see you."

Caution made her think long and hard before eventually agreeing to answer the summons, but she recognised that this was the perfect opportunity to resolve her outstanding issues with Rimmer, so after tying up some loose ends at the Priory, she booked a flight to Johannesburg expecting to find him on the mend. Upon her arrival at the clinic however, the story took a further twist.

His endearing parents, David and Carol met her in the lobby with an update on the current situation. David did the talking while an ashen Carol put on her bravest face alongside him.

"Things aren't great with Gordon, Sue. The bullet hit him from point blank range in an area between his right shoulder and chest, resulting in a serious wound. The good news is that it's been removed safely. Everything was going so well - he regained consciousness after the surgery and even gave a statement to the police. Then complications arose, and he developed a blood clot. I don't know the ins and outs of it, but this affected the flow of blood to his brain, and he's now slipped into a coma." Susan froze on the spot. "Please try to remain calm - he's stable at the minute and your being here will help him immensely."

"Why do you say that?"

"Because we've been told that he kept asking the medical staff to contact you before his turn for the worse."

She was grateful for Mr. Rimmer's kind words, but this latest drama was almost too much to bear. Despite her anxieties, she took comfort from seeing the elderly couple again, and with typical consideration they led her to their son's ward, then withdrew to give her some space for reflection.

She surveyed Rimmer's glazed expression, hoping to see some response; the merest flicker of acknowledgement that he was aware of her presence. None came.

Oh Gordon, please give me a sign that you're on the mend.

Anything will do…

A tear ran down her cheek.

This would never have happened if you'd stopped working for Marcus-bloody-Botha when I asked you to.

Why oh why didn't you listen to me, you idiot?

How could you find the courage to give up on us, yet when it came to standing up to him you were such a meek little lamb?

In the awkward peace and stillness of that moment, she recalled her only meeting with the fascinatingly formidable Bothas. It was at one of Elizabeth's glitzy, black-tie functions, a prize giving ceremony for young achievers, where Rimmer, who was still working at *The Focus* at the time, had been asked to present an award to a Cub Reporter of the Year. Typically, the invitation carried an ulterior motive, for Marcus wanted to sweet talk him into accepting an extremely lucrative offer to become *The Horizon*'s Chief Sports Correspondent. On the way home, he bragged to Susan of winning the evening's biggest prize, but she remembered feeling uncomfortable in the company of the billionaire couple. During the evening, she even joked that, "those ice buckets for the champagne are pointless - if Mrs Botha stares at the bottles they'll chill on their own."

Once he had accepted the Head Honcho's offer, her relationship with Rimmer began to unravel. She quickly recognised that the new role was affecting his mental wellbeing, but when she raised her concerns with him, he refused to acknowledge the problem, and the inevitable consequences followed.

It all seems so long ago now.

I'm always encouraging my patients to look beyond their regrets and recriminations, so I should see that stuff as yesterday's news and move on…

Her thoughts returned to the present predicament. The media, both locally and in the UK, inevitably focussed its attention on Marcus Botha's sudden heart attack, while the shooting of Rimmer passed largely without comment. Usually when one of their own gets gunned down on manoeuvres, the press provides comprehensive coverage of the incident, but here, a publisher and an employee from the same paper had suffered near-death experiences at the same time, so the story to follow was that of the boss.

I bet The Horizon won't even bother sending anyone here to find out what's happened to Gordon.

At least Susan felt confident that the South African police would take an interest in him; after all, a black man had attacked a white man, so she expected them to conduct a comprehensive criminal investigation into the circumstances of the shooting (she was equally certain this would not be the case if the assailant was Caucasian and his victim dark-skinned).

Hopefully, they will have cleared this mess up by the time he's back in the land of the living, then when he comes to terms with what's happened, maybe I'll find out why I had to fly five and a half thousand miles across the world to be here.

A plausible answer to that question is the least that I deserve…

Elizabeth Agnes Botha cut a pensive figure as she surveyed her husband's elegantly appointed private suite at the London Bridge hospital. She knew that while wealth can buy friendships, influence, sex, power, or anything else the heart desires, it can do nothing to bring the unconscious to their senses. At least the plush surroundings reassured her that he was receiving the very best care available.

Hour after hour she sat impassively at his side, occasionally flicking glances towards the heart monitor perched on a shelf above his bedside table. Just like Susan Somerfield, she had many questions to ponder.

You're famed for resilience Marcus, so why, in the middle of a fight to preserve your professional reputation, did you choose this moment to keel over?

It was the first time in all their years together that he had exhibited the slightest sign of weakness, and the experience shook her.

They met at the University of Cape Town, where both achieved Masters qualifications in business management. The two unique individuals were instantly drawn to one another; Marcus recognised her as a thoroughbred winner and Elizabeth Viljoen (as was) found his earthy confidence hugely attractive. While the other students in their peer group problem-solved by endlessly procrastinating over theoretical blueprints, Botha just got on with things. He was pro-active; a doer; a visionary; and Elizabeth admired his ability to take difficult decisions without fear or favour.

Her background was in livestock (daddy was one of the country's most successful ranchers) and she intended to take over the reins of the family business when her father retired. The farming community doubted whether she could survive in such a testosterone-fuelled environment, but she saw herself as a trailblazer for women in business and was determined to challenge their antiquated attitudes.

Like Botha, her father was a tough individual, yet Marcus had something else in his locker; something extra; an almost pathological drive to succeed; to win at all costs. While Mr. Viljoen knew how to fight hard, he also fought fair; there was a dignity in the way he conducted his business dealings. The new man in her life was a very different kind of player who had no interest in boardroom pleasantries. He intended to crush the broken bodies of anyone who stood in his way, and this aspect of his personality gave her tingles down below. However, Elizabeth was a fully focussed young woman, not some flaky child, and although their courtship was inevitably carnal, she never allowed sex to disrupt their studies. Success provided their greatest mutual satisfaction.

After graduating, they became long distance lovers as Botha immersed himself in the mining industry and his girlfriend returned to her father's farm. They kept in touch through lengthy phone conversations or written correspondence, and as neither of them bothered with the hearts and flowers aspects of relationships, their time was taken up with discussing strategies for process improvements in the workplace (much to the thinly disguised amusement of colleagues and family members). Ridicule failed to cause them undue duress though, for they cared nothing about the opinions of outsiders.

The Beast from the Bush rapidly rose through the *TMMC*'s ranks, and within five years he had achieved a corporate status that met with his girlfriend's exacting expectations, opening her mind to new possibilities. To the amazement of her father, she suddenly abandoned her own business dreams and announced her intention to marry. Elizabeth was a shrewd operator with a sharp eye for the main chance and although there was financial security in ranching, she knew that in tandem with Marcus, her future was limitless.

At no point over the intervening years did she question the validity of suppressing her personal business ambitions, because by adding polish and *panache* to the Botha brand she played a pivotal role in enhancing its stratospheric progress. Her organisational talents created spectacular charitable events that raised impressive fortunes for good causes, and the resulting positive publicity helped to deflect attention from her husband's incessant belligerence.

The business world often disparagingly referred to Elizabeth as 'Lady Botha,' (likening her to Macbeth's scheming *femme fatale*) and it was certainly true that when she spotted her man's potential, she clung on fast for the ride, but there the similarity ended. She was never the engine of the machine, driving the pistons on; instead, she contented herself with a subtle supporting role, acting as the staff that he leant on whenever the going got tough. Their personalities dovetailed perfectly, ensuring that ego clashes were never an issue in the pursuance of their objectives.

Neither partner had ever felt any desire to raise children; Elizabeth's own early years were proof positive of the damage that offspring can do to parental ambitions, and she did not intend to suffer those same slights herself. As for Marcus, he looked on with barely stifled amusement at the desperate lengths taken by other entrepreneurs to install (usually unsuitable) progenies into family businesses and he would have hated to produce a failure (or worse still, an even greater success!). A Botha child could never hope to receive the necessary love and attention to thrive; the couple's cable car ride to the stars was strictly a two-seater conveyance.

They performed their good cop/bad cop routine to perfection; Marcus was the devil dog, a Rottweiler who got his own way through snarling, barking, and biting at his opponents until he wore down their resistance, while Elizabeth's cool, calm glamour attracted the paparazzi's flashing lenses like moths to a flame. It was a dynamic partnership, inspiring awe and envy in their rivals, but after decades of almost continuous success, they now had a crisis of huge proportions to address.

When the Head Honcho collapsed, the banks finally lost patience with *MJB TV*'s financial woes and withdrew their support, destroying his broadcasting ambitions. The news staggered Elizabeth, for although she had an uncanny gift for spotting icebergs on the horizon, this time she had failed to see the danger, thinking that the network's trading troubles were surmountable. To make amends, she became doubly determined to show the same fighting qualities as her warrior husband.

Thanks to a legally binding contract drawn up by the pair years earlier, she assumed temporary control of *Marcus Botha Publishing and Communications* and her first task was to convince concerned shareholders that the present difficulties were nothing more than a manageable inconvenience. Rescuing the finances and reputation of the holding company would require every ounce of her considerable business nous, but to get to grips with its problems, first she needed to know precise details of the root cause …

With a panther's grace, she rose from a bedside chair to linger over her husband's prostrate body.

"You're far too smart to have just let this happen Marcus - you must have an ace up your sleeve, yes? Tell me I'm right, you old rogue. Speak to me!"

Looking anxiously towards his heart monitor, she counted the time elapsing between each electronic beep and contented herself that the gaps remained consistent. Her gaze shifted to his face and with enormous relief, she suddenly noticed a flicker of recognition in one of his resting eyes; it was tell-tale evidence of his tentative return to the conscious world. Gradually, colour returned to his formidable features, and the Beast relinquished his shackles of slumber. For once, the ice maiden dropped her guard and a rebellious tremor rippled across her chin. This momentary weakness incensed her, for she did not want to let Marcus see her defeated in the struggle over her emotions.

"Hello old man, you've been gone for a while - I was beginning to think you might not come back to me." This was as close as Elizabeth could come to a show of sentimentality. He looked up at her, expressionless, but *compos mentis* just the same, and she wasted no time in switching her attention onto matters of business. "You know that I wouldn't normally question your working practices, but I'm minding the store now as our acting CEO, so I need to know how you've got us into this TV network mire."

He listened intently to his wife's concerns without reply, for his condition left him unable to defend the expensive failure of his strategic actions.

Elizabeth continued to explain her predicament.

"I have to steady the ship, at least until you get back on your feet again, and to do that effectively, I'll need you to co-operate with me - that will mean full disclosure. We're in this together, as always - I won't let the side down. Just give me a nod, a wink, any kind of sign that you can help me to find that missing ace."

No response was forthcoming, so she sat down again, resuming her vigil with stoic resignation. "You're a stubborn, stubborn man."

Lying motionless on his hospital bed, he just wanted to ponder and plot in peace. Every rival media outlet had hacks camped in the hospital lobby, and even though reports of his demise were greatly exaggerated, the vultures still lay in wait with obituaries at the ready, in case his condition should take a fatal trajectory. He was vulnerable and powerless to fend off negative comments about his faltering health and business acumen, so *en masse* the national newspapers carried front page headlines joyously raining on his parade.

HEART HELL FOR HEAD HONCHO
BOTHA'S BUBBLE BURSTS!
BYE, BYE, BOTHA?

What fun they had!

Elizabeth internally raged at her husband's detractors. As news of his troubles surfaced, she developed a siege mentality and refrained from issuing any public statements relating to *MJB TV* until she had positive information to use as ammunition in a counterattack. With Marcus temporarily unable to offer any assistance, patience became her watchword.

When the time is right, we'll show them all - we're vengeful people, you and I, so let's make sure we have the sweetest of revenges here...

Those backstabbing bankers and jealous editors can do their worst, but they won't finish us off - oh no - there's plenty more gas left in our tank!

Meanwhile, in a quiet corner of a Maidstone chapel of rest, Ruth Shackleton stared impassively at the embalmed mannequin before her, thinking that it bore little resemblance to the man she had loved and honoured for more than half of her cursed existence.

Since Barry's AIDS bombshell blew up in her face, she had struggled to come to terms with his hitherto unknown darker side, and the ghastly way the press chose to assassinate his character only served to compound her misery. Legal red tape in Las Vegas prevented her from bringing his body home for over a week, and during that infernal wait they vilified him as a pervert, liar, and cheat; a diseased monster who had led a double life of public respectability and private depravity.

What a mess all this has turned out to be!

The people who wrote that horrible rubbish had never met you, but after everything that's happened, I can't say for sure that they were wrong now, can I?

Cindy Shackleton, the couple's eldest daughter, had driven Ruth to the chapel and on the way there, she parked her battered Ford Fiesta outside a local newsagent's to buy a packet of calm-inducing cigarettes. At the door, she passed two middle-aged men who instantly recognised her face from a family snapshot splashed across the front page of that day's *Horizon*. They turned to gawp at her grieving mother hunched in the passenger seat of the car and with a display of extraordinary impropriety, one muttered to the other, "I bet she took it up the wrong 'un from Barry an' all!" Their target shuddered uncomfortably, straining to maintain her composure in the face of base ignorance. Such are the unconsidered ordeals suffered by loved ones when tabloid newspapers disembowel the rotting carcass of a disgraced celebrity.

The chapel viewing was a family-only affair, but the younger Shackleton children were still coming to terms with the seismic disruption brought on by their father's demise, so only the two adults attended. Ruth was grateful that Rita and Faye had broken up from school for the summer holidays, sparing them from the merciless taunts of unsympathetic playground bullies.

Standing over her husband's coffin, she spoke softly, with a despairing voice that began to falter.

"Oh Barry - what was going on in your head? Did you ever stop to think about us - your wife and kids? Did you ever really love us?"

She turned to Cindy and motioned her head towards the door, indicating that it was time to leave. Before going, she turned to look one last time at this mystery who had once been her husband, and, struggling vainly to suppress a tear, muttered, "You confused, mixed-up, silly, lovable… stupid, stupid… bastard!"

41.

A torch rekindles

Susan Somerfield routinely checked the time on a large wall-mounted clock in the cafeteria of the Brenthurst Clinic before glancing at her own watch to see if it told a different story. Her life was temporarily in limbo and there was no possibility of jumping on the next plane home to await developments from a detached distance, because those developments depended on her staying put.

The medics on Rimmer's ward assured her that he might regain consciousness at any moment, but from her own experience, she knew how vague such estimations could be. Back at the Priory, some issues had arisen relating to her reallocated workload and the logistics of her situation meant that they could only be remedied through regular, lengthy telephone dialogue. This additional inconvenience added to her omnipresent unease.

I need Gordon to recover now!

I've got to know why I'm here!

Although she had his parents to lean on for company, David and Carol lacked the stamina to maintain a constant bedside vigil, so they would occasionally return to their hotel for some much-needed rest. That was when the time really dragged.

Eventually the monotony of her situation was broken by a visit from two policemen who turned up at the clinic hoping to find Rimmer fit enough for further questioning. Disappointed to have made a wasted journey, they introduced themselves to Susan as Detective Inspectors Sneddon and van Hoosen and casually enquired about her relationship to the comatose invalid without showing any discernible interest in her answer. She guardedly described herself as, "a friend". Their dismissive attitude annoyed her, so she asked them a question of her own.

"Have you managed to find out anything about the young man who did this?"

DI Sneddon chose to reply.

"Oh, he was just the usual rubbish from the township."

"Can you be more specific please? After all, when Mr. Rimmer regains consciousness, it will be a great comfort to him to know that your investigation has been thorough."

Gordon's been the victim of an unprovoked attack here – surely these morons can do better than this?

"Miss Somerfield –"

"I prefer Ms."

The two men exchanged furtive glances which Susan computed as, '*Bloody feminist!*'

"How about Madam?" Sneddon was determined not to concede ground.

"That will be fine, thank you." Having neither the energy nor the inclination to start a protracted debate about gender politics, she let him have his little victory.

"Well then, Madam – he was a tearaway from Soweto who got his kicks from waving a gun around and trying to steal white men's money. Luckily for your… friend, the assailant's weapon of choice is unlikely to cause a fatality unless it's fired into the head or guts – .25 caliber Browning's are popular with hustlers because they're small, lightweight, and easy to hide, but they're not particularly powerful, even at close range, unless the shooter knows what he's doing, and this kid clearly didn't."

Inspector van Hoosen then added his own opinion of the deceased Lenka Molome.

"He was a hopeless stick-up merchant – he'd tried to knock over another innocent bystander at an ATM machine in the same area a week earlier. That poor guy had a heart attack on the spot and when he fell over, the dumb black bastard took off without getting any of his cash!"

Susan despaired that the two men made no attempt to disguise their abhorrent racism, but she valiantly tried to get them to concentrate on the details of the attack.

"Are you sure this was just about money then?" She was determined to dot all the *i*'s and cross every *t*.

"We believe so Madam - the gunman had never met Mr. Rimmer in his life before, so what else could the motive have been? As I've said, he'd been active in the area recently and it looks like he was hanging around that car park waiting to steal the first vehicle that pulled in. If he'd managed to get away with it, that VW would have been sold on by the end of the day - opportunists like him are quick off the mark. None of these *kaffirs* seem capable of looking for a proper day's work to get what they need. Christ help us if they get into power - I'll be on the first plane out of here, that's for sure!"

Susan had heard enough and decided to challenge van Hoosen's opinions.

"So tell me then, Inspector - where will you go? And when you get there, are you still going to look down your nose at anyone who looks different to you, or have you stopped to consider that people beyond this white supremacist bubble might not appreciate that sort of thing?"

Her unwelcome expression of liberal tolerance clearly hit its target, but the DI's professional training taught him not to rise to the bait.

If I bite back, she'll only put in a complaint about me at the station, so I'll have to hold my tongue 'til we can get out of here.

Jesus, I get so sick of stroppy bitches like this one!

Van Hoosen tried in vain to make a sharp (if undignified) exit, but she had not finished with him yet.

"Before you leave, did you say that the young man who shot Mr. Rimmer was active on the streets the previous week?"

"That's correct Madam."

"Then how did you allow him to get away? Surely delinquent black boys are easy to find in one of Johannesburg's main thoroughfares?"

DI Sneddon tried to regain the initiative for his partner by answering the question with similar belligerence.

"For your information Madam, we did apprehend him for the ATM shake-down, but our judicial system dropped the ball and he got released on bail. I presume his criminal friends scrambled the bond money together from some of the ill-gotten gains they've made mugging white folk."

"Or from doing a proper day's work, perhaps?"

Both men responded with another look that said more than words, before Sneddon curtly drew the malicious exchange to a close.

"Well, I think we're done here for now - thanks for your time, Madam and good day to you."

Once they were out of her earshot, van Hoosen tapped his partner's shoulder and sneered.

"Can you believe the cheek of that smart-arsed English cunt! Coming over here and trying to tell us how to behave? She needs to fuck off home and take that cabbage next door with her!"

While it brought Susan some satisfaction to vent her spleen at the bigoted detective inspectors, her deep frustrations remained, until finally, on day three, a breakthrough moment arrived.

Outside, rain politely pitter-pattered against the windows and a passing nurse suggested to Team Rimmer that, "This is a sign - God is nudging your man to wake up." He was still being drip-fed intravenously and Susan read to him from a local newspaper's coverage of the *Sun City Snooker Showdown*. As she recited from the clumsy correspondence, she gently held on to his free hand, and just then, a weak but imperceptible twitch transferred from one of his fingers to hers. Gradually, the trigger movement became a gentle grip and she realised that this was the first sign of a cautious re-awakening. Calmly, but firmly, she asked his father to call the nurse back to observe proceedings. Carol Rimmer looked on closely and suddenly saw her son's eyes flicker, then uncontrollable tears of relief rolled down her cheeks as she embraced Susan in a hug of triumphal relief. Their ordeal was over.

The recovering patient spent the next couple of days gradually coming to terms with his brush with death, and as soon as he felt strong enough, he finally put an end to Susan's misery by explaining his reasons for their break-up. He revealed how Marcus Botha wanted to use her inside knowledge to dish the dirt on the Priory's celebrity clientele, and then owned up about his financial difficulties.

"I had to split us up to keep that bastard from bothering you and it wasn't possible to just quit *The Horizon* there and then - without my fat paycheque every month I'd have lost the Notting Hill house - I'd be bankrupt. You can see the pressure I was under, can't you?"

"Christ almighty, Gordon! How could you think of putting money before what we had?" she asked, in anger and disbelief at his life choice.

"But Sue, I'm Scottish! That's what we do!"

She appreciated his reassuringly familiar self-mockery but could not understand his weakness.

"You should have said, *'To hell with the house - we'll downsize and make do!* You know I'd have supported you - I couldn't care less about that place!"

"But there was so much else going on in my head - Botha held the keys to my career. I've worked hard to get to the top of my trade, and I know that means I let my ego control my decision making, but I just couldn't think straight, ok? Jesus, we're all fallible, aren't we? Pressure sometimes leads us to make stupid choices - you must hear that from your patients all the time."

"Oh Gordon! You selfish idiot! So you're saying I had to deal with all that distress and anguish because your reputation and your wallet came first - really?"

Love versus career and cold, hard cash - such a Thatcherite dilemma!

"You're wrong Sue - you were always my top priority - I was trying to protect you, I swear it. I had to find a way of keeping the Head Honcho at arm's length."

"You don't honestly think I would *ever* betray a professional confidence, do you? I'd have reported him to my board of directors immediately."

"I'd expect nothing less, but a scandal like that would hit sales of the paper and some decent people might have lost their jobs as a result. Can you see the hole I was in? God knows, it's not that I didn't love you anymore - my life has been pure torture since we broke up."

This new consideration caused Susan to think a little differently.

So he's telling me our parting was a prudent tactical withdrawl?

'Live to fight another day,'- that seems to be the gist of his pitch anyway...

I still think his motives were shallow, but I've got to acknowledge his bravery in trying to stand up for me – in effect, he sacrificed a limb to save the rest of the body.

Is he my modern-day Mr. Darcy after all?

Perhaps…

"Look, you know me well enough to understand that I'm not some silly little airhead who'd normally drop everything to come running at the click of your fingers, right?"

"Of course."

"So what were you thinking of, dragging me thousands of miles across the world like this? Your parents were already here when I arrived, so you were hardly short of company."

"I thought this might be my last chance to say I love you! There it is – it's out in the open now, for better or worse. You're my whole world, so if I was going to check out here, I wanted to go with you by my side."

"Gordon, slow down – I need a moment. For months I haven't heard a word from you – nothing at all since our split. I may as well have not existed. Then you go and get yourself shot –"

"Almost killed!"

"– and I'm supposed to write off all that hurt, am I?" The cogs whirring around inside her head were almost visible. Quietly, rhetorically, she said, "How the hell am I supposed to react to all this?"

"You're intelligent enough to work that out for yourself Sue, but all I can say is that I've just stared death in the face and everything's clear to me now. You're right – you always were – you always are! To hell with the house! Let's downsize and make do. I'm asking – no – pleading… look, I'm bloody begging you if I have to!" He took a deep breath, then with reckless confidence, blurted out the words he had wanted to say a long time ago. "Susan Somerfield…will you do me the honour of being my wife? Marry me, Sue. Marry me. Please?" A trickle of tears started to run down his face that soon turned into a flood of expunged emotion. "Only don't expect me to get down on one knee just yet!"

Susan was finally getting some of those *i*'s dotted and *t*'s crossed, and after much deliberation, she responded with familiar, considered orderliness.

"No Gordon, I can't do it – for all I know, this is just a crazed reaction to a shattering event, and I won't fall victim to a whim brought on by your having a second chance of life." His heart missed a beat and he suddenly feared that this moment might be their final reckoning. After a brief pause for breath, she continued to speak, and to his huge relief, her tone was more conciliatory. "Let's take a step back - wait and see where we are in a few months' time, ok? I won't agree to marry you until I can recognise the man I used to know - if, over time, you prove you're serious, then you can ask me again."

Obviously, the answer was not what he had hoped for, but on reflection, it was typical of Susan. For their reconciliation to be meaningful, he needed to acknowledge the extent of the hurt that he had caused her.

After a mutual drying of moist eyes, their excruciatingly difficult arbitration process had produced peace, harmony and understanding. If only industrial disputes could be resolved as impressively!

Because of the high emotions on display during the lovers' reconciliation, sensitive hospital staff were careful not to rush Rimmer's recovery for fear that he might slip back to a comatose state. Their concerns were groundless, for now he faced the future with confidence. He would forever bless his True Love for dragging him from the darkness into the light in that tender moment when her hand touched his. Her presence was the elixir he needed to mend his broken body, but soon she had to return to England, and then he felt his jabbing, stinging, burning gunshot wound more intensely.

His parents were a great comfort during this period, and they remained in South Africa until he was fit enough to fly back to the UK. As they helped him gingerly stumble through the **ARRIVALS** gate at Heathrow airport, Susan raced forward to greet her returning hero with a welcoming hug of pure love, and from that moment on, the couple resumed their relationship in defiance of the great fissure that had once split it asunder.

Rimmer reluctantly put his house up for sale and moved into her cosy Camden Town apartment while he plotted his exit from *The Horizon*. Fortunately, he was able to take time away from the stresses of the sports desk thanks to the paper's employee health insurance policy. Marcus Botha offered his troops a generous protective umbrella to shield them from unwelcome financial downpours during periods of enforced absence (though in reality, it was rare for anyone to match the criteria for a successful claim and his wounded correspondent only qualified for assistance due to the exceptional circumstances surrounding his incapacity).

The Las Vegas and Sun City scoops had raised his stock, and several publications made surreptitious overtures for his services. Rival red tops were now prepared to match his earnings, but he decided to leave the tabloid world behind and pursue offers from the less lucrative (but infinitely more prestigious) quality papers. Susan supported his move of course, but when he sold his home at a large loss, the hit to his ego still stung like that bullet from Lenka Molome's pistol.

Back in Johannesburg, the police investigation quickly concluded that the shooting was a failed carjacking attempt. Case closed. At first, Rimmer felt relieved to put the entire incident behind him, but gradually his curiosity returned. He wanted to: -

a) understand what motivated his assailant to take such a brutal course of action, and

b) finish his enquiry into Marcus Botha's dubious past.

There was only one option open to satisfy his need for closure. He must face his fears and return to South Africa.

42.

Laments for the dearly departed

B arry Shackleton's funeral descended into an appalling media scrum. His family had wanted to mourn in peace, but the paparazzi turned the solemn ceremony into a shambolic scramble for snaps of a beleaguered, grieving widow and her shell-shocked children. All in the name of *'serving the public interest'*.

The saddest, maddest thing about the unedifying spectacle was that every participating newspaper enjoyed a surge in sales for their efforts. Once again, an apparently civilised society had opted to gawp at completely innocent victims of extraneous events. *The Horizon* felt particularly entitled to linger a little longer on their distress, because its fat cheque for the rights to Barry's story sat securely in his widow's bank account. Ruth and her children remained vulnerable for as long as that vile and vengeful magnet for moronic curiosity wished to treat them as its personal spittoon.

Eventually the Shackletons got welcome breathing space to repair their shattered lives when the circus found itself another tragic clown to ridicule, but the savagery of its intrusion into their private world left them with scars that would never truly heal…

Far removed from the insanity of a first world burial in the maelstrom of the media's spotlight, Bettina Molome and her daughter Dikeledi shed copious tears in the quiet of the Avalon Cemetery in Gauteng Provence as the body of their wild, misanthropic Lenka was laid to rest. There were no cameras on hand to record the occasion; no random bystanders aiming abuse at the deceased; no one threw brickbats of innuendo and ignorance from the pages of the national press.

Nobody cared at all, save for the poor, put upon remnants of the Molome clan.

The sun shone brightly over the near-deserted plot, but its rays did nothing to lift the atmosphere of gloom. Flies quietly busied themselves amongst the flowers that hung despondently against Lenka's tiny tombstone. His feral friends were conspicuous by their absence from the funeral; neither the Hitman nor the rest of his shameless crew dared to emerge from the shadows of the township, fearing that they would raise the suspicions of a plain clothes policeman who was respectfully observing proceedings from a discreet distance.

So for now it was bye, bye, Lenka Molome, the wayward wannabe who had bitten off more than he could chew in pursuit of his small-time criminal dreams. Bettina would soon be back at the same spot to say a final goodbye to her beloved daughter too, and then her descent into a bottomless pit of depression would be complete. She would see out the rest of her days alone, lonely, and unwilling to embrace the challenges of the New South Africa that she had once longed so hopefully for.

Then there would be nobody left to cry, to hurt, to mourn....

On their exit from the cemetery, a tall, lean, intelligent looking young white man with blonde hair and a copper complexion approached the weeping females. His open expression and clear-eyed demeanour gave a suggestion of honesty and trustworthiness, but Bettina had no approving smile to send his way, for he was the representative from the police force that had mercilessly gunned down her boy.

"Mrs. Molome? My name is Cornelius Carter - Detective Inspector Carter. Would it be possible to have a word with you? It's about your son."

Her anguished expression told its own story.

"I do not want to talk to any more policemen. You've just watched me bury the boy you want to speak about, so I can see no point in any of your chit-chat. He is dead, Inspector - understand? You cannot bother him anymore and as I have done nothing to hurt anyone, I don't want you bothering me either."

Dikeledi cut in.

"Please, can't you leave us alone? We answered hundreds of questions at the police station. My mother wants no more of this now."

"Well, can I offer you a lift home? My car is just around the corner?"

"No, thank you, we'll walk."

"But you're not well enough to walk. Please?" Bettina could see the logic in the inspector's offer, so she buried her pride for the sake of her daughter's wellbeing and accepted the lift on behalf of them both. In the car, Carter explained that he had attended the funeral service at the request of his brother Dominic. "He was the arresting officer during the failed armed ATM robbery - he managed to talk your son into giving himself up safely. He's very sorry about how things have turned out since then. He wanted to attend the service himself, but work commitments prevented that possibility."

"Do you think he deserves a medal, just because he feels bad now? He might very well be sorry, but neither of you can imagine my own sorrow and I have no gratitude for any policemen after the way they beat my boy so savagely."

Carter tried to explain that Dominic had defended her son against the rough treatment meted out by his colleagues, but mamma Molome .was in an unforgiving mood. When they reached the family home, the doggedly persistent detective inspector invited himself in and asked once more for assistance in his enquiries, because he was struggling to understand why the young man would pursue a second hold-up while he was already on bail awaiting trial for an earlier offence. Despite Bettina's contempt for the South African Police Service, she reluctantly decided to answer his questions in the hope that once they were over, she might be allowed to grieve in peace.

"Could you tell me something about Lenka - had there been any change in his behaviour recently?"

"Of course! One day he was full of life - too much so for his own good - and the next he was dead. Killed by a policeman's bullet. How much more can a person change than that?"

For the rest of her days, she would speak bluntly to establishment figures without fear of any consequences. Carter felt the deepest sympathy for the distraught woman, but he was unapologetic about the right of his colleagues to protect the public and enforce the law.

"Madam, those officers performed their duty by bringing down your son because he was attempting to evade capture. He had committed a serious crime - that's an essential fact to remember in all of this. They didn't shoot him out of cussedness."

She looked into the inspector's eyes and said, "Well that hasn't stopped your kind before! You know it and I know it, so do not give me any of that nonsense about duty. They shot an unarmed eighteen-year-old boy!"

"He was only unarmed because he dropped his weapon at the crime scene, and they had no way of knowing that. With respect, the man he put in hospital is somebody's son too."

It was almost too painful for Bettina to imagine another mother (and a father too, perhaps?) suffering like her because of Lenka's senseless act of brutality. At that moment, she could not help but feel jealous of those unknown parents, for while their son hung on to life in a Johannesburg hospital bed, they still had hope that he might return to them; all she was left with were her memories, and even those were tainted.

"Look, I do not want to know about what Mr. Rimmer's family are going through - all I care about is that a policeman shot my son when he was only doing what your people told him to do."

This odd response took Carter by surprise and clearly required clarification.

"*My* people Madam?"

"Yes, yes, you know what I mean Inspector, er... I've forgotten your name already!" Bettina was still looking at him, but in a confused and flustered way as the events of the day began to take their toll on her powers of concentration.

"It's Detective Inspector Carter."

"Oh yes ...well, you know my boy was acting on government orders when he shot that man."

"Government orders?"

"Do not play dumb with me, that won't do. When I told your friends at the police station that his first arrest was part of a Secret Service plot, they just looked at each other and smiled. You're probably all in it together. I didn't see you outside my house the night before the shooting, but I did see the other two men."

"What other two men?" His failure to understand Bettina made the poor woman all-the-more irritable.

"The men in the saloon car - the thick set one in the passenger seat and the bald driver. The fellows from the Secret Service who told my son to shoot Mr. Rimmer!"

Carter was sure that these were the ramblings of a distressed mother struggling with her sanity in the wake of a huge loss, but as some details were emerging from her accusations, he pressed further.

"Mrs. Molome, I give you my word that I know nothing about any kind of… *conspiracy* - if that's what you're talking about."

"Then that just proves that the statement I made at the station was ignored. What a surprise! You people are all the same."

He side-stepped her bitter criticism and dug deeper.

"So you're saying that your son had been contacted by people from the South African government to shoot Mr Rimmer? If that's the case, did he receive any payment to do the job? And if so, what happened to that cash?"

"Do you take me for a stupid woman Inspector? Perhaps you expect me to give those men their blood money back?"

"Well how am I going to know you're telling me the truth if you don't have proof of this transaction taking place?"

"I don't care what you think! That night Lenka handed me an envelope stuffed with sixty thousand rand in notes and said that it was an advance payment from the government for doing a certain task - he did not say what it was because I would have stopped him from doing it! That money has all gone towards his funeral and buying medicines for my daughter. If you don't believe what I say, then how else do you think I could afford to do those things? Or do you think *I* am a thief now? If you do, you will have to take me away too, but while I am locked up don't expect your spells to work on me like they did on my boy! Look where they got him!"

Carter decided to shelve any further questions about money and instead focussed on her allegations of government paymasters.

"What can you tell me about the two gentlemen that you saw with Lenka?"

"The thick set man did all the talking while the bald one just fidgeted behind his steering wheel. It was him I noticed really."

"This bald man - can you give me a better description of him?"

"No, it was dark, but I know one thing - he does not like to face up to the fact his hair has gone. He was wearing a baseball cap, but when he took if off to scratch his head, I noticed that he quickly put it back on again afterwards. A bald head, eh, what is that to worry about? That's just silly - stupid vanity, isn't it? If that is the worst of his problems, he is a very lucky man."

"Are you sure you didn't notice anything else in relation to the bald man? Please think." Carter was keen to see where this grieving (and possibly delirious) woman's fantasy was heading. Just then, a light bulb switched on in her head, illuminating a mental picture of the mystery man.

"Wait a minute; there is something else...he wasn't just hiding his bald head...he had an ugly scar on the side of his skull, like a massive birth mark. Yes, I remember that now...very strange it was...I remember it really stood out in the dark - that's how unusual it was. I can't understand why I did not think of it before."

"That's perfectly understandable, you can hardly be expected to think straight, today of all days, but I thank you for trying so hard for me."

Bettina's face hardened.

"Don't try to butter me up Inspector. I have absolutely no desire to help the police out now or ever again, for the rest of my life. I just want to tell you the truth so that you will leave us alone and not come back. I do not want your kindness or gratitude; I just want my son and there is nothing you can do about that is there? Even if you wanted to."

"I'm sorry Mrs Molome - please forgive me for my approach, I certainly meant no offence. If I uncover anything from what you've told me, I'll be in touch."

"And what good will that do me? Lenka will still be dead, and I do not care for revenge. I just want to hold him in my arms again and that can never be. Will you leave us alone now - please?"

With a resigned sigh, Detective Inspector Carter duly left the distraught mourners to their misery.

That evening he rang his brother with news of the funeral and Bettina Molome's story.

"I think the poor woman has lost her marbles a bit Dom - she was giving me a load of nonsense about her son being involved in a government conspiracy to murder Gordon Rimmer!"

Both brothers began to chuckle at the notion.

"What? Are we recruiting teenage spies from Soweto now? I didn't see that one coming! And why would our government want to kill Mr. Rimmer anyway? I shouldn't mock, Corny, but I don't imagine that Scottish sports reporters come high on our list of national threats!"

"I only wanted to offer my condolences in your absence really, but she came out with all this stuff about her boy getting sixty thousand rand as a down payment for the hit. I drove her home from the cemetery and the place was full of heavy-duty medication for her daughter. That must have cost a hell of a lot - more than the mother could afford to buy on her wages anyway. Did you know the girl has AIDS?"

"No, I don't know anything about Lenka Molome or his family at all. I expect the medicine money came from his petty criminal activities, eh?"

"With that kind of stockpile knocking around, those activities weren't so petty, but yeah, I reckon so. It'll all be untraceable now anyway and his mom and sister have suffered enough without me snooping around hassling them further."

"So how did this conspiracy thing come up then?"

"She said that his original arrest by you and the two goons from the station was set up to justify his involvement with these government people. It was crazed - very sad really. She did mention one thing that struck me though. She described one of the men who ordered the hit as having a bald head and a distinctive scar on his skull."

"What, like Chrome Dome Daalmans?"

"Yeah, that's what I thought…Wasn't he at the station when the kid was brought into custody?"

"You know it brother - he chewed me out for scrapping with the other officers, remember?"

"Yeah, yeah, I remember…I expect mamma Molome saw him hanging around the courthouse when her son got bailed and his scar stuck in her mind - it'll be something like that anyway…what I can't figure out is why a township thug was let back out onto the streets in the first place. That was unusual, eh Dom?"

"Well it wasn't exactly smart when you think that after his release he proceeded to carjack a notorious Scottish spy."

"Less of that!"

"You've got to have sympathy for his mother though - her head's probably in a terrible place right now. I know Daalmans is a nasty piece of work and I'd think twice before sending him a Christmas card, but he's no government special agent! And Lenka Molome didn't strike me as a black double-0-seven either!"

"You're right…But I'm still going to ask old Chrome Dome what he knows about that young man."

The next morning, Douglas Daalmans was heading out of the CBD station house with his partner DI Wolters in tow when Cornelius Carter caught up with him.

"Can I have a quick word with you? It won't take long."

"What about - we're on a job, so hurry it up." Daalmans's attitude was familiarly abrasive.

"Kevin, can you give us a minute please?" With that, Wolters lit up a cigarette and meandered down the street. "I just wanted to ask you about the kid who was gunned down after that shooting at the *TMMC* building last week?"

Daalmans met the question with a lengthy silence before finally replying, "What's he got to do with you? You weren't assigned to that case so mind your own bloody business. If you want to know anything about him, ask DI's Sneddon and van Hoosen, though I doubt they'll have much to say either. That was a simple case of a greedy blackie trying to roll a tourist over - end of story."

"Quite so," said Carter (neatly side - stepping the racist element of the reply). "I'm only asking because someone answering your description was seen speaking to him in Soweto the night before the shooting. Would you know anything about that?"

He sensed an anger welling up in Daalmans and anticipated his furious response.

"Fuck you, Carter! Don't try any of that shit on me! What do you take me for? I'm not in the habit of chatting to darkies in the township late at night, least of all ones who carry pistols around with them! Who said they saw me?"

"Calm down Inspector, I fully expected it to be duff information. I only wondered how anyone might have managed to put you and the young boy together, that's all."

"How should I know? Now are you going to tell me who's been spreading this sort of crap around or not?"

"That I can't do."

"Then get the fuck away from me before I lose my temper! And you can expect a call from our captain about unwarranted bloody harassment too!"

"That's a bit of an over-reaction to a couple of simple questions, isn't it? Oh, and before I go, can you tell me whether you were in the court room when Lenka Molome got bail?"

"No I wasn't - why would I be? Now fuck off and leave me alone!" With that, the brief but lively conversation abruptly ended.

Back at his desk half an hour later, Carter received a severe reprimand from his superior, Captain Mackenzie, with strict orders to concentrate on his own cases in future. As a follow up, he must never question the integrity of another police officer without corroborating evidence. No further discussion was encouraged on the subject.

PART FOUR

PERSUASION, EVASION, AND BAILING OUT

43.

Rebuilding Brand Botha

The Head Honcho's untimely heart attack left a huge burden of expectation on the shoulders of his wife Elizabeth.

His London Bridge hospital consultant warned her that his recovery would be a slow process, so when he returned to their palatial Georgian period Hertfordshire mansion, she hired a small team of private nurses to provide him with round the clock care. This seemed like an extravagant indulgence, but there was sound reasoning behind the move, for it allowed her to concentrate on raising enough money from disposable assets to keep *Marcus Botha Publishing and Communications* viable.

Her first major decision was obvious; with liquidation looming large, she had to jettison *MJB TV*, knowing that, realistically, Rupert Murdoch would be the only interested bidder.

Recognising the strength of his bargaining position, the wily Australian made a derisory offer to underwrite ten per cent of the company's losses in exchange for its subscription business; to rub salt into an open wound, he also promised to scrap its defective satellite dishes and replace them with his own state of the art models. This was a take-it-or-leave-it, non-negotiable proposal, and Elizabeth wasted no time in accepting the terms.

Disgruntled investors (including Michael Brookes on behalf of *The Horizon*'s print union) were unimpressed with the deal and threatened legal action, claiming that Botha's prospectus fraudulently underplayed the financial risks involved in establishing a television network. MJB himself was by far the largest shareholder in the failed enterprise, so his own cash reserves were now severely drained, and his wife feared that expensive litigation might finish them off.

Yet more pressure!

She worked fast to amass a significant fighting fund, divesting thousands of shares held in companies that were not under her husband's direct control, while keeping a firm grip on those owned in his core businesses. Her judgement calls displayed impressive business acumen, though she still harboured concerns over how he would react once he emerged from his enforced furlough.

To make a problematic period even more difficult, she faced an orchestrated media campaign that portrayed her as an imbecilic wrecker of the Botha fortune (despite unequivocal evidence that she was, in fact, its pragmatic saviour). If the malicious abuse caused her sleepless nights, nobody could tell; her ice maiden image remained flawlessly intact in front of board members, employees and creditors. For weeks, the fortress walls of Brand Botha took a relentless battering, but their sturdy buttresses withstood the assault and in due course, the financial institutions began to realise that *MJB TV's* collapse was an isolated aberration rather than being symptomatic of a more general malaise.

Elizabeth insisted that the couple's mansion was exempt from consideration during the great sell off, and one sedate Sunday afternoon, as Marcus sat quietly reading a newspaper in their sitting room, she decided to raise the thorny issue of the network's mysterious funding once more.

I have to find out how that unmitigated disaster got its cash!

This task clearly required discretion, so after relieving his nurse of her duties for the rest of the day, she began to dig for the truth.

"Come on then, you crafty old rogue, it's time you told me where that money came from to keep things ticking over when the problems arose. This is a matter of the utmost importance, and it simply won't wait - I need to know if there's anything left in your secret vault to pay off our outstanding creditors."

Botha brushed aside his wife's concerns.

"Ah, I'm afraid those coffers are empty now my dear. Relax - there's an annoying boil I still need to lance in that regard, but it'll be dealt with once I get back on my feet."

A familiarly frosty glance found its way towards him, but something happened to it along the way; from nowhere, the glacier exploded into volcanic fury.

"Marcus I'm insisting here! I haven't suffered the traumas of the past few weeks to be patronised by you now - tell me the truth, dammit! I have the right to know...I've *earned* the right to know where you found that money!"

He remained unmoved.

"It's a private matter and that's all I have to say. Let sleeping dogs lie."

Elizabeth reacted to this brusque dismissal with almost apoplectic anger.

"Who do you think you're talking to? We only kept this roof over our heads because *I* managed to put out a fire that *you* mistakenly lit! Don't you DARE try to pacify me like that!"

Her husband was astonished to be attacked with such ferocity while he was still so fragile, but the issue had now taken on the same significance for her as it had for him during the weeks preceding his collapse. Undeterred, he continued to fend off her request with the slipperiness of old.

"I wouldn't dream of playing such games - it's just that the situation is extremely complex, and I don't have the paperwork at hand to go through the finer points...when I can concentrate properly, I'll let you in on everything."

"That's not good enough - I want an answer now! An enormous amount of money seems to have landed on your lap out of fresh air and the cack-handed way it's been used has almost destroyed us. I need to know how you got it, where it came from and, now that it's been wasted, what your plans are for replacing it!"

These impassioned demands were insufficient in themselves to force him to reveal all, but he realised that her financial advisors may also be hunting for the source of the mystery millions and if they uncovered his misappropriation of company pension funds, the implications would be disastrous. On reflection, he decided that confiding in his only trusted ally was the lesser of two evils.

"Ok, ok, I'll tell you what you want to hear - but you're not going to like it." This was an extremely uncomfortable moment, but through gritted teeth he finally began to explain the dilemma he had got them into. "I took the money that you're looking for from our employees' pension scheme in the belief that Murdoch's mob would go bust at any moment. I'm sure they were only a whisker away from ruin when those idiotic bankers pulled the plug on me."

There it was. No apology, no guilt.

Elizabeth assessed the revelation with a mixture of distress and admiration; the first reaction was obvious, the second less so. On the one hand, she worried at the seriousness of her husband's criminal activity, but on the other she admired his sheer audacity.

"How on earth did you think you were going to get away with that!"

"It was simply a case of borrowing money from Peter to pay Paul in the short term - if *Sky* had gone to the wall, I'd have been the only player left in pay-per-view broadcasting. That's a business that will grow and grow, and I would have had it all! Once we were moving in a profitable direction, the pension payback would have been easy to deal with."

He pointed out the vast potential of a successful television network in financial and political terms, but still she fumed.

"Oh Marcus, you're such a chancer - you put our entire portfolio in jeopardy just to win a silly boy's game of chicken! That's what it was really all about - you wanted to see who would blink first! Your reasoning sounds plausible, but it didn't work, did it? YOU LOST OUT! I simply cannot believe that you of all people adopted a losing strategy! The millions recklessly gambled - the threat to our future - I can accept all that, but when you take a risk, I expect you to WIN. You are a winner…it's what you do. Never forget that."

Her venomous criticism stung, but the Head Honcho was too tired, too weak to fight back; all he could do was absorb it. She then asked him how and when the fraud had taken place.

He thought about the long-term implications of his answer, for Elizabeth's ignorance of the details would help her to avoid prosecution as an accessory after the fact if the whole thing became public knowledge. Balanced alongside this consideration was a primal instinct for self-preservation; under United Kingdom law a wife cannot be forced to testify against her husband, so her knowledge of his skulduggery would not implicate him.

I can't put this off any longer- it's time to open my Pandora's box of secrets!

"To tell you *when* I moved the money is an easy question to answer - every time the network needed a cash injection, I simply dipped into the pension pot and transferred the necessary amount. *How* I did it was rather clever though, if I say so myself." A mischievous smile broke out across his previously anxious face. "The whole thing was child's play really. Go to any park and observe the behaviour of infants when they're parents allow them a bit of freedom to run and chase. You'll see that some like to spin around and around until they make themselves dizzy - they love that sense of disorientation. Constant irregular motion creates confusion, whether it's inside a child's head or on the pages of a balance sheet. Now, the pension fund rests within my *publicly* traded companies, and I own between 50 - 70 % of the capital in most of them, yes?"

"Yes, that's still intact, though of course I've had to offload a lot of your non-core business assets to keep us afloat."

"Alright Elizabeth!" He preferred to ignore the bitter reality of their reduced circumstances. "I'll sort those issues out when I'm better, but you want to know how I continued to finance *MJB TV* don't you?"

"I do. Please carry on."

"Well, I simply moved cash and other assets, in particular, pension fund money, from those *public* companies to my *privately*-owned ones. Now here comes the smart part in all of this. I made sure that the public and private businesses operated on different accounting year-end dates - April 1st to March 31st, or January 1st to December 31st - so when money was switched around between them, the banks and shareholders had no idea where it all was at any one time."

This all seemed too easy for the sceptical Elizabeth, whose background in ranching came from trading livestock, not share options.

"Surely questions were asked at boardroom level as to why you were moving company assets?"

"I like to keep everyone second-guessing, that's the trick! Let's deal with my privately owned companies first. Whenever a decision requires ratification, I'll call a meeting at short notice and if any board members manage to show up, they only receive key documents an instant before we commence. I retrieve the paperwork immediately afterwards, so they don't get time to reflect on the details of any items raised. Those idiots are kept spinning like the dizzy children I mentioned - do you see? It's by maintaining this state of confusion that I eventually secured the power to make key decisions alone. I argued that the newspaper industry requires on-the-spot action, rendering collective discussion redundant. Now I call the shots, signing all the significant cheques, and everything is rubber-stamped at board level retrospectively."

"Ok, but in the publicly owned companies, plenty of prior notice is required before board meetings take place, so how do you disrupt those?"

"I'll call them off at the last minute and re-convene at times when the members find it difficult to attend. Once again, everything is in a state of flux, with one ringmaster - me - in command of the timetable. When it comes to financial matters - like syphoning off assets - legal requirements might force me to announce details of a specific share deal or transaction and in those situations, I am, shall we say, less than forthright in my responses. I've had to fend off some awkward questions at times, but in the end, with my reputation for success, I'm never scrutinised too closely."

As these revelations tripped from his tongue, he found a renewed energy; perhaps confession was good for the soul after all. Even one as dark and empty as his.

For Elizabeth, extracting the information felt like pulling out a decaying tooth, but in the end, the effort was worth it.

"By Christ, you're a subtle swine."

"A swine, am I? That's as may be, but I'm going to have to rely on you to keep up the family tradition 'til my strength returns. Are you up for the challenge?"

She would have to re-stock the pension fund by redistributing big money from his remaining successful enterprises, and that risked eroding City confidence once more. Also, now that many of his assets had gone to appease creditors, opportunities to bamboozle his auditors were uncomfortably scarce.

"It's a Herculean task, but with such a cunning husband to turn to for advice, I'm sure that, in time, I can replace everything that you've, 'borrowed'."

Significantly, after satisfying herself that they could escape detection, at no point did she question the lack of morality in her husband's actions.

They were indeed a remarkable pairing.

44.

The rusting of an Iron Lady

For more than a decade, Margaret Hilda Thatcher had held centre stage as the most charismatic and formidable figure in UK politics. She possessed an uncanny ability to convince people that she was always right (even during times when they knew her to be very, very, wrong) and her single-minded belligerence sparked a social revolution. Thatcherism created many success stories, particularly in the south of England, but the game of life inevitably throws up more losers than winners and the economic divide between rich and poor increased considerably during her three-term tenure as Prime Minister, with huge numbers of people sinking into long-term unemployment.

Undeterred by criticism, the Iron Lady continued to vilify anyone who failed to embrace the go-getting entrepreneurial spirit of the age, but over time, her fanatical fervour began to irritate the silent majority. Her policies grew ever more draconian (culminating in her infamous Poll Tax legislation) and as the sunlit uplands of her rhetoric faded to dappled reality, many previously loyal supporters lost faith in their heroine.

During her dramatic reign, Thatcher won countless gladiatorial skirmishes in the Westminster Colosseum, but as a consequence, she left a trail of vanquished opponents licking their wounds with simmering bitterness, and by November of 1990, self-seeking government plotters began to emerge from the shadows, determined to slay their Caesar.

The seeds of her downfall were sown four years earlier when she ignored the Defence Secretary Michael Heseltine's advice to sell the ailing aircraft manufacturer *Westland* to a European consortium (she preferred a rival American bid). With his authority undermined, he sulkily quit the cabinet and retreated to the back benches, until finally, with public confidence in her abilities fading fast, he saw his opportunity for revenge via a leadership challenge.

Under the terms of the contest, the successful candidate needed to secure a 15% majority of votes cast by their fellow Conservative MP's, and to Thatcher's amazement, she came up short. Several quivering dissenters hedged their bets during the ballot, but after seeing how many of their colleagues were prepared to abandon her, they let it be known that they would follow suit in a second vote. The game was up.

Still she refused to accept the inevitability of defeat until close-quarter cronies advised her that she faced humiliation by fighting on in a losing cause, and so, after much anguished soul-searching, the *Grande Dame* reluctantly fell on her sword. Eternally divisive, it is reasonable to speculate that as many people cried as cheered when she left Downing Street as the nation's leader for the last time.

Heseltine naturally expected to claim the victor's spoils, but his role as chief executioner left a bad taste in the mouths of her remaining devotees and they were determined to look for a more palatable successor, so two new names were added to the second ballot paper: the Chancellor of the Exchequer John Major and Foreign Secretary Douglas Hurd. Eventually, Major, an unremarkable politician with minimal cabinet experience, got the nod to govern the country.

A greater contrast in leadership styles could hardly have been imagined: Thatcher, bold, colourful, confrontational, and Major, grey of hair, and of temperament; the Monochrome Man.

This changing of the guard was very bad news for Lewis Neeves. He had spent his entire Parliamentary career sucking up to Mrs Thatcher and now suddenly found himself a relic of a bygone age, a reminder of times past. He needed to show the right people that he was still politically relevant, but his association with Marcus Botha made that problematical, for many of his colleagues at Conservative central office had publicly approved *MJB TV*'s broadcasting license and its embarrassing collapse left them distinctly red faced.

Given the Head Honcho's current toxicity, how do I find a way into John Major's inner circle?

Let's look at the positives first – we can probably expect a boost in the opinion polls after our change of leader.

Will that be sustainable though?

The next general election is less than two years away and if that goes against us, we'll ditch Major for sure, so I need to be careful not to get too touchy-feely with the new broom just yet.

I think I'll spend the next few months edging towards the centre ground without abandoning my original views entirely – just in case the political landscape changes once more.

This trick required great delicacy, for there were many eggshells to walk over along the way and only the fleet of foot might avoid making a mess. Thatcher's policies left little room for manoeuvre, even for the most astute of politicians; on the good ship *Margaret* you either served as a loyal crew member or walked the gangplank, and Neeves preferred the creature comforts of his cosy cabin to a dip in the briny sea any day. With mutineers now in command of the vessel, it was imperative that he avoided, 'Davy Jones's locker' long enough to eventually worm himself into the officer ranks.

So how do I catch the new PM's eye?

Major shared the aspirational philosophies of his predecessor; he promoted a vision of a "classless society" where anyone could rise to the top and the Westminster well-wisher passionately endorsed this view (in principle).

It's idealistic nonsense really – talk of a genuine meritocracy is just a pipe dream thanks to our insufficient funding of the education system – but an empty promise is something I can happily get behind!

For other issues, common ground was harder to discern.

The public backlash against Thatcher's Poll Tax had effectively finished her off and John Major wanted to introduce a fairer rating system, requiring Neeves to perform a three-point turn over his enthusiasm for the original levy.

I'll have to say that I've seen the error of my ways and now wholeheartedly agree with the government's rethink.

On aspects of foreign policy, he found himself caught between a rock and a hard place.

Westminster is suddenly pro-Europe, so I'll embrace this spirit of, 'entente cordiale,' by nodding approvingly in the Commons at any mention of greater economic integration with our partners across the channel - I can easily feign memory loss about that if Major's reign proves to be short-lived.

As for his desire to see free elections in South Africa, I need to make a few discreetly favourable public comments about Nelson Mandela and the ANC - I won't over-do it, but I do want to appear open minded and statesmanlike.

The stench of his hypocrisy was rank indeed.

Of course, this new approach won't sit easily with Botha back at The Horizon - oh, if only that heart attack had killed him!

The old bugger will be back at work soon, breathing down my neck if I write anything that he objects to.

For the time being I'll stay on there, but I must be prepared to walk away if the subtle changes in my outlook meet with Major's approval.

When the new broom announced his first cabinet reshuffle, Neeves unsurprisingly found himself out in the cold. Nobody saw this move as any great slight on the part of the incoming Prime Minister; it was simply a case of political expediency; it made sense for him to put a junior minister with strong Thatcherite connections out to pasture for the time being. The party's hierarchy had no enthusiasm for another period of in-fighting, so the demoted MP was advised to keep his head down and vigorously support the government at every opportunity.

Naturally, this arrangement sat very well with the new regime, but Neeves wanted a little bit of *quid pro quo* to ensure his compliance. He promised to sit tight and be a good boy, so long as there was a reward for his loyalty with a return to the cabinet (preferably in a position of influence rather than his previous role as a minor cog at the Foreign Office) once the furore over Thatcher's ousting settled down.

If I'm patient and play my cards skilfully, I can emerge from all this upheaval very creditably indeed...

Marcus Botha had deep concerns over the Iron Lady's removal from office. To his immense frustration, he was still convalescing at home when the crisis unfolded and therefore could not influence public opinion in her hour of need.

My target market - the kind of people I can easily sway through a well written editorial – were starved of my guidance.

I would have comfortably corralled those wayward sheep back into their pens before they got out of control if I had the chance!

Although John Major upheld traditional Tory values of low taxation and support for business, he had a less radical approach to government than his predecessor and the Head Honcho much preferred Thatcher's dynamism.

Despite my misgivings, I've no choice but to back the new leader – the prospect of an alternative government is simply intolerable!

With Labour in power, we might see the return of trade union influence and those knots have been successfully untangled – I don't want them re-tied!

On international matters, he was distinctly nervous about Major's keenness to see the end of apartheid in South Africa, for he was acutely aware of the possible danger to his long-term future, should the ANC win power in his native land. Mrs Thatcher had been notoriously reluctant to condemn the government there, and her stance was very good news for Botha, for it meant that awkward questions about his past remained unanswered. As far as she was concerned, he was a United Kingdom domicile employing UK workers; they paid UK taxes and spent their wages in UK shops (mostly) on UK goods and services. Those things mattered more to her than the dubious history of a one-time mining man from the colonies.

Now she was gone, and with Lewis Neeves shunted into the sidings too, the Head Honcho no longer had a 'go-between' conduit in government to remind the new PM of his worth.

To avoid any possibility of my extradition, I need to force Major and his advisors into a rethink of their attitudes towards those black bastards back home – that's got to be my top priority now!

45.

Getting back in the saddle

Gordon Rimmer's life changed significantly in the six months after his return from South Africa. Those stellar performances in Las Vegas and Sun City had made him hot property and several plum offers came his way, the most attractive of which was an invitation to join Rupert Murdoch's *News International* empire as Chief Sports Correspondent at *The Times*. While Marcus Botha relied on tabloids and regional papers for his daily bread, Murdoch's publishing portfolio included a healthy mix of high and low brow titles, so he consequently attracted a greater breadth of talent, from vocational journalists to the vain, needy or just plain greedy. Rimmer happily admitted to ticking every one of those boxes, and once he was fit enough to resume work, he journeyed beyond *The Horizon* without a second's hesitation.

Some of his former colleagues grumbled that the move was a callous betrayal of the Head Honcho, and this made his decision all the sweeter; their jealous judgements satisfied him immensely. Of course, he remembered Pieter Hertzog's dire warning back in Las Vegas that his former boss took great umbrage at displays of disloyalty, but beating a hoodlum's bullet can embolden a man, and anyway, Mad Marcus was still recuperating from his own brush with death, so he was hardly in any position to cause trouble.

The new job paid less than the king's ransom Rimmer earned at *Horizon Tower*, but his drop in salary was more than supplemented when another prestigious opportunity came along to anchor a new sports magazine programme for the *BBC* called, *"The Tale of the Tape."* This particularly pleasant commission boosted his bank balance and ego in equal measure, all of which made him the very picture of contentment at home, where his idyllic partnership with Susan Somerfield grew even stronger the second time around thanks to the absence of Botha's omnipresent interference.

1991 may have been a meteoric year in Rimmer's orbit, but as autumn chilled into winter and shop fronts took on a festive façade, his thoughts turned back to sunny South Africa and the shooting. The more settled he became in his new surroundings, the more he wanted to confront his anxieties over the past, and to that end, he began to spend time at the British Library pouring over Johannesburg's newspaper coverage of the incident. To his dismay, he discovered that an important element of the story had gone unreported; there was no mention of the fact that at the time of the attack, his assailant was on bail from a charge relating to a previous gunpoint robbery.

The South African authorities take a dim view of black criminal suspects, so why did they release a dangerous thug like Lenka Molome before his trial for that original hold-up?

And why did the local press fail to pick up on something so unusual?

Most accounts of the first incident mentioned that it was followed by a seemingly routine arrest, but one crime reporter, Felix Nel of the *Johannesburg Journal,* suggested a different picture altogether. Buried away at the bottom of his piece was an ambiguous hint that the arresting officers became embroiled in a fight amongst themselves before taking the youth away.

How could a claim like that receive so little attention?

Rimmer decided to contact the author responsible for this remarkable footnote and made the necessary enquiries with great haste. It only took a couple of calls to deskbound staff at the *Journal* to obtain a contact number (he was intrigued that a regional paper was so relaxed about revealing the personal details of its contributors; national papers were certainly more circumspect in this regards).

"Hello, is that Felix Nel?"

"At your service sir! To whom am I speaking?"

The South African's lofty tones immediately reminded Rimmer of the grander correspondents at his new workplace, but he was gratified to hear such a friendly voice on the other end of the phone.

"My name is Gordon Rimmer and I'm a brother-in-arms so to speak from the UK - that's to say I'm a fellow journalist…I write for *The Times.*"

"Oh my, oh my - you're not offering me a job, are you? I must say that would be a turn up for the books!" Nel was obviously a playful fellow.

"No such luck Felix."

"Pity. Ah well, onwards and upwards. What's on your mind then, this fine and sunny day?"

"I'm interested in an article you wrote some months back in which you mentioned that a fight might have broken out between some police officers during the arrest of an armed mugger."

"Oh yes - an incident of which we dared not speak."

Immediately this comment intrigued Rimmer.

"What do you mean?"

"I take it you've read the piece?"

"Of course."

"As a journalist yourself, you must have seen it as a complete fudge?"

"Well I don't mean to be critical, but yes, it's not exactly clear whether anything actually happened. Can I read back what you wrote?"

"It's not what *I* wrote Mr. Rimmer - I was determined to lead my story with the disclosure of that unfortunate *contretemps,* but in the end, I had to accept its inclusion as a mere footnote following a ludicrous editorial re-write prior to publication. Feel free to remind me of my boss's handiwork if you will."

"Ok then, I quote - *'eyewitness accounts suggested that punches were exchanged amongst the arresting officers, but later reports confirmed that the melee resulted from difficulties in restraining the suspect.'* Considering the kind of government you have there, I'm surprised your paper got away with that much, though the backtracking is obvious, as you admit."

"The whole thing was all so frustrating! That dust-up was something of an exclusive for me, but once the authorities got wind of what had happened, they issued a terse denial, making my account look rather foolish. Originally, my editor ordered me to remove any mention of the punch-up from the report, but I insisted upon its inclusion as a point of principal. In fact, I (rather flamboyantly) offered him my resignation over the matter. He backed down, assuring me he'd find a compromise, and that mealy-mouthed rubbish at the end of the piece was it."

"Why were you so determined to write about this at all?"

"Because one of the officers involved is a young lad for whom I have the greatest respect, and I wanted to highlight his bravery in trying to uphold correct arrest procedures while his colleagues were letting themselves down. I'm a good friend of his father and I have high hopes that his commitment to duty will be the way forward for the policing of black suspects once the blight of this wretched apartheid nonsense has gone."

"Can you tell me his name?"

"Yes, it's Dominic Carter and he works out of the Jo'burg Central Police Station. My paper wouldn't go so far as to allow any mention of him by name in my report, but in truth, that may not have been a bad thing - as his father said to me, the resultant publicity might have made him a target for reprisals amongst his fellow officers. Under those circumstances, I'll accept a compromise, but restrictions on what I can write normally go beyond the pale.

Did you know my fellow reporters and I were also discouraged from mentioning that Officer Carter's suspect subsequently got released on bail and went on to attack an off-duty British journ...wait a minute - of course! That was you, wasn't it? He held you up too! So that's what this interest is all about?"

"I won't lie Felix, I'm trying to understand how a black guy who had been charged with a serious offence managed to get bail under your regime. The bond must have amounted to quite a sum I would imagine?"

"I'd expect the terms to be significantly prohibitive, yes indeed."

"So who put up the money then, and why?"

"There you have me sir, for once again, someone on high had stern words with our editors here to prevent them from pursuing that line of enquiry. They were told that his release was an 'administrative mistake'. Our legal profession gets very tetchy at even a whiff of criticism, so when an error like that leads to a dangerous black gunman's release from incarceration... well, I'm sure you can appreciate how that sort of thing would make the white folk very nervous. Particularly now that the ANC is readying itself for power."

Rimmer saw the logic in such reasoning.

"When I was over there, it seemed that a lot of whites - mainly the older generation - were just itching for an excuse to slap down Mandela and his militants, so I can understand the authorities' wanting to keep negative race stories from emerging in your press. As it is, you're only a mis-placed comment away from civil war, so why fan those flames, eh?"

"Be that as it may, suppression of facts is stifling debate in our country, I'm afraid to say. I know I'm an idealist, but I prefer to see everyone's cards on the table - it avoids nasty surprises later in the game. There are good and bad stories on both sides of the race divide, and sugarcoating the bad stuff just leads anyone with an agenda to make mischief. We have an opportunity to start again here with a clean slate, but it'll only work if we accept that neither race has a monopoly on goodness or mistakes. Home truths need to be exposed for everyone's sake."

"Spoken like a true newspaperman."

"Well it's in my blood - I can't help myself! I expect that you feel the same, though I'm sure you don't have struggles over freedom of speech at an esteemed publication like *The Times*, eh?"

"Let me assure you pal, when it comes to making compromises, I've got plenty of personal experience from my days as a tabloid journalist! I have to say though Felix, that I'm not completely convinced by your outpouring of altruism - doesn't part of your frustration come from the fact that you're being denied the opportunity to profit from exclusive scoops?"

"Absolutely sir - I'm guilty as charged!"

"I knew it! For a minute I thought I was speaking to a real one-off - a reporter who believes that the story is the be-all and end-all."

"Let me be honest with you Mr. Rimmer - when the apartheid dam breaks, there'll be a flood of big stories to be had here and I want to top up the old pension pot by cashing in with my share. Remember the mint Carl Bernstein and Bob Woodward made from breaking the Watergate scandal in the *Washington Post*? They got film rights, book deals, TV and magazine interviews - those boys were set up for life. They showed us all how a major revelation can line a sharp reporter's pockets. Now I know my work isn't ever likely to bring a President down, but I can dream, can't I? There's one big payday out there for me, I'm sure - why not live in hope for something like that, eh?"

Rimmer had really warmed to this wily old rogue.

"Why not indeed, my friend. But while you're waiting for that jackpot, I still need to speak to this young policeman…Dominic Carter, wasn't it? Can you help me there?"

"I tell you what - I'll give you his father's phone number and if the old man's happy for you to chat to Dom, you can take things from there. That would be better for the lad than if you started to ask awkward questions of his colleagues at the station - there are a few ball-breakers down there who might become fractious if they knew that his actions had drawn attention from the foreign press."

Both men agreed that this suggestion was the smartest way to move forward, and they wrapped up their productive conversation in a spirit of mutual respect and kinship.

That evening, the patriarchal Mr. Carter received Rimmer's call during a family dinner, and a short conversation followed to establish the precise nature of this sudden interest in his son. The young buck then received a few preparatory words of advice from his father before taking centre stage.

"Hello Dominic, my name is -."

"I know who you are sir - I remember you getting shot over here a few months back. You sound in fine voice now - I trust your recovery is going well?"

"Thanks for your concern, aye, I'm getting stronger by the day. I'm sure your dad has already mentioned that I've got a few questions to ask you about my attacker?"

"He has and I'm happy to help. I'm sure that you're aware I'd arrested him only a couple of days earlier after he held another man up at gunpoint in the Central Business District - that's my patch. May I say that I'm sorry he was back out on the streets to try his luck again, but these things happen from time to time, I'm afraid. He shouldn't have been let out of jail, but sometimes the odd slippery fish manages to wriggle out of our net. No judicial system is perfect - not even yours in the UK."

Dominic's mature way of speaking amused Rimmer; he was blunt, but honest, and his vocational enthusiasm shone brightly.

"I'm trying to understand why I got shot, so I need to get a better picture of what was going on in that fella's head. I'd like to find out as much about his background as I can. To that end, would you tell me why you had a fight with the other arresting officers at the scene of the first incident? Did you know him previously, perhaps?"

"Absolutely not sir - when I lashed out, I was simply trying to stop a suspect from getting beaten up in a police car. That's not the sort of thing I want to be involved in."

"That's very idealistic of you."

"So I keep being told, but there are right ways and wrong ways of doing this job and I'm not going to conform to the wrong ways - it's as simple as that. Look, I don't want to get sanctimonious about all this, Mr. Rimmer - I just wanted to do things by the book and my colleagues didn't. Lenka Molome's punishment was for the courts to decide, not us, and we should have been happy enough to make the arrest and take him off the streets for a while. I'm sorry to say this, but I think that little dust-up may have indirectly led him to you, because it looks like somebody took pity on him for getting a beating - maybe they paid his bail bond after reading about what had happened in one of our local papers. In hindsight, I'd say whoever did that made something of an error of judgement, wouldn't you?"

"I'm not going to argue with you there!"

"Anyway, that's as much as I know, except that he was killed a couple of days later trying to avoid capture after putting a bullet into you. If you want any further information, give my older brother Cornelius a call - he's a detective inspector at my station and he attended Molome's funeral. As the assailant had been gunned down by a member of the SAPS -"

"SAPS?"

"That's the South African Police Service, sir."

"Oh, sorry, aye, please carry on." (Ignorance of these kind of acronyms reminded Rimmer of why he reported on sport rather than *real* news).

"Well, as he'd been shot by one of our men, I thought that someone should represent the force at the funeral as a mark of respect to his grieving family, but nobody else seemed to be too bothered with that idea. I decided to go myself, but unfortunately, I couldn't get anyone to cover my shift, so I asked Corny if he'd take my place. Afterwards he spoke to the lad's mother, and it seems that the poor woman has gone a bit nuts with the shock of everything, 'cos she had some crazy conspiracy theory about why her son was going around Jo'burg toting a deadly weapon. My brother can give you the full story and that might tie up some of your loose ends."

The words 'conspiracy theory' are enough to ignite any reporter's curiosity and Rimmer's went into overdrive as he jotted down the elder sibling's number. When he contacted Cornelius Carter, he found him to be as refreshingly upstanding and honest as young Dominic, but over the phone it was difficult to ascertain from his deadpan delivery whether he thought that there was more to this simmering mystery than a simple case of carjacking by a Sowetan hoodlum.

To discover the truth, Rimmer knew he would have to organise some face-to-face meetings with the peripheral players. He needed an excuse to return to the land of his darkest nightmares, and as luck would have it, a major story emerged that would do the trick.

46.

Who's who?

Sport is often instrumental in breaking down barriers of prejudice, and now that South Africa's beleaguered government had finally begun to dismantle their despised apartheid system, the International Cricket Council offered them a welcome olive branch; after much earnest deliberation, the game's administrators decided to restore the national team's test match status, allowing its players to grace the world stage once more. Marcus Botha's *Sun City Snooker Showdown* may have generated plenty of domestic interest in competitive sport, but this was the real deal; a globally significant gesture bringing an end to two decades of international isolation.

Rimmer reacted quickly, convincing *The Times* to book him onto a Johannesburg-bound flight so that he may capture local reactions from social, cultural, and racial perspectives. Whilst there, he would make further use of his time by: -

a) resurrecting his original enquiries into the allegations concerning Botha.

b) soliciting Cornelius Carter's help to investigate the circumstances surrounding his own assault.

With his concerned partner Susan's advice still ringing in his ears to, "just be super-careful!" he hoped to find the experience both cathartic and enlightening.

Upon his arrival, he checked into the Sandton Hilton hotel to the north of the city and wasted no time in contacting Carter.

"Any chance we can meet up for a chat this evening?"

"Ok sir, but I must insist that we keep it brief - the long hours of a detective inspector aren't conducive to family life and whenever possible, I try to be home before the kids are in bed." They arranged to meet up at an unassuming bar on Rivonia Road and Carter wasted no time on small talk. "So why were you in town that day - after all, shouldn't you have been in Sun City?"

Rimmer replied evasively.

"Oh, I wanted to follow up a lead on another story." He was reluctant to discuss the precise nature of his enquiries without corroborating evidence, though he did name the source of his interest. "I came here to see a man called Pieter Hertzog - he's the Operations Manager at the *Transvaal Mineral Mining Corporation* building. As I drove into the visitors' car park there, this Molome kid appeared from nowhere, pointed a gun at me and opened fire. Tomorrow morning, I'm going back to try and figure out why that happened."

"Will you be seeing this Hertzog fellow?"

"No, not yet, first I want to know how it feels to be reminded of that crazy day. Tiny steps, eh?"

"Mind if I tag along? Returning to a crime scene can be tough and you might appreciate the company. If something jogs your memory, I could advise you on how best to proceed."

"Thanks for your consideration, Inspector - I realise you're going out of your way to help, but you're right, I would appreciate having someone with me. I'll meet you in the lobby of my hotel and you can drive me into town, if that's ok? Shall we say 9 o'clock?"

"Sounds good to me." With that, Carter rapidly downed the remains of his beer. "Now I have to get going!"

The next morning, he called the station complaining of a painful toothache that needed immediate attention, then skilfully picked his way through the rush hour traffic to reach the Sandton Hilton on time. The two men headed towards the Central Business District in good spirits, but as they approached the *TMMC* building, apprehension gripped Rimmer.

"I've got to tell you, Inspector, this is giving me the heebie-jeebies - I'm quivering like a jelly here."

"Don't worry sir, that's a perfectly understandable reaction, but there's no need to be nervous - remember, your assailant is long gone, and he won't ever be coming back. Now that we're here, can you visualise exactly where you were when the shooting occurred?"

From the security of DI Carter's vehicle, the not-so-intrepid reporter pointed out the specific spot, but he was clearly still traumatised by his surroundings and had no further insights to impart.

"Can we leave now please - maybe park somewhere out of the way 'til my heart rate gets back to normal?" They found a side street nearby. "Christ, I could really do with a whisky - or ten!"

"I suggest you save your thirst 'til you get back to your hotel. Would you mind staying in the car for a couple of minutes while I quickly check out a few things by myself?"

"Do what you like pal - I'm happy to stay put."

Carter entered the building's busy foyer and was immediately confronted by an imposing brass plaque listing its various business activities; the Operations Department was situated on the twelfth floor. He asked a receptionist whether anyone by the name of Pieter Hertzog worked there, and she studiously checked her employee roster before replying in the negative.

"Well, can you kindly tell me who the Operations Manager is please?"

"That would be Mr. Louw sir - that's him right there."

She pointed to a brochure sitting proudly on the desk in front of her entitled, **'TMMC Team Talk'**, which appeared to be a quarterly staff magazine, containing stories about various activities being undertaken in and around the business. On its cover was a picture of a large, somewhat drawn, yet still thick-set man, sharing a wide smile with a bespectacled black woman dressed in agricultural clothes. Together they held a giant mock-up of a cheque to the tune of fifty thousand rand, which, according to the magazine's blurb, was a gift from the company to an impoverished Northern Cape village farming community for the construction of an irrigation system. The cheque was signed -

Allan Louw, on behalf of the Transvaal Mineral Mining Company.

"Could I take this copy?" Carter asked.

"Please do - we encourage members of the public to see how seriously we take our social responsibilities here."

As he walked away, he considered the *raison d'etre* behind such admirable altruism.

Good deeds like these are terrific public relations opportunities, and at a fraction of the cost of a concerted marketing campaign, but how else does the TMMC benefit?

The article says they have a mine close to the village, so the irrigation project will buy a lot of good will, making it easier to recruit local workers for the dangerous, back-breaking, low paid jobs below ground...

There really is no such thing as a free lunch.

Back at the car, he showed the brochure to Rimmer.

"Do you know this man on the cover, sir?"

"Of course - that's Pieter Hertzog. He's lost a lot of weight since last year, but unless he's got a thinner twin, that's my man." There was no hesitation or uncertainty in the reply.

"I'm sorry, but you're mistaken - his name is Allan Louw, and as you can see from that signature on the cheque, he's the *TMMC*'s Operations Manager."

"Well that's definitely the man I spoke to in the States a fortnight before I got shot and whatever he calls himself over here, his name was bloody Pieter Hertzog over there!" After this unexpected turn of events, Rimmer decided to reveal more about the nature of his intended meeting with the man in question. "Look, the lead that I was following up came as a result of a drunken conversation I'd had with this guy in a bar at the Sands hotel in Las Vegas. He'd spun me a highly unlikely yarn about being involved in the murders of some troublesome mine workers back in the sixties. Marcus Botha was the boss of the firm back then and my man accused him of sanctioning the assassinations, so during a bit of down time at the Sun City tournament, I set a meeting up with Hertzog - this fella here - to discuss his comments in greater detail. That's why I was in the visitors' car park when Lenka Molome put a bullet in me."

This was the first time that Rimmer had spoken to anyone else about his extraordinary scoop, and from Carter's expression, he was clearly sceptical.

"I have to say that doesn't sound like the kind of everyday chat I would be having with somebody I'd never met before. Surely it strikes you as slightly odd too?"

"Of course it does - I'm not a complete fool! I made that two-hour trip from Sun City to establish the facts."

"You were going up to his office then?"

"No, he told me to meet him at the front desk downstairs."

"Mmmm."

"You don't believe what I'm saying, do you? Did you see what's-his-name in the flesh? Is he in there now? Let me prove that I'm not lying!" Rimmer's pale cheeks had reddened with frustration.

"Calm down sir! Even if he is in the building, there's no way he'd see us without an appointment - you know that from the last time you were here. You need to start thinking rationally and you're not in the right frame of mind to do that now. Let's take a step back, ok?" Carter took a long pause before speaking again to take the heat from the moment. "Now if you'll pardon the pun, may I suggest that you hold your fire for a while where this particular individual is concerned? I have an idea in mind that might help us get to the bottom of all this. Will you put your trust in me?"

Rimmer nodded, confronting his demons had been an uncomfortable experience. For the present, he would concentrate on his work for *The Times* without upsetting distractions cluttering his headspace.

"Can you drop me back to my hotel now, please Inspector? This has all been a bit much for me to take in."

Carter duly complied with the request, and once he was alone again, he analysed the events of the morning.

What should I make of all this?

It's possible that those guys did bump into each other in Las Vegas - if their paths did cross, I'm guessing there was a mind-blowing bar bill at the end of it all!...

Any 'confession' from Louw would surely just be the words of a drunken fantasist - no one in their right mind assumes another identity and admits to multiple murders over a few drinks with a total stranger!

But what if everything Rimmer says is true?

By meeting up in the TMMC's reception area instead of his office, Louw had the opportunity to conduct their discussion in some quiet spot outside without giving away his real identity...

This whole thing is just bizarre, especially when added to Mrs. Molome's ramblings about a government-backed assassination plot involving her son...

Could the man I just dropped off have been the victim of the professional hit she talked about – was he lured to a meeting that was never intended to take place?

No, I don't think that's likely – he didn't come across as a national threat when he was shaking like a leaf next to me in the car!

So who really is who here?...

If I'm going to make sense of this, I need to know more about the people involved.

He sought out a street payphone to make a couple of calls. Discretion was needed, for his enquiries were off the clock and he felt guilty about neglecting an already extensive caseload to pursue a vague investigation that had little prospect of producing charges, but he wanted to test a barely imaginable hypothesis that was a long shot at best. First, he contacted the *TMMC* offices requesting an interview with the Operations Manager. To get the attention of Louw's PA, he had to provide details of his business.

"This is a police matter concerning the shooting of a UK citizen outside the building in June of last year. A new eyewitness statement has come to light that requires investigation."

If Louw has anything to hide, this is certain to set off his alarm bells.

Next, he made an international call to the London offices of *The Horizon*, asking to speak to Rimmer's former Sports Editor. Harry Ellis replied immediately; something about the combination of a police enquiry and Gordon Rimmer's name appealed to his impish sense of humour. Carter dispensed with rambling introductions as he watched his small change rapidly disappearing into the payphone.

"Can you tell me what business your Chief Sports Correspondent had in Johannesburg on the day he was gunned down? Wasn't he supposed to be in Sun City a hundred and twenty miles away?"

Ellis's answer conveyed a lingering animosity towards his former reporter.

"I can't help you there, Inspector – the fella is a law unto himself and if I had the authority to do so, I'd have sacked him on the spot for wandering off from his job. Whether he ended up getting shot or not is immaterial, that was a dereliction of his duty, plain and simple."

"You don't sound too sympathetic about what almost amounted to a fatal attack."

"Listen, I don't like the big-headed prick, but don't imagine for a minute that I wanted to see him get killed! All I'm saying is that he was paid to report on our *Sun City Snooker Showdown*, not to go sight-seeing around South Africa.

The Head Honcho - that's what we call our boss here - must have already known that Rimmer was a rat, because he requested full details of the guy's whereabouts throughout the course of that assignment - everything from his flight times to the hotel room he was staying in - the whole nine yards. Mr. Botha even wanted the registration number of his hire car! Originally, I thought the boss was on the scent of an expenses scam - that man doesn't miss a trick if he thinks someone's trying to get one over on him - but in hindsight, I reckon he suspected Billy Big-Bollocks of moonlighting on another story for one of our rival papers.

I don't know if you're aware, but after his shooting, Rimmer spent months convalescing at our expense before buggering off to work for Rupert Murdoch at *The Times,* so I wouldn't be surprised if he'd already been stabbing us in the back on the sly."

This information did not stack up correctly in Carter's head.

"Isn't it highly unusual for the boss of a national newspaper to take that kind of interest in one of his journalists?"

"Well, Rimmer was in another city instead of being at his post, so it turned out that the Head Honcho was right to keep tabs on him, wasn't he?"

"So if what you're telling me is true, then Mr. Botha must have got wind of the shooting pretty quickly?"

"You're kidding, aren't you? He had a much bigger crisis of his own to deal with that day - a few hours before we heard about Rimmer, the boss had keeled over after suffering a major heart attack. He was on death's door - didn't you hear about that?"

"Of course, Mr. Ellis - I can assure you that he is a very famous man in South Africa."

"Oh yeah - sorry, I should have realised that. Anyway, I've already said that he's normally as sharp as a tack, but I saw him that morning and he didn't look right at all - he was really on edge, so I wasn't surprised to hear he'd collapsed not long afterwards. If only he'd heard that Rimmer had gone missing from his post by then - that would have been a perfect stress-buster - he could have kicked the arsehole out of the door and might not have been taken ill himself!"

"When you say you don't like Mr. Rimmer, you're not joking are you!"

Christ, how tough must Botha be if this is how his editor acts over the shooting of an employee?

"Look, what you see is what you get where I'm concerned. I'll say one thing about your man - he's one lucky, lucky bastard. He goes missing in action and rather than face the Head Honcho's wrath, he gets away with it 'cos Mr. Botha is waylaid by his own health issue. Tell me that's not lucky!"

Carter had heard enough.

"Ok, thank you for your input, sir. I'm getting a picture of the kind of man Mr. Rimmer is now."

"No problem at all, Inspector."

Harry Ellis wanted to leave the young DI with an impression of a despised Prima Donna who was too big for his boots, but contrarily, he saw a diligent professional who just might have been onto something very big.

I would have chased that murder lead to Johannesburg in the very same way if I'd been in Rimmer's shoes.

The fact that Marcus Botha had been acting strangely on the day of the shooting only increased his intrigue.

He knew the registration of the victim's car too...

47.

An Inspector calls

Allan Louw looked distractedly out of the window of his minimalist office while his PA Jill Smit ran through his outstanding appointments for the week. Suddenly, the mention of one particular item brought his attention back into sharp focus.

"A Detective Inspector Carter from the CBD station wants to arrange an interview with you - apparently, there's renewed interest in the shooting of that man in the car park last year. I've freed up some space in your diary on Wednesday morning if that's ok?"

Her boss instinctively flinched.

"What? Who? Oh, yes, of course - very good. Did he say specifically what he wants from me?"

"No Allan, but surely it's a bit late in the day for the police to ask questions about all that isn't it?"

"Quite! Still, it won't hurt our organisation's good name to assist them with their enquiries, eh Jill?" He gave her a tired smile, but the minute she left the room, he got on the phone to his friend Douglas Daalmans complaining of unwelcome harassment. "Who's this Carter character at your station Doug, and what does he want to know about the Rimmer business?"

"Search me - he's one of these young do-gooder types - thinks we're all terrible people who pick on our black brethren too much. I remember he was snooping around at the time of the hit, asking questions, but I warned him there and then to mind his own business."

Louw felt distinctly ill at ease.

"I'm telling you, this scrub fire needs to be extinguished before it gets out of hand and burns down the whole bloody veldt!"

"Don't lose your cool Al - Christ, I've waited years to be able to say that back to you! Rimmer's long gone, and that dumb darkie is deep in the ground too, so we've got nothing to worry about, right? I'll sort this nosey prick out at work - a few well-chosen words from me should stifle his enthusiasm for re-opening closed doors."

"Be sure that you do clip his wings then - I'm getting old and don't have the same stomach for a fight that I used to."

Shortly after arriving back at work from his bogus visit to, "the dentist's chair," Carter's desk phone rang red-hot, and he received a barrage of abuse from an irate Daalmans.

"I've just taken a phone call from Allan Louw of the *Transvaal Mineral Mining Corporation*, asking me if I know about an investigation you're conducting on the carjacking of that British reporter outside their building last year. What the hell is wrong with you? I'm pretty fucking sure I told you that the case was closed - are you some kind of *kaffir* loving Sherlock Holmes, looking to find ways to exonerate them from their low-life crimes?"

Carter tried to calm the excitable detective inspector down.

"Look, one or two things have come to light that may force a re-think on what happened and that's why I want to talk to Mr. Louw."

"What things?"

"Things of a private nature. Now, as none of this has anything to do with you, I suggest that you let me conduct my enquiries without further interference."

Daalmans paused, moderating his belligerent tone somewhat.

"Listen to me for a second - Mr. Louw is an important man in the mining industry and it doesn't do to rock the boat just for the sake of satisfying your curiosity over Christ-knows-what. He's also a personal friend of mine - has been for 30 years and I can vouch for his good name."

Carter quickly reacted to this throwaway comment.

"I'm sorry, but I don't think I brought his reputation into question - I didn't say he was suspected of anything did I?"

This reply threw Daalmans, and he realised that he had been wrong-footed in the most elementary way.

"Well if he hasn't done anything wrong, why are you trying to bother him?"

"I've already told you, this is a confidential matter. Now I'm sure you've got other things to be getting along with, so could you kindly leave me in peace to do my job?"

The older man turned sour again.

"Now look here, you cocky fucker, you're starting to sound like your self-righteous little brother. You need to get a grip on the way things are done around here."

"I think you'll find there's going to be a shake-up of, *'the way things are done around here,'* once Mandela starts running the show."

Unsurprisingly, this comment provoked a further challenge.

"Nothing's changed yet, you smart-arsed nobody, and you might not be around long enough to show me or anyone else how to do things differently!"

Carter stood his ground.

"Are you threatening me Inspector?"

Again, Daalmans paused to consider his reply.

"I'm just telling you not to cause any embarrassment to the force. If you still feel the need to speak to my friend, make sure you show him some respect."

The call ended, and the veiled threats of Daalmans only made Carter more determined to continue with his investigations. For his next step, he needed to reacquaint himself with the redoubtable Bettina Molome.

Many of his older colleagues struggled to get to grips with computer software, but he embraced every advancement in modern policing and had stored reference information onto a floppy disc marked POFI (discrete shorthand for "Possibly Of Further Interest"). In seconds he found the address of the Molome residence and ascertained that the house was not connected to the city's telecommunications network (luxuries such as a telephone were scarce in Soweto). To speak with the lady in question he would have to drive there personally. On his way out of the office, he picked up the copy of the *TMMC*'s corporate magazine that had been staring back at him throughout his difficult conversation with Daalmans.

It was late in the afternoon by the time he reached the Molome residence; if the mother was not yet home from work, he would wait in his car until dusk for her return. This proved unnecessary, for after breaching the rickety gate that offered little in the way of either privacy or protection from the outside world, he peered inquisitively through a window and saw her sitting quietly in the tiny front room. A passing neighbour spotted him and angrily called out.

"Leave the poor woman alone! Can't you see she has enough on her plate without being bothered by the likes of you!"

When white people paid visits to the township, they were usually authority figures looking for trouble.

"What do you mean? What's happened here?"

The neighbour was a young woman pulling a petulant small boy by the arm.

"She's had to arrange the funeral of her daughter Dikeledi - now why don't you go away and let her be!"

God, not again! What has this poor lady done to deserve so much tragedy in such a short space of time?

Just then, the door opened, and the drawn, forlorn face of Bettina Molome stared back at him. It was already too late to walk away and leave her to her thoughts, even though he realised that his presence must have felt like a knife in her side; a physical reminder of the day she said her final goodbyes to her wayward son.

"Oh it's you - you are the bad news boy, aren't you? What do you want, Mr. Policeman? Have you come here to torment me once again? Always showing up when I am wiping tears of sadness from my face. Well this is the last time you will be able to mock this poor Soweto wretch - I have no more children left to lose."

He wanted to leave her to her misery.

"Please accept my apologies - I came here to ask if you could identify someone who might be of interest to both of us, but I can come back at another time....I am so sorry for your loss Mrs. Molome."

"Save it - Inspector...?"

"Carter, madam."

"Forgive me for not remembering your name, but I'm sure you can imagine that I have had other things on my mind - save it then, Inspector Carter. Spare me your sympathies; I do not care for anyone's grief but my own now. The last time I spoke to you, when I put my other child in the ground, I told you everything I knew about your friends in the government - wasn't that enough? Now my precious girl has gone to meet her maker too, and as you can see, I am all alone, so I do not care about your questions. Please go."

"As you wish madam."

He turned away, but as he reached her gate, she called him back with an air of weary resignation writ large upon her face.

"Inspector, I am sorry - now that you are here, you may as well say what you came here to say."

With gratitude, he accepted the opportunity to show her the magazine photograph.

"Could you please tell me if you have ever seen this man before?"

"Of course I have - you know full well that he is one of the people who told my baby boy to shoot that British spy. He gave Lenka the gun and a bag of money."

"Are you sure mamma - are you quite sure?"

"Do you think I could easily forget his face? I see him and the other man in my sleep every night. I can never forget who they are or forgive them for what they did."

The answer confirmed Carter's suspicions.

"Did Lenka ever happen to tell you the names of these men?"

"Only this one. He said the man in your picture was called Pienaar."

"Pienaar? That was his name?"

"Yes, yes, I'm hardly likely to forget it, am I?"

"Thank you, madam, but as you can see from the magazine, it says here that he's called Allan Louw."

"Pienaar I say! His name is Pienaar." Her agitation was as evident as it was reasonable.

"Pienaar it is then. Thank you for your assistance. I hope I never have to bother you again and please accept my deepest condolences for the loss of your daughter."

"I told you to save your grief for someone who appreciates it Inspector - now go please. Go."

Carter could only imagine the hurt he had stirred up for the poor woman, but it was important to establish the facts of the case he was building against his suspects. If what Bettina Molome had said was true, then Louw (probably with the help of Douglas Daalmans) had somehow influenced her son to shoot Gordon Rimmer.

Louw's liking for aliases has now been corroborated by two people, neither of whom have ever met.

I can't wait to hear what this guy has to say for himself!

48.

The bad blood bargain bucket

In the shade of his overgrown back garden, Allan Louw nursed a cold beer and reflected upon the sins of a life badly led. While no longer in his pomp, he was still a rugged example of the Afrikaans breed, and within that sturdy frame lurked the soul of a bully; throughout his mean-spirited existence he had felt a deep-seated entitlement to humiliate non-whites, homosexuals, or anyone of a passive or sensitive nature. So long as his strength held up, he would continue playing the aggressive tormentor, but there are twists and turns in every long journey, and during the spring of 1990, a challenge presented itself that, to his bitter frustration, he could not overcome…

An extended spell of sickness and fatigue had laid him low, and when unsightly blotches began to appear on his body, he decided to seek medical advice. Dismissively, he attributed his maladies to pressure at work, but his general practitioner Dr Malan gave him a thorough examination and drew an altogether different conclusion.

"I'm going to need a sample of your blood to send to our lab for further analysis and I'd advise you not to have unprotected sex until the results come back."

"Why? What do you think is wrong with me? Come on man, out with it."

"Look, I'm reluctant to unduly alarm you Allan, so let's wait for the lab results before I commit to a diagnosis."

"But I want to know what you're thinking!"

Intimidated by this combative behaviour, the distressed doctor reluctantly decided to forego his usual professional caution.

"Alright then - brace yourself, because you're not going to like what I've got to say. I suspect that you are HIV positive and may have developed the early stages of AIDS."

Louw found the suggestion utterly absurd and sprang from his chair in disbelief.

"What are you talking about?"

"You must understand, this is an initial impression, but these types of lesions are becoming an all-too familiar sight in GP's surgeries. I've seen other patients who have tested positive after coming to me with similar symptoms to yours."

"Are you calling me a fucking *poofter*?"

"Please - we don't use that sort of language here."

"Just answer the bloody question!"

Dr Malan needed to cool the overheating atmosphere.

"Your sexual persuasion is none of my business, I have no interest in speculating on that. What's important here is for us to establish the root cause of those blemishes, so will you roll up your sleeve for me please?"

"Absolutely - let's get on with it! The sooner I find out what's really wrong with me, the happier I'll be."

By then, both men were keen to end the fraught consultation as quickly as possible.

A week later, Louw received a summons to discuss the sample results, and to his utter disbelief, they confirmed that he was indeed HIV positive.

"This is bullshit! How can I have a queer's disease?" At that moment, the stigma of suffering an illness associated with the gay community outweighed his concerns over its implications.

Calmly ignoring this latest explosion of bigotry, Dr Malan insisted that the results were conclusive.

"I've looked over your medical history Allan, and I have a theory about how this may have happened. A few years ago, you travelled to the United States for a serious operation, didn't you?"

"I had some cancerous tissue cut out of my stomach in 1983, yes."

"May I ask why you went to America for this procedure? Don't you trust our own surgeons?"

"Of course I do - I'm fiercely proud of this country! I didn't want anyone at work knowing my personal health details, that's all. I told them that I was flying to Las Vegas for a much-needed break. That was true too, though obviously the main reason for the trip was to have my operation. It was performed at the Lindsay Buckton Medical Centre - and seeing as you're so interested, it cost a lot more money than if I'd had it done locally. What's this got to do with anything anyway?"

"Were there complications?"

"Yes, as it happens - I lost a lot of blood."

"Mmmm. If I were you, I'd look into any transfusions you received because there may have been a problem with them."

"What do you mean, a problem?"

"It's common practice for US hospitals to use walk-in blood banks to replenish their stocks. The system involves members of the public making donations in exchange for cash, and these facilities inevitably attract interest from drug-addicts and the sick - people who will willingly swap one resource to receive another. Recently, reports have surfaced in the media about blood contaminated with the HIV virus infiltrating some transfusion procedures."

Louw scarcely imagined that such a thing could be possible, but in the poker game of life, we rarely know when the Ace of Spades will come to the table.

"If you're suggesting this is what's happened to me, then how come it's taken until now for any symptoms to show up?"

"It's not unusual for HIV to lie dormant in the bloodstream for this period of time."

The patient remained unconvinced.

"I want a copy of those test results - I'm going to check this nonsense out for myself."

"As you wish Allan, but I must insist that you refrain from sexual activity. I'm sure you know the dangers and unless you can disprove our findings you must behave responsibly." Sexually, Louw was a threat to no-one; excessive drinking had led his long-suffering wife to the divorce courts and other women found his overbearing personality repulsive.

He immediately set about researching data on the transmission of HIV from infected blood donations and discovered to his horror that Dr Malan's hunch was correct; the Lindsay Buckton Medical Centre faced two separate ongoing legal proceedings over the same issue.

Taking time from his duties once more, he returned to Las Vegas looking for trouble, only to run into a brick wall when the facility's obdurate administrators advised him to join the back of the queue pursuing justice through the courts. That option was impossible without someone back home discovering his illness and he feared that litigation might be viewed there as a smokescreen to disguise secret homosexual tendencies. Left powerless to punish those responsible for his predicament, the bully had been beaten; exasperated, he would carry their error to his grave in silence.

In his room at Binions hotel overlooking Freemont Street, he opened a bottle of Jack Daniels and began to drink himself into a depressive stupor, when suddenly the phone rang to shake his senses. The caller was Marcus Botha with an unwelcome, yet familiar request.

"How are you Allan? I've had a devil of a time finding your exact whereabouts!"

"How on earth did you manage to track me down Marcus?"

"I'm a very resourceful man - but then you already know that."

This contact came completely out of the blue, for the two men had barely spoken in recent years; they had little enthusiasm to keep in touch without the common ties of company business and murderous intent to bind them. Louw tensed up, fearing that the Head Honcho might know of his fate.

"Look here, I'm sure you haven't gone to the bother of looking me up just to ask after my wellbeing, so what's on your mind?"

"Sounds like somebody's grumpy today! Are the blackjack tables being unkind?" Botha knew that his former Mr Fix-it liked the occasional game of cards and had a singular ability to lose when playing. "I'd like a favour and you are in the right place at the right time to do what needs to be done. I have a troublesome reporter on my team here in the UK and as luck would have it, he is currently in Las Vegas, just up the road from you, staying at the Sands hotel. He works for *The Horizon* newspaper and he's covering the big darts event that my television network is staging there."

Louw breathed a quiet sigh of relief, knowing that his virus would have been brought up immediately if Botha had known about it.

"Marcus, are we talking about an, '*employee relations*,' issue here? The kind of thing we used to take care of in the old days?"

"We are."

"Then may I remind you that the solutions I used to find were way-back-when, and our lives have taken different paths since then?"

"Absolutely, of course, but there's no-one else I'd trust to do what's necessary without creating any mess afterwards. I wouldn't expect you to help me out without the benefit of a little reciprocation - some appropriate backscratching as it were - but hear me out first. My problem child thinks it's a good idea to defy me whenever the mood takes him and we both know that sort of behaviour is not conducive to my health, so I want to see him, '*disciplined*,' for his insubordination."

"Would this, '*discipline*,' result in him leaving your employment permanently, or do you just want to make him aware of your displeasure?"

"The former. There is a twist however - when he's finished on my darts extravaganza, I want to utilise his talents one more time before we have our little parting of the ways. My *Sun City Snooker Showdown* tournament starts in a week's time - you know about that I suppose?"

"Of course, everybody's talking about it back home."

"I certainly hope so Allan - I have a lot riding on its success, so I need my best man out there encouraging the UK's armchair sports fans to subscribe to *MJB TV*."

"This guy is your best man? If he's that good, can you really afford to lose him?"

"I can afford to lose anyone who crosses me," Botha replied chillingly. "The annoying bastard is reluctant to support the event - he has commitments to follow the football World Cup in Italy, so I'd like you to come up with a plan that will tempt him away from *la dolce vita* next week and get him to South Africa instead. You'll be waiting for him - I checked with your PA and she told me that your vacation is over in a few days - presumably you'll have handed over enough cash to the croupiers and card sharks by then, eh? Once he's done what he does best there, I'd like you to do what you do best. Am I making myself clear?"

"Perfectly." They had an almost telepathic understanding where the performance of dark arts was concerned. "We've taken this kind of disciplinary action on many occasions in the past, but as I've just said, that was a long time ago and done for the good of the *TMMC* - it was in both of our interests to get those…problems solved."

"Not always, Allan! Have you forgotten about that little shipyard 'accident'? The one you performed to perfection for me back at *MJB Maritime*? You weren't on my payroll then…"

"Look, I owed you that one, Marcus, and you know it. When you used your influence to get me off that hit-and-run charge you saved my life, never mind my career. I always knew you'd call the debt in some day."

"And why shouldn't I? That girl you ran over was sixteen, and white - she had her whole life ahead of her. You were lucky it happened on the edge of town and the street lighting was poor, but even then, if I hadn't gotten the local officers to alter those witness statements, you would have been finished for sure. Drunks really shouldn't be behind the wheels of fast cars, late at night…"

Louw winced at the memory.

"I only took to drinking so heavily after sorting out your *kaffir* problems at the mines."

"Excuses, excuses!"

"Look, none of that stuff matters - I paid off my debt, so let's get back to business. Why should I help you now? How are you going to scratch my back, Marcus? What's in it for me?"

"Very good Allan - keep that focus, I like that. Consider this - we both know that radical change at home is unavoidable now, yes? As soon as the opportunity arises, Mr. Mandela and his cronies will want to get their own back on the likes of us over some of those, er, '*problems*,' that we solved in the good old days."

Louw defiantly grunted.

"I'd like to see them try."

"Trust me, things are likely to get very difficult once the ANC take control." Botha had his man's full attention. "I have friends in the government here in the UK, and I'm currently working with the utmost vigour to ensure that any acts of vengeance on the part of those tricky black bastards stay well away from my door. Now, if they fail to get at me, wouldn't you agree that they'll almost certainly try to pin something on you instead?"

"I don't doubt that, but surely if you find yourself in the clear then I'll be sitting pretty too, so how could I possibly get any extra value from helping you with your current problem?"

"Oh Allan, come on now - I'm surprised you can ever see the bigger picture with those blinkers on!"

"What do you mean?"

"With my help yes, you will indeed be sitting pretty, as you say - but extricating myself from their investigations is one thing…pulling you out the mire too is quite another. Remember this…I didn't get *my* hands dirty while solving our little problems, "way-back-when," - any incriminating evidence will lead directly to you. Without my intervention, you'll be facing all the awkward questions, the accusations…the murder charges perhaps? Oh, I'm sure the ANC's lawyers will be happy to hear that you were only acting under orders from on high, but if it comes to a straight case of your word against mine, I think you'll find that I'm pretty fireproof thanks to my well-wishers in Westminster."

The same old Marcus.

The same old Bastard Botha.

After pausing to think for a minute, Louw clarified the deal in front of him.

"So if I help you with your present little difficulty, you can categorically assure me that I'll be free from prosecution over anything I - or rather, we - have done in the past?"

"Absolutely."

"You're certain that can be done?"

"As certain as I am that day follows night. In all our dealings, have I ever been anything less than 100% reliable?" Botha had indeed been a resolute ally to Louw throughout their relationship, ably facilitating his enforcer's rise through the corporate ranks, then protecting him from prosecution over the involuntary manslaughter of a young girl whilst driving drunk.

"Alright Marcus, I'll do you this favour - this one and only, very last favour, ok? Let me know who this man is, where I can find him, and leave the rest to me." This readiness to accept the commission was driven by his sudden change in circumstances; it is easier to be reckless and brave when one is inexorably confronted with, *'the dying of the light'*.

That afternoon, Louw transferred to the Sands hotel with the aim of luring Gordon Rimmer to South Africa and a deadly date with destiny…

Over a year had passed since Lenka Molome's shooting of Rimmer and in an almost farcical twist of fate, the renewed police interest in the incident gave Louw increased confidence that Botha would honour his promise of protection. If DI Carter was as bright as he was nosey, he might very well connect the Head Honcho (a former leader of the *TMMC* and Rimmer's employer at *The Horizon*) to the case, leaving both men on the receiving end of his unwelcome attention. Louw decided to call the old boy at his mansion and warn him of this possible threat.

Unsurprisingly, he had to absorb an expletive-laden dressing down from his bitter ex-boss over the botched assassination before finally getting a chance to spell out his concerns. Initially, because Rimmer was still alive, Botha threatened to renege on their pact, but after a short assessment of the situation, he saw no alternative but to promise that he would: -

a) pull every diplomatic string at his disposal to stifle Carter's curiosity.

b) stand by his original offer to keep the ANC's hounds at bay.

To Louw's dismay, these reassurances were uttered by a weak, weary man, rather than the thoroughbred bulldog of days past. An anxious shiver washed over his bones as he suddenly felt exposed to the very real possibility of facing justice for his complicit (and latterly, complacent) crimes.

49.

The Captain and the kid

The following morning, Cornelius Carter's hopes of slipping into work unnoticed were immediately dashed when he was confronted by the steely stare of his superior, Captain Brian Mackenzie.

"I'd like a word in my office."

"Sure thing, boss."

Inquisitive glances from nosey colleagues passed around the room with a nonchalance disguising their true intent, for Mackenzie was a patrician type of leader who took immense pride in the promise shown by his protégé and inevitably this favouritism (whether real or imagined) drew jealousy from some quarters at the station.

To keep their conversation confidential, neither man spoke further until the captain closed his office door, then Carter took it upon himself to break the awkward silence.

"What's up skipper? Is this about me not being at work yesterday morning? I rang in to say I had to see my dentist - you were busy when I made the call, but I asked for the message to be passed on - you got it, didn't you?"

"I was in a meeting, but somebody did tell me about your appointment, yes. How's the sore tooth?"

"Oh it's out now, the damn thing had been irritating me for days. It was a wisdom tooth - see?" With a pantomime gesture, Carter pointed to the back of his mouth, though he could see that Mackenzie had no interest in checking his gums for gaps.

"This isn't about your absence son - well it is, kind of, but only indirectly. I'm not buying your dentist story, but I'll let that slide, because I know you were busy with something else. This is about what you were really up to. During the meeting I just mentioned, I had to bat off a bit of heat regarding you're interest in someone from the *Transvaal Mineral Mining Corporation*...would you like to tell me what's going on?"

"I just want to ask their Operations Manager Mr. Louw whether he has any connection to a man who was shot outside their building last year... surely a simple question like that can't stoke any fires for you, can it? The last thing I want is for you to face any flak on my behalf."

Mackenzie was evasive with his reply.

"Look, he isn't the sort of guy you ought to be bothering, so what do you think he's been up to? What case are you working on that needs this kind of information?"

Carter trusted his captain, but he had to tread carefully, particularly as his suspicions also pointed an accusing finger towards another detective at the station house.

"I haven't got anything tangible to report yet, but I'll be as up-front as I can. I felt the original investigation into this incident was wrapped up too quickly - not enough effort had been taken on the why's and wherefores surrounding it."

"But it wasn't your case, so what's that got to do with you?"

"Well only a couple of days earlier, the assailant - a teenager called Lenka Molome - had been involved in an armed mugging at an ATM machine in the same area and my brother Dominic was one of the patrolmen who gave chase as he tried to get away. I'm sure you recall that dust-up between Dom and two other officers last June? Well, this kid was the catalyst for that happening, because he received some heavy-handed treatment during his subsequent arrest."

"Yeah, I think we all remember that right enough - your brother needs to be less headstrong if he wants to make progress here - we've got a public image to preserve. I hope you told him that?"

"I did, but be that as it may, sir, it was Dom who then drew my attention to the second attack - the one at the *TMMC* building. This time Molome was gunned down by our armed response team before he could take off." Shrewdly, Carter decided against asking Mackenzie if he remembered the killing of a black felon as vividly as he recalled Dominic's passionate adherence to upholding correct police procedure. "The thing is, I can't figure out why he was back on the streets again so soon, so I attended his funeral to find out if there was anything unusual about him - whether he was more than just a street thug. I spoke to his mother afterwards and she had all sorts of ideas about him being caught up in some government-led assassination plot."

"And you believed her? Have you gone nuts? If you've fallen for the delusional ramblings of a bereaved parent, then I'm gonna rapidly lose my faith in you, lad!"

"Of course I didn't believe her, but Mrs. Molome told me that she'd come into the station to make her claims and nobody from the department was interested in what she had to say. The very least we should've done is to take her statement and follow it up with a quick question and answer session from various witnesses."

"How do you know that wasn't done?"

"I checked at the time. We have no documented evidence of that happening."

"Well that's probably 'cos she's crazy like her son and made the whole thing up. You should know better than to waste time on this."

In his gut, Carter suspected that Bettina's statement had been destroyed, but he continued to explain his interest in the case without referring to possible police impropriety.

"I didn't give the thing another thought sir, until the man who was shot - a UK citizen by the name of Gordon Rimmer - contacted me recently, asking questions that have opened up some interesting lines of enquiry. He's examined local newspaper reports on the two hold-ups and initially got in touch with Dom looking for further information. I got dragged into it because I'd spoken to the boy's mother, so as a matter of course I talked with her again yesterday and she's still sticking to her story. Not only that, but when I showed her a picture of Louw from a *TMMC* company magazine, she pointed him out as the man who had given her son the weapon used in the Rimmer assault."

Mackenzie admired Carter's diligence and certainly felt intrigued by his far-fetched yarn, but he had orders to rein his detective inspector in.

"Ok, I've had enough of this nonsense, so it stops right here - you've got your own investigations to work on and I want you to focus your mind on those. Leave Mr Louw alone, because he has some very powerful friends…I don't know whether you're aware, but back in the '60's, he was a close colleague of Marcus Botha. You know Botha, don't you?"

"Of course - who doesn't?"

"Well, that nasty bastard might have left this country when it got too small for his head, but he still has a lot of influence around here and his say-so can stop an enquiry dead in its tracks."

"Are you saying that Marcus Botha himself wants to stop me from talking to one of his old pals?"

"Did I say that? I only said that someone like that can bring a lot of pressure to bear in support of a friend if it suits him to do so and it looks like you're treading on some delicate toes with those big feet of yours."

"So he is involving himself in this then! But what gives him the right to interfere with a criminal investigation over here, skipper?"

"Because powerful people can son, and he's a very powerful man." Despite the gravity of his warning, Mackenzie's instincts told him that the headstrong Carter would press on regardless with his enquiries. "Look, I can see that you've got the bit between your teeth here, so let's agree to this. How you choose to spend your time *after* work is entirely up to you. I want you to understand the chance you're taking with your career Corny - and listen to me when I say *your* career, because I'm not about to risk *my* pension by endorsing *your* harassment of a very well connected member of our business community. If you're still stupid enough to poke your nose into this man's affairs, then at least take some good advice: proceed with caution and put the elements of your equation together correctly - two and two must end up making four, and not five." Before concluding his lecture, a rare twinkle then appeared in the captain's eye. "Having said all that, if in the end you do manage to find a rat in the kitchen, I'll be happy to pass you a broom to beat its brains out with - all I'm asking is that you make sure you get a direct hit on its head, ok?"

Carter broke into a beaming smile.

"My mouth's too sore to eat anything, so I'm staying well away from bloody kitchens, boss!"

348

His cocksure attitude belied the butterflies dancing around in his stomach. He had much to ponder.

50.

Truth and reconciliation

The Allan Louw conundrum continued to distract Detective Inspector Carter as he spent the next couple of hours reviewing his ongoing investigations. Eventually he decided to focus his attention on the *TMMC* man and contacted Jill Smit to confirm that their meeting would proceed. When she reminded her boss of the diary date, his blood turned cold, for he realised that Marcus Botha's intervention had fallen on deaf ears.

Carter needed to work late to prepare for the clash, so he dutifully rang home and let his wife know.

"Kim? Bad news hun - I've got a lot on here at the station house so I'm going to have to miss dinner. Oh, and by the way, it can't be helped, but I need to take tomorrow off as annual leave to conduct some extracurricular police business."

She was predictably upset.

"What? You're always saying that your time off is precious and should be spent with the family! Give me one good reason why you're putting the job before the kids and me - and it better be special!"

"You know I don't do these things lightly, but there isn't any other way - I might have a career-defining case on my hands and I need to be off the clock to see things through to their natural conclusion. Trust me here, love, ok?"

Kim sensed that her obstinate husband must be taking a big risk somewhere to chase up a line of enquiry in his own time. She suddenly grew concerned for his safety, though she kept her own counsel to avoid distracting him from the task at hand. With a frustrated grunt, she replied, "I don't suppose there's anything I can say to change your mind, is there?" When no answer was forthcoming, she stiffened, then whispered, "Just be careful…I love you Corny."

Throughout the evening, he slaved away at his computer, researching police responses into, 'accidental,' deaths of *TMMC* mine workers during the 1960's. Before calling it a day, he examined the company's financial results and shareholder details to get a more complete understanding of its size and status.

When he eventually got home, he slept badly in anticipation of the adversarial contest to come. Like a cabaret illusionist, he intended to create an atmosphere of unease and confusion, culminating in a rabbit-from-a-hat moment when he would introduce Gordon Rimmer to his bewildered suspect, and with only a sketchy mix of supposition and hard facts at his disposal, his strategy and tactics needed to be flawless.

In the morning, tired but determined, he drove out to Sandton to release said rabbit from the confines of his hotel hutch. Knowing that this would be a big day for each of them, Carter issued a pep talk to his jumpy accomplice.

"Ok sir, today we're going to speak to Mr. Louw - or Hertzog, as you know him - and I don't want you to get spooked by the prospect. Can you promise to stay cool? I'm going to take some chances to try to unsettle our man, and everything needs to go as smoothly as possible. Any maverick behaviour from you might wreck things, so follow my lead, ok?"

"Whatever you say Inspector; I'll help in any way I can. I just want to know why I got shot."

They replicated their last sortie to the Central Business District, parking up in the same side street, but this time they entered the *TMMC* building together, via a side door. Without ceremony, a busy receptionist sent them up to the twelfth floor, where they made themselves comfortable in Jill Smit's cosy little waiting room adjacent to the Operations Manager's office. Her beady eyes fixed determinedly on Rimmer as he thumbed through a copy of the company magazine.

"Who's this? I was under the impression you were coming alone."

"Oh, he's just here to say a quick hello to your boss - they're old friends."

"Mr Louw is a very busy man - he hasn't got time for unsolicited social calls."

"Trust me, he'll be speechless when he sees this guy!"

Just then, her desk phone rang.

"Has the Detective Inspector arrived yet Jill?"

"Here's here with me now Allan."

"Excellent, send him through please."

Before she could mention Rimmer's presence, Carter sprang towards the connecting door while gesturing for his companion to stay put.

"I'll call you in when the time is right to join us, ok?"

"No problem."

Upon entering the room, the observant policeman quickly took stock of his surroundings.

From here Louw would have had a clear view of Rimmer's vehicle as it approached the visitor's car park on the day of the shooting.

It's a good job we entered the building from a side door today – there's no way he could have seen us arrive.

The Operations Manager's smile was friendly but cautious, belying an inner turmoil as Carter got the obligatory introductions out of the way in a business-like manner.

"Thank you for giving me your time sir - I know what a precious commodity that is for someone like yourself."

"Don't mention it Inspector, I like to think that we do everything in our power here to assist the police whenever it's possible to do so. Now what can I do for you?"

"Well firstly, given those impressive words, can you explain why you were so reluctant to meet with me today?"

Louw did not expect such a direct opening question, and he tried to buy some thinking time to compose himself.

"Oh come now, let's not get off on the wrong foot, eh? Why don't you have a seat, then perhaps we can talk in a more relaxed manner?"

"Thanks, but I prefer to stand."

"As you wish." This passive-aggressive statement of intent was not lost on its target, who, as a result, found himself having to look up at his guest from behind his desk. "You must understand that this is an international operation, and we have to address business needs before creating space to *parley* with our friends in the force."

Despite his discomfort, he tried to project an air of conviviality, though the tactic failed to pacify his contemptuous inquisitor.

"I'm sorry, but I can't say I'm convinced that business needs got in the way of our *parley* as you put it. If you were happy for this interview to take place, then why did you ask one of your, 'friends in the force' - Detective Inspector Daalmans - to warn me from coming here?"

Louw responded with a nuanced show of flattery.

"Christ, you're a plucky lad! I'd almost call your attitude rude, though I'm sure that's not your intention…"The comment met with a stony silence. "Look, we obviously don't want a police presence in our building if we can avoid it - it's not good for our corporate image, you see? I've already said there was nothing sinister in my initial reluctance to meet you - I don't want valuable time being wasted answering trivial questions, that's all. You've said yourself that time is a precious commodity here - it's almost rarer than the minerals we mine for!"

"Sir, who is it exactly that you're referring to as, 'we'? Do you mean the organisation you represent, or Mr. Marcus Botha? When I decided to ignore the little threats of DI Daalmans, I believe you got your old boss (of all people) to intervene - that's right isn't it?"

"Well, yes, it's true that Marcus did indeed have a word with your superiors on my behalf. He's been a good friend of many years standing - as I'm sure you know - but that's not why he spoke up. He's simply keen to see that my working hours are spent pursuing profits. He still has a significant shareholding in the company and wants to know that everyone is focussed on pulling their weight!"

Carter knew this to be a lie.

"I've been doing some research on Mr. Botha, and actually, he doesn't appear to have any financial stake here anymore, so I doubt if he cares about who does what."

"You're wrong there - you obviously haven't done your homework properly."

"Be that as it may, I believe his interest in my investigation is much more personal."

"What do you mean?"

"Oh, I was hoping you could tell me something about that, Mr. Louw…or is it Mr. Pienaar?" One heart in the room temporarily stopped beating. "Or even

Mr. Hertzog, perhaps?"

Now Louw's strained conviviality disappeared altogether, and the Transvaal tough guy stirred himself for a fight.

"Inspector, you can't come here and throw strange names around expecting me to know what you're talking about - either make your point or you can get out of my office right now! And you'd better make the most of your chance 'cos I've got a feeling you won't be getting another!"

Carter responded to this counterpunch with another haymaker of his own.

"It seems I've touched a nerve sir, and I'm not surprised - after all, I've got witnesses who can put your face to those names regarding a conspiracy to commit murder."

"Oh, this is all just so much crap!"

"I believe that you and your accomplice Detective Inspector Daalmans set up a township hoodlum called Lenka Molome to kill a man outside this building last year. I'll go further and say that the hit was sanctioned by Marcus Botha!"

This was the gamble of a lifetime.

"Are you mad, boy! Have you lost your wits completely? Do you actually expect to keep your job after spouting rubbish like that at me?" Louw's face reddened with anger. "How the hell did you arrive at a conclusion like that? And what in Christ's name makes you want to squeeze Marcus Botha into your ridiculous equation? I reckon you've been watching too many American cop shows on TV - I'm right, aren't I? Well I've heard enough of this now, so it's time for you to bugger off! Go on! I don't want to see you again unless you bring your handcuffs and make a formal arrest, though I'd love to know how you're going to manage that when you're getting kicked off the force tomorrow!"

Carter faced this mocking rant impassively, but when he reached the door, he merely beckoned in his rabbit.

"Sir, are you going to deny that you've ever seen this man before?"

Louw's eyes met Gordon Rimmer's and his jaw dropped involuntarily.

"Deny knowing him? Of course I do, absolutely! Who the hell is he?"

"This is the man I was speaking of - the one who was gunned down in the car park."

Rimmer could not hold his tongue.

"Are you seriously going to pretend that we didn't meet in a bar at the Sands hotel in Las Vegas last June?"

Louw resembled a pummelled boxer, desperately clinging onto the ropes to avoid a trip to the canvas.

"What?..No, never...Not me...I've never been to Las Vegas...Never in my life…"

Carter chanced his arm again.

"You're quite sure about that?"

"Didn't you just hear me?"

"So your credit card statement won't show any transactions from there and I won't find your name on the Sands hotel register on the date that this man alleges to have met you?"

"No, no, no, not...er…Well, alright, if you must know, I admit that I did visit the city last year."

"Why did you just deny it then?"

"Just give me a minute! Let me explain, will you?" Louw began unravelling under the pressure. "I had an operation over there a few years earlier and returned to discuss some…long term issues relating to my surgery. It was a strictly private matter. I don't want my staff poking their noses into personal business like that, so I'm trying to keep quiet about it all."

"So now you deny meeting Mr. Rimmer, but you do admit to being in Las Vegas when he was there?"

"Yes, yes...but thousands of people were there at that time, it's a bloody tourist trap, isn't it?"

Carter paused.

"I didn't mention the date when Mr. Rimmer said he met you, sir…"

"What? Of course you did - you fucking did! It was when that bloody silly darts player collapsed with...with…" Louw's voice trailed away as he remembered that Barry Shackleton had faced the same losing battle with the deadly HIV virus that would bring his own days to a premature end. While he was still reeling, the wily young inspector struck again.

"Well, Mr. Rimmer here is prepared to testify in court that you introduced yourself to him as Pieter Hertzog. What's really important about this alleged meeting is that he accuses you of boasting about doing away with trouble making *TMMC* employees for your old boss Botha."

"As if that's likely! This is just too ridiculous!"

"I couldn't agree more, so I'm wondering if blabber-mouth chatter like that might be drink induced…do you have an alcohol problem sir?" The ability to hold one's liquor is a staple building block in defining a macho man's character and this question was designed to puncture Louw's sense of worth.

"Everyone who knows me will tell you I can hold my booze - I can drink you under the table boy, any day of the week!"

"Then could there be another reason for making such an outrageous statement? Mr. Rimmer is a journalist, so he obviously wanted to corroborate something like that, but circumstances prevented him from seeing you again in Las Vegas. Now as luck would have it, his next assignment was here in South Africa, at Sun City. That's quite a coincidence, wouldn't you agree?"

"Make your point Inspector."

"You were back in the country by then and he says the pair of you arranged to meet up - downstairs in the lobby of this very building."

"The guy is crazy - he's making all this up!"

"Really? Then why did he undertake a two-hour drive from Sun City to be here on the day he got shot?"

"How should I know? I'm telling you, the fella's nuts!"

"Or was the whole thing an elaborate ruse to lure him to his death?"

"You're both off your heads. Are you on drugs?"

"Sir, I could understand your denials if Mr. Rimmer was the only person accusing you of putting this assault together, but he isn't. A township woman by the name of Bettina Molome has come forward too - she's the mother of the boy who fired the shots and she tells me that you gave him the gun. She knows you as Mr. Pienaar - shall we see if she can pick you out of an identity parade?" (This line of enquiry was pure bluff, for that poor embittered lady had steadfastly refused to cooperate further with Carter's investigation).

"You're pissing in the wind - it'll come down to my word against hers… some stupid fucking *kaffir*! I'll take that one on all day long! You're relying on accusations and hearsay…you're nothing but a parasite trying to further your career by sucking my blood, but you won't get me, sunshine! Are my fingerprints on the weapon?"

"The forensic results reveal no prints on the gun at all - not even young Molome's. It was wiped clean, which suggests either police incompetence or a cover up to me - perhaps by one of your 'friends in the force'?"

"So you're turning on your own people now? You're some piece of work!"

Rimmer had tried to keep quiet, but emotion got the better of him.

"Look pal, the inspector knows you did this to me! And he hasn't even started on the murders at the mines!"

Carter quickly jumped in to calm his witness down.

"I was coming to that sir - will you please leave this to me?"

"Sorry - I got carried away."

"On the subject of your 'friends in the force' Mr. Louw, I know that you and Detective Inspector Daalmans first met thirty years ago when he was an impressionable young policeman in Kimberley. You worked as the *TMMC*'s safety officer reporting directly to Marcus Botha, yes?"

"So what?"

"I've checked the company records and whenever a fatality occurred at one of your mines in that region, the same two people - yourself and Daalmans - were always on hand to lend your signatures to the accident reports."

"Well of course I had to sign those reports - who else do you think would have the authority to investigate an accident occurring on our property? And the police had to confirm that our safety checks were all above board too - that's standard legal procedure - you should know that, you fucking simpleton!"

"Be that as it may, but every time there was such an accident - and let's be honest sir, there were quite a large number - it was Daalmans who always seemed to turn up at the scene to represent the police. And every statement he wrote is identical - word for word - indicating that his sweeps of the accident scenes were hardly methodical. None of those reports ever apportioned any blame to the *TMMC*...Quite a cosy arrangement, I'd say..."

"I take it you've never been to one of our mines! They're dangerous places at the best of times, but we do everything we can to ensure the safety of our workers, so that's a perfectly reasonable conclusion for him to draw."

"If the sites were dangerous places to work at for everyone, can you explain why so many of the men who suffered fatal accidents had recently been issued with disciplinary warnings accusing them of militant behaviour? I have their Personnel files on my desk at the station, detailing the fines or suspensions they'd received for inciting fellow workers into industrial action. Those disciplinary files and police accident reports are physical evidence - not accusations - not hearsay. There's enough in them to charge you with multiple murders of Kimberley miners in the 1960's."

Louw was quieter now, replying through gritted teeth.

"You won't get a conviction from our courts."

"I wouldn't be too sure about that, sir - the world will be watching when Mr. Mandela takes over here and right now the justice system is readying itself to listen to a number of high-profile cases of white corporate misbehaviour. You can be certain that those cases are going to be tried fairly and squarely."

"Who are you trying to kid? Mandela and his black bastard mates won't get anything past the white elite running our legal profession …it's still us with all the money, all the power…"

"The money, yes, but the power? If the 'white elite,' as you call them want to hang on to their cosy jobs, they'll have to play ball with the new power around here…and that's going to be the ANC. They're not through the doors of the Parliament building just yet, but now that all races are free to vote in our elections, we're obviously on the cusp of black rule - and you think our judiciary will turn a blind eye to your malicious killing spree because you're a white man? Who are *you* kidding? Your trial will be a test case to see if justice is possible, post-apartheid."

"You're in cloud cuckoo land boy - your liberal, darkie-loving one is not a land that I recognise, and remember, I'm not without influence around here. I know important people!"

"Are you referring to Marcus Botha again? Our prosecutors will be gunning for him too! He couldn't even stop me from showing up today, so how is he going to save you from facing a jury?" This deception was Carter's final gamble, for Botha had indeed prevented his meeting with Louw from taking place in an official capacity. The detective daringly avoided mentioning that he was actually off duty as they spoke. "Since his heart attack your old boss has become an irrelevance, and the UK government won't stand in the way of an extradition application for him - trade links between our two countries will soon be opening back up and their Foreign Office won't scupper business opportunities to help a tired old has-been escape justice."

The fight had finally drained out of Louw and he visibly sank into his seat.

I was so stupid leaving those old employee records open to scrutiny!

And why couldn't Daalmans be bothered to change a single word on any of those accident reports?

What an idiot!

Then again, no one in their right mind would ever suppose that an upstart detective might come sniffing around, running checks on such things.

Not in my South Africa!

But this was no longer his South Africa. Mention of the ANC's thirst for revenge had a ring of authenticity about it and Carter's appraisal of the Head Honcho's fading powers mirrored his own concerns too.

The Operations Manager was dazed and downed; he would rise from the canvas no more. Though the evidence against him was speculative and circumstantial at best, he faced spending the rest of his days in a drawn-out, debilitating courtroom battle trying to secure a worthless freedom, and that prospect depressed him deeply. He decided to call time on the pretence; the subterfuge; the lies. Raising his hands in submission he spoke softly, but with surety.

"Enough, Inspector. I've heard enough... it's over. You have me. There, I've said it, I'm done - are you happy now? Do your worst. Would you like me to come with you to the station, or do you want to pick me up later after you've boasted to your colleagues about the size of the fish you've caught? My advice is to reel me in now boy, before I change my mind."

It was the triumphal moment Carter had hoped for and he did not intend to let his catch off the hook.

"Thank you for seeing sense sir - I'd like to take you into custody immediately. Mr Rimmer, you should come and make your statement too."

Over the next few hours, Louw sang louder than a Cape crow, concisely reciting a damning confession that accused Marcus Botha of being the ringleader in a series of murders, with Douglas Daalmans included as a co-conspirator. Details of the gruesome crimes soon emerged in a press statement, and shockwaves spread across the globe.

Cornelius Carter had taken a huge chance with his career and won. During the course of one extraordinary day, his fortunes had turned around completely; at dawn he risked becoming a sacrificial lamb on the altar of his superiors, but by dusk he was the toast of the station house, and media outlets from here, there, and everywhere frantically sought him out for comment. When he finally got a moment to himself, he called home to share his news with Kim and she shed a relieved tear that everything had gone so well. As they idly chatted, he watched a defiant DI Daalmans being led from an interview room to a holding cell and a wide, satisfied smile broke out across his exhausted features.

51.

With a little help from my friends…

Marcus Botha sat in the drawing room of his mansion, angrily brooding over the calamitous setbacks that had destroyed his grandiose ambitions to become the world's premier media influencer.

The Fates are conspiring against me!

Those idiot bankers started the rot – they lack the long-term vision to understand that concepts like MJB TV require enormous finance to establish themselves.

My protracted recovery from heart surgery has been another cataclysmic obstacle to overcome – it's left me looking on helplessly while Elizabeth struggles to keep the rest of my empire intact.

And now – if all that's not enough to deal with – I'm facing extradition to South Africa on charges of conspiracy to commit murder!

What a crock of shit!

In the contrary world of politics, any interpretation of history is fluid. Following Allan Louw's bombshell allegations, the South African Police Service forwarded a warrant for Botha's arrest to the UK's foreign assistance division, and the ruling National Party, under pressure from Nelson Mandela, enthusiastically welcomed the move as a positive step towards building bridges and righting past wrongs. Unsurprisingly, the Head Honcho considered the warrant to be another cowardly betrayal of values that had helped him thrive.

At the time of these so called, 'crimes,' I don't remember anyone having issues with my management of the mineral mines …

Nobody cared if a few blackies got killed back then – after all, they were obstructing the running of a highly lucrative business, weren't they?

The government used to love all the money I generated for them through exports and tax revenues, yet now they're standing side by side with those ANC fuckers, trying to bring me down.

Hypocrites, the lot of them!

Adversity requires a positive response and the Head Honcho dredged up every ounce of his faltering strength to meet the challenge. Looking to leverage influential support, he brought his pet poodle in Parliament, the Right Honourable Lewis Neeves, to heel for a consultation.

"I believe you expect to return to the cabinet now that the dust has settled over Mrs. Thatcher's despicable removal, yes?"

"All being well, Marcus."

"That's excellent news and no more then you deserve, for you're a very skilful orator and right now I'm in need of those persuasive talents myself. The government must be dissuaded from getting into bed with the ANC - perhaps you can start the ball rolling with some anti-Mandela comments in your column?"

Neeves' response was less enthusiastic than Botha had expected.

"Of course, I'd like to help, but that would be an act of political suicide on my part at this time. While it's true that I expect to return to the top table in due course, there are no guarantees, so with my future in the balance already, I feel it's necessary to put my family's considerations ahead of your own. Prudence requires me to align myself to the policies of our leader, and he is a man who warmly embraces the impending regime change in South Africa, so as I'm unable to support you, with regret, I have decided to put an end to our professional relationship by resigning as *The Horizon's* political columnist forthwith."

Botha took a moment to absorb the MP's declaration of betrayal, then his mood music suddenly took on a more menacing tone.

"My, oh my, you really are a slimy little bastard, aren't you?" His notorious fists began to clench with a resemblance of their old power. "You take the fucking biscuit alright. Do you expect to walk out of here with my best wishes and a pat on the back? Forget it - I want my pound of flesh!"

Extreme discomfort spread across Neeves' perspiring features.

"What on earth are you talking about? As a Member of her Majesty's elected government, I don't have to stand here and be threatened in this manner. I've done all I can for you, but I'm afraid that we have come to the end of our road over the South African issue - my party now has a policy of conciliation with the ANC and there is really nothing I can say or do that will alter that fact one little bit."

"Oh, that's rich! You wanted to give them a kicking nine months ago when you had Mrs. Thatcher to hide behind. Where's your backbone, you tepid little turd? You have an obligation to me, and I demand that you speak up, opposing the Mandela love-in. I don't want any ifs or buts about this!"

Neeves struck a ministerial pose to disguise his diminishing confidence.

"I have told you my position and if I may quote from the Great Lady, *'I am not for turning'*."

Botha glared.

"Which Great Lady are you quoting from? Do you mean Mrs. Thatcher, or the prostitute in Wigmore Street that you visit every second Thursday in the month? The dark-haired dominatrix who whacks you across the arse with a riding crop?"

"That's a lie! A gross, baseless lie!"

"Is it? Well perhaps I got mixed up between her and your mistress in the Home Counties? Silly me! Is she the one who spanks your bare buttocks then…?"

"This is an outrage! I'm being set up!"

"Listen Lewis, I'm not the one with the peculiar sexual tastes here; it's not me who's stupid enough to risk my career by frequenting whore houses."

"I do not visit whore houses! That woman in Wigmore Street is a respected chiropractor who treats me for a severe back condition!" Though this protestation of innocence was voiced with great passion, it carried a hollow ring of deceit.

"Do I really have to go through the formality of showing you the photographs? Do you honestly want to hear the tape recording? How does it go? *'I've been such a bad, bad, boy etc'….*" A mischievous smile broke out on Botha's grizzled face. "What's her name again…Mistress Penelope, isn't it? Well, I think pretty Penny will prove to be a very expensive mistake if you don't make a public statement against the ANC for me. And while you're at it, I want you to pull some strings amongst your old friends at the Foreign Office as well, to keep those black bastards off my back."

"This is nothing more than blackmail! You're behaving like a Chicago mobster!"

"Oh, don't act so naïve, you idiot! You swan around with some of the worst dregs that privileged society can muster - Christ, Westminster is the most notorious haven for backstabbers, shit-stirrers and double-dealers on earth - yet you have the cheek to cry, *'foul'* when the school bully bashes you in the balls! Let me spell it out to you once and for all - you seem to have gotten yourself into a bit of a pickle *old boy*, and if you don't speak up, you'll be finished as a politician."

Though Neeves was severely rattled, his ego forced him to fight back.

"Finished? Me? How do you arrive at that conclusion? After all, it wouldn't look very clever for you to publicly smear one of your former employees, would it?"

His tormentor ignored the question.

"If I say you're finished, you are, simply because I say you are. I make the rules around here and it's little lackeys like you who follow 'em, so let's not waste any further time pissing in the wind to see how far our spray spreads - here's the deal. You can choose to ignore me - that's your prerogative - but if you take that course of action, then your family will be reading about your little perversions in my paper in the morning. That's option one…" Botha revelled in this sort of sadistic baiting. "Option two is to do what I fucking tell you to do, then nobody ever needs to know what you get up to behind those sordid little closed doors of yours."

An involuntary twitch appeared on Neeves' tormented face. "Poor old Lewis…perhaps you can get one of your incorruptible friends in the Commons to stand up and defend your good name? The kind of Honourable Member who always puts the interests of their constituents above those of wealthy benefactors offering them cash for Parliamentary favours - good luck finding such an idealistic angel! Maybe you could persuade some of those naïve activists amongst the Young Conservatives to back you instead? There's a particularly boisterous group of them who gather at a Knightsbridge cocaine convention every Tuesday evening - would you like the address? I'm sure they'd understand your need to, er, blow off a little steam. I have the names of every member of that happy troupe!

If you decide to look for support from some of your former cabinet colleagues, I'd be very careful about who you choose…You'd be wise to avoid the one with a taste for wife-swapping - he's probably too busy playing pass-the-parcel to spare you the time of day anyway. As for that minister who gets his kicks in a secret Chiswick dungeon, poncing around in stockings and suspenders while being manacled, beaten and buggered by rent boys - well, an endorsement from him might prove to be a little… uncomfortable, eh?"

By now Botha was really getting into his stride. "Don't you get it? I've got slurs to cover most of your crowd, enough to erode the credibility of John high-and-mighty Major so badly that he loses the next election. Do you want that on your conscience? Oh, I remember now, Members of Parliament don't have those. Let's say this then - I'll let your law-breaking, drug-taking, philandering and fairy chasing colleagues know who set them up in the first place. Once that becomes common knowledge, your friends, your family and your party will all turn their backs on you.

I know you expect to walk into a comfortable job in the City if your Westminster ambitions aren't realised, but try cosying up to your cohorts there once they discover you're responsible for toppling a government that lets them get away with so much."

Neeves valiantly resisted an urge to cry whilst trying to stave off his inevitable ruin.

"Marcus, may I remind you that you haven't exactly done badly out of our policies yourself? If we fall and Labour returns to power, you'll still be done for, because they'll support Mandela and the ANC in their witch hunts too."

Botha bluffed away those concerns with obstinate bluntness.

"I'll take my chances - if I get no joy from you, I may as well look to them for protection. They're just as susceptible to being cajoled - or threatened - as your mob. Even if they did throw me to the wolves, I'd still have the satisfaction of knowing I trod you into the ground like so much shit on the heel of my shoe first. Obviously, I'd prefer not to have to go down that road - that's why I'd like you to bite the bullet and do as you're told. I'm just laying your options on the line."

He then allowed silence to wash over his threats so that Neeves could fully grasp the despairing emptiness of his position. After what seemed like an eons-long pause for reflection, the calculating politician suddenly had a *Eureka!* moment.

"...If I do criticise the ANC for you - if I cast a shadow of doubt over Mandela's party and their post-election intentions - we both know there won't be any way back into the cabinet for me. My only chance of a return would be if another shake-up takes place at the top of the party...Of course, at this moment in time, we are behind Labour in the opinion polls by several percentage points, and it's possible that we may not be able to claw that gap back...if Mr. Major can't arrest our slide, *I* won't be targeted for blame like his sycophants. By remaining unapologetically Thatcherite and upholding her principals and opinions - including such things as her support for the current South African government and antipathy towards the ANC - I could emerge as the authentic right-wing voice of my party. That might play out rather well with the electorate...I might emerge as an antidote to arrest our party's malaise!"

This was much more in keeping with what Botha wished to hear.

"That's the spirit - I'm delighted to see that you're thinking properly now! I could print some of my scandalous stories about your colleagues and establish you as the man who refused to compromise his principals in return for a cabinet post alongside such wretches."

"Er...steady on - I wouldn't want things to go so badly that we Conservatives end up done for!"

"No, no, exactly - I'll just spread enough muck to see Major out of the door and give you a chance to go for the top job. With the right friends, you're never truly dead in politics - even if, like me of late, you may find yourself occasionally comatose! You're smart...so for now, use your communication skills to create unease over the implications of a black government in South Africa and drum up some public sympathy for my fight against extradition, ok? Do this for me and I guarantee that your spell in the wilderness will be a temporary one."

The colour that had drained from the cheeks of Lewis Neeves now began to return.

"I've made up my mind - I'll do it! I won't leave the paper - my column will paint a lurid picture of the ANC as a bunch of rogues who are looking to terrorise their white neighbours. You're an incredible man Marcus - your blackmailing tactic may just prove to be the stimulus that saves my career!"

"Please Lewis, blackmail is such an ugly word. Political manoeuvring is all I'm doing - shuffling the cards to deal myself a better hand."

With that, brim full of self-congratulation for the brilliance of his negotiating skills, Botha ushered the malleable MP out of his home.

In the United Kingdom, European extradition cases took precedence over those concerning other countries, but to get the ball rolling, prosecution lawyers prepared a preliminary case against Botha, and it was at this eleventh hour that Neeves finally managed to pull some strings on his behalf. *The Horizon's* anti-ANC propaganda campaign had unsurprisingly put distance between himself and Conservative party strategists, but his private discussions inside the Foreign Office did harvest dividends, for with a Machiavellian nod and a wink, he persuaded Whitehall mandarins to employ delaying tactics by asking their South African counterparts for more detailed information before any decision could be made on handing the accused man over. First, they required written assurances confirming that Botha would not face a death penalty on his return home, then they argued that his weak heart brought into question his ability to undergo the rigours of a trial.

Months of interminable legal wrangling lay ahead, but at this moment, the Head Honcho got a lucky break; Allan Louw's health deteriorated rapidly, and independent medical examiners declared that he was no longer fit to testify.

The case against Botha had been flimsy at best, based around circumstantial evidence and the say-so of the prosecution's star witness, so to save valuable taxpayers' money on a lost cause, all charges against him were dramatically (if very reluctantly) dropped.

He had survived this brush with disaster by the skin of his teeth and was understandably relieved, but ultimately invigorated too.

I feel unstoppable again!

The damage to my professional and personal reputation has been immense, but I'm the master of my own destiny once more and I'm going to take back the reigns of my businesses with a renewed confidence.

It's time to plot my Second Coming!

52.

The Fates

In November of 1991, '*Gay Plague*' hysteria hit the headlines once again following the AIDS-related death of *Queen*'s flamboyant lead singer Freddie Mercury. Reactions to the rock legend's passing were predictably varied; around the world, his legions of adoring fans wept tsunamis of despairing tears, while religious fundamentalists from every persuasion saw his demise as a divine judgement.

During the same month, another victim of that accursed disease also drew international interest, though in this instance, the cause of his death raised less of a furore than the tales of corporate killings that accompanied him to his grave. Allan Louw's fighting spirit had been broken during DI Carter's intense interrogation and he passed away five days after the cessation of criminal proceedings against him.

As we have seen, the collapse of the prosecution's case allowed Marcus Botha to settle back into his old role as Head Honcho of a major corporation; free to repair his damaged reputation and make life familiarly miserable for those around him. But what of his remaining accomplice Douglas Daalmans? The crooked cop had endured brutal remand conditions in the Johannesburg Correctional Centre while preparing for his court appearance, yet upon his release, his demeanour was one of frustration rather than relief.

Thanks to Louw's big mouth, I'll never be accepted back on the force, so an early retirement – with a generous pension package – is my only option.

I don't want to be forgotten though – I'll see to it that my friends at the station house make life hell for those Carter boys.

They can have that as a parting gift from me!

So far, so bad; guilty men had avoided punishment for their long-hidden misdeeds, but time has a habit of righting wrongs, and if one waits long enough, the reward of just desserts very often finds those it seeks...

While Louw's death ended any hope that the South African Prosecution Service might secure convictions relating to the murders of the Kimberley miners, separate charges for the botched hit on Gordon Rimmer remained open (provided strong enough evidence could be brought before the courts). That prospect seemed a distant possibility at best, but against all the odds, justice suddenly received a helping hand from the most unlikely of sources.

Bettina Molome's frustrations with the world finally boiled over when she heard about the trial's collapse and after a few days of intense soul searching, she appeared at the CBD station house asking to see Cornelius Carter for a face-to-face chat. He was upstairs in Captain Mackenzie's office discussing another case when the desk sergeant notified him of his unexpected visitor, and he was so taken aback that he brusquely burst out of the room to meet her.

"Mrs. Molome - this is an unexpected surprise! What is it that you want to see me about?"

"Detective Inspector, I have decided to help you. I want vengeance for my boy's death."

In a state of bewilderment, he ushered her into an interview room so they could speak freely.

"If I recall, you were adamant that you didn't want to participate in my investigation. What's brought about this sudden change of mind?"

"When we first spoke, I thought you were just like every other policeman in this country, but now I believe you to be a good man."

"There are a lot of good police officers here Mrs. Molome, though I'm grateful for your kind words."

"You won't convince me about the rest of them, but be that as it may, I have seen the news - God knows I've tried to avoid it, but that's impossible - and I realise that you were sincere in wanting to put those killers behind bars. I cannot pretend that I am sorry that this Pienaar -"

"Mr. Louw, you mean."

"Pienaar, Louw - whatever his name is. The Devil I call him. I cannot say I'm sorry he has gone to hell - for I know that is where he is - but the idea that his sidekick, this Daalmans fellow, is a free man is too much for me to bear. If he cannot be sent to prison for killing all those poor men in Kimberley, then I want to see him punished for his part in what happened to my Lenka. I want you to make him pay."

"Well with your testimony I'm sure we can get the Rimmer trial up and running again, but I'm afraid it's not up to me to send him to jail, that's for a judge to decide."

"You can at least let everyone know what I know. What I saw."

She made a statement under Carter's supervision, then Daalmans was re-arrested and charged with conspiracy to commit murder. Once again, the evidence was circumstantial, but before the case came to court, intrepid Felix Nel of the *Johannesburg Journal* managed to shed some light on the defendant's character. With the accelerating pace of change in South Africa now allowing for greater press freedom, he got his editor to publish all the identical accidental death reports relating to the original trial. Those revelations had no bearing on the Rimmer shooting, but their timely exposure did have an adverse effect on the public perception of the under-pressure former policeman.

In the dock, he defiantly faced his accusers alone (due to the fragility of their case, the prosecution decided against going through another lengthy extradition process to include Botha this time) but his self-confidence proved to be misplaced. Astonishingly, the testimonies of Molome, Rimmer and Carter somehow convinced a jury that Daalmans was complicit in the assassination attempt, and to his utter dismay, he received a three-year prison sentence. He could not be held accountable for the subsequent gunning down of Lenka Molome, but at least some semblance of justice had been conferred, to the (partial) satisfaction of those most closely affected.

Meanwhile, in the UK, Marcus Botha was back in his big chair at *Horizon Tower*, but if he thought life would become easier thereafter, he was in for a seismic shock.

On September 16, 1992 (a date notoriously referred to in the City of London as, 'Black Wednesday') international speculators engineered a run against the pound. Panic spread in the money markets as the value of sterling plummeted below previously agreed minimum European Exchange Mechanism rates, and consequently, by the close of business, the UK was humiliatingly forced to withdraw its membership of that august institution. Traders saw share prices nosedive, and this drastically reduced the value of Botha's portfolio, forcing him to temporarily mothball the redistribution of his finances.

After a day of extreme turbulence, his problems were about to get a whole lot worse; without warning, the Serious Fraud Office announced that it was taking an interest in his holding company's pension fund accounts. He had overcome gargantuan challenges to his health, wealth, and freedom, but this was yet another devastating hammer blow.

With the swiftness of a hungry bird of prey swooping upon its feast, government legal eagles sequestrated his financial ledgers and Botha, who had proved to be so slippery in wriggling out of his South African difficulties, found himself powerless to prevent the process. He knew that once the authorities traced what went where, he would be done for. Thinking time was needed.

Now that the threat of extradition had gone, he was free to roam the globe with impunity, so he took himself and his wife off for a weekend break to the Mediterranean on their yacht, the *Lady Elizabeth*. Staring out at the shimmering sea from his private rooms below deck, he recalled some of the confidential conversations and shady deals that had been cut with despotic rulers of banana republics within those oak panelled walls. Try as he might, his calculating mind could find no solutions to address his current troubles; threats of violence or bribery would cut no ice with the unimpeachable accountants at the SFO.

His had been an astonishing run of misfortune by anyone's standards, but he was satisfied with his Herculean efforts to mitigate the damage to his reputation and businesses. He did not offer similar credit to his subordinates.

When the banks stopped backing MJB TV, I was smart enough to fund it by diverting money from my company pension scheme.

When my heart tried to spite me, I found the strength to beat that.

When the South African prosecution service tried to extradite me, I got the better of them too!

At every turn I extinguished the flames that threatened to turn me to cinders...but can I make the same claim for anyone else?

No!

Edmund Cornell has failed to prevent the gradual decline in sales of The Horizon, resulting in lost advertising revenue and reduced profits.

Gordon Rimmer defied me when I wanted exclusive insider celebrity revelations from his lover at the Priory – then his copy from my darts and snooker tournaments failed to drag people away from their obsession with bloody football.

Lewis Neeves was expressly procured as my insider at Westminster, but he did nothing to dissuade the government from encouraging friendly relations with the ANC and in the end, I didn't need his help to avoid extradition because that traitor Louw died before he could damage me.

All those useless bastards let me down – in an ideal world I'd make them pay for their incompetence, but it's too late now – that time has gone.

So what of my ever trustful, unquestioningly loyal wife and her part in this fiasco?...

She lacked the dynamism required to run my business empire properly – she constantly questioned the way I worked, constantly found ways to gum up the process of moving company money around.

She squandered cash on endless meetings with bean-counters trying to sort out what she saw as a mess, but which was really a carefully arranged plan of concealment – I'm only under investigation because she poked a gaping hole of transparency through my 'creative accountancy' methods.

Just like the others, she's become a liability.

He was done with his ponderings now; a decision had been made and he summoned his valet.

"Michael, can you find Mrs. Botha for me and ask her to come here please?"

True to form, he had kept the current crisis to himself, so Elizabeth was on deck soaking up the sun and de-cluttering her mind from her fraught fight to restore Brand Botha to something like its former glory. She duly glided into the room, reclining elegantly on its sumptuous leather chez lounge.

"What do you want Marcus? I hope to God this won't be a business discussion – I've had about as many of those as I can stand. I'm happy to leave the sleepless nights to you now."

"I bet you are."

The acid delivery of his comment made her sit upright.

"Do I detect a certain air of irritation in that remark?" she enquired.

"You do."

"Out with it, old boy, what's afoot?"

"What's afoot?...What is afoot?..." His temper was set to slow burn. "How shall I put this? Oh yes, that's it...we're done for. Board the lifeboats - we're going down!"

"What on earth are you talking about?"

"Don't you know dear? Well, let me enlighten you. On Friday, the Serious Fraud Office took my accounts away for scrutiny...I'm sure you know what that means to us? How many fucking number-crunchers did you have poring over what goes where? Well, it looks like one of 'em has realised that two and two doesn't always make four where I'm concerned, and they've blown the whistle on me."

"Oh my God! What are you going to do?"

Elizabeth's impassioned question hung in the air and the only competing sound came as her husband carefully opened his desk drawer to remove a Colt Anaconda .44 Magnum revolver. Her jaw dropped and a shiver ran down her spine while she listened intently to his reply.

"I've been sitting here all afternoon considering every possible permutation and scenario, and each one leads to the same conclusion. We're done for. I have been a fighter all my life, but The Fates have finally beaten me. My body won't stand the ordeal of a trial, so there really isn't any other way out..."

"No! Surely something can be done! I believe in you - you've always been able to navigate a way through...sticky situations."

"This is far more than just a, 'sticky situation,' my dear. It's true that whenever shit has hit the fan in the past I've managed to come up with an answer, but I'm afraid one can never fully cover for the incompetence of others..."

Elizabeth sought clarity from his comments.

"Are you referring to me when you talk like that?"

"Well, if my recovery had been better supported by you, none of this would have happened."

"Exactly what are you trying to say?"

"I'm saying that your constant criticism of my business strategy nearly finished me off! You undermined my confidence to make decisions at vital moments. You kept me weak when I needed to be strong."

He waved the gun around in a distracted manner as he spoke, vaguely pointing it in his wife's direction every time he uttered the word, "you". His look of half melancholy/ half madness disturbed and frightened her in equal measure.

"Don't be ridiculous Marcus! You can't honestly think I would try to wrong foot the only person I trust in the world? Where would the sense be in that? Now put down the gun and let's talk sensibly."

"DO NOT PATRONISE ME WOMAN!" His eyes flashed as he came back at her like a dog barking at his bitch. "Don't make the mistake of thinking that you can control me...I'm too long in the tooth to fall for the *femme fatale* bit! I will not be told what to do - not by you, not by anyone. Not anymore! Just look at how things turn out when I do! I repeat again, if I'd been on my guard, none of this shuffling of our finances would have come to light."

Like her husband, Elizabeth was uncomfortable with criticism. Unbowed, she bravely faced his irrational behaviour and went on to the attack.

"I refuse to allow you to pin the blame for all of this on me! It was YOU who threw our money down the drain chasing an egocentric dream - get that into your stupid, stubborn head. I WAS NOT TO BLAME! Throughout your illness and recuperation, I desperately sought solutions to problems YOU caused and if it were not for my diligence, we would've been finished long ago. It was YOUR irrationality that put our finances in peril and YOU who stole the pension fund money from your employees. Have I made myself clear?"

Botha's frown hardened and he bared his teeth.

"You're never wrong, are you? Nothing's ever your fault, is it?"

"Oh, I'll admit to my failings - I don't like to be reminded of them, but I will acknowledge them. Having said that, I most certainly will not accept any part in this catastrophe - you've brought the whole thing down on yourself. You took that money."

Still Botha sought to justify his behaviour.

"Jesus Christ, woman - it was MY bloody money! MY MONEY! I own the pension scheme! That money would have turned into a golden investment for everybody - you, me, the little people - everyone."

At this point Elizabeth understood the extent of his delusion. A sense of omnipotence had led him to believe he pulled strings over things that were legally beyond his control; he saw himself as above the law. She realised that this really was the end; the finish of life as she had known it. Standing before her was the same cold, calculating man that she had admired (and even idolised) for the largest part of her time on earth, but his usual reassuring self-confidence had been replaced by an insanity that defied reason.

She could be as hard-headed as he when it suited her, but in the deepest recesses of her own chilled heart there was still some semblance of humanity; her charitable work attested to that. Suddenly she wondered if he had ever felt any tenderness or compassion for anyone and for the first time it crossed her mind whether he had ever really loved her, though deep down she hoped that he must; at some level anyway. The possibility that she may never have understood her husband at all would need to be dealt with at another time though, for the immediate issue was to part him from his gun.

"Look Marcus, whatever the rights and wrongs of this, nothing can be settled until you put that weapon down, can it?" She stared into those mad, huge eyes, frightening in their despair, frustration and anger.

Is he listening to me?

He looks as if nothing and no one can diffuse the ticking time bomb inside his mind, but I have to try.

"MARCUS, PUT THAT FUCKING GUN DOWN!"

Ashen faced, he simply fixed her in his sights and took aim.

BANG!

Blood splattered in a random fashion across the ridiculously expensive furnishings and Elizabeth fell to the floor. She was dead immediately; gone before she hit the ground. A smell of cordite filled the room and Botha's valet burst through the door, scrambling towards him. In a glance, the Head Honcho could see that Michael would try to disarm him, so without a second to spare, he turned the revolver towards his own temple.

BANG!

More blood: brains dispersed in the opposite direction and another lifeless body thudded onto the lavish carpet.

Confusion reigned for several minutes as an uncoordinated melee of crewmembers piled into the private apartments, all of them desperately trying to ascertain the precise details of what had transpired.

Once everyone had calmed down, the ship's Captain took control of the situation and contacted the Spanish Coast Guard. He was given instructions to sail the yacht into nearby Cadiz harbour and relinquish authority to local law enforcement officers. Within minutes, global media outlets were issuing their first sketchy reports on the deaths of the tycoon and his wife.

Unsubstantiated rumours spread like wildfire: -

- There was some sort of onboard mutiny.

- South African terrorists had stormed the yacht.

- The couple had agreed to a suicide pact.

After a forensics team had completed their investigations, the police issued a statement saying that the Bothas were involved in an angry quarrel and Marcus had shot his wife before killing himself.

Speculation abounded regarding the motive for such behaviour, until back in London news of the Serious Fraud Office's investigation into his business accounts uncovered the gaping hole that he had dug in the employees' pension fund. Quickly two and two added up to four.

In due course, the *Lady Elizabeth* received a spit-and-polish deep clean before being sold off to a Saudi Arabian prince. The couple's magnificent mansion was quickly snapped up too. To further appease creditors, the rest of the couple's vast array of treasures and trinkets were submitted for auction at *Christies* in a blaze of publicity that the Head Honcho would have been proud of. Perversely, all the sale items achieved a premium price thanks to the macabre notoriety of their previous owners.

During the years that followed, Marcus Botha became the subject of endless revelatory television documentaries and paperback books, produced by a plethora of vengeful or curious investigative journalists. His deeds and misdeeds were recounted with varying degrees of accuracy (mirroring the man's own approach to journalism) but none could ever adequately describe the utter selfishness, unbridled ambition and raw cruelty that lurked within his dark and damaged soul.

53.

Read all about it!

Although most of the events in this book are fictional, a very real tragedy on an overcrowded football terrace in Sheffield exposed the callous nature of a newspaper industry that routinely misinforms its readers and sensationalises situations to increase sales. For more than three decades, the families of Hillsborough's ninety-seven victims have contemptuously derided the print media for distorting the narrative of that terrible day, because their fight for justice was seriously derailed by those deceptions. I set *The Horizon* up as a prime example of gutter journalism, but shamefully, many genuine examples exist.

The UK establishment has a sorry record when it comes to punishing its own, and the legal profession is equally culpable in failing to bring those responsible for the disaster to account. A coroner's inquest in 1991 ruled that the deaths were accidental, and six years later, Lord Justice Stuart-Smith rejected requests for a new enquiry. Undeterred, the campaign to apportion responsibility continued.

Eleven years after the tragedy, the Hillsborough Families Support Group brought private prosecutions against the police match commander David Duckenfield and his deputy Bernard Murray, but despite the best efforts of those concerned, they ended in failure. Still the bereaved fought on.

In 2012 an Independent Review revealed details of police efforts to shift blame for the incident onto the fans, and the authorities finally admitted that some of their officers had been involved in a cover up (in all, sixty-eight police statements were altered to disguise the force's failings). Although this led to the verdict of accidental deaths being quashed, it still took another four years and a second coroner's inquest to conclude that those supporters who perished were unlawfully killed.

Eventually, six people had to answer charges ranging from manslaughter by gross negligence to perverting the course of justice. Five of the accused were acquitted on technicalities and only Graham Mackrell, the stadium's safety officer, received any form of punishment (he was fined £6,500 for failing to have sufficient turnstiles open to accommodate such a large crowd).

No custodial sentences have been issued to anyone for their part in the deaths.

From that painful reality I return to matters of a fictitious nature.

At the pinnacle of his career, Marcus Botha watched Communism crumble in Eastern Europe and dreamed of a global capitalist economy of free markets and rich pickings. He saw an opportunity to shape events through a broadcasting venture that would revolutionise the communications industry and increase his power and riches, but he disastrously underestimated the competition.

The time comes to us all when we begin to falter from the peak of our performance: an athlete's reactions to the sound of a starting gun fade; a night club doorman suddenly fears the drunken reprisal of an ejected customer; a *gigolo* no longer commands the attention of his fair maiden.

Tempus fugit.

Arrogantly, Botha followed his gut instinct when going head-to-head against Rupert Murdoch in their broadcasting skirmish without making an accurate financial assessment of his rival's ability to stay competitive when the going got tough. He entered the race too late, anticipating that Murdoch would overstretch himself in creating the infrastructure required, but he underestimated the depth of his rival's resources, meaning that he had to dig ever deeper into his own money pit as the finishing line came into view.

Is it always the fastest, the strongest, the best equipped competitor who ends up victorious? Not necessarily. Sometimes the winner owes their place at the top of the podium to good old-fashioned luck: a rival may trip up, perhaps, or get injured. In the case of our tale, the Botha hamstring tweaked, leaving Murdoch to take the tape with an unchallenged stroll.

For a while, the Head Honcho had realistic chances of becoming a true multimedia giant; uptakes for *Sky TV*'s subscription packages were poor, and Murdoch's venture was in serious trouble. Then external events turned in his favour after he struck a canny deal to broadcast *Cable News Network* content in the UK.

During the early months of 1991, Iraqi dictator Saddam Hussein's occupation of Kuwait was repelled by a US-led international coalition of armed forces, and *CNN* had both the manpower and knowhow to deliver twenty-four- hour rolling news coverage of the action as it unfolded. For the first time, breaking stories were screened as they happened, irrespective of scheduling constraints, and the domestic audience found this approach very much to their taste.

Had Botha agreed terms with Ted Turner first, *MJB TV* might have won the satellite broadcasting war, but as he recovered from his heart attack all he could do was look on with bitter envy. By then of course, with his network's finances in crisis, his wife had duly washed her hands of his dishes and subscription contracts.

While bad luck certainly played its part in his defeat, he also chose to run with an imaginative but fatally flawed strategy. He understood his demographic well and knew that sporting coverage would be the perfect bait to capture their attention, but then chose to back the wrong horse. Murdoch hijacked his business model by prioritising sports fans too, but it was football, not *MJB TV* endorsed snooker or darts, that catapulted his network *Sky*wards. So how could Botha have made such a critical error?

In his native South Africa, white men played rugby or cricket, and football was only popular in the black townships, so when attendances at English matches dropped, he failed to appreciate that the fans' passion for, 'footy.' was merely lying dormant, waiting for something special to stir it into action. He correctly recognised the detrimental impact of hooliganism on attendances, but failed to acknowledge that sophisticated police surveillance tactics and government legislation was gradually beginning to clip the wings of those barbaric thugs. Even during the fallow period for match-day crowds, television audiences remained reasonably strong, so enthusiasm for the game itself had not been terminally impaired.

Back at *Italia 90*, England's World Cup hopes came crashing down to earth after a heart-breaking semi-final penalty shoot-out defeat to the eventual winners Germany, but the spirited efforts of all concerned had restored a collective sense of pride in English sporting prowess.

Their struggles getting past the qualifying group were forgotten, as was the fact that, with sixteen teams left in the competition, they only defeated a dominant Belgium side 1-0 thanks to a wild swing of David Platt's right boot in the last minute of extra-time. So what if they also needed two dubious penalty awards to squeeze past the underdog Cameroons in the quarter-finals? Ironically, that defeat to Germany was the only game in which they had actually played well! By the time they were finally eliminated, nobody cared that the team had once again failed to win the damned trophy, or even reach the final! No country on earth celebrates a plucky loser like the English.

The players returned home to a hysterical reception, the like of which had not been witnessed domestically since the heady days of Beatlemania almost thirty years earlier. An open-top bus led them through a crowd of 300,000 revellers outside Luton airport, and at the centre of the shenanigans, cheeky, chipper Paul Gascoigne, the ultimate 24 hour-party-person, danced and pranced before the throng wearing a pair of false plastic breasts bought from a joke shop. Here was a new type of celebrity for a new type of public: irreverent, idiotic, and irrepressible.

English football was cool again. For the first time, significant numbers of women took an interest in their partners' leisure obsession, while in school playgrounds, previously disinterested young boys heartily chanted the names of Gascoigne, Lineker, Barnes and Beardsley. The huge disparity in earning power between players and their fans on the factory floors no longer mattered because the heroes of *Italia 90* were major celebrities now, on a par with their rock 'n roll counterparts (in fact, they *were* pop stars when their recording of the song, "*World in Motion,*" with indie band New Order became the biggest hit of that landmark summer).

Rupert Murdock's opportunity to cash in on football's upsurge in popularity arrived two years later, when England's top clubs decided to break away from the restrictive practises of the old Football League and begin their own competition, the vainglorious Premier League. *Sky* astutely paid them £304,000,000 over five years to secure live and exclusive broadcasting rights, outbidding the *BBC* and *ITV* in the process. This was a marriage made in heaven; advertisers fell over themselves to purchase slots during matches and soon, serious cash began to fill the company's coffers. Each subscriber received *Sky News* as standard, and the wily tycoon now had a growing audience to influence as he saw fit.

Meanwhile, thanks to misfortune and a diminishing business acumen, Marcus Botha was left with insurmountable debts and the certain prospect of a lengthy prison sentence for his company pensions grab: the destruction of a lifetime's work. He would be forever lampooned as an unscrupulous thief whose ego and greed destroyed the future of thousands of his employees. The stakes were high, but his hand was piss-poor, yet still he played on in the expectation of glory.

What a time to lose the plot!

So how did our other major players react to the Head Honcho's downfall?

Gordon Rimmer despaired when he heard about Botha evading South African justice, but the edge was taken from his reflections after his personal circumstances improved so dramatically.

I may have been cheated out of seeing that psycho behind bars, but in hindsight, I suppose the whole experience has turned out very well for me.

I still find it astonishing that he wanted me killed just for standing up to him over that Priory business, but ironically, if I hadn't been shot, I'd never have had the chance to get back with Susan.

I might not have been given my own show on the TV, or my plum job at The Times either.

Maybe I should be thankful that he came into my life after all!

Then again, probably not!

Susan Somerfield gave a small prayer of thanks at the news of Botha's suicide. She was acutely aware that as a medical practitioner, this was an unprofessional guilty pleasure, but since the revelation of his involvement in Gordon's shooting, she had felt burdened with a sense of impending danger, never knowing if or when the madman might try to strike again. The dread shadow he cast was all too real, not some theoretical case study, and now that he was gone, she could rest easily.

Would I class him as criminally insane?

Absolutely!

Then she considered Elizabeth the Ice Maiden.

Oh, to be a fly on the wall as their final scene played itself out!

Soon enough, her mischievous whimsy dissipated, and she chilled thinking of Elizabeth breathing her last at the hands of her crazy husband. With a shudder, she speculated that those bullets may have been initially reserved for Gordon; maybe even for herself too.

Like Professor Somerfield, Edmund Cornell's only genuine emotion upon hearing of Botha's death was relief.

The man's considerable successes commanded respect, but he was a cruel bully whose every edict carried dark overtones for its recipients.

In truth, I'm very glad he's gone.

The Horizon quickly found itself under new ownership, and once again, Cornell was given a chance to resurrect it from the doldrums of its latter-day mismanagement. As he had done in the aftermath of the Head Honcho's heart attack, he could once more run things without any stifling interference from above, and gradually he guided the floundering behemoth from the very real prospect of liquidation towards a profitable future.

The embezzlement of pension fund money came as a bitter blow to Father of the Chapel Michael Brookes and *The Horizon*'s print workers.

I always hated Botha - never trusted him an inch - but even I struggled to come to terms with the depths he plumbed.

Eventually, most of the losses were recovered in the High Court, but those successes came too late to console Brookes, for his heart gave up before the conclusion of the legalities. In his own way he had become another casualty of the Head Honcho's greed.

Everything changed for Barry Shackleton's family after *The Horizon* hung him out to dry, and his despairing widow Ruth felt overwhelmed by the challenge of keeping everyone together. Problems began to emerge among the younger children, particularly with regards to their behaviour at school, and she had to assume the positions of disciplinarian, councillor, and role model alone, while trying to suppress the heartbreak of her own shattered life.

I'm not sure I can handle all this by myself.

I suppose I should be grateful to Marcus Botha for the money he gave us for Bazza's interview, but once everybody knew about my husband's secret life, we were all done for.

The kids and me get shouted at in the street and I even had some religious nutter spit in my face sayin' it must have been my fault that my fella liked other men.

What did I have to do with it?

I didn't know about any of that 'til it was too late!

Oh Baz, we wouldn't have needed Botha's money if you'd stayed well away from those rent boys and their diseases.

We don't need this stress!

Page Five Filly Danielle Lae's walk on the wild side in Sun City was a step too far for *The Horizon's* (predominantly male) readership. They were a fickle bunch who wanted their topless teases to project an image of cheeky fun, but her cocaine-ravaged high jinks with Ben St. Claire managed to upset many a repressed sensibility at home. Consequently, the Essex Barbie doll's insubstantial career, constructed from nothing more than simply being famous for being famous, disappeared as quickly as it had emerged.

Everything was going sweet for me and Ben 'til Gideon Judge turned up at our hotel room and spoiled it all.

Marcus Botha dropped me like a stone after that with not so much as a, "thank you," for all the papers I helped him shift – that's gratitude for you!

Soon the offers for modelling work dried up, then the personal appearances went too – before that story broke, I used to get a grand a pop for adding a bit of glamour to a movie premier or a product launch.

As for dear, sweet Benny, he was such an insecure individual without class A drugs, and when he started losing, his backers walked away.

Naturally, I moved on too – I was too used to the high life to start dropping my standards!

Deep into her 40's however, she did have a brief comeback as the subject of a, **"WHERE ARE THEY NOW?..."** Sunday newspaper supplement. She was traced to a lavish villa on the, "Costa del Crime," in sunny Marbella where she lived with her husband, the notorious former armed robber Jamie Knoxx. Following on from the renewed media exposure, she tried to foist herself into the emerging reality TV circuit, but those ambitions were summarily squashed by his underworld connections, who suggested that such a move would prove unwise as it might shine an unwelcome light on their own closely guarded private lives.

My whirlwind romance with Jamie led to an unplanned pregnancy and to keep him happy I decided to have the baby - we rushed into a registry office wedding before the bump showed.

I got some good snaps out of the big day from the paparazzi - that was my last tabloid splash as it turned out.

Everything was pretty good at first, but then we had to leave London sharpish 'cos of his problems with the law.

Sure, Marbella's a party town, and thanks to Jamie I'm never short of a bit of sniff to liven things up, but we always see the same old faces and all they ever talk about is who's getting out of the nick back home, who's going inside, who's planning a new job.

It's so boring!

I'm slowly going nuts here - our eldest, Brianna, joined a hippy commune and became a tattooist, bless her, but the youngest girls Amber and Jade are still under my feet being typical stroppy teenagers, so I never get any time to myself to sneak off and play with those fit young men down at the beach!

God, I really miss the old days…

In South Africa, Cornelius Carter's failure to see Marcus Botha convicted of conspiracy to murder would always be a cause for personal regret.

I came so close - if Allan Louw had stayed alive long enough to give his testimony in court, I'd have netted the biggest fish in the whole bloody sea!

His disappointment was tempered however by the subsequent conviction of Douglas Daalmans, which ridded the CBD station house of its most toxic troublemaker. Carter's vigilance, devotion to duty and sensitivity in dealing with multi-ethnic issues showed the way forward for post-apartheid policing and after the ANC won the country's first free election in 1994, both he and his headstrong younger brother Dominic became agents for positive change, rapidly rising through the ranks into positions of authority.

Last, but not least, how did Lewis Neeves react to the Botha shootings?

I hardly knew Elizabeth, so my only response to her murder is one of utter delight that it completely discredited her husband's name.

Once his extradition fears were over, he went back on his promise to attack John Major's allies and I can neither forgive nor forget such treachery.

In April 1992, the Conservatives managed to claw victory from the jaws of defeat at the ballot box, and as Neeves correctly surmised, his political column's radical far-right rantings destroyed any lingering hope he may have had of a return to the cabinet. After bitterly accepting his fate, he let significant acquaintances know of his desire to quit politics for a high-profile position in the private sector, and soon received an outrageously profitable offer that eased the pain of his defection from the Westminster whirlpool.

A carefully worded press release soon followed:

It is with enormous sadness that I have taken the decision to resign forthwith from Her Majesty's government.

I have accepted an opportunity to assist UK businesses with their international expansion plans as an executive member of the Investments team at Goldman Sachs bank.

Regrettably, the long hours that I must devote to this task mean I will be unable to continue my Parliamentary and constituency obligations.

It goes without saying that I wish John Major and my Right Honourable friends every success in the coming years.

As soon as he abandoned the Commons, Botha terminated his newspaper contract, describing him during a daily briefing as, "a nobody masquerading as an irrelevance." Neeves fumed from the comfort of his new surroundings after hearing about that savage slight, and vowed revenge. He did not have to wait long.

That man effectively brought the curtain down on my political ambitions, but even ex-politicians get to hear things to their benefit now and again, and when an accountant who had been hired by Elizabeth Botha at The Horizon tipped me off about possible irregularities appertaining to the company's pension fund, I recognised an opportunity to make trouble.

When I left the paper, the decision was supposed to be my own so I could save face, therefore my informant thought I was still close to the bastard who let me go.

He told me of his concerns in the expectation that I might help Botha fashion an escape strategy, but instead, I discreetly contacted the Serious Fraud Office, advising them to sequestrate his financial ledgers with immediate effect.

Little did I realise that my decision would culminate in those dramatic scenes on the Mediterranean, but events often take on a life of their own.

Oh, vengeance was so, so sweet!

Throughout his loathsome and mean-spirited life, Marcus Botha had made enemies with complete indifference, but like his former ally Margaret Thatcher, in the end he simply lost sight of the fact that a foe who has been badly bludgeoned can sometimes fight back.

....

Collapse has been a recurring theme of this book: history shows us that safety barriers gave way with horrific consequences at Hillsborough and a Conservative *coup* brought down Margaret Thatcher's Premiership, while my fictional characters experienced similarly devastating downfalls. The exposure of Barry Shackleton's secrets left his broken widow and bewildered children flailing amongst the rubble of their shattered lives; the embryonic careers of Daniella Lae and Ben St. Claire went into terminal decline curtesy of their Sun City frolics, and finally, Marcus Botha's empire crumbled after Lewis Neeves surreptitiously exposed his financial chicanery.

Collapses sometimes produce very positive outcomes too and it is worth thinking about some of those instances mentioned in the story:

The fall of the Soviet Union allowed a spirit of entrepreneurship to prosper in Eastern Europe and the end of the apartheid system in South Africa created economic opportunities for the country's black majority. On a more intimate level, frank and open dialogue demolished the emotional barriers that had driven a wedge between Gordon Rimmer and Susan Somerfield.

But for the removal of this last obstacle, there would be no happy ending to finish this tale on, and that simply wouldn't do, would it?..

54.

And finally...

In a quiet country church on the outskirts of Kirkoswald in Ayrshire, near to the Turnberry golf course where Gordon Rimmer's career began as a local sports correspondent, the now acclaimed journalist and television presenter celebrated his marriage to Professor Susan Somerfield in a modest ceremony attended by their families and close friends. The occasion lacked the kind of ostentation and pomp of a modern media wedding and was all-the-more enjoyable for it.

A formal feast was held at the hotel on the grounds of the famous old course, and afterwards most of the guests repaired to the garden area as the tables were cleared in preparation for the evening's revelries. Gordon and Susan joined their guests for pictures on the lawn, then the groom doubled-backed to the banqueting suite alone to quietly savour the magic of the moment. Early evening sun shone golden and clear through the windows, illuminating the room which was festooned in wedding paraphernalia. Icing sugar models of the happy couple stood guard over the remnants of a traditional wedding cake decorating the top table.

A flitting fly caught Gordon's eye.

The busy insect danced between the husband-and-wife figurines, almost kissing each in turn, as if it were blessing the joining together of life partners. It brought to his mind the flies of the African bush, and the indelible stamp that his experiences in that continent would have on the rest of his life.

During the evening reception more guests arrived; the women to ogle Susan's dress and the men to address their pangs of jealousy towards her husband.

Eventually the loving couple retired to their suite, leaving the good-natured tumult downstairs. Two years of conflict and resolution had resulted in this most perfect of outcomes.

In the calm of their room, the newlyweds gazed lovingly into each other's eyes and recalled their magical Presbyterian ceremony and the lyrical wedding rhyme written by their jolly presiding minister.

"Rows in a marriage are like kindling – they combust!

Please be wise and compromise – just as we discussed.

Love conquers all when you stay patient and show trust,

And consign disagreements to history's dust!"

Giggling, Susan looked at her husband and yelled, "Amen to that!"

THE END

Printed in Dunstable, United Kingdom